THESE LONELY VICTORIES

Brian Colman, an Intelligence agent in Berlin, refuses to surrender an innocent girl, Adele, as part of a prisoner swap. She is the wife of an East German agent, but is frantic that she should not be sent back to East Germany. She learns that her husband has been killed, but she does not realize that Colman was directly responsible for his death. Brian is determined to find some channel among his underground contacts by which she can escape to the West and to safety. The two soon find themselves deeply in love as they flee across Europe to avoid arrest. The chase is breathtaking as time after time they narrowly avoid capture, and the gripping narrative builds up to a climax which is both thrilling and intensely moving.

Also by
ELLIOT WEST

★

THE NIGHT IS A TIME FOR LISTENING

THESE LONELY
VICTORIES

*

ELLIOT WEST

THE
COMPANION BOOK CLUB
LONDON AND SYDNEY

THE COMPANION BOOK CLUB

The Club is not a library; all books are the
property of members. There is no entrance fee
or any payment beyond the low Club price of
each book. Details of membership will gladly
be sent on request.

Write to:
The Companion Book Club,
Odhams Books, Rushden, Northants.

Or, in Australia, write to:
The Companion Book Club,
C/- Hamlyn House Books, P.O. Box 252,
Dee Why, N.S.W. 2099

*Made and printed in Great Britain
for the Companion Book Club
by Odhams (Watford) Ltd.*
600871703
1·74/270

With love for Jed and Diana

Author's Note

TO ACHIEVE the hoped-for dramatic impact in telling the following story, I have taken certain liberties with actuality. The problems of the ordinary defector from East to West in Germany do indeed exist as set forth in the passages referring to them specifically. The liberties consist in my use of East Germans to illustrate the situation. The Federal Republic of West Germany has never considered citizens of East Germany anything but Germans, automatically conferring upon them West German citizenship when they have managed to arrive from the Communist side. All people regarded as defectors coming from any other Communist country constitute a burden to be painfully assumed and are therefore subjected to long and difficult processing periods during which they are considered stateless. Only German characters could effectively serve my efforts to create a certain spirit inherent in the situation and convey the proper tone and the emotion required. Aside from this, the story, while fiction, is as accurate sociologically, politically, and historically as I am able, within my own limits, to make it.

Part One

CHAPTER ONE

HE HAD BEEN SITTING under the café awning watching the hypnotic disorder of people endlessly passing by in the sunlight as if he had nothing better to do. He looked like one of those well-groomed, footloose Americans contemplating his next liaison, the night's pleasures-to-come, getting along in Berlin somehow; not old but in the over-thirty category, shorthaired, clean-shaven, nonrevolutionary; a good-looking, quiet type women might like and trust. It happened he liked women; but he was always very careful with them. One had to treat them well but never too candidly, for their own benefits as well as one's own.

When Gerda arrived and joined him, he listened while she told him all the things she had learned about the traitor in their midst. It was his business to have found out, to have employed almost any means in this regard. Gerda had worked out very well. Her lies and deceit had served an unquestionably good cause. Colman had done his best to make this clear to her. Her admissions of guilt and confessions of weakness were spoiling his efforts. He listened to her out of kindness but was bored and faintly irritated. He was a fourth-generation career Army man and he was bred to believe in Them and Us. He found no value in letting things prey on one's mind. There were contradictions in everything, inconsistencies everywhere; a job like this was not for moralists: the soul, whatever that meant to each individual, had to have been well searched by the time one got to this job; nothing should have come as a surprise by then.

Yet here she was—both betrayed and repentant. Women were able to reconcile the two. He didn't resent her for it; he accepted it as one accepts any other natural phenomenon.

9

The two of them sat there on white wrought-iron chairs with red padded back cushions. Colman watched her, a tall, pretty young woman of an immense and somewhat muscular beauty, someone who might be able to run and jump well. And he let her talk as if they were ironing out an old misunderstanding, his eyes sympathetic, his impatience under control.

Her eyes were moist, her apple-cheeked face a mask of regret. 'It makes me feel sick,' she was saying. 'I didn't think it would, I thought I could take it in stride. . . .' She spoke with a faint German sibilance in otherwise good English.

Colman continued to look at her and didn't move.

'After I began the whole thing, even though it was all for you,' she said reflectively, 'I began to wonder what *you* would think of me. . . .'

But he had never given it a thought and now merely waited for her to go on.

'And what *do* you think of me, Brian? Now that I've done all of this? . . .'

He didn't turn away from her insistent and oddly innocent gaze. He said, 'You've been indispensable.'

'But what do you *think* of me?' she persisted, then considered the case against herself in a quietly rueful voice. 'I searched his pockets, listened in on his phone calls, read his mail—spied on him . . . all the while he was making love to me—believing me completely. . . .' She shuddered slightly, looked at him again. 'What *can* you think of me—no matter how pleased you are with the results? That I'm . . . *eine Dirne*.'

'You did an important and difficult job,' he said, 'and you did it well.'

'Would that it had been someone else,' she said, as if a terminal illness had overtaken her.

'There was no one else,' he pointed out. 'Someone had to get into bed with Don to be close enough for what we needed. We couldn't have got within a hundred feet of him; he's one of us and he knows everything we know, every trick.' Colman looked into her eyes as if this were all for her benefit. 'Only someone he'd go to sleep in front of would have had a chance— and that had to be someone special. Because Stebbins is a lot of things, but he's not a fool and he's very particular.'

'I know. . . .' She obviously took no pleasure in the thought, perhaps didn't even believe it.

'Webber,' Colman said with deliberate significance, absorbed by whatever implications that name held. 'He's the one we have to get. And now we've got the chance. Thanks to you and you alone.' He nearly said 'darling' but instinctively stopped short of doing so. It wasn't his kind of word anyhow. 'Without you,' he went on, 'we wouldn't even have known of Webber's existence.'

'It's rather like a game,' she said with wistfulness and supreme disappointment, as if she had expected something else.

'It's not a game to me.'

'Then does it prick your conscience, does it hurt, because of the method we used?'

'Why should it?' Colman said. 'We're talking about some-one who has sold out. Betrayed his country, his friends, the lives of dozens of people he was sworn to protect. He has no claims on anyone's conscience.' He looked at his wristwatch. 'I just hope he doesn't turn into a folk hero.' Then: 'I'm going to have to leave now. . . .'

'Will you call me?' she asked gravely, with soft, demanding eyes.

'Do you want me to?' he said, wishing it hadn't come up.

'Yes,' she said. 'I'm sorry about carrying on this way.'

'You can't help your feelings.'

'Yes. But I should keep them to myself.'

'Do you have plans to see Don before his plane takes off?'

'We've an afternoon appointment.'

'Keep it. And don't give him any reason to be jumpy.'

Like an injured player ready to return to the game, she said, 'I'll be all right by then.'

'Good. Come. We'll leave together.'

Thirty-eight years old, a touch over six feet tall, dark-haired, even-featured, blue-eyed, Colman walked with a measured step at medium speed in unison with big, golden Gerda Hantzmann. She was honey-haired and high-breasted, her long legs covered only to mid-thigh by a moderated miniskirt. She and Colman made an attractive couple as they walked towards the waffled walls of Europa Centre, the damaged tower of the old Kaiser Wilhelm Church looming in front of it. There was everywhere that air of prosperity now long world-renowned. People bustled back and forth or strolled here and there as if each of them were responsible for the achievement of an exquisite premature spring day. In a moment Gerda and Colman would separate and experience its glories far apart and in different ways. 'I think I must get out of all this some day very soon, Brian,' she said as they stood at the corner crossing, the noise of the traffic creating an enclave, an odd sort of privacy.

Colman saw what amounted to a cry for help in her eyes. He realized for the first time that she was in over her head and he felt sorry for her. But there was nothing he could have done about it. 'Does it ever make you feel unreal?' she asked. 'Does it ever feel . . . unnatural?'

'I never let it,' he said, without bothering to explain his own understanding of its purposes, something she could never share anyhow. 'I'll call you in a few days.'

'After it's over?'

'*If* it's over—yes.'

He was ready to turn away when she stopped him. 'Brian,' she said, something vital on her mind.

He waited attentively and she then told him: 'Whenever I've—been with Don—whenever he would hold me . . . I've always imagined that it was you. . . .' There was a touch of triumph in it.

Colman looked at her and she returned the look steadily. Then she crossed towards the big shopping centre and was lost in the streams of people. She had left him with a flourish and he remained standing there for a moment or two afterwards. She had wanted to take something from him that may have been rightfully hers but which he was unprepared to give.

He began walking in the opposite direction, consciously pushing her from his thoughts, considering only the crucial information she had delivered. In twenty minutes he was entering an office building off the Kochstrasse, teeming with prosperity and the diverse commerce of advertising, publishing, and manufacture, two hundred different corporations and companies listed on the nonreflective glass directory in the lobby. He might have been a research chemist, a salesman, an executive of one of the American companies with branch offices in Europe; not someone excessively feared or admired for what he was and the willingness with which he led his hard and relentless existence—just anyone in the so-called normal scheme of things, as he stood in the elevator with several other anonymous travellers.

His face was chiselled and swept clean of any uncertainty or tension. He seemed calm, even as he had talked with poor Gerda, in some ways almost phlegmatic, as if he couldn't easily be moved by his own discomfort or even grave personal loss. Yet the coldly blue and steady eyes were not quite carefree on close inspection. And faint tracks, as if made with a thin stick, ran from the cheekbones down like hints of doubt. But no reliable man was utterly convinced of anything, and only idiots didn't have doubts.

He got off at the fourth floor and went to the door of the offices of Compound Development Ltd. It was here that Stevenson awaited him.

Stevenson was a candidate for legendary, the kind that originates in the annals of a specialized field and is ultimately, and with often dubious intentions, turned into a book about master spies, criminal lawyers, or old-fashioned city editors. He had a flat-nosed, asymmetrical face with glittering hooded eyes and what Colman always thought of as a Chinese smile. Into his fifties, he was markedly short and compressed and quick. Everything about him was like the tight-collared white shirts with the sparkling French cuffs which he wore invariably and for so many years that they had the semblance of a deep personal conviction. He was hard, good-humoured, and impatient. You always thought, if you were one of his people, that he would have a solution no one else could come up with.

He waited and listened as Colman said, 'I think we've got Stebbins leading us to it. He's flying to Stuttgart tonight. Six-o'clock plane. From there he goes to Blauengen by train, about an hour away. We can only assume he's going there to meet this Webber, whoever that may be. Anyhow, we'll be there ahead of him, waiting.'

13

Stevenson said, 'It sounds good—on paper anyway.'

'You can trust it,' Colman said flatly.

'Oh, I do,' Stevenson assured him, strolling to the window with a view of the Wall at the Friederichstrasse crossing, looking down briefly as if to be sure it was still there. 'That girl couldn't have done a better job,' he said and then moved back towards his desk. 'I had my doubts to begin with. The Mata Hari routine has its limitations. I wasn't at all sure someone like Stebbins would fall for it. The type that does usually has wet eyes and a fat lower lip. Don't ask me to explain that. . . .'

'I won't.'

'Anyhow she did the job. Dirty but not regrettable. No less than Stebbins deserves. My hat's off to her.'

Colman said, 'She's not feeling exactly carefree about it.' He felt moved to say a good word for her, recalling with a touch of sympathy Gerda's misgivings and afterthoughts. 'She wouldn't do it a second time.'

'I'm not taking her lightly,' Stevenson said. 'I won't even ask you why she did it for you.'

'I got her from the *Bundesnachrichtendienst*. Highly recommended. It was her job. She's sorry now she didn't turn it down. But I never promised her anything. I never slept with her, never even touched her. It doesn't matter, because she's decided she did it all for me anyway. So now I owe her something I can't pay her.' He shrugged faintly. 'I can't worry about it or I might as well quit.'

'That's okay. Tell it to her, if you have to, not to me.'

'You wanted to know.'

'That's right. But I didn't ask you. I just hope your conscience and your job stay together most of the time, Brian, and that you don't lose too much sleep about anything.'

'Sometimes they do.'

Stevenson waved the topic to a close. 'Let's talk a little bit,' he said, walked behind his desk, remained standing, frowned thoughtfully. 'Stebbins is only a minor factor now—the dirtiest, but still minor. We are interested in him only in relationship to other things. The major factor is getting Mankin back from the East Germans. That's objective A. Everything else is subordinate to that.'

'Nothing from the East Germans—no feelers, no hints?' Colman asked.

'Not yet. We can pretty well assume it was Stebbins who betrayed him. He's willing to do it to a whole list of others, so why not?'

'We can fix the leak in any event.'

'Yes, but there's more, that's just the point, and I don't want you to lose sight of it. We need this Webber, we need him in an airtight case, because that's how we'll be able to get Mankin back from the DDR; that's the blueprint. And Stebbins is the key to Webber, we hope. After that you can throw him away.' Stevenson had come around the desk again to where Colman was standing and he put his smallish but strong hand on Colman's arm. 'Look, there's plenty behind this, Brian. This department is sitting with eggs in its pockets right now. You're bright enough not to need anyone to draw pictures for you; you know partly what's up. We're on the most urgent and generally nasty detail we'll ever pull in all likelihood.' He used the Army terminology simply because he was speaking with Colman. 'I could be fired. That's right. And I don't want to be fired. Why? Easy. Because that will leave Steve Major to take over Llewellyn's job when Llewellyn steps down—and I happen to know that the move is imminent.' Stevenson's eyes glittered with desperate energy, his voice vibrant and all-knowing. 'As an American citizen that would bother me dreadfully, Brian, simply because Steve Major has shit for brains and cannot discharge the responsibilities or carry the burdens imposed by the position. He doesn't even have the political gifts and personality Llewellyn has. As a matter of fact, knowing as much as I do, the thought of Steve Major in charge of operations over here not only worries me, it terrifies me. . . .'

He released Colman's arm, having underscored the point, and Colman said, 'Are they pressing you?'

'In subtle ways. Because *they*'re being pressed. Because ignorance and self-deception are historical commodities. Because people want to stay in office, so they play it safe and avoid nasty facts that might make a mess for everyone.'

'I'm glad I'm where I am,' Colman said. 'I might quit if I had to be in your spot.'

'I'll wait to be fired,' Stevenson said, walking back to his desk, moving like a gamekeeper through his preserve. 'Too many people complain about the quality of the people who serve them in governmental departments of various kinds. But they do nothing about it themselves, even when they're certain they could do what's required better than it's being done. That's why I'm in this job, Brian; not because I'm thrilled by it, but because I feel it's a job to be done and that I can do it well—and not many other people can or will do it. And at my stage of life there's nothing in the world to stop me. . . .'

Colman said, 'One thing—since you've opened up with me like this—just one.' Stevenson began to light a cigar, as if waiting for someone else to play a card. 'What *is* it about Mankin? What makes him so high grade?' Colman said, knowing better. 'Can I ask you that?'

'You can ask,' Stevenson said, drawing on the match flame, 'but I won't answer. You don't get enough money to carry anything like that around with you.'

Colman nodded. 'I'd better get going,' he said.

'Don't talk about it to anyone, not even to Joe Fox,' Stevenson told him. 'It might help you to know a little bit about what's on my mind, but no one else needs to.' He had confided just that much and it had to be enough. 'And one other thing,' he then added. 'The girl. Women like that can be unreliable, I don't need to tell you.'

'So can certain men,' Colman said.

'We don't want this thing showing up in *Time* magazine or something. I trust you'll be exceedingly careful with her.'

'I will be.'

Colman then walked out. They hadn't talked much about Stebbins. Maybe it was too soon. He had left behind him disunity and poison. The man next to you never looked quite the same again. For this alone Stebbins deserved to be the sitting duck that Gerda had made out of him. She had passed herself off as a grade-A girl, gave him her body, her promises, took his trust, and then stuck a knife into him, lied to him and double-crossed him—in other words, gave him exactly what he had given the others. Colman wanted to feel it was absolutely fitting, absolutely just, and he told himself that it was.

16

Stevenson sat there by himself for a moment or two after-wards, glad he had a soldier like Colman he could count on. So few others understood patriotism and what it was that was expected of them. The Russians understood it, as did the Chinese and the Israelis. We, on the other hand, seldom did. Because our lives were too easy, too successful on the whole. That was the uneasy truth of the matter. We bred rebels, recalcitrants, and cynics. Stevenson was glad that Colman, at least, was none of these.

CHAPTER TWO

THE AFTERNOON FLIGHT to Stuttgart was just fifteen minutes away and a cluster of passengers was poised expect-antly at the appropriate bay gate to await boarding. With a measurable sense of distaste Colman approached the refresh-ment bar where Bork was standing as if he was secretly the most important man in Germany.

A look of studied scepticism on his face, his cigarette dangling far too nonchalantly, Bork had seen Colman, but doggedly continued to read *Stern* to show he was unimpressed. He was a man at pains to flaunt an air of independence which no one was interested in enough to challenge or threaten in the first place. About forty-five, clay-faced, round-shouldered, heavy pouches under his eyes, Bork was nasty goods but the best to be had under certain circumstances.

'Looks as if you can board the plane now,' Colman told him, the Stuttgart departure announcement just having come over the PA.

Bork lowered the magazine and slowly removed the cigar-ette from his mouth.

'Don't sit with us, and stay away from us on the train to Blauengen,' Colman told him. 'I don't want us to look like a mob, you can't be sure who might be watching.'

'They sent me all the way from Munich for this,' Bork said in his thick Berlin accent, as if admiring a work of art. 'So I must have something special to offer. But as a representative of

17

the Federal Intelligence Agency, I cannot help wondering why it is you who are in charge of things.'

'You just keep cool and stay happy,' Colman said, 'and you'll serve a useful purpose when the time comes. *Verstehen Sie?*'

'*Versteht sich*,' Bork said, his normally saturnine face grotesque with forced good humour. 'I just thought I would mention it. You mustn't take it to heart. What the hell. Have your day.'

Colman let him leave without a rejoinder and turned to see Joe Fox entering the rotunda. They met halfway and sauntered to a line of public lockers. 'We have a West German agent along with us, name of Bork,' Colman said. 'He has arrest powers we're going to need—not for Stebbins, for this guy Webber.'

'I'm a blank about most of this,' said Fox, who was a couple of inches taller than Colman, about thirty, blond, hard-muscled, his physique that of an offensive end which he had in fact been in college. 'All I know is that we're going somewhere to wait for Stebbins.'

'Right. Blauengen. Stebbins is going there because he's been told to by Webber. That's an educated guess.'

'How educated?'

'Very highly.'

'Do we know Webber yet or are we still in the dark?'

'No, we don't. But according to Baumler, the German we've arrested, Stebbins and Webber have never met either.'

'Is that good?'

'Yes, that's good,' Colman said wryly, suspecting he was being tweaked. 'Maybe you'd like to know why. I'll tell you. It's because we can therefore assume that Stebbins hasn't any idea of what he's supposed to do or where he's supposed to do it until Webber gives him the word—*after* Stebbins arrives in Blauengen. Follow?'

They were now moving towards the passenger gate leading to the tarmac as Colman continued: 'He goes to Blauengen and waits to be contacted. It's almost impossible to think of it working any other way.'

'Do we let Stebbins see us?'

'Not us. Bork,' Colman said as they walked through the gate

and drew closer to the Lufthansa two-engine Caravelle. 'Bork plays Webber. He contacts Stebbins immediately and buys the list. There isn't a reason in the world why Stebbins would be suspicious.'

'Theoretically.'

'That's right.'

'What if there's a password or an identification speech?' Fox asked with sobering logic.

'It will make things that much harder,' Colman conceded as they continued walking, separated from the few stragglers who were also moving towards the waiting plane. 'We're counting on surprise.'

'If there's a password, he's not going to be argued out of it.'

'It won't be as neat, but we've got him anyway on Baumler's accusation,' Colman said. 'All of this is in order to nail Webber. Stebbins is finished either way.'

They reached the passenger ladder, passed the check-in, and boarded the plane in silence. Bork was situated forward, Colman glimpsing him as he sat down and out of view. Colman and Fox remained in the aftersection, a sea of empty seats in their immediate area. 'We're much stronger, no doubt of it, if he sells that list to Bork,' Colman summarized. 'We're assuming he suspects nothing.'

'And that there's no password.'

'If we get that far, he'll accept Bork.'

'If Bork doesn't screw up.'

'He's good at this,' Colman said. 'Likes to trap people, has a room full of trophies for causing downfalls.' There was no flippancy in the words, no admiration, merely a hard appreciation of the function of Bork's malicious energy. 'Mainly we don't want Webber spooked. I think he will wait—maybe hours or even overnight. He won't move in on Stebbins immediately. If I'm right, we'll have plenty of time to put Stebbins in a press and squeeze him—if he makes us squeeze him. If necessary, until he begins to ooze.'

The seat belt and no-smoking signs came on and the engines turned over, their breathless shrieks filling the cabin. In three minutes the plane was airborne and levelled off at about eight thousand feet, flying along the southwest corridor over East

Germany. The captain's greeting came through, first in German and then in English. After ordering coffee from the flight's single hostess, the two men sat in the extending silence until Fox finally said, 'I can't think of a way out of it, but I'm not looking forward to it no matter how smoothly it may go. I almost hope he doesn't show.'

Colman had mixed feelings about the basic decency of Fox's nature, the absence of pain or hardship in his life altogether apparent. 'Feel sentimental about him, Joe?' Colman asked.

'No,' Fox replied. 'But I like bad guys to be strangers . . . nobody I ever knew; or if I knew them, nobody I ever liked or trusted. That's all I'm saying.'

Colman said nothing and Fox added, 'It's a stinking job.'

'That's right,' Colman said. 'That's why I always try to keep in mind, at times like this, something my father used to say. There are reasons for shovelling manure. Not one of them is pleasure.'

'Good saying,' Fox said and then said no more.

It was four o'clock when they landed at Etcherdingen, outside of Stuttgart, and five thirty when they arrived at the valley station in Blauengen, whose sign read 1,304 metres. Thick coats of dazzlingly white snow covered the rooftops of the baroque buildings, and there was snow in the streets, horse-drawn sleighs among the Mercedeses, the Peugeots, and the Volkswagens. Less than three hours later, from the window of the hotel room they had checked into, Colman and Fox were observing the approach through pools of cold lamplight of a tall, thin man in his late thirties, his steps across the hard-packed surfaces of snow easy and unconcerned. Fox saw the familiar, quite evidently unsuspecting, figure. He clenched his jaw as if now, for the first time, it had become real. 'Let's get it over with,' he said.

'Let him reach the hotel entrance,' Colman cautioned, watching Stebbins draw closer.

In a moment the tall man, wearing horn-rimmed glasses and reminding Colman, as he always had, of a small-town high school basketball coach who was basically a maths teacher, had gone into the Blau-Berghaus, a small hotel in whose vestibule Bork awaited him.

Colman and Fox then departed their own hotel and walked towards the Blau-Berghaus across the snow, like glass underfoot, the night air like ice. A horse-drawn sleigh, its tinkling bells sharp as frost, glided by, its passengers, four holiday-makers, happily ignorant of whose path they had crossed.

'Is it too fast?' Fox said with freezing breath as they reached the hotel's threshold.

'No. He'll either have flopped by now or got Stebbins upstairs,' Colman said.

Bork had not flopped and was joining them a few minutes later in the vestibule, hands in pockets, his face a mask of grim success under a slightly angled hat brim. 'Was *this*'—Bork produced from his pocket a white envelope—'what you wanted?'

Colman perfunctorily inspected the contents, two plain pieces of white bond paper covered with names and addresses. A careful scrutiny wasn't necessary. 'Yes,' he said. 'This is it. He accepted the money from you?'

'He did.'

'He took you for Webber?'

'The name alone was the password. I had him totally convinced. Webber must have left things wide open.'

Fox then joined them where they were standing in back of the old-fashioned grill-enclosed lift and said, 'I had to tell the innkeeper we were on police business.'

'I will attend to him,' Bork said.

'It's okay,' Fox said. 'I convinced him nothing terrible was going to happen—just routine questioning of one of his guests.'

'Let's catch Stebbins before he leaves his room,' Colman said.

Colman, the other two men behind him, went upstairs and knocked at the door to Stebbins' room. When Stebbins' voice said, '*Wer ist es?*' Colman replied, 'Open up, Don. It's Colman.'

Only seconds elapsed, an eternity for all, before Stebbins stood before them just inside the room, tall, serene, a soft smile on his lips. His patient eyes behind the glasses, his hands jammed casually into his trouser pockets, he looked at them, and they looked at him, the threshold between them, and there was silence. Even Bork waited expectantly. Finally Colman said, 'We've got you cold, Don.'

Stebbins answered cordially, 'Come on in.' It was momentarily disarming. He might well have been welcoming a delegation that had come to persuade him to take charge of some urgent task because only he could save them.

CHAPTER THREE

THERE WERE no prolonged manœuvres, no denials, but rather a fatalistic and simple admission of the facts. 'You've got me cold, Brian, just as you say,' he said like a gracious loser, standing before them without a speck of discomfort or fear. 'You've done your jobs and saved the day.' He was genial, too flawless, of course, too superior. 'You're unsung American heroes. . . .'

'Thanks for the memory,' Fox said.

'I say it sincerely,' Stebbins told him.

'No one gives a shit,' Fox said. 'You're a despicable son-of-a-bitch, Don. Either that or you're out of your skull.'

'For being nothing more or less than what you yourselves are, for doing nothing more or less than what you yourselves have done and continue to do. . . .' He laughed and put his hand to his forehead, an almost delicate gesture. He grew sharper, some of the mask peeling away as he went on: 'Unquestioning and obedient and duty-bound; every base act a noble sacrifice, every thievery or betrayal a heroic duty performed. . . . Except when the *other* side does it: then it's despicable or crazy. Double-cross, trap, cheat, and ensnare— all splendid deeds if they come from *our* side. . . .'

'Nice hypocritical speech now that you're caught in bed with the other side,' Colman said.

'Brian, old chum,' Stebbins said with a caustic smile, 'you're faced in the wrong direction, thinking along a straight, well-conditioned line. I *am* the other side. I always *have* been. . . .' A man purified by enlightenment, Stebbins stood there with complete certainty. 'That's just the point, and it changes things quite a lot, doesn't it?'

Colman and Fox looked at him with growing intolerance

and disgust as he continued to reveal himself. 'I'm talking about spirit and sentiment now, nothing else. And *mine* have always been with the other side, as we so smugly refer to it— yes, always. But my first opportunity to work for it came along only recently. As to the money, I took what your German handed me, thinking he was the real article because I had no reason to think otherwise, and I didn't even bother to count it —something he can verify. But he could have had that list of names for absolutely nothing—just for the asking. . . .' His tone was restrained but proud.

After a moment Colman said, 'We get it. But you don't need to bare your soul, it would only bore everyone.'

'Would it?' Stebbins' mouth tightened, his eyes fixed on Colman. 'The agonies of three-quarters of the human race don't bore *me*; American subversion of the aspirations and desires of emerging peoples doesn't bore me; people kept in bondage and ignorance for the benefit of capitalism for hundreds of years doesn't bore me either. . . . Sorry, Brian, if it bores you. . . .'

'You put the finger on Mankin, didn't you, Don?' Fox said. 'That could accrue to him some of that agony you're talking about. Rubber hose, glaring lights, seventy-two hours without sleep. . . . Even when we stick you in the brig that's the kind of experience you won't need to have because it seems to take place only in workers' paradises.'

'Are you trying to suggest to me,' Stebbins began with a toweringly righteous and deliberately slow cadence, 'that people's rights in the great American democracy haven't been *violated*?'

'They've been violated everywhere,' Fox granted.

'. . . that brutal police methods haven't been used—third degree, intimidation, beatings—usually on a black person or a Mexican—legal assistance withheld? *Come on.*'

'Not as a matter of government policy,' Fox said.

'Unspoken,' Stebbins said. 'The clean, circumspect gentlemen who look the other way. . . .'

'Do you think it will happen to you?' Colman asked.

'If it suits someone, if enough is at stake,' Stebbins answered. 'Someone like Stevenson.'

'You'll say *any*thing, won't you, Don?' Fox said angrily. 'Neither logic nor facts mean a damn to you, do they?' He would feed stray animals, never crib on exams, and help elderly ladies across the street. But he would trample you on the next play if you had clipped him from behind on the previous one. The hot-eyed, wet-lipped rage to be seen in that face told the story. 'You don't give a damn who you put on the rack, do you?'

Stebbins had moved to the window, as if to evade Fox's mounting anger, pained by the impossibility of conveying his thoughts to those who could not and would not understand. 'I do not want anyone killed,' he began in a voice suddenly muffled with emotion. 'I don't want anyone *punished*. I just want them stopped from committing atrocious crimes.'

'Don, you know that Brian was a prisoner of the North Koreans——'

'Yes.'

'——and that they tortured him.'

'Yes.'

'That's enough of that,' Colman said, unwilling to put any of it on exhibit.

But despite the injunction Fox plunged ahead. 'Do you consider that not to be atrocious?' he said, winning the case and achieving nothing.

'Drop it,' Colman said, disinterested in shaking Stebbins anyhow. 'Don is ideological. And when you're that way you never let stories about broken bones or crushed testicles spoil anything for you.'

'How about defoliated forests?' Stebbins shot back.

'What about three thousand people buried alive in Hue?' Fox countered, thrusting his jaw forward.

'Let's can it,' Colman said. 'Let's talk about something else. Let's talk about Webber.'

'Why don't we first talk about how you used a woman's body to get to me, Brian—since we're talking about relative virtue and decency?'

'You can always find a way to look like the good guy-victim, can't you?' Fox snorted with contempt and then looked at Colman, who said nothing because he had nothing ready.

Stebbins, talking in the same faintly accusative and superior tone he had now brought to bear on all subjects, went on: 'About how you made her whore for you like a pimp on the Reeperbahn. Did you think I didn't know it the minute I heard your voice outside the door?' Now Stebbins' bitterness was scarcely contained. 'I can easily understand the forces that overwhelm a girl like Gerda,' he said, staring reflectively, recalling earlier, fonder impressions. 'She could hardly be expected to rise above them . . . everything good in her lying defenceless, unnourished, and slowly dying. She needed fresh air and she didn't get it. She's a victim—one of the millions you and all the others like you are responsible for.' He turned his eyes, swimming with rage behind the lenses, back on Colman. 'What a nice, clean-limbed, American thing to arrange. . . .'

Fox maintained a sudden, ambivalent silence as Stebbins spoke, and Colman stood there watching without any inclination to offer an apology or express regret. 'I wonder if it's worse than the back-alley knifings and canal drownings you were about to arrange for at least half the people on this list,' he said.

'They're gangsters,' Stebbins replied, 'just like you. . . .'

Fox looked as if he wanted to hit Stebbins, and Colman, unruffled, said without theatrics, 'Listen, Don, when Webber tries to contact you, you play along and do as he says so we can nail him. That's what we want of you. And it may be the best offer you get for a very long time.'

'Are you threatening me?'

'Yes, I am.'

'Well, screw yourself, you jackbooted tin soldier,' Stebbins snarled. 'You want to think it's that cheap, don't you, so you can feel safe and secure about it. You don't want to think that faith can't be napalmed or thumb-screwed or bribed out of existence. It kills you to think it can't, doesn't it?'

Colman didn't answer and Stebbins turned his back, fixed in the role of religious martyr, convinced he was better than he was, cut to the quick by the corrupt use of passion to bring him to ruin at the same time he was ready to doom fifty others to his own fantastic insistence on how the world should have been. It deeply disgusted Colman. But maybe it *was* faith.

Quietly Fox said, 'What do you want to do, Brian? It's ten minutes to nine. . . .'

'Stay here. I want to check on Bork.'

It was the excuse he needed to take a breather and think things over. He went downstairs to the small, nearly deserted lounge where Bork was seated smoking a cigarette, hat and coat removed, coffee and brandy before him, enjoying a clear view through the open doorway to the vestibule. Obviously Webber had not shown up. 'I hope to receive a lot of credit in your report to Munich,' Bork said. 'This could never have been done without me.'

'You can count on all the credit you want, Bork,' Colman said, sitting down on the chair next to him.

The German sat on a divan, back stiff, arms folded across his chest, his pitiless eyes and his vulpine air like the marks of his trade. He couldn't have been appealed to and he enjoyed the victim's plight.

'Have you contacted the local police?' Colman asked.

'I know them all,' Bork said, dipping an ash. 'But what about the next move? Are we simply to sit here and wait? I would prefer to circulate, use my powers of observation.'

'That's interesting,' Colman said. 'How?'

'In the bars around the town. I bet right now Webber is sitting in one of the *Hofbrauhäuser*—waiting. That is, if he hasn't been frightened away.'

'Yeah? And how would you know him?'

'How would I know him?' Bork's lips parted in a compellingly ugly smile of self-esteem. 'The same way I shall know him if he walks in here. I have a sense for that sort of thing—a radar.' He shook his head. 'Yes, that's right. If you were to put Webber in a *Polizei-Musterung*—a line-up—with a dozen others. I should pick him out.'

Colman half believed him. 'We may be able to use your gift some other time. For the moment, stay on guard right here. How's the manager?'

'In line. I know just how to deal with people like him. Most of them are mice. But look, don't keep me down here too long, Mr Colman. One of you can sit here, if that's the way you want to do it. What kind of luck are you having upstairs?'

'We'll see. . . .'

'Doesn't sound too promising.'

Colman left Bork without further conversation. Bork had seemed more willing to crowd him than he had been up till then. He undoubtedly could sense that Colman had to wait and rely on luck, that he couldn't really control events. There was no sure way at the moment to trap Webber, no actual plan. Just a loose confederation of rough ideas.

Colman returned to the room and his hand was on the handle when Fox suddenly pulled the door open from inside, evidently about to rush from the room, tight-lipped, an awed, angry look on his face.

'What the hell is it?' Colman said.

'Stebbins—'

Colman swiftly barged into the room and could see for himself as Fox said. 'He's dead—he took hydro—got it into his mouth before I even knew it——'

'Jesus. . . .'

'—there was nothing I could do, nothing. It's incredible—it works in seconds—just seconds. I knew he had it. I tried to grab him, force his mouth open. I couldn't do a thing. He smiled, told me to go fuck myself, and died.'

Colman nodded. 'He meant every word he said.'

'I couldn't believe it. He must have been nuts—unbalanced —he must have been. You had to be here and see it to know what I mean.'

'Yeah. . . .'

'He was sick.'

'Maybe.'

'He probably should have been in a hospital—under observation, getting psychiatric treatment——'

'Don't give me that,' Colman said, hard, intolerant. 'Come on, let's get him off the floor.'

In a moment, without a word, they had placed him on the bed. As one walks through the doorway to a room where nothing of consequence awaits one, Stebbins had bitten down on the hydrocyanic capsule they all sometimes carried with them—had done it that unhesitatingly, that casually. Now his face was that of a sleeping man frowning at a troubled dream,

27

his lips ajar, his teeth together, his eyes shut behind glasses as if unremoved because sleep had taken him by surprise. The smell of peach blossom was unmistakable. 'It works fast,' Colman muttered finally. He wondered fleetingly if somehow it could be kept from Gerda, the futility of the idea immediately apparent.

'I couldn't believe it,' Fox said, as if Stebbins had proved to be a real disappointment.

'Why? What do you think we're doing? Selling vacuum cleaners?'

Fox felt the sting. 'I didn't see the outcome this way, that's all. What was it he couldn't face?' His big hand made a vague gesture to accent the question. 'That he was a caught traitor? Or what the girl did to him?'

Colman gave him a blank look and said nothing.

As if he had been forced to follow it to a logical conclusion, Fox went on: 'I think he couldn't take the truth about Gerda. I think he was really in love with her.'

'Which means nothing to us. Nothing, Joe. What does mean something to us is getting Webber. Just that. Nothing else. Right now. Later on you might like to apply for a transfer to Analysis and Evaluation.'

Fox looked at Colman, the man in charge. 'What do you want to do, Brian?' he asked and waited attentively.

Colman felt himself struggling to keep things together, but he talked in a cold, authoritative voice. 'First, get him into the local morgue—quietly, very quietly. Bork can arrange that. Then wait for Webber. I still think he'll try to contact Stebbins. Nothing that has happened, as far as *we* know, could have altered that. It's the same blueprint. We have to get him into this room to make the transaction. He's got to buy that list in front of witnesses so that Bork can make the arrest.'

'That *will* be a trick.'

'We'll have to wait and see how things go before we know how it's done. Maybe it can't be done. We may have to finally abandon it, abort the whole thing. But we're going to dig in for a while before that happens.'

The anger and indignation of the scrimmage with Stebbins long gone, Fox gazed down with reflective eyes. 'Do you feel even a little sorry for him?' he said, compelled by the sight of sudden self-destruction.

'Not even a little,' Colman answered. He had been very close to this kind of death before. More momentous was the fact that Stebbins had overpowered them. He had left them to stumble around and pick up the pieces if they could.

It was the next day before the man called Webber made any move.

CHAPTER FOUR

HE WAS STILL, after just under one year, deeply aroused by his wife's seductive air, her quiet, sensuous beauty. At the age of twenty-six she was cleanly curved and lithe, and her breasts were very full and prematernally firm. She had dark-blonde hair, not quite to the shoulder, her eyes a light, elusive colour, green or vaguely blue, a still-waters look to them.

With more than enough time before he had to leave, he approached her, the blinds drawn against the blue skies and the midday sunlight. But she wasn't thinking of him, her mind wasn't on it, he could tell. She looked up at him like a sympathetic witness, indulgent, at his service, but reflecting a benefactor's sense of satisfaction rather than passion. She gave him unstinting help, but it wasn't enough. His pride didn't totally rule him, he was too practical for that. Yet he was left with a residue of dissatisfaction. He had failed to touch the core of her once again. A faint stab of ego defeated his better judgement, and as they lay there side by side in the softly dimmed room, he said, 'I have the strangest feeling that I am a patient and you are a dutiful but dispassionate nurse. . . .'

He was watching her face in the quarter-light, her pensive gaze trained upwards, calm and presently as unfathomable as a deep pond he couldn't bring himself to pass by and leave untouched. 'And I have the feeling,' she said, 'that we are both merely people who don't even exist . . . just shadows.'

'What are you talking about?'

'You know what I'm talking about, Martin,' she said and rose from the bed and put on a wrapper, tying its sash tightly.

'You're a child, you deceive yourself with every breath you take. You believe in nothing and you think you can live by your wits forever.' She looked at him, suddenly without mercy, her expression thinly tranquil, anger just beneath. 'But I can't. I need more than that—something different. . . .'

'Adele, my darling,' he said with incredible civility, getting out of bed and covering himself with a bathrobe simply to protect against draughts. 'You should try to be more of an existentialist. That would mean you finally understood the absurdity of the universe and you would achieve a certain measure of freedom from anxiety over moral conventions.'

'Such *dreck*, Martin.'

'Is it?'

'I'd rather be able to walk past a policeman without holding my breath.'

'Adele, my love, we're out of the Zone, and I am making money,' he argued in a reasonable, pleasant tone.

'Yes, but I can't make love very well when there are three people in bed: the two of us—and the person who is going to arrest you some day. . . .' She added in a deliberately premonitory whisper: 'Or kill you. . . .'

'Oh. . . .'

'He is always there.'

'Risks are part of life,' Martin said, his hands in the pockets of his robe, superior understanding on his aquiline young face, a white-blond strand of hair on his forehead. 'Where would you be if we hadn't taken them to get out of the Zone, Adele? Where would you be if *I* hadn't been willing to take them, if I had been a more *normal* and conventional type, a nine-to-fiver?'

She had to stand up to the deliberate manipulation of what was an essential truth. 'I thought you were the finest, most courageous person I had ever known, Martin,' she said forthrightly. 'But it's turned out to be the fire after the frying pan——'

'Oh?'

'—and time is running out, Martin. You've got to be able to see that.'

'Such drama.'

'Don't take it lightly, I beg of you.'

'You're blackmailing me.'

'I wouldn't know how.'

'By turning frigid.'

'I am distracted, not frigid,' she said. 'I think that must be common among women in hiding.'

'In hiding?' A sneer appeared. 'Aren't you overstating things just a bit?'

'No. We are unprocessed defectors, Martin. We have never reported to the Federal authorities. We could be deported at any time. Of course, we are in hiding. What else would you call it? One false step and we are through. How do you build a future on that?'

'The present, Adele, the present. Who talks of futures these days?'

'And if a woman is pregnant?' she said and waited for his reaction.

Carefully he said, 'Are you pregnant?'

Whether with regret or relief it was hard to say, but she answered, 'No, I am not.'

'It wouldn't have been a very good time for it,' he admitted.

'Will *any* time be a very good time for it?' she asked. 'We must go to the authorities and report our defection, Martin, before they discover that we haven't done it.'

'Do you think there is some kind of magic in that?'

'I think it means that you are finally out in the open.'

'After a year, or even two years, in a resettlement camp while they *process* us.'

'Maybe not that long.'

'Of course, it is.'

'But does it matter? We are not old. What does a year, or even two, mean if we are free at the end of it?—to live as we please, to go anywhere and do as we like, to be like anyone else——'

'Who wants to be like anyone else?' he said with amused disdain.

'To be as free, I mean,' she replied angrily.

'No one is free altogether,' he told her with that same superior understanding. 'No one is free at all without money.

And I am making it now. Because I am walking around, un-processed or not.' He began to pace and show signs of impatience at last. 'It is there for me now. Two years from now it might not be. Free, yes. Free to work your ass off in someone else's business for a fixed wage and a lousy two-week holiday every year. I can't quite leap at such an opportunity, *liebchen*.'

'Perhaps you'll wish you had some day.'

'Listen, don't press me now, please. I have to have time to think about a great many things that aren't as simple or cut-and-dried as you might imagine. And right now I *haven't* the time. So just put on some coffee like an angel, will you, and quit all of this.'

'And you think that does it?'

'I can only hope.' And then he was off to the bathroom from where a moment later could be heard the rush of shower water. No matter what the business, for some people a bath and fresh linens to begin the day were mandatory.

She let in a flood of daylight and stared out the window at the wide avenues below, seeing nothing, thinking only how deceived they had been if this was the purpose of it all. There had to be something more to hold them together than their memories of the East Zone and the restrictions imposed by their new lives. The thought continued to absorb her as she sat at the kitchen table with Martin, blond, lean, handsome, sparkling from the effects of his shower. 'Listen to me,' he said to her in a sober tone. 'I don't expect to change you on the subject. You've the principles of the middle class, bourgeois square; though how you came by them I don't know. Maybe because your mother was a Gestapo whore and then a *Vopo* whore and you are simply reacting—I don't know. . . .'

'Is that necessary?' she snapped. 'What are you trying to accomplish talking that way?'

'I apologize. That was very inappropriate. A lapse on my part. I suppose I bristle when I think of how little she considered you.'

'How little *she* considered me? But what has changed?'

'Everything,' he insisted. 'What I am saying is that you are what I want and no one else will do. Call it sex, I don't care.'

32

'That doesn't move me very much.'

He smiled. 'Are you becoming uncompromising?'

'Why not?'

'Don't, I implore you,' he said, as if advising someone much less experienced than himself, almost paternalistically. 'We are meant for each other. And listen to this: Once I've made our pile, I'll go into the resettlement camp—walk the straight-and-narrow, think pure thoughts. I'll do it all gladly. No matter how long it takes, I'll go through it with you.'

'Once you've made our pile,' she repeated with the half-humouring derision reserved for the prophecies of a five-year-old. 'You know what that sounds like, don't you?'

'I'm in contact with a CIA agent,' he confided, trying to make his case stronger. 'It's a magnificent situation.'

'What if you are caught?'

'Very unlikely. It's child's play really. All that I do is take information from him and pass it on to a man in—well, never mind where, I'm telling you too much as it is. But it couldn't be more simple.'

'It makes me shudder. You say it all so casually.'

'It's a matter of buying and selling. That's the heart of everything.'

She shook her head almost pityingly. 'And you look down on my mother. . . .'

He didn't care for the allusion. 'At least,' he said with a cutting, angry hiss, 'I did not use you for bait to hold on to a bored lover——'

The ringing doorbell ended the discussion and startled both of them, not incomprehensibly. A knock at the door or a ringing bell where they came from seldom meant you had won a prize. Adele, without any wish to pursue the topic, opened the door to the postman, who stood there with a small package for Mrs Stransky, the lady in the flat across the corridor.

'She must be in at this hour,' Adele insisted somewhat coldly, her wrapper gathered at her neck in a tight fist, the postman innocent of her various apprehensions.

'I have rung the bell, *gnadige Frau*,' the man insisted in return, then looked at the package. 'Something from Israel . . . not that it's my business. But it is too large for the letter box.'

'Well, I can't accept it. Leave it at her door,' Adele said and returned to the kitchen, repentant immediately and angry with herself more than with the postman or with the neighbour for having someone to send her packages from Israel. One had to withdraw from even the most innocent of circumstances, coming, going, forming no attachments, saying *guten Tag* but not smiling. In the billowing consecution of thousands and thousands of others in the immediate surroundings, one could live a lifetime without credentials and attract no attention, providing one was never the victim or committer of either a public accident or a revealed crime. Martin had logically explained this to her.

'Have you encouraged anyone around here?' he said, slightly wary, his eyes narrowed.

Adele answered, 'The postman doesn't realize that perfectly normal behaviour can be upsetting to some people.'

'You handled it very properly,' he said and took her arms in an almost comradely way. 'Remember what I said. Think existentially. Don't be hoaxed by any of it.'

'It won't work for me, Martin,' she said. 'I have nothing but ordinary, commonplace ideas.'

'We'll discuss it further, I promise. . . .'

'The time for discussion is past,' she said, staring into his eyes with a fateful steadiness.

He kissed her and squeezed one of her breasts. 'We'll sort it all out,' he said. 'I promise.'

He was gone in just a few seconds and she immediately felt terribly alone, left with nothing but wisps, rudderless in the vast sea of a small three-room flat within the teeming ebb and flow of West Berlin. The sounds from the streets below came up like whispered conversations she was not intended to hear. She stood there abandoned and motionless in the centre of the living room, her eyes on the door through which he had departed like a bright young executive off on a business trip, having kissed his wife good-bye with expressions of faith and ardour, surely to return and resume the cycle of youth and love and money once his transaction was completed.

In the stall shower she let the warm needles of water beat on her and stream along the surfaces of her body, the illusion of

34

peace and safety a very thin one which vanished as she stepped from the stall a few minutes later into a momentary chill, her flesh contracting with horripilation. She got dressed, applied her lipstick and eyeliner, and brushed her hair with only casual vanity. Wearing the new black raincoat Martin had bought her at Ka De We the week before, she walked out of the apartment and in the corridor saw the package from Israel placed in front of Mrs Stransky's door. It was one o'clock.

One had to practice caution and go unnoticed—that was a cardinal rule. But the package was alone and unattended. It could easily be stolen, perhaps by one of the kids in the building; the fabric of even German discipline was wearing thin these days. Adele's teeth raked her lower lip as she stared at the package and made her rash decision.

She picked it up—it had to be dried fruit of some kind or preserves in paraffin containers. She rang the doorbell twice, to no reply. She was about to return the package to her own flat for safekeeping when Mrs Stransky's door unexpectedly opened, revealing that lady like some long-anticipated but finally forsaken arrival from a distant place. 'Yes? *Guten Tag*.'

She was a small, unprepossessing woman of sixty, wearing a bathrobe, her face pallid, her eyes spilling with age, troubled and rheumy at the moment with a flu or some other illness.

'This arrived by post,' Adele said, afraid to be any more than civil and polite, her smile minimal and brief.

'How good of you. But I would not want you to come close to me—I am down with an infection, not terribly serious, but I have been in bed. . . .' An air of self-effacement emerged from her like a scent and Adele was immediately on to it. 'I shall go inside and you can simply put it down. . . . I was asleep and did not hear the post. Thank you, you are very kind.'

Adele gave Mrs Stransky, with whom she had never exchanged more than a muttered and forbidding *guten Tag*, a pinched and uninviting smile. She then walked the few intervening steps to place the package on the doormat, no sense of satisfaction or gain in the small generosity she was extending, eager to quickly disassociate herself, yet overpowered by the spectre of helplessness Mrs Stransky conveyed. Quite by herself evidently, undoubtedly a Jew, and bound to have few if any past friends and acquaintances left, Mrs Stransky presented an appealing and diminutive figure, an object of pity, despite Adele's determination to resist such enticements. Giving help was often like an addiction. Adele could scarcely believe the sound of her own voice at first as she heard herself saying, 'I am going to market. Is there anything I can get for you?'

'Please, don't trouble,' Mrs Stransky said from behind her door, open a mere fraction of an inch.

'I wouldn't volunteer if it were trouble,' Adele said. 'It can't be a great deal, of course. . . .'

'I feel so guilty. . . .'

Adele smiled dimly to herself and thought, Why? Haven't you had enough done to you yet? 'Don't be silly,' she said. 'What do you need?'

Self-protection and withdrawal finally became septic and one had to wash them away—at least, from time to time. This woman's distress would have preyed on her mind, it was that simple, Martin wouldn't need to know.

And as he walked briskly along the Hohenzollerndamm he could not have guessed. His psychology was already that of the forager among others who were the same, his mind on things only indirectly related to Adele right now. His hat and over-coat, heavier clothing than required for the sudden and un-seasonable warmth, were fully appropriate for where he would finally find himself and now distinguished him from the drift of hippies and students in leather and lambskin and from the various other iconoclasts of the day and placed him firmly in the entrepreneur class. He was one of the suit-and-tie people, with their ostensible devotion to regulations and procedural purity, to rules and honesty and dependability in their dealings, but buying and selling no less ruthlessly than himself and taking far fewer risks. Marxism, on which he had been gorged, made essentially the right assessment of all the fine gentlemen with the ties and suits. Trade and manufacture for profit was a matter of murder and theft. But when Marx transcribed his nightmare he either deliberately left out or simply didn't recall that the have-nots are never satisfied with a fair share of any-thing any more than are the haves, because no one has ever known precisely what a fair share is. As to murder and theft—these were abstractions because they took place far away from the board rooms where they were conceived as other things; and in a Marxian world without God and where a fair share was ill-defined there could be no retribution, only possible retaliation. And without retribution there was no fear of judgement; and without fear of judgement there was no sense of guilt. And without guilt only quick wits and one's own definition of a fair share were necessary.

In a kiosk at the busy Fehrbelliner Platz, Martin, in perfect safety and anonymity, made his crucial telephone call. Surrounded by numerous buildings containing various government offices, Martin trained his eyes arbitrarily across the open space towards a façade of multicoloured tiles making a dominating tower building. He watched absently as he waited to hear his party's voice. Then he announced himself, smiling, cheerful, his eyes never removed from the fixative pattern glistening in the sunlight. 'This is Webber,' he said. 'Yes, that's right. I simply wish to confirm our engagement. Ah, yes. Very good. I shall call you again this evening.' All in English except for *auf Wiedersehen*. That was all there was to it; Mr Stebbins would complete his end of it, for whatever his reasons.

He then paused in the plastic recess, observing with a certain unexpected longing the bourgeois normality of the pedestrian traffic, the passing back and forth of people who almost certainly did not live in the shadows. Whatever else these putty-faced and flat-eyed squares were, they were not nonpersons; these credulous louts, deceiving husbands, red-cheeked buffoons, and oppressed little secretaries were not stateless. Any one of the queer, long-haired fauna advertising their political puberty and historical paraplegia by the wearing of anarchic rags and patches could have produced an *Ausweis*.

A moment of wistful vertigo came from the unsuspected depths of him and then, like a vapour, wafted away in a vagrant breeze as he stepped from the telephone enclosure and began to walk across the open square. The unsettling supposition deferred, the hard business ahead, Adele would have her way eventually. He strangely enough found the prospect not only interesting but even inviting.

CHAPTER FIVE

THE SECOND TELEPHONE CALL to the Blau-Berghaus came early that evening. And the rendezvous was arranged.

'You're going by yourself?' Fox said.

'If I don't, this man will never show his face,' Colman said. 'He was pretty clear about that just now.'

'And we just sit here and wait?'

'That's about it.'

'I'm starting to feel like the wallpaper.'

'That's too bad, isn't it?'

No one's nerves had improved overnight.

'Good luck, Brian. . . .'

Colman nodded. 'This too shall pass.' He grinned faintly, hit Fox on the arm, and walked out.

He had already changed into the boots and anorak he had brought along. At the appointed time he sat next to a window in a half-filled local bus beginning its thirty-five-minute journey to the Swiss border, on his way to a meeting high above the world, away from crowds, from narrow streets, from closed-off rooms. Evidently Webber was a nervous type.

Blauengen, with its little lights, was finally reduced to a toy city left on the living-room carpet. Colman alighted at the bus stop at Brughaffen and then climbed from the mountain pass across a two-inch surface of snow through the tall pines trailing up the incline in endless formations of silent and unconquerable giants. Bright moonlight came through the branches. The enemy was neither mythological nor the creation of diabolical press agents. When he reached the hut above the timberline someone behind him said, 'That's far enough. Don't turn around. I am pointing a nine-millimetre Mauser at your back.' The English came easily, the voice accented and faintly contentious.

'You don't need to, I assure you,' Colman said, afraid not for his own safety but of failing in what was to come. 'I have no weapon.'

Martin circled to a position facing Colman and immediately knew something had gone wrong. He was suddenly over-extended. The man was looking directly at him and now would

38

always know him. Within a minute or two that man would be dead. It was a matter of survival, not being caught and destroyed. He would never tell Adele, of course. He stood there with tight, cold lips, measuring the target, capable of his first and, he hoped, his last killing—capable beyond doubt. He could feel it. There would be no hesitation.

'I'm Stebbins,' said Colman. 'But I'd like to be sure of who you are.'

'Webber,' Martin said. 'Where is it?' he asked as a matter of ritual.

'I have it at my hotel,' Colman said. 'In my room.'

'In your room?'

'I was afraid to chance it before I was sure. And now I am sure. We can go back together, if you like, and I will give it to you. You may not care, but I'm not doing it for the money.'

'Turn around,' Martin said, giving Colman a new look, the eyes embarrassingly insolent, the mouth an insinuating flexure. 'And move to the hut.'

The Mauser was a deadly efficient extension of his hand and it was trained on Colman, who knew that what *might* have worked had *not* worked, and he needed no explanations as to why. 'I think,' Colman said, as if it were absolutely true, 'you may be jumping to a false conclusion.'

'You can drop the act,' Martin told him scornfully. 'Do you really think I would not know what Stebbins looks like? What did you expect me to be? An imbecile?'

Colman had not yet obeyed the command to turn around and move. He managed to look taken aback.

'I had a photograph of him taken by Baumler when he didn't even know it. I have a certain set of techniques. I never deviate from them. That's why I'm still walking around.'

'I can still get you that list,' Colman said, dropping the pretence. 'It's true, I'm not Stebbins. But he's not the only one you can deal with.'

'You're one of his CIA friends.'

'Why lie about it? Yes.'

'Where is he?'

'He's dead. He killed himself. Incredible as it may sound. But he told me all about this before he did it.'

39

'You're lying,' Martin said, his anger, and perhaps fear, increasing now, the time drawing near.

'No, I'm not. He's dead. And I have that list. Fifty important American agents, names and locations—the very list Stebbins was going to hand over. He and I thought alike on this. What's the difference? I can give you the same thing—fifty American agents.'

'Even if you were to be trusted, it would not be worth the risk to me of returning with you to Blauengen. I've most of those names already—yes, that's right. This list of Stebbins' could have provided no more than half a dozen unknown to me, merely to complete my file. I can wait for them—or forsake them altogether.'

'Have you passed them along yet?'

'It won't make any difference to you.'

Martin was about to kill Colman, his chest tightening, the compulsion to do it surging through his veins. Colman knew it was coming and it caught in his throat. From his slightly higher position on the incline, he hurled himself in a low diving block at Martin, hard enough to knock himself cold and break his collarbone or an arm against a stone wall. He had little to lose by making the effort. It was more effective than the elaborate lies.

He hit Martin with such force that the sound of bone moving in its socket was clearly audible, the impact of the two bodies terrific, the gun firing into the air with a faintly bell-like twang, the sound dying quickly in the hills.

The two men fell down hard in the snow, Colman solidly on top of Martin and wrenching the gun from Martin's grasp. There was no way to put cunning or intelligence to work now, only physical strength, and Martin had to relinquish the gun. He was crushed by his failure to kill Colman, felt like a fool for having lost a fight so quickly and easily. Had he perhaps hesitated that fateful split second?

Colman got up swiftly from the victory, the gun now in his possession. He aimed it at Martin, who was struggling to his feet in the snow, his hat gone, his pale-blond hair revealed, snow and ice clinging to his coat and trousers, his breath short from the violent exertion.

'Don't make a move,' Colman said, panting just a bit, his cap still in place on his head, his body tense, his eyes fixed and unflinching. He had reached the age where his ability to fight anyone more formidable than Martin was growing questionable.

'You were saying something about fifty American agents,' Martin said, as if they had been interrupted by a phone call.

'Just as you were about to put a bullet through my brain, yes,' Colman said. '*Now* we'll move into the hut.'

As they walked towards it, Martin said, 'Listen, there's an alternative to everything. For me, it is only a matter of money —I don't care who wins the war between the East and the West. And I have just changed sides.'

Colman found Martin's unabashed opportunism almost refreshing, almost amusing—but not quite. Underneath, showing through the skin, was easy dishonour, not a vestige of scruple to be seen.

'You don't need to admire it,' Martin said. 'We all have different ideas about life. I am being practical. If Stebbins is finished, obviously Baumler was finished even earlier. That leaves me badly off from a business point of view—Baumler was my source.'

The hut smelled of bottled-up cold air, the place lit by a kerosene lamp on a rudimentary piece of furniture passing for a table and situated between them. It was mere shelter from the elements, not more, bare but for the table, two wood bunks of simple sacking, and a cold fireplace. Martin was still talking, earning a living, as they entered and positioned themselves. 'You have to remember that people can't always afford to be what society asks them to be,' he said with unlimited tolerance for all miscreants, presenting what he hoped was a likeable and reasonable personality. He was tough and aggressive, even with Adele, up to a point; and then he was always ready to bargain. 'Nothing is that simple. . . .'

But this CIA automaton was exactly what one saw. 'That's not what I want to talk about,' he said. 'Tell all that to a priest.'

'I am not trying to rationalize anything I have done. But I was eight years old when the Russians got to Berlin. My father was dead and my mother, after successive rapes by the noble liberators, became a *Traumerfrau*. . . .' It was a wounding recollection. 'Obviously I had a chance to grow up seeing things differently than perhaps yourself . . . more able to swallow my disgust than I might otherwise have been. Except that you don't mingle with the best of people either, do you?'

'That's right,' Colman said. 'But what I do I don't do for money.'

Martin sneered. 'Ah, yes. The higher purpose. . . . Some day it's more than possible that you'll learn there is no such thing—on *any* side, under *any* flag, or any set of ideas—that those who think so are masturbating. And that's something I don't do.'

'You're doing it right now,' Colman told him.

'That's not so,' he snapped. 'I'm offering my services, not asking you to approve of my character.'

'How many names of American agents do you have in your possession?'

'Forty.'

'Have you passed them along yet?'

'I promise you I have not. They are still safe and they shall remain safe.'

'What about Switzerland?'

'It's merely the third-country technique,' Martin replied willingly. 'I came over from the East Zone—for a better life. . . .'

'What does that mean?'

'I crossed over—defected—ran—call it what you like. And I want to stay out of the reach of the East German security forces. So I simply do business with the operational people on neutral ground. I have not even felt safe in West Germany.'

'Why not, if you're able to get them good items?'

'Because there are competing forces at each other's throats in the German Democratic Republic,' Martin said knowingly. 'And a certain Colonel Emmering, whom I am sure you know of, is head of internal security and has no interest in the business of espionage or spies in the West. His sole concern is with policing the citizens of the DDR. And he hates defectors—particularly he hates me—it doesn't matter why. . . .'

'Maybe it does.'

'Take my word,' Martin said with restrained urgency. 'What counts is that if he could get his hands on me somehow he would do *any*thing. . . .'

'Emmering?'

'Yes. Even if it meant that the Communists would lose the Third World War. That's his craze, his obsession.'

'He must have quite a grievance,' Colman said.

'My HVA contact is in Zurich,' Martin went on. 'He handles everything. And there is no chance of Emmering putting his hands on me—not in Zurich. I don't need to move into the East to pass my material and HVA needn't take any unnecessary risks in the West. It is no more mysterious than that.'

'Sounds like *Les Miserables*,' Colman said.

'Emmering is not Javert; that's too pure, believe me.'

'Where did you cross?' Colman wanted to know suddenly.

'I'll talk about that later,' Martin answered. 'I will tell you only that it wasn't easy. One doesn't walk through walls.'

'And I'd say you avoided being picked up by the West German police,' Colman concluded.

'I would have as soon gone back to the East,' Martin said with contempt for the thought. 'What? Let them hand me over to every Western intelligence organization in Germany, put me on the Voice of America, and then kick me into a refugee camp for up to two years while the Federal Republic of Germany gets ready to absorb me? Shit, I would die first.'

'So that basically you're stateless,' Colman said.

Martin shrugged. 'Yes, but you could fix that up for me with no trouble at all. That's why I'm putting all my cards on the table with you.'

'It might not be that easy, Webber,' Colman said pleasantly.

'Why not?'

'We may not want it that way. Just anyone can hand you over to the police as a refugee without papers. That's what we want. But we weren't looking for it. It comes as a pleasant surprise.'

Martin's face went slack, his eyes stilled suddenly with the realization that the last train had just pulled out of the station,

43

that a door had blown shut unexpectedly and locked him out. 'What do you mean?'

'I mean, you don't need to be charged with espionage or tried or any of it. And what a hell of a lot of trouble we could have saved everybody, you included, if we had known from the start. You're there for the taking.'

Martin was appalled. 'There for the taking? But *why*?'

'Because that's the way it suits us.'

'After I have been so honest, so completely truthful and goodwilled with you?' he said, his voice stretching with emotion.

'We need you, Webber.'

'Now wait——'

'No, Webber, this is it. Let's move,' Colman said, motioning with the gun.

'I cannot understand,' Martin went on, deeply distressed, holding down his panic with tremendous effort, 'with all that I can offer you that you would choose to do this. . . .'

'You have nothing to offer,' Colman said.

'My contact in Zurich,' Martin said quickly and desperately, childishly innocent in his willingness to sell out anything or anyone. 'A man named Harquist, Sachs Harquist, the jeweller. You see? What greater show of sincerity could you want than that?'

'It can't help you now, Webber,' Colman said, satisfied and casual. 'Not now. Some other time maybe. . . .' The bad guy was caught and things might now be set to right. 'Don't make it tough—let's get going.'

'Wait, wait, wait, I beg of you. . . .' Martin sank to his knees, abject, frantic, a shocking sight suddenly.

'Get up, Webber,' Colman said, pained, 'and stop behaving as if you're going to be tortured to death.'

'You must listen. There is someone else. I am not alone in this. . . .' Martin heard himself but didn't know where he was going with the thought, mocked by the recollection of advising Adele to become an existentialist, uncertain now of just what he had meant.

'Yes?' Colman said. 'Someone else?'

'And if I am not there to prevent it,' Martin continued,

doing penance on the cold stones, the words spilling out of him, 'he will turn over the names to HVA, now that is the truth. . . .'

'It had better not be,' Colman said, not believing Martin anyway, sure that this was a solitary animal.

As Colman spoke he saw the steady and cold burn of Webber's eyes. It was not the expression of a man genuinely reduced to his knees. And then the wooden table came flying at him, sent through the air in a single upward heave, without a windup or a back motion of any kind. Martin let out a cry of both rage and fear as he made the move meant to surprise and unsettle the enemy. There was a kind of insane jubilation in it and it came up from within him like an explosion.

Colman saw it coming and managed to block it on his forearm as it knocked him off balance and caused him to stagger backward. But he had a clear shot at Martin's sprinting figure before Martin was through the door of the hut, a shot he deliberately did not take. Maybe Martin had suspected he might not. Colman resorted instead to shouting, 'Webber, it's no use, you can't get away,' recalling the same familiar warning as it echoed through a thousand adventure movies on as many lost Saturday afternoons.

Martin ran across the white copse under the moon and dashed fiercely towards the incline above the trees in an obvious attempt to get to the top. His chances of escaping to the road were nil. His speed was very great, even through the snow and under the burden of the overcoat, his Homburg marking him as if he were one of the suit-and-tie people being pursued from a board meeting by enraged stockholders. But his entire life was suddenly a race in which he would win new freedom and a sensuous fairy queen to go with it or die in the attempt. It was too early to call it quits. Later perhaps, but not now, and not like this.

Colman followed, lunging as hard as one can lunge uphill through two or three inches of snow, hoping to get close enough to overtake Webber with a tackle. When Webber suddenly raced into a peripheral line of trees, the last of the wooded area at this height, Colman slowed his pace, stopped, stood still for a moment, and then scanned the summit. In order to reach the other side, where there were more trees and a downward run towards Switzerland, Webber would need to cross the opening at the top of the glade once again; he could not do anything else. The only other egress from this point was back towards the Blauengen road. Colman was betting Webber would not choose it.

He moved quickly across the open area and into the trees and placed himself behind one of them, night deeper here than in the clearing where the moon still beamed down from a cloudless sky crowded with luminous and shimmering stars. He went into a crouch, one hand on the bole of the tree, one hand gripping the nine-millimetre Mauser, and he had a good command of the open area leading up to the crestline. He felt cold now as time shortened, and depressed because of the way things were going. But it had to have been worse for Webber: his whole world had been blown to bits.

Colman took a breath and shuddered with cold. Just fifty or a hundred feet away, Webber must have now lurked on the verge of his next move, gunless, cold to the bone, and desperate.

Colman shifted his feet and then stopped to listen. The wind hummed softly in his ears for several moments and then fell silent. He looked overhead as if for a sign and then back to the clearing and the crest of the hill. After a moment he rose from his haunches and began to move in a straight line towards the place where Webber had disappeared to slink and hide, Colman going from one tree to the next for concealment, a necessary tactic even in the darkness. He moved carefully, cautiously, and with a certain amount of rigidity, the automatic in a firm grip. He stopped, peered, could see only the dimly frosted trunks, branches, and pine needles, the tortuous paths between the trees. He continued moving.

He stopped short. Webber was pressed behind a tree not ten feet away. There was no sound; the narrowest edge of Webber's coat caught a prism of perfidious moonlight—there simply wasn't enough room for total concealment, though it might not have betrayed him to less avid eyes.

'Come out, Webber,' Colman said quietly, the end of the line reached.

Webber didn't hesitate. He left the bosom of the tree without a word and began to run away. Colman was ready to follow. A tree root sent him sprawling on his belly and left him with no further chance, he knew, to win a race with Webber. He watched Webber running away as if demons followed. It was then, from a position on the ground, that Colman shot him dead.

CHAPTER SIX

WEBBER'S BLOOD seeped from within, a thin flow spilling over his lower lip and down his chin with the compulsion of water coming from a ruptured main, his eyes close to death. The bullet had pierced a lung and probably the aortal artery. 'I didn't think . . . you would shoot . . . to kill.'

'I didn't. . . .'

'Listen, whatever your name is . . .'

'Colman.'

'There's someone . . . Colman . . .' Webber said that much and then died.

Colman, crouched on one knee, looked down at Webber's cold, dead face. He found he didn't hate Webber or regard him as an enemy. Instead he felt a chill of solitude he had never felt before. This was the only person, outside of war, he had ever killed. There *was* a difference.

He went quickly through Webber's pockets.

He found a set of keys whose locks were God knew where, a billfold containing about two hundred D-marks, a Swiss driver's licence and a Swiss passport, both made out in the name of Martin Fischer of the Hotel Splendid in Zurich, age twenty-nine, height six feet, weight seventy-eight kilos—statistics with the quality of a footnote. Webber—or Fischer—was for the moment a rough diagram; not more, not less. And the chances were that the Hotel Splendid would reveal nothing beyond that.

Colman pocketed the few items and then moved downhill with Webber slung in a fireman's lift on his shoulder, Webber's head drooping like a blossom from a broken stem, the hair hanging straight down in soft yellow strands, a handkerchief forced between his teeth to dam up the flow of blood. Colman lugged the body along, his footprints like a trail of guilt which would be covered by another fall of snow before anyone would have a chance to see it and wonder at its meaning.

Within five minutes he had come down the hill and moved as quickly as he could across the road like a thief who had stolen no more than a sack of flour. He dropped the body on the other side of the stone guardrail and swung himself over immediately after.

Just a few yards away the steep descent to the ravine began, undisturbed, snow-covered, the nearly sheer line leading several hundred feet down to a narrow gorge accessible only to climbers and apt to remain without visitors until after the snows. Colman found he was sweating. He pushed Webber over the edge.

The body sank, crashed through the branches of one of the densely growing pines, and, leaving muffled, snapping and cracking sounds echoing behind, disappeared.

Colman took Webber's hat from inside his anorak and threw it like a wreath to follow its owner. He had done what he must. He began to walk back towards Blauengen, turning all of it over and over in his mind.

Webber—Martin Fischer may or may not have been his real name—had been rapacious, deceitful, treacherous, certain to have caused the deaths and downfalls of others had he been allowed to escape. There were those who would have perhaps said to Colman, 'And did *you* not murder?' And he would have answered, 'I killed. But I am not Christ. I prevented the murders of comrades in the only way possible.' Had they then said, 'Are not your comrades the same as those who would murder them?' Colman would have remained silent. There was no answer that would either satisfy or persuade in the face of such a devout refusal to see life as it is.

CHAPTER SEVEN

AT THE EXACT MOMENT Colman walked towards the
viaduct and those occasional moving jots of light from passing
vehicles, Stevenson had entered the presence of three men,
each one of whom was substantially taller than he was.

There was Llewellyn, with his faintly Rooseveltian air and
his instinct for running an organization by keeping himself out
of reach; Steve Major, bald, undeviating, humourless, not
nearly up to the business of being an operational chief; and a
third man, well past his keenest appetites and best health,
whom Stevenson did not know and who continued grimly to
regard a massive night view of Berlin through the window of
the penthouse office even after Stevenson had arrived and
exchanged greetings with the other two men.

'This is Senator Arthur Davis,' Llewellyn said, towering
over Stevenson, who had long ceased to equate status and
potency with tallness. 'The Senator wants to know what we're
up to, Michael,' Llewellyn continued, going to an eight-place
board table. 'And so do I.'

Stevenson, fifty-two, positive and polite, his smile sagacious
and always accompanied by the squint of tolerant but faintly
sceptical eyes, stood his ground. Every morning at seven
o'clock, while Llewellyn and his patrician ass were in the sack,
Stevenson was shaved, showered, dressed, done with breakfast,
and poring over the surface of a wide slant board to which were
pinned the circumstances of his special existence. Reports,
placements, opinions—the various flags—checked, cross-
checked, and rechecked. Little else commanded his attention.
Looking directly at Llewellyn he merely said, 'If I may ask,
with what specific Congressional interest are we dealing at the
moment?'

'There's a growing doubt, Mr Stevenson,' the elderly and
joyless Senator began, coming a few rather onerous steps away
from the fascinating view, 'concerning the efficacy and the
desirability of maintaining a vast intelligence agency at all.'

Stevenson raised his eyebrows, pursed his lips, then nodded
his head. 'I trust that the Senator finds the idiocy of that
growing doubt as conspicuous as I do.'

'The issue, Mr Stevenson, is what does a nation get for its tax dollars,' the Senator said, undeterred. 'A lot of people think that the CIA in general goes around stirring up trouble. You've got to reckon with it, because if you don't, *I* can't when the clamour begins. . . .'

Steve Major picked that moment to become influential. 'Michael,' he said, as if they were discussing the hanging of drapes, 'why don't you tell Senator Davis, in broad terms, what your department's function is, in case he doesn't know. That might help to clarify things.' He hadn't convinced anyone that the thought had just occurred to him.

'Why don't you have a seat, Senator?' Llewellyn said.

'I don't want to insult your intelligence, Senator, with recitations of the obvious,' Stevenson said, the centre of all eyes as he spoke. 'So forgive me if I do. My section is called Two with a Roman numeral. It does the job of a watchdog. *Like* a watchdog, it pounces on intruders. At the very least it barks and saves the valuables. That's the object of counter-intelligence. More specifically, the putting together of numerous bits and pieces in order to find out who is going to hit you, with what, and just where. I think it's an important job. I think it's urgent. I might even add, I think it's a matter of life and death.'

'But you are not empowered or even organized to send agents into the East Zone, Michael,' Steve Major wanted to make clear to the Senator. 'That's the work of Section One.'

'We want the Senator to understand, Michael,' Llewellyn said, 'that the Mankin incident came about accidentally—that is, because basic operating procedure wasn't strictly observed.' And then standing up, looking like a Roman proconsul in a double-breasted suit, he continued: 'I don't want to see this agency emasculated in the Congress through misunderstanding or lack of information.'

'I couldn't agree more,' Stevenson said amiably.

'With that in mind, the Senator has got to know that you, Michael, not the organizational machinery, balled up.'

Stevenson smiled faintly through his own and the mild shock of the others, and Llewellyn added, 'If I may put it that way.' He returned from a stroll around the table to his chair.

'I'm willing enough, Mr Llewellyn, that Senator Davis carry that impression away with him if it will help matters,' Stevenson said and looked at Senator Davis and continued. 'You see, Senator . . . a long-standing policy of the East Germans and the Russians has been the infiltration of U.S. Army bases, the placing of agents in jobs as civilian kitchen help, filing clerks, electricians, typists, motion-picture projectionists, and so on. They haven't been exactly unsuccessful in that regard. And I think it is safe to say that in no situation is the function of counterespionage more classic and significant. Root out the spy—if you can. Because he's not there for the salary the U.S. Army pays him. . . . Excuse me.' He stopped to relight his three-quarters-smoked cigar while they all waited in silence. Then he continued:

'Without going into too many details, my people turned up evidence that a list of just such infiltrations existed in one of the offices on Normannenstrasse, which is headquarters, Senator, for East German Intelligence. I think you can readily see the connection between getting possession of that list and the work of my section.' He puffed on his cigar and the others watched. 'Well—we failed to get the list. And Mankin got caught.' He splayed his small but firm hands. 'Do I shrug off the loss of a man or regard it as part of a game? Not for a moment. But I know at the same time that the value of that list hasn't diminished a fraction of a point simply because a man got caught and we're embarrassed by it.'

'I understand that much,' said the Senator, 'but there's a mood today that definitely doesn't favour you, Mr Stevenson —the ins and outs of your procedural problems aside.' And he continued wearily. 'Maybe it's because people are not quite sure of what you're doing and why.'

'I can understand the overlap to some extent, Michael,' Steve Major said, 'though something about it definitely puzzles me. But you should have cleared it with me. It was definitely not your move.'

'Maybe not, Steve,' Stevenson said. 'But it was done. And that brings us to what you, Mr Llewellyn, like to call my department scandal, which I assume you have already mentioned to the Senator——'

'Rather than having him read about it in the New York *Times* or *Newsweek*—yes, Michael,' Llewellyn said.

'It won't necessarily appear in either of those august publications,' Stevenson said, placing one hand in his back pocket, the other holding the cigar, 'if our best efforts are accompanied by one or two good breaks.'

'Tell us, Michael,' Llewellyn said, 'was it Stebbins who put Mankin where he is?'

'Probably,' Stevenson answered. 'According to the German civilian we've arrested—or rather, the Germans have arrested for us—the answer is yes.'

'Is this man Stebbins in your section, Mr Stevenson?' Senator Davis asked.

'Yes, Senator. He's very enterprising. He was working to uncover Communist agents we had reason to suspect were placed in the three-hundred-and-fifteenth-ordnance battalion in Zehlendorf.' He paused, then went on. 'Well, he uncovered one, all right. But he didn't bother to let anyone know it, kept it strictly to himself. You can understand why after you know that he decided to go into business with the very Communist agent he'd uncovered, one Kurt Baumler—not much, a nondescript, a drone, but the key to Stebbins' heretofore unsuspected ambitions. Stebbins, in a nutshell, had things to sell, and Baumler was only too happy to put him in touch with the right customers.'

'Was this man Stebbins in a position of trust, Mr Stevenson —that is, was he considered trustworthy?' the Senator asked.

'As much as any of us, Senator, or even yourself.'

'Incredible. . . .'

'He had good papers. Smart, courageous . . . loyal—we thought.'

'Why haven't you arrested him?' Llewellyn asked.

'We're about to, Mr Llewellyn,' Stevenson said. 'We've been waiting for him to make the move that would lead us to his contact, the key East German agent in the whole affair, someone called Webber. We think the moment may be at hand.'

'It seems to me,' the Senator said, 'that there's a tit-for-tat quality to so much of this business: they take one of your people, you take one of theirs. I mean, do you really achieve anything by it? Why not simply arrest this Stebbins without delay and be damned to the rest?'

'Well, it's too late for that anyway, Senator,' Stevenson said, his resentment cloaked by a warm, tolerant smile. 'But consider the two possibilities and perhaps you'll see the logic in it. One, this agent of theirs might have valuable information to give us. We might find out where some underground burrowing is going on just in time to keep a building from suddenly falling in on us.'

'Perhaps they would stop burrowing if we would stop burrowing,' Senator Davis said heavily.

'Well, while we're awaiting that Utopian day, sir, consider the second possibility—that of an exchange. We might be able to shut their mouths about Mankin and even get him back in trade . . . if Stebbins leads us to this other man, this Webber. Under the circumstances,' Stevenson said, looking steadily at the Senator, 'I think that will have been worth waiting for.'

'What, specifically, was Stebbins trying to do?' the Senator asked.

Stevenson answered, 'Sell the names of our people who are operating in the East. We know he has the list in his possession. Some fifty names of American agents and where they can be found. Not very pretty.'

The Senator heaved a huge sigh. 'I think,' he said, 'you have a mess on your hands—simply in terms of the nature of what you have to deal with, perhaps. But wherever I look, frankly, I find . . . signs of incompetence or questionable activity. Forgive me, gentlemen. But that's the impression I've been getting for days.'

Stevenson smiled at the Senator almost pityingly and Llewellyn sat as still as if he had been struck dumb, his long, proficient-looking fingers steepled six inches in front of his face, his eyes in the fixed stare of a man who has heard a guilty verdict rendered on his actions.

'Wouldn't you say, Senator,' Stevenson reasoned, 'that getting to Baumler and finding out about Stebbins, disconcerting as it may have been, is a sign of *some* competence?'

'I don't think any of you quite understand,' the Senator

53

began, rising heavily from his chair. 'There's a growing sentiment for disengagement—even limited—from the Cold War. A great many Congressmen, as well as plain citizens of *all* persuasions, are, ideologically speaking—deeply fatigued. I mean, it all begins to look unnecessary—as if it has gone on of its own accord long after its objective was either reached or simply became obsolete.' He looked from one to the other and concluded: 'Think of a tractor ploughing and reploughing the same field and you can see what I'm driving at.'

'I'm certainly sorry about the ideologically fatigued among us, Senator,' Stevenson said, smiling good-naturedly. 'I'm sure we all sympathize. I personally wouldn't consider arguing the point with them. But I would like to ask what they would have us do, if anything, about the enthusiasm with which some of the tractors from the other *side* seem to be ploughing and reploughing the same field.' A deep frown finally overtook Stevenson's smile at the end of his speech, though his voice, that of an experienced presentation lawyer, remained steady and controlled. He had tacitly been put in charge of the defence, not just of himself but of an entire point of view.

The Senator picked up his grey Stetson and said, 'For all that, there is the opinion—not necessarily my own—that so much of this sort of activity begets more of the same, not only in the CIA but elsewhere. Certain situations are put into motion and go on endlessly with no visible purpose.' A little sadly he added, 'We may all be victims of that, gentlemen—serving nonexistent causes long after we should have realized as much. . . .'

'Senator,' Llewellyn said, standing up and coming slowly around the table, 'that is a very portentous statement. Are you trying to tell us that we're . . . unnecessary? Some sort of a boondoggle?'

Stevenson winced inwardly at the choice of word, and Senator Davis said, 'I am just one United States Senator, Mr Llewellyn, and I don't subscribe to sweeping and irrevocable pronouncements about anything. If I ever did, I do not now. But I do say that your function is under scrutiny, along with all sorts of others things that are being re-evaluated today. My committee happens to be concerned with you, but you are simply part of a whole new pattern in the rethinking of national interests and priorities.'

'Then actually whether the agency operates smoothly or not is purely academic,' Stevenson said.

'Not at all,' the Senator answered. 'Paradoxically, your severest critics, when it comes right down to it, expect you to operate smoothly in the way for which you were activated.'

'Senator, I'm suddenly not sure of what's disturbing the Congress,' Llewellyn said, good-humoured but perplexed.

'Mr Llewellyn,' the Senator said, 'my message to you is that in this time of flux, people who belong to anything that can be considered an old concept have to be exceedingly efficient, circumspect . . . and cautious. They must try hard not to appear foolish . . . clumsy . . . or insensitive to new ideas or the demands of minority groups. And above all . . . their spies mustn't be caught.'

No one spoke, and the Senator, who was undecided about many things after a long life and wide experience and was clearly trying to keep an open mind, seemed a bit played out. 'Gentlemen, I must return to my hotel now,' he said. 'I think we've covered enough for the moment. I'll be in touch with you before I leave Berlin, Mr Llewellyn. Remember one thing, gentlemen—I am not your enemy. I am your friend. But I am your realistic and practical friend.'

A moment after one of Llewellyn's staff had escorted Senator Davis from the office, Stevenson said, 'There's some confusion these days about who is at fault—the burglar or the victim for providing temptation,' and stuck the dead cigar into the corner of his bulldog mouth.

'I'd say they suspect that we're the ones who keep things going,' Llewellyn said soberly, his dignity and bearing now accented as he walked to the window and looked out from the irresistible height to the night scene, streaked and pinpointed colours on a black background. 'They think,' he continued, 'that we are the sentinels of the East-West conflict, that we are out to prolong the Cold War, that all our efforts and activities are a matter of self-interest—even at an unconscious level.' Deeply philosophical, he added, 'Can any of us swear that perhaps a little of that isn't motivating all of us?'

Stevenson saw the side of Llewellyn that usually lay submerged beneath political layers and felt a measure of fondness for it. But he said, 'Yes, I can. At the risk of sounding smug. . . .'

They both looked at him, and Steve Major, having no philosophical bent whatever, went to the core of his personal irritation. 'Michael, you've stepped on a lot of corns with this Mankin thing. And I can't quite understand why. *We*'ve known about that list of their agents on our Army bases also. It doesn't make sense to me. Was there any other reason you sent Mankin in?'

'I've told you all there is to tell, Steve,' Stevenson said.

Coming away from the window, his reflections at an end, Llewellyn said in an almost declamatory voice, 'We're stuck with Mankin, we're stuck with Stebbins. We have to minimize the effects if we can, get out from under.' He shook his fine large head with critical distaste. 'We look bad, no mistake. We look like a pack of wahoos, Dick Tracys, blunderers, sadists, deranged personalities—playing games, stirring up trouble——' He stopped short and began to pace, looking for that ultimate executive decision. Steve Major smouldered with a new cigarette, his hairless skull still flushed. Stevenson let his attention wander just long enough to keep his mind from running down—ten or fifteen seconds usually did the trick. 'House-cleaning is always a nauseating task,' he heard Llewellyn say, and he refocused his attention. 'Get it done, Michael. And don't compound the felony.'

'It's under way, Mr Llewellyn,' Stevenson said. 'Unpleasant, but under way. . . .'

'I think Stebbins must be mad,' Llewellyn said. 'Why would he have done this?'

'Because your conscience and his conscience are not the same conscience,' Stevenson said, quoting Nietzsche. 'But I'd say he did it for the money. Anyhow, you'll have a chance to ask him personally soon enough.'

No one said anything more and Stevenson walked out and travelled by elevator to the underground garage where Kagen was waiting to chauffeur him from the British Zone back to Rose Bowl, just two blocks away from Checkpoint Charlie.

Kagen wore a modified livery and an American police .38 underneath the jacket at his hip. He had been with Stevenson for five years. No serious purpose had yet brought the gun from its holster.

Stevenson sat in the back seat as the car moved into the Tiergarten along Strasse des 17 Juni, Berlin's nightly restlessness and pleasure drives fully evident. He was not really a part of the place. He usually travelled in a straight line connecting the underground garage of his apartment building in Charlottenburg with the underground garage at Rose Bowl at the other end of the West Zone. But he knew it well and his sense of sodality with it was unquestionable. This was ironic, of course. Stevenson had been one of the youngest prosecutors in the secondary trials at Nuremburg, and he had zealously, and even vengefully, pursued the abominable defendants—the gauleiters and the camp commandants. Nothing had rescinded that—not the economic miracle, or the emergence of a blameless generation, or any of the new hatreds. And nothing ever could. Not even the Russians, about whom he had thought constantly and for so long. Every waking minute of his life included the unshakable belief that their foreign policy constituted the world's most purposeful evil. But not even that could dim or nullify his old convictions.

Bob Brannigan, a fiery red-faced man of fifty who was Stevenson's deputy and liaison with the two allies and also the West German authorities, awaited him at Rose Bowl, which consisted of three connecting rooms on the fourth floor of a new building in the old newspaper quarter. Stevenson walked through the door bearing the legend COMPOUND DEVELOPMENT LTD. 'Anything from Colman?' he asked, for that was the only reason he had returned at this hour.

'Nothing yet,' said Brannigan, a man who still jitterbugged with his wife whenever they could find the appropriate music and the time. Watching his chief wander, coat and hat unremoved, to the window, Brannigan said, 'How was your meeting?'

'Every question got an answer to a question that wasn't asked,' Stevenson said. 'No two people in the room were talking about the same thing.'

'Did they ask about Mankin?'

'Steve Major twitched a little bit about it. Something about it bothered him. He was actually having perceptions of some kind. Maybe I've misjudged him. Not by much—around five per cent. . . .' Stevenson's eyes were trained on the Friedrichstrasse, on the stone wall that had thrilled Khrushchev so much. 'Wanted to know if there had been any other reason for sending him in. . . .' The Wall was lurid, without an ethic of any kind, a rank symbol of antagonism one had almost to admire even while despising it. Stevenson did not take a detached view of it any more than he had of Hitler's Jewish policy. 'According to Senator Davis, we're ideologically fatigued. . . .' He could feel acceptance of that evil setting in everywhere as a result of dogged promulgation on the one hand and on the other the desperate weariness embodied in the Senator's rather pithy description. 'And maybe he's right. . . .'

Brannigan kept his eyes on Stevenson and said, 'What did you tell them about Mankin?'

Still watching the checkpoint, Stevenson said quietly, 'All the right lies. . . .'

A moment or two went by and Stevenson said, 'I'm going home. Call me if anything comes through from Walters. I don't want to sleep through it.'

'Okay, M.J.'

But before he could get out of the room, the green flash came, accompanied by its buzzer. Brannigan was closer to the desk than Stevenson, who said, 'That's him. Pick it up.'

Brannigan did as told and listened to the voice at the other end briefly. Then he said into the mouthpiece, 'Where is he now?'

Stevenson, near the office door, studied Brannigan's face with an expectant squint, motionless and waiting for answers to all the obvious questions.

Brannigan finally said, 'Okay, I've got it,' and replaced the phone receiver. 'Walters has heard from Colman,' he told Stevenson.

'Yeah?'

'Stebbins is dead, and so is the other guy.'

Stevenson was disappointed rather than shocked.

'How the hell did that happen?' And then he didn't even believe it.

Brannigan hesitated. 'He killed himself.'

Stevenson believed it completely now, and with marked impatience he said, 'What other guy?'

'The East German—Webber.'

Stevenson felt a surge of anger even as he knew how futile anger was, how self-belittling. '*Both* of them?' he said resentfully. 'What about Colman?'

'He'll be back tomorrow, early.'

'Is that all?'

'We supposedly will get the details when he gets here.'

'That's great. So far I count up to minus two,' Stevenson said, knowing he would not sleep decently that night, not caring but deeply uneasy about having to wait to find things out.

'Not exactly,' Brannigan said. 'We just found out something I was going to mention to you later.'

'What?'

'Webber has a widow. She is one now, anyway. Right here in Berlin.'

'How did you find that out?' Stevenson asked.

'From Baumler—one of the finest canaries in captivity. It could be interesting . . . informative. . . .'

Stevenson was faintly grudging, almost as though not to build up to any letdowns. 'We'll see,' he replied noncommittally. And then he went home.

CHAPTER EIGHT

COLMAN, among other debarking passengers, crossed the glistening tarmac through a light but cold rainfall and joined Brannigan just inside the domestic in-flight doors. They said hello and nothing else until they sat side by side in Brannigan's car and began to drive away from the airport towards the centre of Berlin. 'What did you get out of Stebbins before he did it?' Brannigan asked. 'Who was the paymaster?'

'No one,' Colman said. 'It wasn't that way.' He hated to go over the dreary and oppressive facts of the matter. 'He went over because he hated us and loved them. He said he always had. He said we were corrupt, that we were imperialist swine, and all the rest of it. I told him he was sick.'

It evidently struck Brannigan as more sordid than anything else would have. His eyes straight ahead as he drove, he said softly and passionately, 'The dirty bastard.'

'He thought we were worse,' Colman said matter-of-factly. 'What *he* did was fine. *We* were the Fascists, the pimps, the racists, etcetera, etcetera.'

'Sick, just as you say, but no less a son-of-a-bitch for it,' Brannigan said with complete certainty. 'Anyhow, you're back with a terrible score, Brian. I take for granted you did your best and that you're not God. But we needed that East German desperately.'

'He was getting away from me with the names of forty of our people in the East in his possession,' Colman said evenly. 'They'd have been X's if he had made it.'

'Maybe. But don't expect any rewards for it.'

'I don't.'

'M.J. is going to want you to take a long leave—just so you won't be surprised when it comes up.' Brannigan's words were friendly but hard.

'That's up to him,' Colman said, not sure how he felt. 'Where did you leave him?'

'In one of the ravines. It will be spring before anyone finds him.' He touched the outside of his coat pocket. 'I've got his effects with me. His name wasn't Webber, naturally. It was Martin Fischer.'

'We know that,' Brannigan said, still watching the road. 'Because we already have a line on *Mrs* Fischer—his widow.' He glanced sideways and gave an answering nod to Colman's look of inexpectation. 'That's right, he left one. Our friend Baumler opened up a bit wider after you went off to Stuttgart. He has a beautiful voice. She's right here in Berlin, where we can look at her. And that's just what we're doing.'

Fischer's death assumed a new dimension for Colman. He was suddenly sharing something with a person he had never laid eyes on, something that could never be got rid of by either of them. 'To what end?' he asked.

'We'll know it when we see it,' Brannigan answered, and then neither of them said anything more. They drove through the soft rain with the sound of the wipers taking over the silence.

At Rose Bowl Stevenson listened to Colman, scowling, crouched forward at his desk as if presiding over an invisible disarray of parts belonging to a disassembled machine. He felt let down, as if he had perhaps been seeing Colman in the wrong light for all this time, imputing to the ease and unhesitant manner and the West Point background more than they were worth. 'I don't like the idea of having to defend a killing,' he stated flatly. 'Remote as the chances of tracing it may be.'

Colman didn't care for the implications of distrust and misplaced confidence. 'He was running and he was going to get where he wanted to go,' he explained without emotion. 'In my judgement I had to fire. I think anyone else would have done the same thing.'

Stevenson said coldly, 'Maybe they wouldn't have.' And as if no response would have been tolerated, he immediately added, 'You didn't tell Fox or the FIA man anything about it, did you?'

'No. Only that Webber hadn't shown up for the rendezvous. They came back to Berlin on another plane, by the way.'

Stevenson approved. 'Maintain the fiction,' he said. 'You have leave coming to you, as you may recall. This would probably be the best time to take it. Go on one of those extended cruises, recharge your batteries. . . .'

Colman closed his eyes for an instant and nodded. 'Step one in easing me out,' he said.

'Everyone needs a change,' Stevenson said cryptically.

'You think I may have gone zonkers out there and shot that man for nothing,' Colman said. 'You have no way of knowing I didn't.'

Stevenson fixed a relentless, searching eye on Colman. 'Did you?' he asked in a deadly quiet voice.

'I didn't think so at the time. I still don't.'

'How did you feel when you killed him?'

61

'Not like whistling. Not like crying either. He was poison. But I didn't like the experience at all, not one bit. . . .'

Stevenson nodded, seemed resigned to irreversible facts. 'It doesn't really work, laying it off on you,' he admitted. 'I suppose that's what I'm trying to do.'

'Because I was the man in the field and you need an answer to why it all went wrong. You don't want to think it was chance.'

'That's true, Brian. But I'm also asking myself if the same —call it bad luck—would have befallen someone else? Or are you . . . tired? Tired without even knowing it. Why did Stebbins kill himself? Why did Webber run? You're right, it could have happened to anyone. But it happened to you— you, who have made no wrong moves before. Do you see what I mean?'

'I'm not sure it matters whether I do or not.'

'That business about Colonel Emmering,' Stevenson said, frowning. 'I'd like to have got into that a lot deeper. . . .'

'I dropped the ball for you,' Colman said.

'Please, no analogies to sport,' Stevenson said. 'That always grinds me. These are not games.' He went on speculatively: 'But maybe Mrs Fischer can be something to us. She's waiting for a husband who isn't coming home. That could be a big factor. It could force her finally to move—if no one moves towards her first. If she's in on anything, maybe there's even a chance of trading her for Mankin. . . .' He toyed almost wistfully with Fischer's ring of keys as if they were the remains of all his hopes and dreams. 'That's the heart of everything.'

Colman watched Stevenson's brilliantly ugly face reflecting the loss. And he wanted to leave, to get away from the gloom of Stevenson's resolve. It was suddenly suffocating, Colman's own increasing sense of disappointment pushing him towards the gusts of air outside in the street, a drink in silence, a dreamless sleep. He had never known Stevenson to show strain, to exhibit so ragged an edge. He was a tough, quick-witted man, kind and pitiless in a single eye-crinkling smile, the cordial, all-knowing friend who was the best of professional agents. Mankin loomed obsessively in every step, in every word and every thought. Stebbins had been at the bottom of it, the reason for Mankin's arrest. Fischer had been too heavily counted upon.

Colman delayed his departure as Stevenson said, 'I tried to tell myself it was the money that turned him. But I knew I just wanted it that way. Then we could say we had made a misjudgement. But we didn't.' He looked directly at Colman and concluded: 'Stebbins was all the things he was supposed to be. Courageous, convinced, incorruptible. But all for the other side.' He smiled when he said it, depressing truths notwithstanding. 'There was that single difference invisible to the naked eye. . . .'

Colman left him and walked for a block or two in the deepening dusk of late afternoon, the great tower on top of the Graphic Trades Building now throwing its evening messages in swiftly galloping electric lights. Colman didn't look up. He went to a small *Konditorei* not far away and then retired early, accompanied in his withdrawal into silence by the essence of a woman he had never seen, by the abstraction of her helpless position and the possibility of her guilt. He didn't know why. But two days later, through Brannigan's office, he was easily able to obtain certain data necessary to seeking the answer.

By that morning winter had returned to its rightful place in Berlin. Cold air came down from the Baltic Sea across the Pomeranian plains and with brute force drove out the genial air of the past few days and took over the tableland of lakes, canals, forests, of wide avenues and open squares. Gusts of intermittent rain swept through the streets and beat against windowpanes and dampened spirits. By ten o'clock Colman saw Adele Fischer for the first time at close range, the distance between them some eighteen inches to two feet.

She had entered the large market, still impressed even after all this time with the astonishing variety and volume of consumer goods. Twenty-six years in the DDR were not easily got out of one's system. She began with her shopping cart to tour the shelves.

Colman studied her as carefully as he dared. She was standing in the aisle before the coffee section on one of the large counters crammed deeply and piled high with foodstuffs and putting two cans of Maxwell House into her shopping cart.

63

Colman searched for some revelation of anxiety or fear. Faint tension could be detected at the corners of her mouth. Possibly. Maybe not.

As she turned to move on, Colman averted his face and selected a box of Kellogg's Corn Flakes from the parallel shelves, dropped it into his otherwise empty cart, and pushed off in the opposite direction. He had wanted to be certain that Fischer had left behind him a female counterpart of himself— a bitch and a faithless fishwife who was deserving of even worse and couldn't have cared less anyhow, deadlier than even Fischer had been and as ready to profit from the blood of others. He suspected already that this was not the case. It was only after they had passed by each other that he realized she was a beauty.

Again he came face-to-face with her, the two of them passing in opposite directions, Colman pushing his cart carrying the single box of cornflakes slowly in front of him. How much she knew or did not know, how significant to her was Fischer's absence was all still a matter of guesswork. That Fischer had been concerned for her at that last moment was not at all unlikely.

On a short line at a check-out counter far removed from the one Mrs Fischer had chosen, Colman's strange surveillance was uncovered by Bork. 'Having a look for yourself, eh? I wonder why,' the German said, pleased to have taken Colman by surprise.

Colman took note of the carefully affected relaxed manner, the dangling cigarette, the serpentine eyes turned elsewhere, and said, 'Maybe I just wanted to be sure you're doing your job properly.'

'Come, come,' said the other, unruffled. 'You had no idea I was doing a job here. And you still can't be sure. But the fact is, I am. Before I go back to Munich. *Sehr niedlich*, Webber's wife—or Frau Fischer, to be exact. . . .'

The line moved forward, Colman having discarded the cart and holding the box of cornflakes in his hand, and Bork said, 'I notice you're doing some shopping. I also . . . for my dog.' He referred to a package of cellophane-wrapped meat and said, 'Isn't that right, Schnapsi?' A small black-and-white mongrel with one blue eye and one brown one and an appealingly stupid face looked up at Colman and whimpered.

'Expensive taste for a dog,' Colman said, conscious of Mrs Fischer's progress on the other line.

'He makes a good cover. I travel with him everywhere.'

'What are you supposed to be doing anyway?'

'Eventually I'm going to be talking to her,' Bork said. 'That's something I know how to do. I'm very convincing, as you know, and I will find out what's what.' His eyes shut and he drew on his cigarette for a final puff before crushing it underfoot. 'I can also add a column of figures,' he said. 'Though you might not think so.'

Colman knew what was coming. Poor judgement had been exercised in assigning Bork to this job. He listened with seeming indifference as Bork said, 'And someone in Section Two is very sure that the woman's husband . . . is not coming back, that he is away—permanently.'

'Your target is leaving the market,' Colman said casually.

'And going directly home,' Bork said, careful to take no notice of the departure. 'I know every move by now.' Bork's turn to check out arrived. He then awaited Colman at the front of the large store.

Mrs Fischer was being played like a creature in a maze. Her husband was dead and undiscovered in a snow-filled ravine beyond her imaginings. Colman could have led her to the spot. There was no satisfaction in the bond between them provided by that fact. Colman paid for a box of cornflakes he had no use for and walked away from the check-out counter.

Bork confronted him with the pointless cunning and low-brow spite that constituted his entire style. 'Funny, don't you think, that Webber—or rather, Fischer—has not returned home after all these days?' he said as they stood next to the vending machine where Colman had joined him.

'So it's funny he hasn't come home,' Colman said. 'You'd better get going. One of these times she's liable to fool you.'

Bork gave him a nasty smile and a slow, perverse shake of the head. 'She's in a cage,' he said, dreadfully competent in the way a type of cretin can be and as unmoved by the human aspect of any circumstances. 'No one is going to contact her.

And she is going to contact no one. And sooner or later she is going to lose that neat, calm look and go to pieces inside. . . .'

Colman stared at him, said nothing, Bork's enjoyment of someone else's distress unconcealed.

'. . . because her husband is *not* coming home—not next week, not ever. We both know that, don't we?'

'Do we?'

Bork went on: 'She is still hoping. But a day or two from now will be different. The guts will be out of her. . . .' He nodded, took out a cigarette, and concluded: 'I have no way of knowing, of course, but I keep seeing him—whatever he looked like—dead. In the snow. I don't know why. But that's the picture I keep getting in my mind. Maybe I am a psychic.'

He shrugged, smiled, and without another word left Colman standing there with the box of cornflakes in a paper bag. Colman felt as if he had tried to turn a corner that simply hadn't been there.

Bork was one of those embarrassments to which all sides of any cause might be subjected. He may have been the son of a semi-prosperous shopkeeper from whom he had received little praise and upon whom he considered himself an improvement. It wasn't important. He was the dregs of humankind, whether he could help it or not; but he epitomized the genius of deceit that could turn a trick Stevenson now doggedly wished to turn. Though Colman didn't know what the trick really was or how Stevenson planned to use it. Until the following afternoon.

CHAPTER NINE

'ANOTHER DAY OR TWO, just as Bork says, will put Mrs Fischer in very soft condition,' Stevenson said, standing at the window. 'Obviously that bothers you and I can see why. But it happens to be the purpose of this operation. To make her vulnerable, to make her susceptible, so she's easier to deal with.'

'It would be just as effective to bring her in,' Colman said. 'She would tell you anything if she had anything to tell.'

'How do you know?'

'I've looked at enough of these people to know.'

'And let her know her husband is dead, you mean. Maybe you'd like to be the one to tell her about that. Aha, it starts to backfire, doesn't it, when you think it through? Because that's not going to make her too happy either.' Stevenson felt he had made only a small impression. 'What you've got to face, Brian, is that basically there is no way to smooth things over, no matter what.'

'She doesn't need to be given details,' Colman said. 'Just that it's all over.'

'Not our obligation,' Stevenson said. 'And sooner or later she is going to realize for herself that her husband is either dead or missing for ever. In the meantime there's an operation to run and it's going to be run with whatever passes for science in this business of ours.'

'And why is Bork in on it?' Colman asked irritably.

'Someone will get chewed out for that. I didn't ask for him,' Stevenson said, going to his private bathroom, leaving the door open, and beginning to wash his hands, perhaps as a device to relieve the tension. 'But I've got to be sure she's clean, Brian,' he said. 'So far there's every reason to believe she is. . . .' He was soaping his hands fiercely as he talked, her cleanliness and his own suddenly forced together. 'She hasn't made a move and no one has tried to contact her. But I've got to be sure.'

'I know,' Colman said quietly, sourly. He simply didn't like the situation; it was a matter of inflicting pain from afar rather than doing the job at the risk of your skin. It made all the difference. The woman didn't even know what was going on.

'I've got to be sure, and do you know why?' Stevenson continued, challenged by Colman, feeling he had to confide in Colman, to let him know just how dynamic it all was. 'Because Mrs Fischer may actually find herself back in the Zone . . . in exchange for Mankin—that's right; there's that very distinct possibility.'

Colman was somewhat impressed. 'Is there?' he said, his eyes narrowing.

'Yes. Because there's been an inquiry about her from over there. Before we could even contact them on our own hook, they got to us. They may be operating on misinformation, who knows?' He rinsed his hands, shook off the excess water, and took a towel. 'Whatever it is, we may be able to capitalize on it.' He came out of the bathroom as he said, 'But I am certainly not going to turn her loose without first being sure she has nothing to give them. And if she *has* anything to give, I'll be able to get our people out from under ahead of time.'

Stevenson swung around his desk and continued. 'Okay. That's the picture. So Mrs Fischer is going through a tough squeeze. In strictly moralistic terms she may not deserve such a trial. Or she may *richly* deserve it. That's not our concern, it never is.' He dug a cigar out of the humidor, some of the agitation visible as he did. 'We sometimes have to get dirty, use people, hurt an innocent party. In other words, behave like everyone else. If we didn't, we'd perish in a fight like this. We may perish anyway. In the meantime, it's a fight I believe in.'

Colman believed in it too: KGB and East German Intelligence were deserving of American antagonism, had deliberately made no other outlook possible. 'But I don't need to go through this litany with you,' Stevenson said and stopped to light the cigar. 'You know what our problems are like. We can't behave like social workers; we need to remember that the people we're dealing with are out to cut our throats and then act towards them accordingly. It doesn't matter that Mrs Fischer is a widow because of us. What matters is that her husband tried to finish you off with a bullet in the back of the head to begin with. It wasn't until *after* that, that, unmotivated by profit, *you* shot *him* because you were forced to.'

'As you say,' Colman said, 'I don't need the manual read to me.' There was nothing to be done, but he couldn't for the moment grant either Stevenson or himself any peace; it didn't seem the thing to do. 'But it stinks,' he said.

'Uh-huh,' Stevenson said, with an understanding if annoyed glare. 'Have it your own way, Brian. I can only tell you that Mankin does not constitute a minor return on the investment. There is still a chance to get him out of East Germany.' He paused, and with an awesome quiet in his voice he said, 'That means more to me than the peace of mind of a thousand Mrs Fischers. . . .' One became sullied not necessarily because of what one had done but more often because of what one knew about and had been a passive witness to. That was true even at nursery school. 'They *shot* Mata Hari,' Stevenson quietly observed, and it seemed to speak, in its obscure and elliptical way, volumes. Then: 'Take your leave. Come back in a month.' He added, with no particular emphasis, 'I may have something to tell you then—something big.'

Colman knew Stevenson well enough to know he wasn't one for idle talk or mysterious airs.

'Two days ago you thought I might be used up. What's happened since?'

'I said tired, Brian, not used up. Go off somewhere and unwind. I've decided that's all you need, after a second look. Take it for what it's worth.'

'I don't need anything, M.J.,' Colman said with a faint, sage smile. 'But I'll get out of your way for a little while, if that's what you want.'

Stevenson sat and stared into space for about thirty seconds after Colman had walked out, old thoughts that waited like importunate creditors thrusting themselves on him. It was as if a gate had been left open and everything were moving through unchecked. He thought of his ex-wife, beautiful Marsha from Back Bay, the mother of his two sons, who had finally come to share with him a deep disinterest in their twenty-year marriage. He thought of how much more desirable it would have been, somehow, if one of them had broken the other's heart instead of both of them simply having grown bored. He thought further of the two boys who looked upon him, despite having no idea of his true vocation, as a desperate captain of a beleagured corruption, racism, and imperialism. They would have found much to admire in Stebbins. The idea lingered like an unwelcome visitor arrived unannounced. Everything was saddening all of a sudden, everything very oppressive. Even Julie, one of the two secretaries in the section, her pink lipstick artfully extended beyond the lines of a meagre little mouth, her patently false eyelashes an attractive nuisance. He wished there were some way to call her attention to the disfigurement without doing injury. But, of course, there was no such thing. People were apt to hurt each other even in minor matters, even when they had only the best of intentions and goodwill.

That was the way life was, made up of ultimate boredom and minor failures, sad rather than tragic.

The gates remained open to these small, soft images he was not normally wont to entertain. Maybe he was the one who needed to go off somewhere and unwind. But even if true, he would not. Who would look after the store if he did?

Colman's opposition and expressions of dismay had made Stevenson irritable. The minus marks had swiftly pyramided all of a sudden. It pushed him into a malaise which persisted until two days later when he visited Mrs Fischer in Moabit prison. They had arrested her because there had suddenly been nothing further to do, no other move to make.

CHAPTER TEN

THAT MORNING a man had come to the door and introduced himself as Klaus Pomerei, said he was a friend of Martin's, that Martin was in danger, and that only she could save him. She was not afraid of the man, but he repelled her, and she never asked him to sit down but continued to stare at him as he talked in an urgent, intimate voice and occasionally paced back and forth.

'First of all, Frau Fischer, you must trust me. Martin needs help—desperately.'

She watched him, strangely detached, as if it all had become a shadow play, a fantasy she was seeing through half-closed eyes.

'You can't know,' he went on, his hat and coat unremoved, 'how important it is that you place complete trust in me. You've been through so very much, it must be almost more than you can bear. But now you must listen and understand.'

'But I don't,' she said tonelessly.

'You must understand one terrible fact,' the man said, looking at her as if his own life were at stake. 'I can't swear to you that Martin will be alive by the end of the day unless the others get what they are after. . . .'

'The others? What others?'

'The people from whom he is in hiding,' he replied in a low voice, hushed with apprehension. 'Now, please try to understand. Try to think this through, because if you can't trust me Martin is doomed. Forget all the suspicions and the caution of other times. Martin's life is at stake, do you understand?'

Adele's mood changed abruptly. She felt beads of perspiration breaking out on her upper lip and forehead.

'They want the list. They will kill him if they don't get it.'

'List? What list?'

'The names. The list he left in your keeping, a duplicate of the one he has with him. Actually he no longer has it and I must take the other one to him—not directly, I must leave it somewhere for him to collect. But there is little time. . . .'

Adele could see him studying her as if for signs of damage. 'You've been under terrible strain,' he sympathized. 'Alone, out of touch, not knowing anything after all these days, nowhere to turn. . . . But now it's different. The worst is almost over. You can save his life. . . .'

She hovered between the possibility of a fall from reality—panic clutched at her momentarily like cold, bony fingers—and a rising wave of outrage. Perhaps she was badly frightened when she looked at him and said, with unaccented but unmistakable contempt, 'I don't believe anything you are telling me. I think it's all lies.'

The effect on Bork was jolting. He froze, as if hurt at first, and then became put out and superior. 'That could be the most tragic misjudgement of your life, Frau Fischer,' he said.

'Get out,' she said, a spark of anger igniting and sending up in flame all of her fears. Nothing mattered now—not the past, not the future, only this moment of indignation at a fate which had been inflicted on her. She resented Martin for it even as anxiety for his well-being gnawed deeply inside of her. 'Get out or I shall call the police,' she told him.

'No need for that, *gnadige Frau*,' Bork told her, oozing sarcasm and bureaucratic *Schadenfreude*. 'I *am* the police.' He showed her his credentials. 'You are without the proper identification and I must ask you to come along with me.'

'I have done nothing,' she said. 'People have rights in West Berlin. . . .'

71

'Rights?' he scoffed. 'You have no rights. You are a citizen of nowhere.'

'I protest,' she said, almost by way of a weak joke.

'You can write a letter about it to Herr Brandt. But first, come along, please, whether you mind or not.'

She wasn't at all sure that she minded. First there had been two extremely long conversations with several American officials. They were polite enough but very insistent, undeterrable men. And now she was about to face yet another.

She was brought from one of the remand-custody cells to a room used for consultations between attorneys and prisoners awaiting trial. The facilities were available to the occupation governments. Stevenson could see immediately that she was not going to be easy to frighten, that a cold and deadly contempt had been built up in her, despite Bork's forecasts of her imminent collapse. She was tall and her back was straight—perhaps a little more than was usual simply for the occasion—her face showing strain and fatigue.

Stevenson had been standing at a barred window looking down to the empty yard when she entered and did not sit down. Not moving, he said to her in German, 'Mrs Fischer, the reason you are in trouble is because you don't exist. You are a non-person. That's very difficult to overcome. It means, Mrs Fischer, you have no recourse to the courts, no right of complaint, no defence against a long incarceration.' He told it in a crisp, authoritative voice, as if instructing a class in legal quirks. He looked at her carefully, determined to exact from her all the assurances he could, ready to spare nothing in his campaign to break her, to turn her inside out. He let all his resentments and anger come to the surface like a smoke screen to obscure his view of her helplessness, her possible innocence, her womanly grace and good looks.

'At least,' he continued, his hands in his back pockets as he paced away from the barred window, 'as far as West Germany is concerned.' He looked at her with appraising eyes, unsmiling, unsparing of the truth. 'You can be detained a very long time, in other words, and no one can do a thing about it,' he told her. 'Kept in prison. You see, it's a government prerogative, Mrs Fischer, to do with illegal entrants as a government sees fit.

72

Usually it will expel such people with dispatch. It may otherwise, in cases of those seeking political asylum, process and absorb. But in either case, the means and the time taken come under no strict regulations.' He met her brave stare with sneaking admiration. 'Do you understand what I am saying? There is nothing to prevent you from sitting in a remand-custody cell indefinitely. You could, according to the law, be left to rot, Mrs Fischer, while a very, very slow investigation of your status took place. I want you to understand that fully before you take any unshakable positions with us. . . .'

She had discovered two days before that Mrs Stransky was a survivor of Theresienstadt. For some reason it now flashed through her mind.

'And this,' she said with a deliberately thin smile, 'is justice in the great Western democracy.'

'Justice has a strange way of looking totally different to different people,' Stevenson said. 'But I see your point. It couldn't have suited you too well on the other side, however, or you wouldn't have come over to grace us with your presence. . . .'

Adele returned his careful look with one of her own, her mind working to convert any left-over or discarded thought to her advantage. But it was a futile effort. All of life was an unending and unanswerable accusation, an illusion perpetuated by men like this one. Always it was men like this one.

'. . . so perhaps you won't mind telling me why you *did* come over,' Stevenson finished, going through the motions of the patient interrogator. 'Why did you and your husband come over, Mrs Fischer?'

'Will you tell me what has happened to my husband?' she said, offering a fair exchange.

'We don't know, Mrs Fischer,' Stevenson answered. 'We actually had him in custody briefly. But he managed to escape the man who had arrested him.'

'Where was this?'

'You went through a lot to get here, Mrs Fischer,' Stevenson said, brushing aside the question. 'Five hours in the cylinder of a petrol truck. . . . Not many people could have taken that. . . .'

73

'Every word is true,' she said, almost privately.

'But then your husband acted as a spy *for* the DDR, using what we call the third-country technique for conveying information—something you could hardly fail to know, Mrs Fischer. An interesting aberration for someone who went through so much to leave the DDR in the first place, wouldn't you say?'

'I have told the others everything.'

'Yes, I know. . . .'

'I have no reason to hide anything, nor anything to hide.

'I'm trying to sort this out, Mrs Fischer,' Stevenson said with a deep frown, ready to employ the necessary amount of cruelty. 'Your husband is undoubtedly a warped human being without a shred of decency or a normal instinct—'

'I will not listen to this.'

'—except in regard to you, Mrs Fischer,' Stevenson said, looking at her without shame. 'I think he may care for you—in his way. . . .'

'You think it is all so very easy,' she said, her eyes now welling up, the smallest catch in her voice.

'Not in the least, *gnadige Frau*; none of this is very easy, because it goes to the root of what's wrong with the human heart and that's where all the world's tragedy comes from. . . .'

'Is that an expression of pity for others?'

'For everyone. As much as I am capable of it; and up to a point,' he said and extended to her a folded white handkerchief. 'Allow me.'

She accepted it almost as if he owed her at least that much, and he went on: 'But I am more alarmed by people like your husband than pitying of them. Because they have no allegiances and they don't stay bought.'

She wiped her eyes, keeping them on him even as she did, and then her nose, listening avidly. 'But then I am alarmed by a great many people these days for various reasons,' he said. 'That's why I am trying to discover what made him tick . . .' A slip in tense like one's footing going out on an icy patch at a perilous height. Stevenson went forward skilfully enough. '. . . and how much you know about it.'

He held his breath until she said, 'Nothing.'

'So you say.'

'Less than you. . . .' She held the handkerchief tightly. 'I'll launder this for you. . . .'

'No, no, don't bother, it's unimportant. . . .' He then took his chance, not certain of what the result might be, but impelled towards it. 'What about Colonel Emmering?' he asked refusing to be distracted by the quiet tears and the running nose his handkerchief had served so well. 'Why did your husband go to such extremes to avoid him? Why is Emmering so anxious to grab hold of your husband? Yes, we know because he told us before he got away, when he thought he was caught for good and was trying to ply us with information and assuage us. . . .'

Her eyes were wide, and her dried-out lips parted, and she stood there exposed to yet another assault. Stevenson had struck at just the right angle. 'Evidently he does mean something,' he said, getting closer to what he wanted, to that achievement of faultlessness he insisted on. 'He does, doesn't he, Mrs Fischer?'

This small, dominant man gave her a feeling of nakedness, probing her like an examining physician, destroying all privacy. She might have wanted to hate him, but she couldn't sustain hate, had never been able to. 'He means something to your husband,' he went on. 'There was no mistake about that.'

Resistance would have provided it with too much importance, given it an intimacy it didn't deserve. 'Colonel Emmering,' she said flatly, 'had designs on me. There. Are you satisfied?'

Stevenson knew instantly that he had his answer; it was as if she had shown him a bottom card that had been face down till then. 'Partly,' he said. 'Just partly. . . .' He didn't want her to think he was altogether pleased at her expense.

'I think you are a man who could never be anything *but* partly satisfied,' she said.

'You may well have summed me up, Mrs Fischer.'

'What more is there? Leave me to rot, as you said before? Well and good. I don't care. . . .'

He said, 'I don't think it will come to that.' She was a fine specimen; he wasn't too old to be aware of it. He looked away and picked up his hat. 'Don't be too pessimistic,' he said rather foolishly. He had what he wanted, had got it easily enough, and was ready to leave. He would stop at nothing, perhaps, but had no stomach for inflicting unnecessary pain.

With a sudden change of heart, Adele said, 'Listen. This morning . . . before I was brought here . . . I was on my way to Tempelhof to report to the police and to ask for resettlement.'

'In spite of your husband's injunction?' Stevenson said.

'For both of us. I took it upon myself,' she said.

Stevenson said, 'There have been cases of people who have asked to go back where they came from after spending enough time in the camp at Zirndorf waiting for resettlement. So the desire—or the fear—has to be overwhelming. It must burn like a torch or you never make it. . . .'

'Am I going to have that chance?' she asked simply, appealing and straightforward. 'Is Martin? . . .'

'Mrs Fischer,' Stevenson began, 'do you really believe that your husband would *deserve* it? Considering all?'

'Why not? If he would change? Pay his debt, as you might call it?' Her innocence was undeniable.

Stevenson said, 'Mrs Fischer, the world is a place of opposing forces. They sometimes change positions. But they never embrace. . . .' It was academic anyway, but she didn't know that, of course.

She said nothing, a deep depression settling on her, a pall on the now silent room. It was all absurd, even weird.

'I may wish to speak with you again, I'm not certain yet,' Stevenson said, wishing it were so, knowing it wasn't. 'In the meantime the prison officials have been instructed to get whatever personal effects from your flat you would like to have.'

She said nothing before she was led away by a matron. She had proved herself with him, perhaps, but the reverse had not by any means taken place. Back in her neatly appointed cell in the women's section of the jail-and-courts complex she sat alone and thought about Emmering because Stevenson had revived him. She remembered his quiet coaxings, his curiously dead eyes in which nevertheless so much tenacity and intransigent desire were visible. He had begun with an avuncular air, and the overtures had been all the more insufferable for that: the proper, decorous posture and the reserved way of speaking—he had known her since she was five years old, after all—were not less intolerable than the crudest imprecations or attempts to paw; just around the corner all of that awaited in any case. Benevolent, a gentleman, if a Communist, always, Emmering conspicuously avoided any reference to power: he bore it on behalf of the State with wisdom and goodwill, this power and authority that had been his for so long. How appealing such a man had to have been, hadn't he? Nothing was improper in any way: her dear mother, after all, had been dead for many months before he had seen fit to reveal his feelings. She remembered it still with, at the very least, dislike. 'Adele, I am only forty-six,' he had said, as grave as a toad contemplating food. 'That is not an old man. . . .'

Stony and obsessive, he persisted and would always have been there until he had crushed with friendship or with love, or with the final functionary necessity to destroy. It took some of that surely to be the head of an internal security force. It was from this that Martin had helped her to flee, bravely and unhesitatingly. An act he then proceeded to nullify in his own way. And now, why had he mentioned any of it to them? She couldn't understand it. It left her so unconcealed.

Stevenson didn't mention it to Brannigan. He walked out to the ante-room where Brannigan was waiting with his overcoat buttoned and a cigarette in his red-freckled hand, and he said, 'She constitutes no risks; she's clean.' They began to walk along the corridor, their footfalls echoing, the building a place of dry throats and sweating palms. 'Strictly Penelope to a road company Ulysses—not more, not less.'

'What do you mean? Oh—the patient wife. I get it,' Brannigan said with restrained satisfaction. 'What about the questions from over there?'

Stevenson didn't break stride or look at Brannigan. 'Tell them they can have her,' he said, 'for the agreed upon price. . . .'

The two men left the building and drove away like visitors leaving the scene of a condolence call.

Part Two

CHAPTER ONE

'IT WILL BE a co-ordinated action, Trauner—yours and mine, on behalf of the state,' Emmering said as he paced the room with the manner of one who decides but never consults, his deep, monotonic voice lending him an air of greater imperturbability than he perhaps possessed.

He was a stolid figure, his shoulders squared and too broad for his height, above average, his round skull thick with straight black hair brushed flat, his face impassive and distinguished chiefly by his deep-set and lightless eyes.

'Though actually the executive decision will be your own,' he went on, glancing at the man seated behind his desk.

'On behalf of the state,' Trauner repeated. 'I find that rather vague, Comrade.' He was an obese man who seemed almost to billow, his chest and shoulders massive, his face vast but keen-eyed, a sybaritic lower lip forming part of a mouth sceptical to the point of contempt, a dauntless and unafraid quality about him. He sat stonily and watched Emmering's every move. 'I always like to know what the specific aims are when I hear that kind of phrase-making,' he said in a melodious and insinuating tenor voice. 'For example, who is this individual you are getting in exchange for an American agent whose release I am supposed to effect on your say-so?'

'I admire you, Trauner, whatever you may think. You are probably brilliant, as I am not.'

'For asking a commonplace question? Or in general?'

'For balancing weakness and strength as well as you do. You observe every procedural demand made on you even when in the end your own needs will come first—because they must. But you do the job that has to be done and can never be accused of dereliction or sloth.'

'That sounds to me like a description of insincerity, Comrade.'

'Not at all. Of a realist. Your sense of duty doesn't mean that you are inflexible. And I'll be happy to tell you who it is we are going to repatriate: the wife of a traitor now in the West—a turncoat, a renegade. It's a woman who may be of great value to us for many reasons.'

He felt satisfaction for having been verbal with Trauner because he rarely was—with anyone. Perhaps a faint sense of elation had spurred him to it. And he now stood with his hands clasped in back of him, his shoulders squared, his back arched almost ferociously. His eyes were on a framed photograph of Herr Ulbricht on the wall in back of Trauner's desk, fleetingly and without interest, of course. He knew that Trauner would do exactly as he was told but needed first to make a show of resistance. Information was like electric power one controlled with a hand rheostat. It came from a catalogue of the foibles and follies of all: the non-Socialist dealings of ministers, the sexual deceivings and cuckoldries of intelligence officers and others, the past crimes and various quirks of the highly placed —the homosexual affair, and murder committed during the Hitler days—he had it all on hand, drawers full of shame and embarrassment; it was his business to have. And whatever wasn't there nevertheless existed in the minds of those who knew themselves and could not be sure of their own secrets. Trauner knew all of this and yet, because of whatever went into the making of his personality and character, he fenced with Emmering and tweaked him with disdain at every opportunity. He was openly caustic and sharper-tongued than the other. But he was hopelessly outflanked in any real sense. There was nothing Colonel Trauner could do but acquiesce, as he knew beforehand.

But he said, 'The wife of a traitor. . . . But no name. Just a category.'

When Emmering merely waited for more, Trauner said, 'My department, Colonel, is charged, as you know, with certain non-domestic matters. And this exchange you speak of has a distinctly internal quality to it. And a very subtle one, as a matter of fact, I don't feel competent to discuss. . . .'

79

'What do you mean by that?' Emmering asked, his tone incapable of change but now revealing some heat by a faint quickening in cadence.

'Comrade,' Trauner said, shifting his bulk, his elbows on his desk, unintimidated but ready to deflect rather than meet anything head-on, 'I am making a witless remark. I really don't know what I mean. But I don't know what you mean either. The wife of a traitor in the West. Who?'

'At the moment, that must remain unrevealed,' Emmering said, knowing that Trauner had been using the services of that very traitor and perhaps already had guessed at the identity of the exchange prisoner. 'At least until after the exchange has been consummated.'

'You've obviously already begun the negotiation,' Trauner said.

'Everything is in position,' Emmering said. He would hold her in the palm of his hand, either to put her in a cage or let her fly away. Think of her astonishment if he were to do that; think of the power implied in such a thing, the strength before which all scorn had to crumble. The gesture would be a gamble and no lasting satisfaction could be expected in the loss: he would have to think twice about it. He would have to think twice, in fact, about what it was he wanted altogether. 'The woman is of importance to all security forces, even to your own two departments. There is absolutely no clue as to how these two people were able to get out of East Berlin. There is no doubt of the importance in finding out about it, much more than in holding on to this CIA agent.'

'I can think of more spectacular possibilities than the one you suggest, Comrade Colonel,' Trauner said with the arch look of an insolent and bored fat man. 'What, for example, happened to the husband—the traitor you speak of?'

'Perhaps the wife will know that also.'

'What if I venture a guess?'

'You're free to do so.'

'I'd say he's dead. . . .' A note of disappointment crept into his voice, his expression suddenly thoughtful and ironic. 'They wouldn't have arrested her if he were still alive. It would make no sense.'

'What do you mean?' Emmering said slowly, taken by surprise.

Trauner looked at him with unconvinced eyes. 'There is no point in all this codifying, Comrade. We both know who we are discussing. The Fischers. And you have allowed yourself to cast aside the fundamental collective outlook all of us try to maintain and without which there can be no true Socialist state. And I am not ready to casually support you in it.'

'One would assume your own collective outlook has been undeviating, Comrade,' Emmering said in that unexcitable bass voice, 'that you've been unimpeachable—eh?'

Trauner was not dampened. 'Fischer was serving a good purpose until recently; a state purpose, a Communist purpose. Not easily, thanks to certain circumstances. . . .'

'Now who is doing the codifying?'

'Thanks to you, then. He was afraid of you even in the West. Be that as it may. I know that his wife, whom I am convinced is now a widow, is of no value. Exchanging her for a CIA agent, whether he is of importance or not, is not building Socialism in my view.'

'Have you more to say than that? I am willing to listen if you feel some purpose can be served.'

Trauner eyed him, now somewhat sly. 'What if I should refuse you?' he said. 'You're not anxious to embarrass me. You would lose something in the process, wouldn't you now? I mean, you would need to be pushed very hard.'

'But there is that point where one thing or the other must go, Trauner. And you never know where it may be. Even I don't know that. I only know that the state must be served by each of us in different ways—because we're all different people with different capabilities.'

'How well you put things, Comrade.'

'You put things even better, Trauner. Perhaps that is why you are chief of intelligence and I am merely a simple policeman.' Emmering paused, then said, 'It's a Marxist-Leninist principle in effect, isn't it? Everyone where he is best suited.' Another pause, and then: 'You will need to begin the release process immediately, Trauner. That is, now that our little conversation is at an end.'

'One day,' Trauner said in a casual voice that carried its own kind of conviction, 'I may decide to go down with the ship, so to speak . . . if I think it's important enough to the state. . . .' He looked at Emmering directly and his sarcasm and jibing criticism had turned to something else, to cool anger. 'I mean that, Comrade. . . .' His blue eyes were turned steadily on Emmering and contained the truth of what he was saying.

'Do you think you've been so burdened, Trauner?'

'I don't like anything that hovers over me for too long. Also, Comrade, I happen to be a good Socialist. Not, it is true, as good as I should be but, nevertheless, convinced. . . .'

'None of us is as good as he should be, we Germans know that,' Emmering said. 'I don't think, in any event, that I am any less convinced than you are, Colonel Trauner.'

'We must discuss it some time,' Trauner said with his first smile, peculiarly cherubic on that wide expanse of face, but unmistakably bitter. 'We can analyse your Socialist zeal for its imperialist characteristics.'

The large man then heaved himself from his chair with surprising alacrity, went to a filing cabinet whose top drawer he unlocked and slid open, as he said, 'I think everything is clear, Comrade.' He removed a folder and added, 'It was nice of you to pay me a call.'

Emmering let him have the final stage of the ritual. It didn't matter. Power didn't reside in mannerisms and posturings or in shows of contempt and defiance; it was measured only by how much one could do, how far one could reach, how great an object one could move simply because of a wish to do so. Trauner's opinions, his low esteem, and even his hatred were incapable of affecting Emmering. They moved nothing, least of all Emmering's heart.

As his official chauffeur-driven car travelled along the wide thoroughfare flanked suddenly on the left by the overflowing Karl Marx Bookshop and on the right by the large Central Sports Club, to which he was far more partial, Emmering was oblivious to everything but the concept of what he was doing and its basic justification. There was surely value in questioning a person who had been able, mysteriously, to penetrate the

Wall; the state could not but be served properly in this much. If the coincidence of a personal connection had prompted or accompanied his action, a footnote would have been sufficient to denote its incidental significance. The intricacies of government even in a Communist country were vast and necessarily filled with moral and philosophical crises. He had every intention of sharply interrogating her when the time came to separate those revelations that lay together in the deeps and which might, admittedly, solve nothing finally. Power had its limitations also. His own might find its level at the moment Adele Fischer, nee Schramm, stood before him.

He stared with those immobile eyes straight ahead of him, his face as impassive as wood, his various desires mingling with resignation to ultimate failure. Nothing would keep him from it. His next step was to grant the terms requested by the Americans, his collective outlook bearing but one more tarnish mark that was hardly noticeable.

CHAPTER TWO

COLMAN'S APARTMENT WINDOW looked down towards the Tiergarten, and the Wall could be seen clearly beyond. Colman looked out briefly, snow flurries scudding across the sky, the Fahrenheit temperature, according to the thermometer nailed outside his bedroom window, 34 degrees. He had returned home two nights before after having had dinner alone in a restaurant near by, wrote a letter to his brother, Jeremy, watched the television screen for half an hour, read fifty pages of Liddell Hart's *Memoirs*, and went to sleep. The day before he had arisen late, wandered without aim, attended an afternoon movie at the MGM-Kino, chosen a small restaurant not far from the Zoo Station for dinner, and attended a second film in Steglitz on the Schloss-Strasse, remaining in unbroken solitude and returning home without an encounter, which had been his objective.

But today was not to be exactly the same kind of day. As he was getting ready to leave the apartment, Gerda arrived unannounced. Without delay he told her that Stebbins was dead by his own hand.

'I knew he was,' she said wistfully. 'Somehow I knew. . . .'

'He believed in the Communist cause,' Colman said. 'Always had. Except I think it was more a case of what he did *not* believe in—what he wanted, for some reason, to tear down.'

'And he knew that I had betrayed him,' she said, perdition in her eyes. 'There is no use in denying that. He had to have realized it.'

Colman said unhesitatingly, 'He blamed me for the whole thing—that is the absolute truth.'

'I wish I had shot him instead.' She looked up at him as he put on his suit jacket, smiling in a dead way. 'I wonder if I would have the nerve for that? It's a much nicer thing to do for someone.'

'Dying was his own choice. He was a traitor. His treason failed. He killed himself.'

'I wish I could look at it that way. How I envy you.'

'There is no other way,' Colman said and sat down on the edge of the chair opposite her own. 'But he put no blame on you—none. He had no reason to. And you have no reason to feel guilty about anything. He was his own master. He took his own path in his own way.'

'I didn't love him, you know that. But I think . . . he loved me. That's the worst of it, in a way. . . .'

'Would it matter if he hadn't?' Because I'm sure you're wrong.'

'Less. But I think he did. And I think he believed I loved him,' she said, smiled, and added, 'I'm an excellent professional bitch.'

'Now listen,' Colman said earnestly, 'you *can* get out of this whole thing. You can have enough to go away and live very comfortably for a few years, perhaps longer. Not in Europe; South America or Mexico. It's been done before; it can be arranged for you.'

'Away?'

'From the whole thing.'

'By myself?'

She seemed surprised and Colman said, 'When we were

standing at the street corner a few days ago—just before we separated—you said you wanted to get out of this. . . .'

'Yes, but—why to South America? What do I have in South America?'

'You couldn't remain in Europe. You'd attract attention. As far as, say, Rio it wouldn't matter. You wouldn't be noticed by the wrong people.'

He had never known her to display rage towards him. She looked at him hotly, scorn in her voice. 'How cold you are, when all is said and done, trying to do the decent thing to balance out an indecent thing, looking for the right pigeon-holes to put people into.' Colman was willing to take it and he let her go on. 'There are certain ones you merely send away. Give them some money and a couple of new dresses and get them out of sight—the farther out, the better. They will get over it, and even if they don't, who cares? At least no one will need to look at them. . . .'

'Maybe that's true, maybe it isn't,' he said. 'But what good does it do to talk about it? The most significant thing I learned in the Army is that most of the time you do not have excellent possibilities but several that rate from one to three on a scale of ten.' He sounded to himself like an instructor in fundamental tactics in a class at the Point. In a less pedagogic tone he concluded; 'I swear to you, that is something I live by, and I try to pass it along to you for all it's worth.'

'It suits you to say that now.'

'What is it I should be saying instead?'

'I don't know what I mean,' she said irritably. 'I'm talking nonsense.'

'What did you think it would be like when you began this kind of work? Things you had seen in the movies? Excitement, romance, no one good ever gets hurt. . . . I suppose you did. And that's our fault. People aren't screened carefully enough —people like you. . . .'

'You're saying I'm either unstable or stupid, and perhaps you're right. But I know what I feel.'

Colman didn't want to be told. 'The question is,' he went on, 'how to choose now, right this minute, so that you experience the least amount of distress.'

She was suddenly resigned, a touch of self-inflicted violence in the way she bitterly shook her head up and down accept- antly. 'Why should I be such a fool and deny it?' she asked herself as well as him. And then she looked at him with the answer. 'But I don't want to go away.'

He shrugged, his expression sympathetic. 'If you want to get out, it's South America or Mexico,' he told her. 'If you stay . . . we won't work together again.'

'Work together?'

'We won't see each other again,' he said. 'It would be bad for business. Too much emotion, too much hangover from the assignment. It would be bad for you and bad for the section. You would need to be somewhere else. . . .'

'I see. . . .'

'You shouldn't rule out going away. You're only twenty-three. . . .'

'And if I don't go away? If I simply . . . quit?'

'I don't know. It could cause a problem, make people uneasy. You'd have to be very careful. I think you'd be much wiser if you went away, safe and well financed.'

'*Really* like a whore. . . .'

Colman said coldly, 'If you're a whore, I'm worse. And I'm not anything like that. If you want to beat yourself, don't do it in front of me.'

'I love you, Brian,' she said, in a last desperate effort.

'You don't,' he told her sternly. 'You can't. I'm unsuited to you in every way. You can't love someone who doesn't love you in return.' He paced away from her, stopped, and said, 'It's simply not natural or healthy.'

'That's part of my problem,' she said almost with pride.

'Nonsense,' he said and knew how stiff-necked he sounded.

'Perhaps it is, but I love you. It's too bad, but I do. . . . There's nothing either of us can do about it. . . .' A kind of mournful glee attached to the hopelessness of it.

'It has to wear off because it isn't love,' he said.

'It's a fantasy, I know,' she said deprecatingly. 'But isn't all love? Don't worry, I understand how things are—finally.'

He faced her squarely. 'Have I ever led you to believe any-thing I shouldn't have?'

'I led myself—admittedly. And if you screened people more carefully you would cut down a big part of your force. Because what sort of person do you think would want to get into something like this in the first place?'

She enjoyed saying as much and added, 'You wouldn't expect someone sensible, someone who knows what's best for her.' But it wasn't satisfying in the long run; she was obviously unhappy.

'I didn't think far enough ahead,' he said, sorrier for her than ever but needing for every reason in the world to be rid of her: no good as an agent, bearing guilt, pining about love that wasn't there—how could she be allowed to remain? 'And I wish I had hit on some other idea. . . .' Had they ruined her? No, not more than she had allowed them to. 'But this is not love, Gerda,' he went on. 'What is there to love in a person who doesn't return it?'

She took a deep breath and said, 'Your own hope that perhaps he finally will. . . .'

Colman said no more and both of them disengaged themselves, she staring through the window at the falling snow, he going into the bedroom to get his fur-lined raincoat and his hat. He had come to the end of his argument, found himself fighting boredom and bad humour and, worst of all, a deep feeling of disappointment—something to which no one past thirty should have been susceptible. He had seen his mother sit in a wheelchair for three years before dying, hopelessly crippled at the age of forty as the result of an accident in a car his father had been driving; his father then drinking himself on to the Army retirement rolls and finally shooting himself through the head at the approach of his fifty-second birthday; and so he knew about the opium dream of happiness, as he had once called it in an abortive attempt to keep a journal in Korea. He knew about death and pain and until now had experienced very little disappointment. He had been trained not to expect anything, innoculated early against sentiment and dreams of undeviating justice. Yet he was uncomfortable with his place in Gerda's consciousness; the prospect of the life he would lead in her waking thoughts and even in her dreams gave him a sense of entrapment.

He looked towards the other room, anticipating sad good-byes and more words that would satisfy no one. But it was empty when he re-entered it. Gerda had, for her own purposes, slipped away without a word. He was surprised and somewhat relieved, and he hoped she had found some satisfaction in it. Perhaps she thought it would gain his admiration. It didn't make him feel a great deal better. He didn't expect to feel very good about Gerda in any event.

CHAPTER THREE

LESS THAN a hundred yards away Checkpoint Charlie could be seen, the opening just the width of the Friedrichstrasse, the wall abutted by concrete pilings and heavy wiring on either side. Stevenson sat in the back of the Mercedes and peered towards the deeply-set sentry posts on the other side, the gathered darkness broken by the watchtower lights which bordered thirty miles of concrete, the cruel bricks and mortar. Brannigan entered the back seat and said, 'They're ready on the other side.'

Stevenson looked at his wristwatch. 'Are they early or are we late?' he asked.

'Walters should be here with Mrs Fischer any minute,' Brannigan said, remaining at the edge of the cushion, and turned to face his boss. 'It's a little distance from Moabit.'

'They have Mankin at the checkpoint, have they?' Stevenson said, knowing he had to do things this way because there was no other way.

'Surrounded by about a dozen *Volkspolizei*,' Brannigan replied.

Stevenson glowered past the back of Kagen's head, his eyes towards the checkpoint, several West German policemen and a U.S. Army jeep containing three MP's in the vicinity. It had stopped snowing but it was cold and the men stamped their feet from time to time as they waited, lights filtering the chill, dark air, almost no vehicular traffic in this area at all. It could all be heard a block away along the Kochstrasse and beyond.

But here nothing went on; only *this* sort of business from time to time and the infrequent crossing of non-Germans into East Berlin. Stevenson's expression was hard and fixed, the idea of Mrs Fischer's discomfort surely not one that appealed to him or one that he took lightly.

Brannigan said, 'Emmering must have a pretty good pipeline. He knew about Mrs Fischer's arrest before she took off her hat and coat.'

'Yes, he must have.' Stevenson spoke without moving his eyes.

'I have to admit it beats me,' Brannigan said, his good-natured red face in a thoughtful frown. 'I went over that woman with Walters like a lawnmower, and you spoke to her yourself. . . .'

'Yes.'

'. . . and there's no doubt she had nothing to give. She had no lists, no contacts, nothing at all to hold her on. All she has done, to all intents and purposes, is defect from the Zone. Nothing more. Even if they don't think much of Mankin, the trade still seems crazy. Like DiMaggio for Ox Eckhardt.'

'You go back a long way, Red,' Stevenson muttered.

Brannigan snorted and said, 'Maybe that's a little off the mark. They presumably have no idea of what Mankin is worth —or might be worth, or better be worth. . . .'

'Look,' Stevenson said, looking at him, 'he's one of ours, no matter what. If they are willing to give him back for a defector who is of no use to us, who wasn't that good a citizen anyhow, whose husband was an enemy agent—well, then, that's just keen with me.' His voice had an aggressive, faintly querulous bite. He didn't like the arrangement much, but the regret needn't be made any deeper. 'He's worth it whether he got what I'm after or not.'

Brannigan, usually a tactful man, took the blame quickly. 'There's no doubt of it. I picked the wrong speech to make.'

'I know. But you're right, in a way,' Stevenson said, looking back towards the checkpoint once again. 'You're thinking that if Mankin didn't represent the mother lode to me I might not have gone into this deal and put that woman on the block— especially with how she obviously dreads going back there.

"What if Mankin didn't come up with it?" you're saying to yourself. How will I feel about Mrs Fischer? Isn't that about it?'

'No one has any right telling you what to do or how to do it,' Brannigan said, taking out his cigarettes. 'Because they wouldn't know how if it was theirs to do. But I'd say you had no other choice.'

'No, Red. I just didn't want to make the other choice. Only *then* did I *have* to do certain things, pay for what I wanted. I wasn't forced. I could have passed. And I'd never have had to remember Mrs Fischer—not ever. That would be trading a hard responsibility for personal comfort. I'm not ready to do that. Maybe someday I'll be old and worn down enough, but not yet.'

'You couldn't have done anything else.'

'I don't get a thing out of it, not even honourable mention in the Congressional Record.' He looked at Brannigan briefly. 'You know what's behind this move, so I don't need to say more.'

'It's the chance of a lifetime.'

Stevenson shook his head, reconciled to his regrets. 'She has no more control over what she is or where she is than a tulip,' he said. 'And yet I had to go after her.'

'I know.'

'I happen to be very sentimental,' he went on because Brannigan knew everything there was to know about him for the past twenty-five years. 'That's not only a character deficiency, it's the deadliest of the slow poisons.'

Brannigan smiled faintly, watched his boss's flattened profile as the latter went on: 'The point is, it doesn't really matter if Mrs Fischer is hurt or suffers or if I have bad dreams. Not if the alternative is the loss of something as significant as this—if he has it. Otherwise she's hurt for nothing.'

'We wouldn't abandon Mankin,' Brannigan reminded him.

'There's nobody who can't be abandoned—not you, not me —unless he has something we need.'

'We'd still want him back.'

'Yes, but we could afford to wait,' Stevenson admitted. Then he added, 'We are doomed to react, Red; and react we must.'

'Yes. . . .'

'Sleepless nights have nothing to do with it.' Stevenson looked again at his wristwatch. 'There's nothing more unreasonable than sweet reason in the face of ill will and brute force. It goes unappreciated.'

Brannigan was impressed but silent. He was very expert in his way, highly efficient. Part of his job consisted of dealing with what was called Contact Material, an important and demanding operation that kept the various intelligence organizations in touch on various nonclassified matters. He was a whip, a beaver, capable of just one punishingly tedious job. His flaws didn't show. He would never be head of anything and he would never be kicked sideways or locked out. He was intensely loyal to Stevenson. 'Why don't I check on Walters,' he said after a moment, 'see what's holding them up. . . .'

'You don't need to,' Stevenson said, his eyes on the rearview mirror past Kagen's cap. 'He's driving in right now.'

Brannigan glanced over his shoulder, then said to Stevenson, 'Do you want to say anything to the woman?'

Stevenson exploded. 'That's a dumb question—why the hell would I?'

Brannigan didn't answer and began to alight from the car.

'Wait a minute,' Stevenson said. 'Did anyone tell her her husband is dead? Confirm it?'

'No. Should we?'

'No, no. She can get that news later on—from someone else.'

Brannigan closed the door and went off in the cold night air to meet Walters. Stevenson didn't look back, simply remained where he was in silence, Kagen's head as still as a mannequin's in the front seat. Stevenson sucked at the end of a new cigar, his sympathy towards Mrs Fischer—the deadliest slow poison of sentimentalism, as he called it—soon sinking from view as his eagerness to see Mankin increased. It could be said that one had drowned in the other. He became transfixed in anticipation of Mankin's appearance, imagining avidly that instant when Mankin would tell him what he wanted to hear. Or would he? What if Mankin hadn't that breathtaking thing to give, those few preliminary words to say, the assurance Stevenson awaited, positively longed for? What if it hadn't happened, after all? What if, like everything else of late, it had fallen flat and the cycle of loss and mischance continued unbreakably? Had he then the right to have bartered Mrs Fischer's future? Had he in any event? The answer was that he hadn't the right. And neither had he the right not to have. It was like a fracture that simply would never heal properly. You finally came to accept it because there was nothing else you could do. So one thing remained untouched: What would Mankin bring with him? To find that out Stevenson might have crossed the steppes of Russia without shoes.

He sat immobile for long moments and waited as if in a trance, while everything slowed and ground like train wheels towards an ended journey. He then began to light the new cigar, hurriedly, without patience, when Brannigan was back, thrusting himself only halfway into the car. 'We don't have her, M.J. She was gone when Walters got to the prison.'

Stevenson slowly shook out the match flame and looked at Brannigan but said nothing. 'Somebody swiped her from us,' Brannigan said, the excitement audible in his voice. 'Colman. . . .'

'Colman,' Stevenson repeated with no sign of emotion or surprise.

'He evidently collected her about an hour ago; came in, signed for her, and took her away. What do you make of that?'

Stevenson said in a calm but rueful tone, 'Perfect sense. And he should have been watched every minute—covered with a day-and-night surveillance until this was all over. But I was looking somewhere else. . . .'

'How the hell could anyone know——?'

'How the hell could anyone *fail* to know? It's so obvious it's suffocating. *Of course* he was going to do this. He's behaved normally and predictably. That's what hurts. I'm not shocked.'

'I am—not just a little. What now?'

'Explain it to the other side, leaving out as many details as possible. Then we'll go home.' He shook his head. 'It was hanging out right in front of me, and I didn't know what it was.'

'Maybe you still don't.'

92

'Maybe Colman doesn't either.'

Brannigan had nothing to add. 'Let me clean this up and we'll get out of here.'

'Yeah, clean it up,' Stevenson said and jammed the unsmoked, only slightly singed cigar into the ash receptacle and left it sticking up at an angle like any kind of a symbol one wanted it to be.

CHAPTER FOUR

A MAN, to whom she gave scarcely a glance, had come for her, and she was ready to accompany him as one does a porter to the door of a cheap hotel room in which one must mark time. He carried her suitcase to a taxicab in the courtyard, and she entered the back seat wordlessly. The driver knew where to go and the man gave him no instructions. Total strangers, together by sheer accident, they drove in silence through a sea of factories and various industrial buildings near the prison. But only briefly; and then he got to it.

'I think you're being unjustly treated, Mrs Fischer,' he said in German, without preliminary. 'I may be in a position to right the wrong that is being done to you—I know all about your situation.'

Unmistakably disinterested in the world around her just seconds before, she was now astonished. She looked at him, an American she would have guessed, and she didn't utter a sound.

'I'm one of the—authorities. Though a minor voice,' he went on, looking away from her skin which had gone dead white from strain and fatigue. 'There is some chance I could persuade them to take another decision. But you've got to want to stay on this side badly enough to take help from me or anyone—regardless of why it is being offered. On face value alone.'

He looked right at her and she said, 'I don't understand. . . .'

'It's simple, believe me.'

'What is it?'

'You're getting a terrible beating. . . .' He would go no

93

further than that, didn't want to be cross-examined, wanted only a sign from her that would make what he was doing significant and not a sham. 'I want to help you.'

'But what am I to you?' And without rancour she added, 'Do you think I have secrets you might discover, after all? Because I don't have.'

'We can get a man out of prison in the East,' he told her, coldly annoyed though completely understanding of what she was saying and why. 'All we need do is hand you over.'

'Why don't you?' she asked with overriding logic. 'How can I believe such generosity?' She knew more about life than that. 'Would *you*? . . . You're an agent, aren't you? You've been trained to trust no one, to take no one and nothing for granted If you were I, would you believe that someone wished to give you a chance like this without expecting something in return? Without more than charity to guide his heart? Would you?'

'What do you think you have to lose?' he asked. 'You're supposed to be sent back to the Zone anyway.'

'I prefer now to later,' she said. 'Not after a false hope I might begin to believe. . . .' She shook her head and closed her eyes in refusal.

'Is that your final word?'

'Yes,' she said, fighting a tug of uncertainty, of loneliness and longing.

'I pity you, *gnadige Frau*. Life has made you small and afraid.'

'Yes, it's contemptible, isn't it, not to be a marvellous sport about it all.' Anger had fleetingly heated her face, and she sat back and turned her head the other way.

Colman sank into dismal silence with her. She swallowed and he could see the peristaltic motion of her thyroid cartilage like a flutter of anguish. The cab continued on its way through the late afternoon darkness of the winter day. 'I am not trying to trick you into anything,' Colman said finally. 'I have no way of proving it at the moment. I'm sorry.'

Something in his voice relaxed her tightly coiled scepticism. 'Are you trying to tell me,' she asked less defensively, 'that you are this—noble?'

'I am trying to tell you I may be able to get you out of the trouble you're in; and I want to try because I don't think you deserve to be in it. In your situation that should be enough for you. But maybe you're one of those people who can't be helped because help gets in their way for some reason or other. They can't bear it.'

'That's untrue. . . .'

'Then what is?'

'Not what you're saying. What am I to you, after all?'

'Didn't you ever want to do something for a person you didn't know?' he said, realizing they were total strangers really. It hadn't been enough to spy on her and know all the things he knew. 'A person who needed help?'

'Something,' she answered sapiently. 'But not anything like this.'

He shook his head. 'Okay, Mrs Fischer. I've gone as far as I can go. I could get on my knees, but I don't think it would do any good. You *are* one of those people. I'm sure you can't help it. Neither can I.'

She could see the tight-lipped, restrained passion with which he spoke, the verge of anger and impatience. 'I don't know what to think,' she said.

'That you've nothing to lose,' he said. 'Even if I'm a fake, you've nothing to lose.'

'I should hate to be used. And I don't want to be knocked down.'

'You would prefer the security of the Zone and the guarantees of happiness they give you over there?'

'If you're a fake I have something to lose—not much but something,' she said. 'And if you're sincere, you're not like many people. . . .'

'This cab is going towards the airport,' Colman said. 'You can get out of Berlin or I can turn the driver around and take you to where they're waiting for you at Checkpoint Charlie.'

'And what about my husband?'

It took Colman by surprise. 'What about him?' he said. Then he looked into her eyes and said, 'He's dead. . . . The East Germans killed him.' He was glad it was out of the way, that it had come about quickly and unexpectedly. Now it was hers also.

95

She couldn't feel it yet. She just stared at Colman.

'You're all you have to think about now,' he said. 'That's the point.'

Dead; of course. What else? She had to cry, but she wasn't sure she would be able to. And then, without warning, a tear spilled down her cheek, the last one she had to shed.

Colman saw it and said, 'I'm sorry. I'm sure you would rather know than live with false hope; wondering and never being sure.'

'Yes. . . .'

He didn't look at her as he said, 'I just happened to think you'd had enough. What difference does it make why? I argued the point with the others. They didn't agree. . . .' He looked at her again. 'They have every logical reason to use you; they don't operate on sentiment or pity, they can't. They know you're harmless, but it doesn't matter. You're nothing to them but a crucial move, a winning tactic—not for trivial reasons, very good ones. It made perfect sense. It was based on bad relations with the Communists and every reason to fear them. But I felt you had had enough. Just that, nothing more.'

She hung on every word now. In that instant, perhaps, her belief began to grow.

'I turned out to be less than I am supposed to be in this particular instance,' he confided openly. 'That's what it comes down to. You do your job impartially and coldly and accept department policy without debate. I did none of these things. Instead I am trying to help you, to get you off the hook I don't want to see you hanging on; and I may not even succeed, understand that. It's just an attempt. But it's solely up to you, Mrs Fischer. What is it you want to do right now? This minute. No matter who I may happen to be or what I am. To stay in the West? Or go back there?'

Her mistrust had all but vanished and vague pangs of caution were replacing it. 'Is it that simple?' she said.

'To me it is. Not easy, perhaps, but simple. Because the road ahead is open, and that's all it takes at this minute. Only an idiot or a liar would say more than that.'

'You are neither, I am sure.'

He looked at her without elation but feeling recompensed.

'It's a chance for freedom as against whatever awaits you in the Zone,' he said.

She had a faintly ironic, even derisive, look in her eyes. 'You mustn't talk to me of freedom,' she said, not aggressively. 'I didn't come here for idealistic or ideological reasons. I might have gone in the opposite direction given the right circumstances.'

'They couldn't exist on this side.'

'We may be talking about two different things. I'm not political—just a simple woman with personal reasons for everything.'

'It doesn't matter, Mrs Fischer.'

'No, it doesn't. . . .'

She grew silent and pensive and Colman knew that she had ceased to resist. He didn't think that she was as simple as she might, for whatever reason, wish him to think. A Bonn-Cologne flight was the first one out of Tegel twenty-five minutes later. They boarded, and shortly after they were in the air, seated side by side, she said, 'Where did my husband die?'

Colman hesitated. 'We weren't told,' he said. 'We know very little about it, only that it did happen. The information came from someone who was arrested by the West Germans. It was some kind of a falling-out, a misunderstanding among people who don't trust each other much to begin with. . . .' He elaborated through habit; the art of quick fabrication was so much a part of him and all the others who were in it. 'That's all that's known about it.'

She looked at him. 'And you feel sorry for me,' she said with an odd, dim smile that quickly died from lack of strength. 'You, of all the others, for some reason think I have had enough. Why are you that kind to me?'

Her fatigue was very apparent and she seemed ready to slip loquaciously into slumber. 'Why not?' he said simply.

'Is it pity?' she said. 'I suppose it is and I'm grateful. But I don't even know your name. And maybe you'd rather I didn't. . . .'

'Brian,' he said.

She said, 'It's such a terrible world, Brian.'

'At least half the time.'

'It's a place of opposing forces, according to your Mr Stevenson. There's nothing people can do but oppose each other. But why?'

Colman looked at her, her head leaned back against the seat cushion, her eyes grown heavy-lidded and dreamy. She looked at him and said, 'Wouldn't it be grand if that were not so?'

Colman nodded ever so slightly. 'Yes.' Then: 'Why don't you try to nap? We've about thirty-five minutes yet.'

She didn't answer but was apparently in agreement, her pale lips dehydrated and parched-looking, the fierce burning within having baked away all the moisture. Her need of liquids—water chiefly—occurred to him. But her eyes were closed instantly and the muffled hum of the engines had absorbed her and carried her off just that quickly.

She didn't awaken until the arrival at Wahn airport, where her acquiescence and trust seemed to be complete, only the barest functional exchanges taking place between them as they proceeded swiftly from the incoming-passenger level to the taxi rank outside. 'Where are we going?' she asied.

'To get you a room for the night,' he said.

'I've no *Ausweis*,' she pointed out.

'It won't be a problem. Don't worry about it,' he said.

A cab took them along the river bank, glittering in the cold winter night, into the city, past its bridges, the lights of its restaurants and nightclubs, always in view of the great twin spires of the cathedral, and finally to the entrance of one of the hotels near the railway station. They entered the lobby, salesmen and their contacts in evidence at every turn.

'Give it a try at the desk,' he told her. 'They may not ask for it—they're more diligent about foreigners than Germans. If they do, I'll be right there to sign you in on my passport. So you use the name Colman.'

The registration clerk didn't request identification, taking only casual notice of her as she calmly signed her name. 'I'm in room two twenty-seven,' she told Colman, who had waited off to one side for the results. 'I said I had misplaced my ID, and he said it didn't matter. So I used the name Schramm, my maiden name.'

98

'That was all right. You must be hungry. There's a restaurant next door.'

She looked at him gravely and said, 'I must go to the toilet before anything.'

By the time they sat in the restaurant she had become reflective, the cutting edge of remembrance drawing blood. She had been eating a plate of *Gulasch* ravenously and then was forced to stop. 'I'm sorry,' she said. 'I had almost forgotten my husband. . . .'

Colman watched her with assumed detachment and said nothing.

'My head is spinning with the same question over and over again,' she said. 'What am I doing here with you, Brian? Should I be here? . . .'

Colman, using a spoon handle, indented a line on the tablecloth between them like a *point d'appui*, looked up from it to confront her, and said, 'You've got to know that for yourself, Mrs Fischer. If returning to the East Zone of Germany doesn't fill you with absolute dread, then I have presumed too much.'

'Existence itself,' she said, 'seems to fill me with dread at the moment. . . .'

'That's too bad,' he said, oppressed by the thought.

'. . . whether here or there,' she concluded and looked at him with what appeared to be yearning.

'Do you want to die?' he said.

'It doesn't frighten me.'

'If you were dead, you wouldn't need to go back there, you wouldn't need to be here,' he said. 'But you wouldn't kill yourself, would you? I can tell just by looking at you.'

'Is it so bad?' she wondered with a philosophical shrug, as people will when death is not imminent.

'It's an end to this. To seeing, feeling, touching—to the commonplace. Bad, no. It's not bad. It's nothing. And it's permanent.' He put down the unused spoon. 'You're alive; that's what you're doing here with me, Mrs Fischer. You're in the process of fighting for a break, of hitting back at your luck.'

Looking at him with both pain and gratitude in her beautifully planed face, she said, 'And what is going to happen to you?'

99

'I couldn't be safer than I am, Mrs Fischer. All I risk is a job and the misunderstanding of some old friends.'

'You are making a great sacrifice for me,' she said with a rise of astonishment, 'someone of no importance to you at all.'

'Skip over that, and think about something,' he said. 'Consider going to England,' he went on in a conspiratorial tone. 'It would take a visa, because I think you would want to work at something. That's not hard, they like girls from the Continent. It wouldn't necessarily be a party, but it would be a haven if you could find the right situation.'

'You mean domestic work?'

'I suppose I do.'

The prospect didn't wholly appeal to her, but she said, 'It's all right; it doesn't make me shrink in horror.'

'Some of those jobs can be less than glorious,' he told her. 'The mistress, the master, the running-nosed kids. And it would be lonely.'

She shrugged softly. 'What do you think my life has been up till now? A Hollywood star's?' she said smiling. Then: 'My mother told me people like you didn't exist.'

He didn't say anything. Dinner was about done for both of them just moments later. 'Don't open your door to anyone,' he instructed her as he helped her to put on her coat and then began to guide her from the restaurant. 'I'll telephone you in your room tomorrow. Stay there until then,' he added as they entered the hotel lobby.

He could see that at the moment she wanted to be led, perhaps out of the sheer exhaustion brought on by fending for herself and taking too many cuts. He could see it in her eyes as they looked into his with an air of obedience and the wish to have it all taken out of her hands, at least for the present. It was rather like a bodily need for warmth, or sleep, or food and drink. 'All right,' she agreed finally. 'And I am not afraid of mistresses or masters or running noses. And I've been lonely . . . quite often.'

Despite the fatigue the colour had resumed in her cheeks, her lips no longer dried out, her face not quite so drawn as when they had boarded the plane so long ago.

He said nothing and departed. A few minutes later he was

in one of the yellow kiosks outside the railroad station, dialling directly through to Stevenson in Berlin. Stevenson failed to hesitate at the sound of Colman's voice. 'Did you forget something? I mean beside your oath?' came the crisp, controlled voice, bristling with barely covered-up anger.

'There's just a chance you'll understand what it's all about after you see me and listen to what I have to say.'

'You must be pretty naïve, Brian. Not that I'm any better. There doesn't seem to be any limit to how often I can be fooled. But even so, you have to have some idea of just what the hell you have done; you *have* to have—or both of us should be certified without delay.'

Colman glanced across the street at the hotel where he had left her and said, 'Yes, I've acted with human weakness. . . .'

'That supposed to put me in my place? You've acted like a fool, nothing else.'

'I'll talk it over with you,' Colman said. 'But you've got to come to me—alone.'

There was a pause and then the one word, grudging and curt: 'Where?'

'The Wahn airport.'

'Oh, Cologne, eh? Or is it Bonn?'

'It doesn't matter, you'd never find her without me, she's too well stashed away. Listen: go to the information desk in the passenger section, the domestic side. There'll be a message addressed to J. C. Bates. Read it and burn it and drop it in the nearest sand urn to be sure no one picks it up after you walk out. Then go to the rendezvous point. I'll be watching, so if anyone follows you, M.J., I won't meet you—remember that.'

'You mean you won't take me at my word,' Stevenson said with angry sarcasm and a leer one could almost see just by hearing the sound of his voice.

'If I did, I don't think you'd want me around after that.'

'I may not want you anyway.'

It was more of the same the next morning when Stevenson came to the parapet of the old bastion on the Königswinter side of the river, broad drifts of cold mist slowly rising from the water. At this height everything seemed as it might have been when chain mail and metal breastplates were the style in which men slew both dragons and each other. Broken stone haunts of distant times were everywhere, but not a sign of litter—not a beer can, not a scrap of paper, not a single discarded matchbox anywhere. The scent was heady, the stillness piercing. Only a bell would occasionally break through from the river. Godesberg Castle was visible through the shrouds on the other side. It was out of season and there were no visitors. Both men stood there with their coat collars turned up and their gloved hands in their pockets.

'I want you to reconsider the trade, M.J.' Colman said.

'That's the gist of your position, I take it,' Stevenson said, his eyes watering slightly, his little figure tightly bound into his clothing, his hat placed squarely on his head as if making an impartial, unsentimental statement of fact. 'You're asinine if you think you can pull this with me,' he said with a growl in his voice as he looked up at the very much taller and younger man. 'Whom do you think you're dealing with? Street pedlars?' He simply couldn't take this from one of his own, and he added with held-down vehemence, 'You want to go on strike, join the Teamsters or become a teacher or enroll at NYU. . . .'

'I'm not on strike.'

'Sure you are,' Stevenson said, almost petulantly, his anger very much in evidence: he had expected more of Colman than of anyone else probably. 'Not for shorter hours or higher wages, no. Yours is a jurisdictional matter. You want a voice in policy, greater compassion for the widows of Communist agents.'

'That's cheap, M.J.'

'Isn't it? And what's all this, Brian?' he said, facing Colman directly, his face blazing with a combination of cold air and anger. 'A grandstand play, pure and simple infantilism. . . .'

'Thanks.'

'You needed a furlough on your back in the sun somewhere, needed it desperately. I could see it in your eyes, I could hear it in your voice,' Stevenson rolled on. 'That's why you've pulled this stunt—you didn't take the antidote quickly enough. And now maybe you *are* used up and not really responsible for what you do. And if you are, all right. There are no penalties. But you're still the only one who can put this thing in reverse and nothing short of that will do, Brian—nothing.'

'You've got it all wrong, M.J. I haven't had a nervous breakdown or anything of the kind, and I haven't gone nuts.'

'Not my kind of word, Brian.'

'Sick, then.'

'You're someone I never knew. I looked at you, I saw stability. Or maybe I just wanted to think so. '

'You think it's unstable,' Colman cut in tightly, 'to shoot someone dead and then feel pity for his totally helpless and innocent widow. Even the Mafia sends a wreath and sometimes puts the orphan through college. . . .'

'Very funny, Brian.'

'You don't shoot someone dead and feel nothing after you've done it,' Colman explained patiently. 'You even indicated strongly at the time that you wouldn't have done it.'

'I was talking about the practical consequences of a killing, not Christian love.'

'Because we're above the law.'

'No, we're not above the law,' Stevenson said angrily. 'But the business we're in has no laws of its own except to carry out certain national responsibilities and raise as little smoke as possible while doing it. It wasn't ever murder in my mind; it was an act of war—the war that has been forced on us. And I don't intend to engage in a polemic about it; I'm talking only about this incredibly morbid piece of romantic rebellion you're wallowing in.'

'It's heartless to send that woman back.'

'There are reasons. You don't need to be in on everything. I can get a man of ours out of an East German prison. That's a sufficient objective.'

'Why? She's of no use. Why should they want her?'

'I don't *care* why. Because they don't like being outfoxed, that's good enough. As if you could really make things right with *this*—the grand gesture of an erratic high-school boy.'

'I hope it's not that. . . .'

'Just an idealist, I suppose, sure,' Stevenson scoffed openly. 'Well, let me tell you something. You are not ushering in an era of liberty and justice for all, and *nothing* will make that woman happy—I know that, I've talked with her. She's one of the bells without clappers and you can't do a thing about it. Except damage, untold damage. . . .'

'There's got to be some other way to get Mankin back——'

'*This* is the way we have in our hands.'

'It couldn't be dirtier or more unjust.'

'I didn't notice that you were so overcome at the time, come to think of it. All you said was that you didn't feel like whistling.'

'I didn't pretend to be overcome, then or now.'

'The point is, you're either part of something or you're not; and you've either got to stand still for certain things that don't make a hit with you or you have to get out—there's no compromise, no in-between. Without strictures, without restraints, and yes—without unavoidable injustices, you have chaos, no matter *whose* side you're on. I thought you, of all people, would know that.'

'I'll die agreeing with you,' Colman said quietly.

'Then what's happening?' Stevenson's anger was edged with incomprehension.

'There are times to show kindness to an innocent bystander,' Colman said.

'Exceptions, eh?' Stevenson said in an unkind and sceptical tone and then removed from under his overcoat a folded handkerchief with which he wiped the moisture from those eyes which were so much like chinks in a crumbling wall.

Colman watched him and knew that the exchange of ideas had reached its conclusion, had never had the potential for anything but new doubts and intensified resentments.

'You're through, Brian,' Stevenson said in a dismissive, low-keyed voice, 'if you don't call this thing off.' There was no question of concession, only a demand for compliance backed by the mercilessness of authority and the personal outrage of the betrayed man who was prepared to use it. 'You've got a little gas left—just enough to get you back where you began. Not more than that.'

The two men stood there and looked at each other in silence for several moments, seeing things they might not have seen before, a boat bell clanging in the distance with eerie innocence.

'You know what to do,' Stevenson said, quiet and final.

Colman didn't answer and Stevenson turned around and walked away and left Colman standing there by himself. He remained there for what seemed a long time after Stevenson had disappeared, and then he fingered the jagged edges of the parapet coping and looked vaguely down towards the river, the mist beginning to lift, the beautiful view beyond his concern. He felt as if he had been flattened out.

CHAPTER FIVE

THE GLASS-ENCLOSED TERRACE of the hotel in Bad Godesberg overlooked the river, the mountains on the other side covered with forests of trees, the snow melting away below the peaks, the Rhine with a brown, glassy surface abiding in the last tingling days of winter. Stevenson couldn't have guessed how close he had been to Adele Fischer, who now sat there and listened as Colman, speaking for the first time in English, said to her, 'He would have to quit his job if he had let me persuade him because he wouldn't be fit for it; I think I knew that before I started. Yet I had to try. And what I found out was what I always knew—that he sees it all as part of a death struggle and everything else is secondary.'

She turned her eyes away from the window where they were sitting in the empty oval room. 'Don't you believe the same thing?'

'Yes, But I don't think we will either win or lose because of you. I don't have that right, but I'm taking it.'

'Brian,' she said with candour, a grateful friend wanting to make things easy on another who had tried to do a good turn and failed.

He gave her his undivided attention and she looked into his eyes and confessed: 'I wouldn't necessarily be put in prison if I went back. I would, in fact, be well treated.' She waited briefly, saw that he didn't stir, and then said, 'The head of Internal Security is—my devoted admirer. . . .' She smiled. 'I'm not without alternatives, in other words.'

Colman now remembered Fischer's references to the arch enemy which he had, naturally, passed along to Stevenson. 'I see. . . . That would be Colonel Emmering, wouldn't it?'

'Yes. I am sure he is behind it,' she said. 'Nothing is of less value than I am on the international market—except to Emmering. Obviously Mr Stevenson was quick to accommodate him.'

She was the evident obsession of a corrupted Communist policeman, and there was a remote air of temptation in her presence now, indirect, accidental. Someone else was stirred, someone far away but constant. The information was purely clinical. 'But I am actually Soldier Schweik in a funny way,' she went on. 'I simply found myself there. Emmering kept company, you might say, with my mother from the time I was five; and though I invited nothing, I can assure you, it did me little good. But that's often the case for all of us, isn't it? Even for you, I'm sure.'

Colman said nothing and she looked down to the river as if it was where she had seen something sink long ago. 'Anyhow, there would be no whips, no bread and water in a dungeon, no usual punishments or humiliation. . . .' She looked at him. 'It isn't fair that you should think otherwise, think you are saving me from something that doesn't exist.'

'I never thought it through. Only that you didn't want to go back mattered to me, not why particularly.'

'And, of course, that's true.'

'Then why tell me that you can go back and be greeted with open arms?' he said.

'Did I put it that way?'

'Not exactly.'

She may have heard the mysterious note of irritation in his tone, but she didn't respond to it directly. 'My mother was his mistress,' she said unhesitatingly, as if it answered everything. 'For years. Until she died. You know the story. It's as ancient as invading armies. A nation is conquered, everything is scarce; and there are the women who need extra allotments of food and protection and privileges that only a few can have. And there are the highly placed officials who can supply them. Even in a Socialist state people behave as anywhere else if they get the chance.' She paused and said, 'I could hardly have avoided Emmering.'

Colman didn't say anything and she said, 'Oh, *I* wasn't his mistress also—not even after I was grown up, I mean. He wouldn't have been so imprudent as to try for that kind of arrangement. No. He waited, just waited. . . .' Her mouth was wry, her eyes recollective. 'I could feel him watching me grow almost from the beginning.' She considered it as charitably as she could. 'My mother dangled me in front of him for all those years; but not altogether consciously, and only because she was older than he and desperate to keep his interest and protective power, as well as possession of our house, and avoid the consequences of widowhood and poverty in the East Zone of Germany. . . . She suspected him of having certain tastes—or certain lusts, to put it more exactly.'

'You were blessed right from the beginning, all right,' Colman said.

'My mother was a poor, simple woman who had an extraordinary figure and the ability to tell herself the lies she needed to tell,' Adele Fischer said. 'A victim of war and the power of other people. She had no control over her own existence. She knew, as she was dying, that Emmering was waiting to come out in the open, so to speak, under his idea of respectable conditions. In the last moments of her life she didn't know how to make up for it. She said only one thing to me about it. She said, 'He thinks you are his legacy. I'm sorry.' Nothing else, just that. It gave her a very bad death.'

Colman listened and said nothing when she stopped talking and absently began to stir the coffee on the little table placed next to them. 'Martin . . . my husband . . . took me out of that situation. We ran away from East Berlin together. We crossed at the Prinzenstrasse, where they transact all the interzonal business. We came in the cylinder of a petrol truck, in a specially constructed metal recess with air vents on the underside, on the bottom curve of the cylinder. It was rather like an airtight closet. And on top of us there was a full load of petrol which was visible to the inspector at the checkpoint—do you see?'

'Yes,' Colman said softly. 'And I'm impressed.'

'From the time we entered the cylinder in Köpenick to the moment we emerged from it in Spandau . . . five hours had elapsed.' She held her voice steady as if fighting the memory. 'The journey itself was two hours,' she went on. 'But after we entered the cylinder it was an hour and a half before the petrol was put in and the journey began. It was a nightmare. Petrol fumes came through the air vents. I became ill.' She arched her back, took a deep breath, and held herself erect as she continued: 'We waited another hour and a half after the arrival in Spandau—I never knew why. The petrol had to be drained before we could come out. Martin's friend had to release the closet catch from outside—it was a safety precaution so we shouldn't trip it from within. It was like being buried alive. We were driven to an open space near the Stadtforst to avoid the West German authorities. That was Martin's wish and I had agreed to it in advance. Then we came out. . . . We were dirty; we were bruised. We didn't speak. We were in shock. We were alone in the world.' Then came the humble triumph. 'But we were in the West,' she said.

'And you thought it was worth it,' Colman said quietly.

She took a breath. 'I could never have done it alone,' she said, as though there was no point in denying it. 'I could never have done it without Martin . . . under any circumstances.'

Colman stared down at the carpet pattern of rococo symbols between his feet, but just briefly.

'Martin was in Emmering's department.'

Something unrevealed until now. 'I attracted him,' she stated and then apologized with a shrug. 'He was very . . . personable; good-looking and kind—yes, really. . . .' She looked at Colman with a further revelation to make. 'You think that your side is right and the other side is wrong,' she said. 'But Martin didn't care about either side. Only whatever benefit there was to be had in the conflict between them. He had no ideals.' It was simple truth; she gave it no colour, no judgement. But with a touch of melancholy, her eyes towards the river, she said, 'And I knew he would be killed. . . .'

Colman waited and she looked at him unwaveringly. 'I think I knew the moment he walked out of the door last week that someone was waiting to destroy him. . . .'

Colman returned her gaze without the slightest show of discomfort, betraying nothing. 'It was that kind of business he was in,' he said.

'Yes,' she murmured, and then said, 'I'm sure that if he was conscious before he died . . . his last thoughts were of me.'

It was certainly not a boast, and Colman didn't know why, if for any reason, she had said it. He could shoot the man but not look into the eyes of the widow or listen to her voice carrying recollective words. It didn't seem like deep mourning; it was more like commemoration and respect for the dead, sympathy for a wasted life.

'Wait here for me,' Colman finally said. 'I should be back late in the day.'

'You're such a kind person,' she said. 'I have never known anyone like you.'

'No, no. . . .'

'It's true.'

'It isn't really. I haven't anything to lose. No one depends on me, not a wife or children, and I don't need the job.'

He was sure her gratitude and admiration would have turned to loathing and contempt if she knew Colman had done what had been done. The gesture might have made it even worse. The attempt to expiate often accentuated the gravity of the act and the weakness of the penitent—as if the irreversible could ever be reversed or death nullified or made acceptable. But whether he was a penitent, whether he was actually trying to expiate anything he wasn't certain. He knew only that he didn't want gratitude in any degree. Everything had to be done as antiseptically as possible. He could see faint disappointment in her eyes behind a soft smile but it didn't matter.

Within the hour, sitting on the Godesberg-Bonn bus jammed into a traffic pattern which daily strangled the city, Colman waited with restraint while an endless string of freight cars rumbled in an agonizing crawl through the centre of the German capital. He was eager to reach his destination. And not long after he reached it.

Spring was just a few days away and already a hint of it had begun to enchant those who were not faced with prison or death or an endlessly debilitating illness.

In a bookshop facing Poppelsdorfer Allee, Colman stood watching through the plate-glass window the passing back and forth of the students and the professors from the university. The number of dogs in Bonn belonging to faculty members was prodigious. The observation drifted idly through Colman's mind never to return again, and other things took its place. These were more sombre, abstract, and vexatious. He had gone bad and let everyone down. He had gone back on everything he had ever stood for, bore only faint resemblance to the soldier he had been in Korea so long before. But he had to be here now and there was absolutely nothing he could have done about it. That was what he had already come to accept —that there was nothing he could do about it. His interest quickened as he suddenly saw the approach and entry of the man called Lorenzo into the shop.

Colman looked at the old, swarthy face full of too much beer and wine and goose-liver paté. 'My friend, I am afraid I must be the one to bear unwanted tidings,' the man said as he and Colman stood next to one of the tables sagging with books. 'Faubrein is dead. . . .'

Colman was shocked but asked quietly, 'When did he die?'

'Last week,' said Lorenzo, the go-between. 'And I discovered it just fifteen minutes ago. I could have saved you the journey.'

'You mean you hadn't been in contact recently?'

'No. He had been ill for quite some time. He was not young, you know.'

Colman said nothing for the moment, his mind racing for an alternative without immediate success. Things would be tight because the word would be out.

'That's fate,' the other said. 'Just a few days too late. If only you had needed this earlier. . . .'

'Is there no one else?' Colman asked. 'Someone Faubrein worked with and trusted?'

'No, no, he was the only one who knew where to get all the materials, especially for the kind of elaborate job you want. He had all the contacts and all the skill.' He shook his saturnine face back and forth. He is, in point of fact, altogether irreplaceable. The man was a great artist.'

'Yes.'

Lorenzo let the cover of a book in his hand fall shut and his expression had grown intensely all-knowing. 'May I be absolutely candid?'

Colman was surprised but merely shrugged slightly.

Lorenzo nodded. 'Well, I had always suspected that perhaps you were not all that you seemed, McNeil. Or that you wished people to suppose.'

'Oh? That's interesting.'

'I had always the distinct impression that you were more interested in who it was Faubrein supplied with his various wares than in anything else.'

Colman didn't really care but found it of academic interest: the cover that one is most certain of is sometimes the shaky one. 'You've changed your mind?' he said.

Lorenzo raised his eyebrows so that his face became a series of cynically etched lines. 'I was surprised at your request . . . if it's genuine. And at your apparent disappointment. If that too is genuine.'

'Why wouldn't it be?'

'No substantial reason occurs to me. Entrapment, if you were what I thought possible, would be too petty. Why would the CIA wish to close in on a harmless old man like Faubrein when he would be of much greater value if left alone? A question of logic.'

'CIA? Is that what you thought?' Colman gave him an admiring shake of the head. 'Very alert. I might easily have been.'

'But I don't think so any longer. It no longer makes sense.' Lorenzo inhaled deeply and seemed to be feeling very satisfied. 'If you still are in need a month from now, McNeil, catch up with me again. There may be some other channel through which we can operate.'

Colman walked out to the sunshine, into the centre of the town past the fruit, vegetable, and flower stalls. He had the strangest sensation of having undergone a transformation marked enough to be apparent to any third party and to create a subtle but definite impression that hadn't been there before. He wasn't particularly moved by it or disturbed. A short time later he experienced again the tedium of the ritual of the freight cars. Soft, damp air drifting from the river clung to him, and the train confronted him like a set of irrefutable facts. Power seldom lay in the hands of an individual, and influence was a thin and not completely dependable resource—not by itself. Pressure was preferable to reason, and he had none to exercise now. This would be the essence of his next report to the waiting Mrs Fischer—beautiful, trusting, unpossessable captive queen of a thousand lonely dreams who now needed a passport and visa to go to England so she could find a job as a housemaid.

He arrived in Bad Godesberg, with its rows of tree-lined streets, its suburban villas and retired civil servants, and he went directly to where she awaited him. They sat once again in the terrace room in view of the steadfast influence of the river and the castle ruin on the Drachenfels.

'I might still arrange it, but not immediately, that's the trouble,' he explained. 'But if you could remain out of sight long enough,' he went on, by no means despairing, '—and you might be able to with some luck—you would finally be able to come out in the open and petition for citizenship. The issue of exchanging you will have to disappear some time and there won't be any pressure to send you back. You'll automatically be eligible for processing as a defector, just as you would have been this time, under ordinary circumstances.'

'Live in hiding, you mean,' she said.

'Do you have any relatives in the Federal Republic?'

'None that I know of. . . .'

'So that you would be completely on your own,' he said, contemplating it realistically. 'It could work. But staying on this side has got to mean everything to you. The other side has got to make you sick just to think of it. That's the only way.'

'I can't simply suspend myself in mid-air.' She looked at him. 'Or you. I mean, I'm already in hiding, aren't I?'

'Yes, you are.'

'I don't know when I shall be able to repay all the money you have spent,' she said hopelessly, suddenly reminded of that also.

'I'll take it whenever you may have it,' Colman said, just to keep things in perspective. 'But I'd be insulted if you mention it again.'

She said nothing and her attention wandered for just a moment, her eyes on some hazy shore of an indifferent new world. There was only one other person in the room now, a tall, grey-haired man of seventy reading his *Abend* and sipping an afternoon *Kaffee mit Sahne*, oblivious to Colman and Adele Fischer after once having said *guten Tag* and seated himself, settled, content, all of his key decisions behind him.

'I think I suddenly believe that each of us has a destiny that really cannot be changed,' she said. '*Geschick*.' She looked into Colman's eyes. 'Do you know what I mean?'

'What you want to do is all that counts,' he said, as if repeating the key instruction in a parlour game spread between them.

She flexed her mouth philosophically, without bitterness, and shook her head slightly. 'It can't work, Brian. I do see that much clearly.'

Colman gave her a deferential gesture with his hands. 'You would have to be the judge of that, Mrs Fischer,' he said.

'It would simply be a matter of drifting—of waiting for something to happen,' she continued. 'Running from Emmering is no longer enough. It's too hard for what it's worth. Do you see?'

He looked at the boats steaming by, conducting remote, anonymous business. 'Yes,' he said. 'You're tired'—he looked back at her—'with every reason to be. And you're ready to make a deal. I don't think you want to, but you will.'

'Never,' she said quietly but with pride. 'I would tell him directly that his attentions are unwelcome. Perhaps that is all it will take, and then he may simply leave me alone. You see, I happen to be a trained laboratory technician, and such people are important to the state. It may be as simple as that, after all. . . .'

In the tone of a man who hated to disappoint someone, Colman said, 'It can't be, Mrs Fischer. If Emmering hasn't a reason to protect you, you'll sit in prison. That's my guess. Then, five or ten years later, you'll be allowed to serve your important function as a good Socialist—not before. It's a very simple principle: you've broken the law that's the cornerstone of their very existence; you've defected. So you'll sit in prison, if Emmering can find no other use for you, because they need examples for others who might be tempted. That's more important to them than a good laboratory technician any day, because a captured defector is not as easy to come by.'

'Perhaps. . . .'

'Granted, that it may be preferable to living in hiding in West Germany and all the pitfalls and problems that entails. But know what you are up against. You won't brazen it through. You'll either be whatever Emmering wants you to be or you'll sit in prison. It won't even be a matter of vengeance; just practical Communist technique.' He spoke evenly, logically, and without any effort to persuade or influence. It was all straight facts, not prejudice.

'It might be easy compared with some things,' she said with almost an air of wilful surrender rather than resignation. 'It takes no effort, and there are no false hopes. I don't need to hide, to be on guard, to tell careful lies, to act as if I have something to look forward to.'

'You can look at it that way,' he granted.

She leaned forward in her chair and looked at Colman intently and with great candour. 'Let me tell you how I was feeling when you came to take me away—when was it? Yesterday, so long ago. . . .' She recalled the sensation with satisfaction, reliving an enriching experience. 'I didn't care. When you led me to the taxicab I was already like an object to be transported from one place to another, not a person. I had no responsibility in any of it. Do you see? If you didn't exist, you didn't need to feel, you didn't need to react or to acknowledge; you didn't need even to think; nothing is required of you any more than of the dead. . . . And it wasn't so bad.'

Colman said nothing.

'I was learning to anæsthetize myself. And now that I know how it's done—I've nothing to worry about. . . .'

'Do you believe that?'

'Yes.'

'It sounds Oriental.'

'Does it? Perhaps. Or existential. What is the difference? If I live, I shall be in the thirties when I am free. Not so bad.'

'You don't ask for much, do you?'

'Only to be smart enough not to play meaningless games—to run and hide without either a goal or a hope of any kind.'

Colman licked his lips. 'You're too smart to be a woman,' he said obscurely.

'Do you resent intellect in a woman?'

'Maybe it's envy,' he said with a marginal smile. And then: 'I'm very sorry to see a Commie policeman reduce you to a state of semi-dead withdrawal. Maybe I admire your attitude towards it, but I am very sorry about it.'

'Can you forgive me for disappointing you so?'

'I'm not disappointed,' he assured her. 'It has always been in your hands, Mrs Fischer. It still is.' He nodded. 'We'll get on a Berlin flight tomorrow morning, if that is your wish. . . .'

CHAPTER SIX

THEY TOOK an early dinner in the nearly empty hotel dining room, the ceiling high and vaulted, only three of the five chandeliers turned on. She had the uneasy radiance of someone who has accepted a death sentence for a greater good. Or maybe that was simply the way Colman was seeing it.

'I shall never forget what you tried to do for me,' she said. 'There will never be a moment that I shan't be conscious of it as of no other thing in my life.'

He wished she would have shut up. 'You're back where you started,' he said cryptically.

'And where are you?'

'Where I've put myself,' he said. 'I'm in control of where I'm going. You are not.'

She looked at him with that serious, admiring expression that he had already seen before. 'Why did you do it?' she wanted to know. 'You still believe in your cause. It pained you to go back on it. And yet . . .'

'I wanted you to get the break I thought you deserved.' He

didn't like the word 'pain' because it suggested inner torment usually associated with youthful poets and middle-aged masochists. 'I don't think I can make it any easier to understand than that,' he said. 'I did what I wanted to do.'

She had brought something new to the atmosphere by terminating his gesture: it hadn't altogether failed, it had been cancelled, even rejected. And now he was anxious to get it all behind him. 'Everything was fine except the result,' he said.

The elderly waiter, fulfilling somewhat easy off-season requirements, came to the table with an air of restrained *gemütlichkiet* and placed plates of duck before them, his breathing audible, his serving of accompanying vegetables and sauce almost devout. 'I am sure you will enjoy it, *bitte*.' He snapped his fingers with surprising vigour and a teenage sommelier arrived with a slim-necked bottle of white wine. 'This is the finest of the Rheinhessens,' he said as the boy uncorked it and handed it to him. 'Excellent with the duck, I think you will perhaps agree.' He poured two glasses for them, said, '*Mahlzeit*,' and departed.

Colman lifted one glass and handed her the other. 'Good luck to you, Mrs Fischer,' he said with the utmost gravity. 'I hope it somehow comes out right for you.'

'I wish you the same,' she said in a quiet, heartfelt voice. '*Prosit*.'

They each drank some wine and then approached their food. She said, 'I know you for twenty-four hours. After tomorrow I shall never see you again. But I shall always think about you as if we had known each other for many years. And I can't believe that we didn't. Isn't it strange? Two days ago I didn't dream you even existed.' She smiled wanly and absently sliced a piece of meat on to her fork.

'You have courage I would never have,' he said. 'I could never do what you are doing. Prison is not easy.'

'Perhaps I'll be luckier than you think.'

'I hope so.'

'Even if I am not, it is better than wandering from place to place, hiding, belonging to nothing and no one—living on a high wire every minute of your life. It is better than that, at least for me. . . .'

'Perhaps.'

'An ordinary and commonplace existence is what I really crave, uncourageous as that may be. It seems so beyond me. . . .'

'You've had anything but.'

'I tried to get my husband to stop what he was doing. And he might have done eventually.'

'You think he would?'

'I shall never know now. I think I might have kept him from that last time. I might have made him quit, then and there, that very day, if I had been more . . . forceful.'

'I have an dea that the cleanest thing imaginable is your conscience. What could you have done? Threaten?'

'It's a despicable weapon. But I'd have used it if I had known. . . .'

'What? Divorce? Suicide? To go to the police?'

'Divorce.'

'Why didn't you?'

She shook her head. 'At the last minute I couldn't. I told myself I would never need to. Now it's too late. . . . I can only speculate on how it might have been.'

They remained silent for some minutes after that, ate, drank, commented casually on the quality of the food. The waiter came to offer dessert but was told to bring only coffee. Colman, finished with his meal by then, took some of his third glass of wine, the bottle now empty. 'You can't change anyone too much,' he then dared to say, though in a respectful tone of voice. 'And you couldn't have made your husband into something he was not.'

She looked at him, wary but deeply curious. 'Why do you say that?' she asked.

'Because I think you believe his death robbed you of the chance to lead an ordinary, commonplace existence, as you call it. And it didn't. Don't mourn for that. It never had a chance.'

She seemed slightly taken aback and even puzzled, and he went on: 'We knew something about him. He was ready to do *any*thing to make money. Anything. . . . That's why he got himself killed.'

'But why do you tell me this now?' she said, frowning, searching his face.

'Because it might have a salutary effect for you to know it, if you don't already. I mean healthy; healing. And it's not idle chatter.'

She owed her dead husband a defence, and it came as no surprise, albeit in gentle, tolerant tones. 'Even if you are right,' she said, 'without the powerful and ruthless men on both sides—without the games they play, without the immorality of governments he should have been something else. In a different world he should have been a different person.'

'And you wouldn't be sitting here with me now, Mrs Fischer, having this conversation,' he said, compelled to go on. 'There wouldn't be Emmering or Stevenson or any of it. But it's not a different world, it's this one.'

Maybe he had wanted to make both of them feel better, minimize her sense of loss, cut the presumptive guilt attached to any killing. Or maybe he at last found Fischer an enemy to be destroyed without remorse, even a second time.

'You'll want to get as much sleep as you can,' he said quietly. 'Tomorrow may be a very . . . difficult day.'

Her eyes had taken on a filmy look as if tears might or might not crystallize; her face was calm. The waiter came to the table as if the occasion had been festive and said, 'I trust everything was to your taste.'

'Perfect,' Colman said.

In a moment they had moved into the foyer and stood at the foot of the carpeted staircase. 'The plane goes at nine thirty,' Colman told her. 'We could move you to a hotel near the airport, unless you don't mind waking up early.'

'It's all right.'

Colman nodded and said, 'I'll meet you right here at eight o'clock. Is that okay?'

'Quite okay,' she answered. The tears had never developed, perhaps had never been there to begin with.

'I hope I haven't upset you,' Colman said. 'It's none of my business to tell you your husband's bad points.'

'He had his good points,' she reflected. 'He was faithful, there were no other women. . . .'

A man passed by with a reserved '*Guten Abend*,' in spite of the English he presumably heard them speaking.

'But just as you say,' Adele went on, 'he would not have changed. I never thought he would—really. . . .'

There was silence for just a moment and then she said, 'I shall be here tomorrow. . . . I hope you sleep well.'

She turned away and ascended the stairs, and he put on his coat and hat which had been placed on a nearby chair. Then he walked out of the hotel and along a colonnade of trees, stripped and cold in the winter night, his footfalls following him, no one else nearby at the moment, the boat engines and those of some of the barges throbbing distantly. A car went by. Colman dug his hands into his pockets and walked on, tasting the bite in the air, his thoughts random but ironic and not unrelated.

It all began because Stebbins turned out to be someone else. Colman recalled all the moves vividly. Cornered, caught dead to rights, not only is he then not remorseful but he actually turns everything around, puts *you* on trial, and pronounces you guilty. You're the one, not him. He's clean, you're dirty and unprincipled. His conscience is clear, you're the gangster. He had been indispensable to the death of Webber and all that had followed with Webber's widow—events he couldn't, of course, have remotely anticipated. Because of him Colman had placed himself across the line from the Great Forces, against Stevenson and the battlements he had always defended. The thoughts formed an obvious chain and Colman soon let it drop.

He reached his hotel, a small place on the river, listed in the guidebooks as 'reasonable,' almost in a direct line with the one where Adele Fischer now waited in lonely circumspection for the dawn. It was impossible not to think about her, and it was a long while before he was able to fall asleep.

For Adele Fischer sleep was to remain elusive for a good part of the night. She lay in her bed acceptantly, her eyes open, her mind like the playing field of a hard-fought game with no winner. She did indeed feel like a high-wire walker, but one who was afraid to be there even though she had insisted on making the attempt. She knew she would never reach the other side and somewhere along the way would fall because of the absence of desire, while he, Colman, watched sympathetically from a restricted distance. That was what being a nonperson really meant. Falling from on high. Or so it seemed as she finally ceased to be awake.

CHAPTER SEVEN

HE WAS AWAKE and ready with the first rays of light. He felt an odd pang of longing—perhaps for recognizable enemies like the commandant of the POW camp at Pak Chee. For just that moment before he got out of bed he thought about the time so long before when his understanding and beliefs couldn't have been breached, when there was no Mrs Fischer but only an enemy to resist or to crumble before and the obstacles of pity, doubt, and guilt hadn't been raised. This particular enemy gave to the acts of debasement and torture a zeal, a rage, a joy, and a passion of religious intensity. All with no apparent motive. And also attempted to induct you into the exquisite concepts of Marx and Lenin at one and the same time.

Colman had remained intact through allegiance not simply to a flag or to groups of words carved on the pedestals of monuments to great men but to himself. In oneself lies the final allegiance when all else is stripped away, when all other consciousness has been blurred by the applied lighted ends of cigarette butts. There were still remains here and there on his body, old autographs that were safe for ever from loss or destruction. Perhaps his escape to the South, one of the few recorded, had come just in time. He would never know.

But Mrs Fischer, innocently, had provided no escape. That she had decided so firmly to go back and thereby rescind Colman's actions didn't change anything. Someone fires a gun with the intention of killing, not aware that the cartridges are blank. The attempt is no less significant for having failed.

He shaved with the Gillette he had bought two days before in Cologne, showered down the hall, and dressed, putting on the new shirt and underwear and socks he had picked up at the PX in Bonn, stuffing the replaced items in a small Lufthansa bag purchased at the airport. He looked in the mirror above the bureau, saw lines at the corners of his mouth, the eyes of someone who didn't want to tell him everything and just stared back steadily.

The morning was cool and crisp, and as Colman made his way towards her hotel he saw a number of cars with CD plates headed in the direction of Bonn. An American fender flag passed him by like a chastisement. He quickened his pace until he reached the somewhat grand entrance to the baroque building and then he slowed, entering and proceeding decorously through the thickly carpeted vestibule. Several of the elderly pensioners who were permanent residents were on the way to breakfast and *guten Tags* were inevitably exchanged. The air was warmed with steam heat. Colman walked to the staircase, ascended, passed a chambermaid coming down, and in a moment or two had reached the door of Adele Fischer's second-storey room.

He knocked and she opened the door to him. 'I was about to come downstairs.'

'It's all right, we have plenty of time,' he assured her, entering and closing the door behind him. 'I don't suppose you slept too well. . . .'

'Not too soundly. And you?'

'The same. I kept thinking about today,' he said. 'I am very sorry to see you going back to the Zone,' he said quietly. 'I'll remember you every day of my life. And the truth is, it will hurt me to think of you . . . it will hurt like hell.'

Her lips parted slightly and her eyes glistened with surprise. 'Thank you.'

'For what?'

'For telling me.'

'It doesn't change anything, I'm afraid.'

'There is no choice. . . .'

'I wish there were.'

'I wish also.'

'It's wrong, this way.'

She nodded solemnly. 'Yes. But so are many things. I've got to look at it in that light.'

'I've always said that. But not now. Oh, it's true enough. But suddenly I'd like to throw the idea away.'

'One can't. It doesn't help to think one's own injustice is the only one that counts. Injustice is everywhere. None of us would recognize the place without it.'

'There's something I'd like to remind you of, Mrs Fischer. You don't need to make up your mind about anything this quickly. You don't need to do anything today—or tomorrow, for that matter. I am not attempting to influence you; but maybe you would like to take advantage of that.'

'Oh, Brian. How impractical. . . .' She smiled a little.

'Is it?' He shrugged. 'I suppose I am doing and saying all the things I might ordinarily sit back and sneer at somebody else for.' He smiled faintly. 'I used to be another person, Mrs Fischer. . . .'

'You've a conscience. You have principles. That's who you are.'

'Don't you believe it.'

'What then should I believe?'

'That someone else has taken me over, got inside my mind and body and made a bad soldier out of me.'

'Because you feel kindness towards me?'

'Because it's more than that,' he said, not looking at her. 'There's more than that on my mind right now. Much more. And that's too bad but none of your fault.' He then looked at her. 'Mainly I hate to see anyone manipulate you like this. I hate the idea of your being in prison or anywhere else you don't want to be. Forgive me for anything else that may have come out.'

'Forgive you?'

'For anything—for anything at all. . . .'

She now seemed somewhat off balance. 'No, no. . . .' She said that much and was obviously uncertain of what to do next, and she looked about the room for an answer. 'Should we leave?'

'Yes,' he said.

But she didn't move. She stood perfectly still, remained in place, and her eyes seemed to change colour, about to fill with tears possibly.

Colman studied her. 'Are you okay?' he asked.

She shook her head. 'Sure. . . .'

They then looked at each other, he near the door, substantially separated from her, and neither of them moved an inch. 'I'll take your suitcase,' he finally said and went to the bed where it lay, light as her life's accomplishments, removed it, and turned to walk out with it. The move had placed them alongside each other, and suddenly, perhaps by design, perhaps not, he was facing her directly. At first they looked at each other with nothing to say. Then he said, 'It was that from the beginning, I think,' as if confessing to a crime, 'not an act of conscience or principle, or righting a wrong. . . .'

'But I was a stranger to you to begin with,' she pointed out, growing flushed, a crisis at hand suddenly, values shifting about restlessly.

'Not altogether,' he confessed further. 'I saw you when you didn't know it. In the supermarket where you shop. I was one of the people watching your moves. Maybe it began right then and there.'

'Oh, Brian,' she exclaimed and then was defeated by the spill of tears; she could take no more and they had won—they had been bound to sooner or later. 'What are we doing? . . .' She swayed just a fraction and his hands went to her arms, the flesh firm through the long sleeves of her dress, and they became two entirely new people. 'Does everything always need to hurt?'

The touch of her increased his sense of longing, his will to influence and take possession. 'No, it does not,' he said softly. 'Not always.'

'Then why does it?'

'It doesn't, it doesn't. . . .' He held her in his arms and patted her shoulder. She was immobile, momentarily stiff, a sob caught in her throat, the keenest sorrow pressing up from her diaphragm to push out the sob. Colman could feel that series of steps gathering force.

She wept not desperately but deeply, the sounds escaping her discreetly. Colman turned her chin upwards to see her eyes, blurred with tears, her cheeks soaked by them like waters washing away years of silt from within. Her lips were loose and as yielding as sponge, and he tasted the moisture and a surprising tang of chloride when he kissed her. 'I'm sorry,' she said. 'I'm sorry for crying like a fool. But I just couldn't help it.'

'Don't. . . .'

'I couldn't hold it in, you see.'

'Who said you had to?' he said and wiped one of the tears away with his finger.

In a few minutes all the questions and answers went out like candle flames, and they made love in the morning light coming through the panes of the high window above the tufted window-box seat. She had lain awake most of the night, injured and alone. Now the injury and solitude were gone, swept away like sandprints by a rush of the tide. They experienced no difficulty or special effort, but rather ease and congruity. With some unspoken prior understanding they were giving into their sexual impulses now as they would have to any other suddenly manifest and irresistible offering; as they would have picked berries and devoured them without let-up in an open field of bursting bushes. The unthinkable thing would have been to leave the field untouched.

'I don't have much conscience *or* principle,' he said when they were done. 'I thought I did. Now I even wonder what exactly those things are.'

'Brian,' she said in a contented whisper, 'all that any of us is supposed to be is kind.'

Her head was on his shoulder, the feel of her hair softly splayed on his flesh. 'I wanted you the very instant I laid eyes on you,' he said. 'Something got caught in my throat as soon as I saw you—that look in your eyes, keeping everything to yourself—things I already knew. . . .'

'And things I didn't know. . . .'

'Yes. . . .'

'That Martin was dead.'

'Yes.'

'Did *that* make a difference to you somehow? Draw you to me?'

Colman waited and then said, 'Why should it?'

'Pity. . . .'

124

'No.'

'And not just a woman, but me,' she mused. 'Is that possible?'

'Don't men fall in love at first sight?' he said. 'I've heard they do.'

'Not love,' she said with a sad note. 'I wouldn't expect that of you.'

'What do you think this is?' he asked without colouration of any kind.

'Your hunger,' she said sweetly. 'I suspect it has been building up for a long time—before you ever dreamed of my existence. That . . . and my own hunger.'

'Sex is not hard to find,' he said.

'I mean hunger for someone who needed the pity and the help you had to give,' she said.

'Do you think of yourself that way?'

'No. But you did. You were ready for this, I think, for a very long time—you must have been. So was I. But I never thought about it. For me it was Martin or . . . well, you know.'

'Or nothing?'

'Or anæsthesia,' she said. 'I told you, remember?'

'Then you wanted . . . something besides Martin.'

She didn't speak immediately and he waited. 'I wanted something he couldn't give,' she said finally. Then: 'Whatever it is that you are giving me . . . but not love. I wouldn't impose on you with anything like that, Brian. I wouldn't ask it of you. . .'

'You're lying,' he said. 'To both of us.'

'How sensible of me.'

'But you don't need to.'

'But have I asked for love?' she said.

'No, you haven't.'

'The opposite really. You can't love me, you needn't, it would be bad for both of us. . . .'

'Then why are we discussing it?'

'We are being complicated,' she said, shifting to face him more directly. 'We can't help it. We're trying to analyse everything.'

'I never do that.'

'Looking for cause and effect, why and how, right or wrong. . . . What sort of woman, just a few days a widow, makes love to a new man? Isn't that one of the questions?'

'Not mine,' he said and began on the spur of sudden renewed fervour to firmly but gently separate her thighs and poise himself above her.

'We shall miss the plane,' she said, her breath short, her breasts perceptibly expanding, the nipples distended, all the involuntary responses ensnaring her.

'We're not getting on the plane, neither of us, not ever,' he told her.

It was like entering into a covenant and Adele said, 'Oh, Brian—if you hadn't said that, I should have died. I suddenly realize that. . . .' And then: 'Oh, how good. . . .'

Colman recalled having once heard it described as the death from which one returned again and again. He couldn't remember who had said it, but as they both abandoned their restraints, as their wills to resist or withhold collapsed, the idea struck him as not altogether insane. One succumbs and so does one's partner or neither has done well.

CHAPTER EIGHT

THE GERMANS are not as concerned with the private lives of hotel residents as the Italians or the English are. No one came to the door and they lay there safely and quietly, no longer strangers in any sense, the rewards and penalties of intimacy achieved, his surging done for the moment, she peaceful at his side. They had ceased to try to define things, to make the situation simple and easy to grasp. Colman was not one to ask for a commemorative copulation or a pay-off from any woman. This was more than an easy column of figures with the possibility of only one total at the bottom. Its conditions were as endless and complex as the flight of sperm to the ovum, whether one called it love or not. 'We're across the line now,' he said reflectively, his eyes on the ceiling. 'Both of us. . . .'

Sleep was making an attempt on her pleasantly for the first

time, perhaps in years. 'Are we?' she murmured. 'I never suspected. . . .'

'What?'

She shifted and stretched herself, staying in the crook of his arm. 'I thought I was only a symbol to you, darling,' she said. 'An abused stray cat or a persecuted Jew without a name. I didn't think for a moment I existed in your mind as a person.'

'You were more of a person to me than people I had known for years,' he said.

'Because I was a woman who attracted you. But what if I had been someone else—a woman of sixty-five, wretched, friendless, in the same circumstances as I, but past her ability to attract you?'

'I don't know. I'd have felt sorry for anyone in that fix,' he answered. 'But you know I wouldn't be here now.'

'And if I had not been arrested?' she went on. 'If Martin had been killed, but nothing had happened to me. And you saw me and you knew me. What would you have done?'

'Why all the ifs? Why not take what there is as it is?' The thing between them, the bond that only he knew about, had not been dissolved. 'The truth is . . .'

'Perhaps you don't know.'

'. . . I'd have ached for you,' he told her.

'But you'd have been hesitant.'

'If they had left you alone, I'd have had nothing to offer you,' he said. 'How would you have liked a CIA agent on the make for you, under the circumstances?'

'On the make? Oh, yes. But you wouldn't have had to tell me.'

'And when you had discovered it? Anyhow, we would have had no reason to meet, nothing between us.'

'Then only my—fix—was responsible—Emmering, really; and Mr Stevenson.'

'That's what they call fate.'

'And we couldn't ever have known each other in normal circumstances,' she said ironically.

'What are *they*?' he said.

'Without policemen; without espionage and prison and murder. . . .'

'To some people in this world, anything else is *ab*normal.'

'If Martin hadn't been murdered,' she observed with awe and revulsion, 'we should never have met. . . .'

Colman disengaged himself gently and said, 'You can put it that way, yes.'

'I suppose that's morbid. I didn't mean to be.'

'You needed to say it for some reason,' he said tolerantly.

'I would need to lose you in order to bring him back to life,' she said, awed by the discovery.

'You're saying you would make that choice: give me up to bring him back.'

'I'm not at all sure that's what I'm saying,' she said, sitting up and shaking her head. 'I should never have brought it up otherwise.' She sat there, her breasts redefined into sculpted bursts, the pain of some vague guilt clouding her eyes. 'I can't believe that I am making love just a few days after my husband has been killed somewhere. . . .'

Colman didn't speak right away, his eyes wandering for a moment, then fixing thoughtfully off into space. 'There is always somebody who has died and left you with a mess,' he finally said, breaking the silence, 'or with feelings of guilt because you weren't all you should have been when he was alive; or because you are relieved now that he is dead, or feeling free because of it.'

'Yes,' she realized. 'I feel freed now. But not at first. At first only squeezed dry. Because I knew he would die, I knew they would kill him.'

'He did it himself. . . .'

'I could say he was already dead for me a long time,' she said. 'Or perhaps I am only telling myself that now . . . justifying myself.'

Colman said nothing, merely encircled her wrist with his hand, gazed towards the foot of the bed, and waited for the topic to lose itself. He then had a thought to help it along. 'You don't need to examine yourself that closely,' he said. 'You can come up with any conclusion that suits you after a while. You can make yourself better than you are or worse. And then what have you got?'

He looked at her and she returned the look. 'I want you to

know one thing,' she assured him with a supplicant mouth and now soft, misted-over eyes. 'I will go back with you to Berlin if you should change your mind tomorrow; or next week . . . or any time. . . .'

'Ready to be stepped on, are you?'

'Not that. . . .'

He put his face next to hers and said, 'Going back will be your option as much as mine. Do you think you will want to?'

'Never.'

'That's a *long* time.'

'Not while you stay with me, Brian,' she said.

'I want to stay with you, Adele,' he said assuringly. He added through scarcely moving lips: 'I've got to be with you.' It was as if he were passing along a dynamic secret, quietly spoken of. 'That's the way it is.'

'And the man in prison in the Zone,' she said, worried. 'He must be of desperate importance to your side.'

'I'm sure he is.'

'And now he will stay there.'

'I can't help that now. They've got to get him loose some other way.'

'Can I balance that kind of loss?' she said, fearful to leave it unsaid.

'They'll find a way,' he said. 'With someone like Stevenson there's always a way.'

'How will you feel if they don't?' she said.

'Very bad. But there is no sense in talking about it now.'

She ran her hand over his shoulder and said, 'I can feel your *Gänsehaut*. You will freeze if you don't cover up.'

'We'd better get dressed. I'm very hungry all of a sudden.'

'With little wonder,' she said, smiling, complimentary and a little sad.

They went to a small restaurant-café on the river, directly across from the lofty Petersberg, ate *Brötchen* with coffee and also oranges, sitting next to a leaded window in full view of the river traffic. The two of them were like conspirators against an unworthy and inappropriate enemy, the outside world of governments, fat-cats, and policemen without souls. 'I have been putting money in the bank for twenty years,' Colman told her. 'I've had no reason to spend very much. There is enough to take care of us for a very, very long time.'

'Darling, I am glad you are rich,' she said with an almost carefree laugh.

'All we need to do is avoid a few key places and certain unfriendly people,' Colman said. 'It can be done. People who want to stay out of reach can do it if they just know a few fundamental rules. And I know them all.'

'That will make nomads out of us, won't it?' she remarked, the thought just having occurred to her.

'For a while,' he said. 'We'll be sightseers. Up the Rhine, the Black Forest, Bavaria. . . . After that we'll see what happens.'

'If I hadn't decided to go back to the East, if I had wished to chance it alone in the West, live in hiding, would you have stayed with me?'

'Don't be so analytical,' he said gently.

'I won't be, I promise you. But I can't help wondering if you wouldn't have left me to do as I wished until I made an issue about returning to the Zone. I mean, you wanted to keep me from going back. You might not have said anything to me otherwise. You'd have gone about your business but for me.'

'Then why didn't I?'

'There was no single dominating reason.'

'And I had no business to go about. I've outlived my usefulness to the people who depended on me.'

'There's something else. Not only must I hide, but so must you simply to protect me.' She looked at him wisely. 'And I only hope I am worth it. . . .'

He looked at her for a moment, as if making an appraisal. Then, with narrowed eyes, his voice low-keyed and deliberately intimate, he said, 'As a matter of fact, you're not. I would rather be anywhere but with you. When we made love I had to grit my teeth to keep from falling asleep.'

She lowered her eyes for a few seconds and then looked at him with a faint smile of longing and said, 'I wish I never had to be without you again. . . .'

She seemed very sure of it; and his own wish to please and protect her was like an embrace, a matter of intention, not in the least vague or uncertain. 'That's a very impressive wish,' was all he said. Her adoring eyes dimmed everything else at the moment. He was not extending sympathy; he was not, if he ever had been, easing his conscience or repaying anything. It had ceased to matter at all how and why they had been brought together.

CHAPTER NINE

WHAT COLMAN HAD DONE was still almost more than Stevenson could absorb to the point of full acceptance, even three days later.

'Is it love—or whatever *passes* for love?' he had said to Brannigan. 'Is *that* it? Something that simple, that unadorned, that embarrassing? Are he and that woman scoring with each other? Something that second-rate and frivolous?' He had paced back and forth, unable to stand still while addressing an unseen jury, Brannigan waiting for him to pause.

'Colman is not someone I would ever call frivolous,' Brannigan said.

'Then what is it?'

Brannigan's analysis carried conviction. 'Sex,' he said simply. 'But not frivolous.'

It was absurd if true. Stevenson, at fifty-two, thought of sex seldom, if ever, and considered it something of a joke whenever he found himself aroused because it always came as a surprise. He was an ugly little man and his passion was reserved for the apocalyptic struggle against Russian espionage and subversion in the West—not for any woman, not now, not this late. Yet so much, so carefully nurtured for so long, could now founder and die on the gonads of one man. Ultimately Stevenson was a realist, and cold acceptance finally took place. New moves had to be made, certain fences mended. Joe Fox became Colman's successor. 'The B Operation is in your hands from now on,' Stevenson told him. 'You'll have to establish your own set of people, some of Colman's might not weather the changeover too well, that'll be for you to decide when you get to it.'

Joe Fox hid his ambivalence in a hard-finish institutional pose as he stood before Stevenson's desk. 'How much of the original operation stays intact? Can we still trust everything the way it was?'

'Sure we can. But we're not going to,' Stevenson said. 'Never, but never, trust an old system once there's been any kind of a leak.'

'Is Colman a leak? What's the department position?'

'Colman is officially suspended and considered unreliable. He is also harbouring a displaced person who is on the wanted list of the West German immigration authorities. That's all there is to that until further notice.'

'You never know about anybody, do you?' Fox said.

'So I've heard,' Stevenson said, walking to the window for one of his periodic inspections of the Wall. 'Get in touch with Walters, he's expecting you.'

'Does he know what actually happened to Webber, or am I going to get the same blank look and mumbled answers I've been getting up till now?' Fox talked with rapidly acquired authority, a tough, unblinking look on his face.

'Going to be the hard-hitting type, Joe?' Stevenson said, not without approval. 'Okay. Just the main points. Webber's dead. He left a widow over in Wilmersdorf. We could have traded her for Mankin. Colman thought it was all too cruel—which it was—and literally snatched her away from us. I don't think you need an adding machine to work it out.'

Fox saw what there was to see and couldn't conceal the little jolt it gave him. 'Then he did meet Webber that night, didn't he? I *thought* there was something that didn't quite jell for me. . . .'

Stevenson said nothing, felt the weight of Colman's departure, and thought to himself, Yes, and I'd take him back even now. All he'd have to do is ask. . . .

'I see what happened now,' Fox said. 'He's either making restitution or . . . I don't know. But whatever it is, I think it cost him a lot to run out. I knew him,' he went on as if a death had taken place. 'This wasn't in his nature. It's a form of cracking-up. So I have to look at it that way. He's a crack-up. . . .'

132

'Talk to Walters,' Stevenson said, terminating the exchange of unofficial ideas and personal regrets.

Maybe they were all crack-ups, Stevenson thought to himself. Maybe he and Brannigan and all the others on both sides were dangerously retarded people trying to sustain inwardly crass lives in a time of enormous historical and social change, pretending to high purposes and import that didn't exist. The return on such philosophizing was small. It usually took place when everything was going wrong, when you were fatigued, when the synapses were worn down. Success was a steadying influence, and it had been out of reach lately. There were lonely midnights and four-in-the-morning heebie-jeebies.

What if you were wrong? What if it was all make-believe? Failure cast grotesque shadows and it had to be got away from finally. Spies had to forget their burdensome significant secrets, women had to be courted and loved. Yes, even that. Stevenson turned to Wanda Mehremberg, the handsome widow of anti-Nazi Count von Mehremberg. This was the woman whose company he occasionally shared and with whom, during the past six months, he had twice slept. And twice been surprised. He now needed not a desperate passion, to which he was resolutely impervious, and which would have been inappropriate anyway. Just a night out; diverting and genial.

He had pleased her greatly without taxing himself terribly. And she was obviously a willing partner. Her poise and social grace were deeply rooted in past generations whose aura was shadowy with the domination of others, something one didn't dwell on in her presence. Tall, call it imperial, yet warm, she greeted him in her Hansa Quarter flat with imperturbable elegance and a brilliant smile. 'Before the theatre?' she asked, amused and perhaps mildly shocked. 'What has come over you?'

'I must leave you immediately *after* the theatre,' he explained straightforwardly. 'And, frankly, I don't know what's come over me. You should really have a young man, Wanda. I'm too old and ugly for you.'

She was drawn to him because he was self-contained and strong; because he apparently sought no one's favour on unequal terms; because he was modest but unhesitant; because

133

he was short and beautifully ungood-looking. 'I happen to be fifty,' was her answer, 'not thirty, my dear.'

For all her experience and intelligence she couldn't have guessed what was going on behind the public face or even the one he exhibited in the privacy of her boudoir. She couldn't have guessed at the magnitude of his responsibilities, the business he was a part of, the daily abnormalities and brutality, the endless corridors of mistrust he had to walk. As far as she was concerned he was simply an American businessman serving as a liaison between American capital investment and the Federal Republic—something she scarcely understood or cared about. This, of course, was what he hoped.

The inconsistency lay in the fact that at least half the people who knew him were not fooled. Not altogether. Not even Wanda really. It didn't matter. It was an age of suspicion. He was something other than what he appeared—so many were— but the specifics weren't apparent. And then, for some reason lost in a vague gesture or momentarily heightened sense of intimacy, Wanda said to him, 'Do you know what I've heard said of you?' Then: 'That you are an agent of the CIA. Are you? Or is that a dangerous question?'

'Brazen anyhow.' He smiled through it; the shock, however, minimal, was there. 'Who told you that?'

'All sorts of people. They merely suggest it.'

They were seated in the back of a cab returning from the opera, which had thoroughly bored Stevenson, one of his major 'weaknesses' a predilection for nothing more musically advanced than Jerome Kern. 'Even if it were true I would have to deny it, wouldn't I?' he said, patting her hand to accentuate the logic. 'And you wouldn't want to know anyhow, would you?'

It was a bad time for it. Behind the air of amusement and the aplomb he felt suspicious and vulnerable. And perhaps incompetent. Maybe he should have worn a sign and had it over with. He was not even sure he could trust Wanda any longer. Finally he was put out with himself to think he had been seduced by the second-rate concept of sexual intimacy as a palliative. A malignant angel had been assigned to him and the world was looking very lousy indeed.

Brannigan awaited him at Rose Bowl in the night light of a back room where a Xerox and a small old-fashioned floor safe sat among some chairs and a trestle table.

'The other side is willing to suspend any action on Mankin pending a change in the situation,' Brannigan said. 'If we can come up with Mrs Fischer, *i.e.*, they are still willing to deal.'

Stevenson mumbled unintelligibly. It was hard to be impressed by anything at the moment.

'They'll wait indefinitely,' Brannigan said. 'And I don't think there's a limit.'

Stevenson walked to the end of the room, opened a connecting door, and entered his own darkened office and switched on the overhead panel lights. Brannigan followed and Stevenson poured each of them a shot glass of Scotch.

Brannigan said, 'We've got the immigration people and the passport and frontier departments alerted; everyone concerned gets photographs tomorrow morning and whatever pertinent data there is.'

Stevenson was fully conversant with such routine procedure and he listened without great interest, his face somewhat blank for just a moment.

'A call to the banking consortium, by the way, turned up a checking account in the Dresdner Bank cleaned out five days ago,' Brannigan continued. 'There was a little over sixty-five hundred marks. A savings account at the Düsseldorf Bank of America had the same fate, in that case for eight thousand. So you can see what he's done. He probably has new accounts in another name, travellers' cheques, marks, dollars—none of it traceable. I would bet he's carrying a money belt too. . . .' Brannigan shrugged. 'Anyhow, he thought it out in advance, that's obvious.'

Stevenson shook his head and sat down behind his desk. 'The best hope we have,' he said, 'is that they begin to hate the sight of each other . . . that they become each other's jailers—if somehow the romantic glow blows a fuse and leaves them with a dead light bulb.' He gazed into space and added, 'If she had known he killed her husband—none of this would ever have happened. She never would have gone anywhere with the man who did that—for any reason; she wasn't the type. And I could have told her. But I didn't have a crystal ball with me at the time.'

'They can't hold out for ever,' Brannigan consoled. 'And there's nowhere they can go if he doesn't have papers for her—except somewhere like Algeria, and that isn't too likely, is it?'

Stevenson didn't answer and they sat there for a minute or more, motionless, soundless, waiting with little hope of immediate solutions. Then Stevenson began to talk in a measured, mellow voice, as if he had finally and painfully come to certain inescapable conclusions about the fate of the universe. 'America can't make things happen any more, Red. We're too healthy, paradoxically too unhappy; essentially divided on all issues. But we will not escape our historical obligations without crumbling in the process. That's something that may have to happen, because there are no divided opinions on the other side, not on strategy or overall aims.'

'When Tom Acker was in Bonn,' Brannigan said, 'he told me if Russia pushes anything anywhere—even in the Middle East—we will give way right up to the point short of a military move on their part. Which comes as no surprise to me.'

Stevenson thought to himself: Two old men lamenting the passing of an old order, the time of decisive, naked power. That's what they sounded like. But he was convinced of the legitimacy of the purposes hidden within that ridiculous aspect. More than the personal prejudices and greed of established orders were at issue. Stevenson believed as much and could only hope that the belief was justified and that his ideas and devotions were just. How could anyone be more certain of anything in this world than that? 'It's too late to back them down,' he said. 'And they know we won't start anything. We had the chance once, but that's long gone.'

'They'd have made a lot more of that chance if they had ever had it,' Brannigan said. 'We never seem to get credit for that from anybody.'

'That's why the only answer, Red,' Stevenson said without even a touch of emotion or colour, 'is to honeycomb the Soviet political and military structures with listening posts, riddle them so completely with security leaks that *nothing*—but nothing—they do is a secret from U.S. Intelligence.'

Brannigan didn't stir and Stevenson went on in quiet, deeply purposeful intonations. 'If we could know in advance all their major diplomatic moves, all their large-scale subversive operations before they take place—something that has always been virtually impossible—we would be able to ensure lasting peace as no other single factor in foreign policy could. That kind of sweeping intelligence would constitute more power than all the megatonnage in the universe, because it would paralyse the Russians. . . .'

Brannigan was deferentially silent, even dazzled for a moment or two. Then he said dutifully, 'And that is where Comrade X comes in. . . .' He knew it, had been the only witness, an adherent hearing once again about the soul of man and the revealed truths in the world of big-power confrontation.

'Yes,' Stevenson said, perfectly still, transfixed by the implications of what he was saying. 'When there is someone that high up who understands, as he does, the value of such a concept—not just to the rival nation, of course, but to his own —then such a thing is within reach.'

'He trusts you, obviously,' Brannigan said. 'Or did.'

'He's unchanged,' Stevenson averred. 'And he's convinced.'

'Do you think Mankin was able to get to him?'

'It's an idle question.'

'I know.'

Stevenson shrugged. 'There was a good chance. The Russian delegation was in East Berlin for several days before Mankin was nabbed.' He considered it, then added, 'I think Mankin has some kind of a message for us. Even if it's only hello from Comrade X, it's top grade.'

Brannigan said, 'I always play a little game with myself about Comrade X. I always find myself trying to figure out which one he is.' He looked at Stevenson candidly. 'There were only three top people in that delegation. . . .'

Stevenson remained silent for long seconds, leaned back in his chair, his eyes slanted up and away from Brannigan. 'Well, then you still know that he is one of the ten most important men in the Soviet Union,' he said finally. 'Continue to leave it at that, Red.'

Brannigan was quite willing. 'Maybe if Colman knew the details it would have made a difference to him,' he suggested.

Stevenson recalled Colman's expressed interest just a week before. 'I'd chance it now,' he replied. 'But I wasn't ready to at that moment.'

'And maybe it *wouldn't* have made a difference to him.'

Stevenson shook his head. 'That's right. Maybe it wouldn't have.'

He poured one more drink and sat there with it, a normally temperate man with a pervasive and compelling set of ideas considered counter-historical in many quarters of expert opinion. He didn't care. He was not susceptible to trends or that mysterious something known as approved thinking. Only to the tides within himself, no less subjective in that respect, he fully realized, than those who may have disagreed with him. 'Mankin may be sitting in that DDR prison with the blueprint for everything,' he mused and took a drink. 'Codes, pickup points, drops, contacts—everything.'

He preferred espionage, to use the crudest term possible, to the alternative of a choice between the use of armed might and capitulation. Espionage whose intended result would be a form of control in which the only hope of measurable peace and relative stability was possible.

'You wouldn't consider asking Llewellyn's help?' Brannigan said carefully.

'I wouldn't consider asking the President himself. . . .' Stevenson sat there with the privilege of an agonizing secret zealously guarded by him and withheld from even the topmost members of the U.S. Intelligence community. 'I would not jeopardize the man in Moscow,' he said. 'And I'd be doing just that if I exposed him to anyone. Only Mankin knows who he is, besides myself. Only you know he even exists. That's as big as the risk gets. Either I do it alone or it doesn't get done.'

'Maybe Emmering would be willing to explore some other avenue. . . .'

'I don't think so,' Stevenson said, almost languidly, gazing off. 'I have an idea it is either this avenue or it is *no* avenue.'

Part Three

CHAPTER ONE

COLMAN AND ADELE spent their first night together in a little *Gasthaus* just outside and to the south of Bad Godesberg. In the morning before going to breakfast, Adele said, 'Whatever happens, Brian . . . I am happier this moment than most women ever are—happier than I have ever been.' Her face was serene, the look in her eyes that of a woman who recalls everything with unconcealed pleasure. 'I could never be the same person I was before—only yesterday. . . .'

'There was nothing wrong with the person you were yesterday,' he said, both of them only just awakened, neither of them ready to leave the sanctuary of the huge quilt which was their sole cover in the rather narrow bed. 'Or the one you are today. I like them both.' He was easily stimulated and his urge to conversation was presently nil. He wanted to make love, and they did. The sturdy oakwood bed frame held fast, and the springs kept the various cadences until Colman and Adele were panting and perspiring in the cold room as if they had just run a race and won it together, as if they had outdistanced a field of envious pursuers.

'I have never been so free, Brian.' She gave to him everything she had to give, spent herself without hesitation or restraint. He returned her love in kind. But love carried obligations and realities. 'But you are safe, sweetheart?' he said, not apprehensively, and even slightly ironical.

Her smile was also ironic. 'Yes, as a matter of fact,' she assured him. 'I take that magic pill. . . . It was the middle of a cycle and I didn't want to discontinue.' She seemed suddenly nonplussed. 'I suppose it is a little too prim to mince words about so natural a subject, and only an ass would do it. But it sounds—I don't know—antipoetic. . . .'

He smiled. 'Knowing it's there should make us feel more poetic than ever,' he said. 'That's the way I look at it.'

'It makes me sound so . . . prepared.'

'Yes, and I couldn't be more glad.'

'I love you, Brian. I'll never love anyone else. No one else will ever have me—not ever.'

'And I love you, Adele. I loved you yesterday too.'

He was referring to the use of that word the morning before when Adele had tried to avoid its conditions, afraid it would be a burden, making an obeisance to gods who might have struck them down for vanity or even in simple spite. He knew she had not had a lover until then—only a husband with rights, the betrayer who was now dead. So there was more than merely the convulsive delights of sex, more than the slaking of thirst; there was the pain whose source no one could really define. The fear of separation soon began to stalk them both.

'If we are caught,' she said, 'I think I would want you to kill me. I couldn't live without you. I wouldn't want to. If you let me, it would be different. But not if we are caught. . . .'

They had climbed up a slope to a stretch of limes, the broken teeth of an old Roman wall that had been finally breached by barbarian hordes from the east. It was silent now but for the river traffic, the afternoon sun pale, the air mild.

Colman said to her, 'Listen; we could get to England with the right papers. Not to go into hiding, but to get political asylum for you. When I failed to get you a passport, you understood that it was only at that moment, that eventually I *would* be able to—perhaps in three or four weeks. I didn't think of it then because returning to Germany eventually was the original idea.'

'Yes. . . .'

'Well, the only thing that hangs over you, Adele, is the unofficial power of the CIA. It's considerable. But outside of the Federal Republic it would carry no weight, in my judgement, because what have you done? Broken an immigration law?' He shook his head, his confidence in the idea growing rapidly. 'Once you were outside of West Germany, the excuse for your arrest would be gone. Which would leave only the CIA. And I don't think there's a foreign office anywhere—not the English anyway—that's going to be quick to accommodate the CIA in something as devious as this. It's too wormy. They couldn't stand the publicity glare. You would merely be asking for refuge, nothing else. If they tried to deport you the sky would fall in on them. It would bring them more grief than it was worth. They don't want details like this out in the open. It would be CIA, not the West Germans, once we were in London. And everyone hates the CIA just enough.'

'And you?'

'Nothing. I could surface anytime. I'm simply written off, nothing else. It's you they're interested in, not me. I only need to stay out of sight until you're free and clear.'

'It would be wonderful,' she said quietly.

'Maybe it wouldn't be. Maybe it would eventually come down to a nine-to-five job and all that goes with it. I don't know.'

'I'll take it. For one day or a hundred; or a lifetime, if you want me that long—nine to five or anything else. . . .'

'There are people in this world who don't need to duck into doorways and look over their shoulders so they can be together, who don't need to hide or tell lies. And they're bored with each other. Can you imagine that?'

'They must be mad.'

'They've never really looked at each other, not even in the beginning. Maybe they've never had a chance even to look at them*selves*.'

This might have been the most telling moment in her life. She felt almost overcome. 'You love me,' she said. 'I can tell you love me. . . .'

'I have never felt this way about anyone,' he told her.

'Yes, I know,' she said. 'But Brian darling, don't ever feel chained. Do you know what I mean?'

'Yes,' he said. 'And stop being one of those tragic Europeans.'

'I'm not. I've never been so happy. Can't you see?'

Life was too sweet for complaints. It seemed sometimes as if nothing could touch them. They remained at the guesthouse several days longer, mere yards from the outer reaches of a well-barbered *Hofgarten* whose tall, deciduous shade trees were just coming to bud. By then everything had begun to thaw. The black earth lost its hard crust and new aromas were released by the relenting soil, giving up smells of sap and herbage that all winter long had been locked up in frost and deadened by chill. The neighbourhood provided its distractions and excursions. And they made a crossing one morning by ferry to the Drachenfels, walking up to the peak, where they had lunch in the restaurant on the castle grounds. On that particular afternoon, as on others, they did what lovers do when they are moved to it and there are no obstacles or injunctions from without. 'Would you object to my growing a beard?' he asked after a few minutes of contented silence.

'No. But why? For disguise?'

'It might be worth it. Just for a time.'

He couldn't forget training and experience or be deceived by love and sexuality and the peaceful surroundings, by the precious intimacy of even the mere grasp of her hand. They could be taken by surprise at any time, with just one bad break, in the midst of the deepest joys and forgetfulness.

'Whatever you think best,' she said. 'You would be handsome in any case, darling.'

She alone could have forced him to forsake the pledges of a lifetime, overpower his ingrained beliefs and loyalty. He had been the one, after all, to leave her helpless and exposed. That *had* attracted him. And then he had watched her secretly and imagined things about her, let a mystery build until she became his creation, in a vague way, and he her own.

CHAPTER TWO

THEY BEGAN TO TRAVEL the next day as planned. They had got on a steamer and sailed up the Rhine from the Königswinter side of the river. About two dozen passengers were swallowed up by the vast accommodations on the big white ship—an unused swimming pool, shops, a hair-dressing salon—the season just about to begin. Two black GI's were travelling with a pair of blonde *Fräulein*, and the rigidity of the other passengers, mostly middle-class, middle-aged natives, was impossible to miss. '*Kleinbürgerlich*,' Adele remarked with an evident lack of admiration as she and Colman walked along the promenade deck towards the stern, a light breeze against their faces. 'The ones who let Hitler come.'

Colman nodded. 'Because he promised them great days that would go on for ever and that someone else would pay for it. And they thought they had the right to expect it.'

'They?' she repeated ironically. 'My own family. My mother and father, my uncles, aunts—all of them. . . .'

Colman wouldn't have expected anything else and he said nothing.

'It makes me ashamed,' she went on. 'I wish they had been able to resist—that they had even died rather than submit to it. And then I feel that just possibly I am a hypocrite, that I have no right to condemn others for giving into an evil that I personally was never confronted with.' She looked at him. 'Is it wrong to condemn them? Is it hypocritical and arrogant to think that *I* would have been one of the few who would have done differently?'

'You are better than anyone I have ever known, in every way and by far.'

'I never knew a Jew personally,' she recalled as they now stood at the railing, 'until last week.'

'Who was it?'

'A neighbour, an older woman, all alone, still living in the place where her life was made a nightmare—a living death. I met her unexpectedly. I actually never knew one to speak to until then.'

'Living in Berlin.'

'She went to Israel after the war. She tried but she couldn't live there. She had to come back to Berlin. She said she was too old and it was too late for anything else. Can you imagine that?'

'I suppose.'

'Every member of her family, excepting the one nephew who took her to Israel, died—was murdered.' The thought moved her to a melancholy smile. 'They alone survived—he Dachau, and Mrs Stransky Theresienstadt.'

143

'Yes. . . .'

'When I talked with her it was the first time that I knew'—she looked at Colman with expectations of accord, her feelings of pity and disgust deep and visible—'really knew what had happened. Oh, they tell us everything in East Germany, not like here where it is all glossed over. But even so, up till that moment there was a screen of statistics and Zone politics that made it all remote.'

Colman hadn't anything to add. Her reactions were more compelling than the subject because her reactions were new to him and the subject was old.

'It is all so long ago and so well known,' she said, 'it seems rather ridiculous that I am suddenly conscious of it and adding my own feelings of pity and horror—as if it matters.'

'You saw what had happened and what was left, saw for yourself at close range,' he summarized for her and felt somewhat foolish a moment later. 'But you can't give her back what she lost.'

'She was sick and I had a chance to be of help to her. It made me feel good, I suppose.' She looked at him. 'I was about to do some shopping for her when I was arrested. The odd thing was I could only think about that—not what was happening to me. Not because I am a saint, by any means. But because I knew that everything that had happened to her was so much worse.' She added, 'I hope she recovers. I feel so very sorry for her, as lonely as a dove on an island of penguins. I suppose because I am no longer sorry for myself.'

She stopped talking as the Lorelei began to dominate the east bank, the ship slowing, a group of the passengers suddenly singing an evidently traditional song about that massive rock. Adele and Colman got off just beyond it in a little town overlooked by a castle ruin converted to a youth hostel, numerous young people in and around the place. Colman had in his possession two passports, one in the name of Richard McNeil whose existence was unknown to the people he had left behind. It was, naturally, the one he chose to present whenever necessary. He had only to add the words 'and family' to his signature. It was easy. He was not a type to inspire officiousness, disrespect, or suspicion in the average Rhineland hotelier;

his air in dealing with desk clerks and buxom *Gastwirtinnen* was politely superior and just distant enough to provide them with no temptation to challenge him unless they had severe cause.

They went to one of the guesthouses in the town itself. It was a quiet place; and as twilight deepened the semblance of six-teenth-century circumscription became dense; it was romantic, even narcotic, certainly lulling. The river could be seen from the window of their room and also some of the houses whose half-timbered façades were painted bright reds, greens, and blues by evidently carefree and sequestered inhabitants. It was all irrelevant and disconnected from reality as reality was commonly defined. The river was marked with passing lights from the vessels, the barges, the cargo ships, and even a paddle steamer. Colman and Adele spent the night quietly, finally succumbing to eight much-needed consecutive hours of sleep.

The next day they walked in the town and stood on the quay at the very edge of the river. The weather was mild, partly cloudy but tempting. A party of young people got into a motor launch and sailed towards Die Pfalz, a gingerbread fortress on an island downstream. Adele and Colman remained there for a while and then found an inn caught in a trap of crawling vines curling past the windows and around the posts upholding a lattice canopy covering the courtyard. Here they ate lunch amidst a few tourists, several of whom were Air Force GI's probably from the base at Wiesbaden. 'How long do you think your beard will take?' she said, observing his three-day stubble.

'About ten days to qualify as a legitimate beard.'

'Will you keep it on after we are in England?'

'Will you want me to?'

'No, I don't think so. I've decided you're much too hand-some for a beard, after all.'

'A lot of men are wearing them these days.'

'It improves them in some cases. Makes them into something else.'

He looked directly at her and said, 'I'll be the same man in back of it that I am now.'

'I'll know you, darling,' she said with a deliberate air of cool confidence and an ironic smile she thought he would like. 'I'll be able to see behind it.'

'But at a glance no one else will. And that's the only reason it'll be there. I hope it doesn't scratch too much.'

She looked at him in the same way. 'I won't mind. Not in the least.'

That night they pored over maps and read parts of the guidebooks and the folders they had accumulated like any other tourists. The landlady, an irrepressible Rhenish woman named Frau Kortner, knocked and asked if they would like anything before retiring. Her curiosity may have been piqued by something about them, by their good looks or the traces of that splendid fatigue left by passion, and it may have prompted her as much as considerateness. It was futile to speculate on whether or not such a person had been an anti-Nazi. She almost certainly had not been, and a cold assimilation, if not neglect, of that historical circumstance was absolutely essential to the urgent travels in this land of those of democratic and anti-Fascist persuasion. Adele looked at her with a smile of appreciation mixed with utter detachment. And after politely declining the offer, Colman and Adele, alone again with their maps, resumed the search for their specially motivated itinerary.

'I think we can slowly follow the river to Mainz,' he said, his finger tracing the line. 'That's about fifty kilometres. But we can take ten days to do it, even longer. We can travel by bus or motor launch. There are a dozen little towns in between—Assmannshausen, Bingen, Rudesheim, Eltville. And then we can touch Frankfurt—stay on a few days or leave as it suits us —come down through Darmstadt to Heidelberg along the Bergstrasse, which is the scenic route, and finally reach Stuttgart by boat on the Neckar.' He looked at her and said, 'We should spend three to four weeks doing that. At that point I'll be able to get in touch with a man who can give us what we want.'

'We have what we want now, darling, don't we? I do.'

'Yes,' he agreed quietly. 'I'm accustomed to thinking in terms of something that lies somewhere just ahead—something that has to be reached. But I know what we have now. . . .'

'If only we never needed to leave this room—I mean, to go on and on within the world of this very moment like people in a photograph. No one could ever touch us. . . .'

'Make time stand still.' He shook his head. 'We don't need to, even if we could. We want all the variations, sweetheart. No one will be able to touch us, don't worry about it.'

'Are you never afraid, darling?'

'Do you want me to say I am, or do you want me to lie?'

'Then you are?'

'Of certain things.'

'Of what?'

'I don't know. Of being helpless. There are ten thousand ways of feeling that. Of pointlessness. Of . . . torture.'

She became solemn, her face still and masklike. 'Torture,' she repeated with stark awareness, her voice above a whisper.

He didn't answer and she said, 'You have been tortured?'

He didn't answer instantly, then said, 'I was interrogated by the North Koreans.'

'And those places on your body. . . . Oh, my darling, how terrible.'

'Yes, it was. It was terrible.'

'I would collapse. I would betray everything. Oh, my God, I hate to think of it, it makes me feel so . . . vulnerable, so untrustworthy. I'm sure I couldn't stand pain.'

'No one can—not indefinitely. But worse than that is the thought of a lingering death. I would be afraid of that.'

'But those are things we can't control, can't run away from.'

'You can get away from a lingering death,' he told her with authority and a sense of security in the knowledge. 'If no one prevents it.'

'You mean suicide.'

'My father was no good to himself or anyone in the world—not even my brother and me—after my mother died. He felt he had killed her—that it was his doing.'

'In the car accident.'

'Yes. He couldn't live with that on top of losing her. For him that was a lingering death. He was afraid to wake up in the morning—when he could sleep at all to begin with.'

'Poor, tormented man.'

'Yes.'

'Was it . . . painful for you?'

'At first, very. And then we knew he had had to do it—that

he had the right.' He shook his head with a tight, mirthless smile not characteristic of him. 'Why talk about that now? How did we get on to this anyway?'

She smiled wanly. 'I said I wanted to . . . freeze time. And you said we didn't need to—that we wanted all the variations.'

'That's right. We just need to be a little bit cautious—nothing more.'

She closed her eyes briefly and then said, 'I can't help thinking that I would crumble under torture, that if it came to the test, I might betray even you, darling. I wish I hadn't thought of it.'

Colman reached over and cupped her buttock in his hand, feeling it and testing its resilience through her skirt, callipygian and enticing. 'Quit scaring yourself,' he said. 'I know what fun it can be when you know the whole thing is a fantasy. But quit it. When a person is under torture he becomes someone else, someone he has never been before.'

She rolled away from the map spread on the bed and sat upright alongside of him, her eyes half closed. 'Will you kiss me?' she said, the little nightmare at an end.

'That's one of the better ways a man can spend his time.'

Two days later in a little university town which they reached by bus Colman and Adele found themselves in the middle of a swirling crowd of left-wing students who had decided to tear up the place, burn an American flag or two, and march for the Viet Cong. It was an occasion indeed to exercise caution.

CHAPTER THREE

THERE WERE about two hundred of them, predominantly male, shaggy, bearded, hair dangling at various lengths and unkempt, most of them brutal and unreasoning, it was fair to say, because one could feel that not even total compliance with whatever their aims and demands would have deterred them from the business of rampage, uproar, and the ecstasy of terror. They filled the cobblestoned market square, their faces flushed, angry, delighted. Colman, for all the experience he

148

had had, for all his lack of hesitance, was a careful man. There was nothing about him imprudent or reckless. 'Shall we get out of this?' he said to Adele as they found themselves on the outer fringes of the gathering.

A tough, thickset, bearded youth had been making a speech from the steps of the City Hall with its Rhineland gingerbread look. This strike against end-of-term examinations was going to make it clear that the youth of Germany, both East and West, were not going to line up on the side of the racism, profiteering, and imperialism of the Pentabonn ass-kissers and their Fascist bosses in Washington, D.C. 'Out of Vietnam,' a girl's voice screamed in English. And the crowd took it up and played it back like a well-directed cheering section. An American contingent, though small, was apparent. The frenzied voices were raised in German and the chant went on for a half dozen salvos, terminated finally by the raised hands of the tough, Saxon-accented speaker who had to have come from the DDR, now standing on the City Hall steps, commanding, virulent, filled with carefully husbanded rage. His lips glistened through the tufts of hair. It had all been seen and heard before.

Before Adele and Colman could depart, the *pièce de résistance* took place. An idiot-eyed Mr Nixon was pulled up a thin pole, dangled in mid-air, and set aflame. A roar of intense joy exploded above the heads of all assembled, such delight and hatred mingling everywhere that the air trembled with yearning for the very reality of such a moment, an *auto-da-fé* for the real Mr Nixon.

Adele turned away, her eyes cynical, her mouth disdainful. '*Proletkult*,' she muttered. 'They will never make anything of value.'

'I thought you were non-political,' Colman said.

'I am. But this is such lunacy. They would never stand for this in East Germany.'

They had begun to walk away. Adele's implied approval of certain repressive measures in the DDR came as a surprise. 'Do you think the authorities ought to crack down on these— students?' he said with quizzical eyes and a questioning tone.

'No,' she answered unhesitatingly. 'I don't want to crack down on anybody, darling.'

He was both pleased and faintly disappointed. And then with little warning the square had begun to empty, and swiftly great knots of the demonstrators were sweeping past Colman and Adele into the narrow cobblestoned tributary leading to the university just a few streets away. 'March, do not gallop,' went up the admonition from the leader and from several of the apparent monitors in the crowd. All eight members of the local green-suited police stood at various postings with watchful but helpless eyes and the throng poured past the baroque old buildings, flowing like fever through the arteries of the little town which was long accustomed to student high jinks but not to the new activism. They were driving towards a collective climax at the university buildings on the hill just above the town and the banks of the river.

In front of one of the town's two bakeries, a man of seventy stood besieged, a roughly formed semicircle of five or six demonstrators badgering him about racism, corruption, and all the rest of it. Not tall, wearing a green Tyrolean hat and an expensively tailored grey-tweed topcoat that followed his unathletic lines to somehow lend them elegance, he defied the students with quiet if somewhat anxious contempt, aided by a Malacca cane held in a hand bearing a pigskin glove. 'You are quite out of your depth with me, *mein Halberstarken*,' he said, his voice quivering slightly. 'You are simple hoodlums, and I never treat hoodlums any way but with a stick.' The Malacca cane was poised for action and the group, a kind of rear guard, moved in on him.

Colman, whose every instinct leaned towards the exercise of extreme caution for currently overpowering reasons, suddenly put himself between the old man and the others, took the Malacca from its owner, and made a sweep of the area. The would-be abductors stopped dead in their tracks. 'Burn another effigy,' Colman told them in German, the cold, unhesitant look on his face an effective deterrent. He had moved fast, and the back-and-forth swinging of the cane with its heavy ornament handle had evidently shocked and cooled the angry heads of the small committee. 'You had better catch up with the rest of the parade,' Colman added. 'I advise you to do that and nothing else.'

The old man watched, grateful but dignified. The five or six committee members were rooted to the spot, suffering an obvious loss of initiative and status. This guy scared them; he could cause trouble and damage and was undoubtedly willing to crack heads in the process. Was taking the old man worth the price at that particular moment? 'Are you one of his Fascist henchmen?' the tall, bony-faced one finally found voice to say.

'Always the worn-out epithets,' the old man said with disgust, 'for those who do not unquestionably acquiesce to everything.'

'Come on, take my advice,' Colman told them.

Adele stood rigidly behind the demonstrators, abhorring the threat of force, her eyes fixed and still, her heart beating fast. He had put aside their vital interest without thinking in order to save another person from harm. He was brave and fair and just; there could be no less a description of him.

The demonstrators turned away as if it hadn't mattered that much after all, one of them shouting. 'This system is doomed no matter what you do, you racist pigs.'

'Just like home,' Colman observed.

'I am Richter von Bleutzen,' the beneficiary said, taking back his cane. 'Ah, there is my chauffeur now. A coincidental arrival, I should like to think.'

There was no trace of fear in him and he was even amused suddenly; and though he was not handsome, his face had that certain distinction common to people who have been bred to believe they are substantially better than others and who are constitutionally unable to think anything else. 'I should like you to dine with me. Are you staying at the inn?'

'Yes.'

'Good. I am actually due at the university just now,' he said as a chauffeur-driven Mercedes 300 rolled slowly towards them from the square. 'I happen to be the chancellor of the coalition of corporations that administer the various colleges.' He nodded. 'That's the root of the . . . emotionalism from which you just saved me.' He nodded. 'It was quite a feat.' He looked at Colman, frankly admiring. 'Selfless and . . . very commanding.'

'It was nothing.'

The man called Von Bleutzen smiled a worldly smile. 'If you insist,' he said. 'You're an American, aren't you?'

'Yes.'

'You speak convincing German. I shall look forward to your company—yours and the young woman's.'

Colman said nothing and Von Bleutzen went off in the Mercedes. Adele said, 'You're magnificent. . . .'

'No, no, don't.'

'It's true. Don't deprive me of saying it.'

'All right. Say it.'

She slipped her arm in his. 'I hate that sort of thing. But you were . . . wonderful. Because your instinct was to help someone, not to have an adventure. And to think you make love to *me*. . . .'

They began to walk. Just ahead was the seventeenth-century inn with its dormer windows and mansard roof. After a moment or two of silence between them, Adele said, 'But aren't they right about Vietnam, darling?'

'No,' he replied, and said nothing more until they had entered the inn.

In the lounge, with its polished wood, thick carpet, and antimacassars, they ordered coffee. Colman's hands were laced together in front of him, his thumbs touching the point of his chin, his eyes scrutinizing her, thoughtful, intimate but not quite readable. 'Have we had our first quarrel?' she said with a lover's tiny but knowing smile.

'Me quarrel with you?' he said. 'About what?'

She smiled again. 'Vietnam,' she answered softly.

'I never quarrel with anyone about Vietnam or anything else like it,' he said finally. 'Least of all with you. You can have your opinions and I can have mine,' he said.

'Even if we sharply disagreed,' she said, 'would it make no difference to you? If I thought America was at fault,' she went on, 'would you care?'

He shrugged disinterestedly.

'If I said America was Fascist—racist—imperialist—and should be destroyed?' She paused and said, 'Could you still love me?'

'And if I said Hitler was a great man?'

'You couldn't. You wouldn't be you in that case.' She shook her head emphatically, the idea absurd.

'That's right,' Colman said, nodding in accord. 'That's my answer to your question too.'

'But are they equal?'

'No, not quite. But anyone who thinks America is Fascist and should be destroyed is either irrational or a dedicated Communist. And you are neither one. You just think that the Commies have a few points here and there because it's a handful of bad people in the West who run everything and deceive and exploit everyone . . . including people like me.'

'I think you've won a little game I foolishly tried to play, Brian.'

He said nothing, watched and waited.

'I wanted to see how far love could go—if it was independent of everything. It's not. Only of some things. But how could it be anything else?'

'Where have I failed you?' he said with a smile.

'I wanted you at my feet just as I am at yours.'

'I am. How could you think otherwise?'

'You're right, I'm not a Communist, and you want me not to be, I know. But could you love me if I were?'

'I wouldn't care what you were. Is that what you want to hear?'

'No matter how strongly we might feel about other things, they couldn't influence our feelings about each other. Do you think that's possible?'

'I would hope you'd have that answer for yourself.'

'I think because I disagree with you so much about—well, Vietnam . . . it frightens me. I wish one of us would change. I wish that you could convince me, change my whole outlook to yours; corrupt me, hypnotize me, I wouldn't care what. I don't want even *that* between us, Brian.'

'Vietnam,' he intoned softly. 'What is that? Neither of us can change it to suit us, can we?'

'No. . . .'

'Then why talk about it? Why should it influence us? All people have differences of opinion—brothers, friends, lovers.'

'I think I am half way to accepting anything you believe.'

'Don't. You don't need to.'

'There couldn't be anything about you that wasn't human, that wasn't understandable. . . .'

He lowered his eyes momentarily and then met her gaze directly. 'None of that can make a difference to us,' he said. 'We wouldn't be here now if it could.' He saw her only in the light of his own desire, as the extension of oneself for which one gave up everything.

'That's what I want to believe,' she said, because it meant everything in the world to her. And then in the exact same tone she said, 'Your beard is beginning slowly but surely to qualify.'

Colman ran his hand over what was there. 'Yes, I'll be looking like those scurvys and motleys out there before you know it,' he said without the slightest rancour or criticism in his voice.

CHAPTER FOUR

IT CAME AS NO SURPRISE that Richter von Bleutzen held a title, that he was descended from Bavarian electors and from envoys of the royal courts of emperors and kings. It was the kind of information that 'emerged' in the course of conversation, was indirectly revealed rather than stated with ostentation or show of pride. He was much too accustomed to his station to care.

He was mostly bald, his thin white hair clinging in neat flat strands to his head, his dark eyes haunted by vanishing privileges and the shadows of time, his mouth a line of mild mockery, the whole face that of an irreconcilable aristocrat who also a cynical humorist, if not a deadpan comedian. 'I can tell you easily enough,' he was saying in accented but perfect English, 'what these people ask for; they always write it down very carefully. But after reading it just as carefully as they write it down, I cannot tell you what it is they actually *want*.' He signalled almost imperceptibly to the dining-room steward, who came swiftly to the table and topped up the glasses with white wine especially brought to the inn from the town *Ratskeller* for the count and his guests.

'Shall I tell you,' he went on, 'the real reason for human upheaval, for riots, for crises in the parliaments and in the kindergarten classes all over the world? Faulty minds which are a result of conditions traceable to nature's blind mistakes. She makes them all the time. And we are left with the inherent inability to think properly. What a shock to finally realize as much. But it's undeniable. Emotion rules us all, not our pretensions to logic. We cannot act *logically*. We recognize logic, yes, but we cannot obey it. It's too boring to abide by.'

'Does that go for everybody?' Colman said half jokingly.

'With minor variations,' Von Bleutzen answered. 'I have been chancellor of the university administrators for six years because someone must be who can afford the time. And as an alumnus, one of *Die alten Herren*, I assumed the responsibility. I shan't bore you with details, but a considerable sacrifice has been entailed, which I now regard as utter waste. And which I have now brought to an end with my formal resignation. I had long begun to feel like the adjunct to a revolutionary future not at all to my taste. It could lead only to the guillotine, and I am very much against that for myself. And other things as well.'

Colman rotated his wine glass one full circle by its stem. The three of them were seated at a round table in the corner of a moderately spacious dining room traditionally frequented by tourists and visitors to the university but hardly ever by students, who preferred the *Ratskeller* or one of the other less formal places in the town. Adele watched the count with concealed scepticism; he was too well kept, dripping with certainty, part of another race. 'All of it is coming down around us like the temple at Gaza,' he said.

'Ordnung muss sein?' Adele said with a smile.

And Von Bleutzen answered in German: 'I don't subscribe to the Prussian implications of that. Order, yes. Silence and fear, no. That is Prussian, and I am not a Prussian.' He laughed with restraint. 'I am a lazy Southerner,' he said, and then, in English, said to Colman, 'And I have an idea that your wife is chiding me. She thinks me intolerant, autocratic: *Blut und Eisen*. Nothing could be farther from the truth.'

'Excuse me if I have given you that impression,' Adele said.

Von Bleutzen's graces were abundant and never out of reach. 'You are young and you are obviously intelligent,' he said. 'And you have doubts.'

She said nothing and the count said, 'I don't believe anyone should be blindly acceptant of anything. That led us to Hitler —to death and ruin. But at a certain point even questioning can lose its meaning and rejection become tyranny.' He shook his head. 'That is my contention—that such a point has been reached. Ah, our dinner is arriving.'

It had all been ordered by the count and carefully prepared for his taste. Chicken and mushrooms fixed in cream served as the central course and was accompanied by the continuous flow of wine. It was the repast of a Bavarian gourmet and the count was one such—an antediluvian epicurean who seemed to have, for all his distaste and resentment, an almost other-worldly forbearance for everything he disapproved of, a resignation to disaster and a measure of satisfaction in recognizing and understanding its sources. As they ate their dinners, the count was at once a stream of antique charm and acerbic commentary. At one point he abandoned his dismay for an airy discourse on the superiority of stag prepared in the way of his hunting forebears in the forests of Bavaria as opposed to how sick it tasted in England, a country for which he otherwise had a fondness. 'In England I feel—not at home, surely, but comfortable. If only the damn cooking were not so dreary— excuse me; in the countryside, far worse than our own, and certainly desperate compared with France.'

He sat there as if oblivious to anything but his role as host and raconteur. But Colman had the feeling that not everything else escaped him, that he had in fact cast them in tentative roles which were not those of innocuous and secure little figures seeing the sights. Colman wasn't convinced that such a liaison was altogether safe.

'I am, at the same time, not at all comfortable in France,' he went on. 'I never really enjoy my travels there, only everything that is French—everything; the cuisine, needless to say, the art, the painting, the chateau country, all of it. I am a Francophile and yet never at ease in France. Make of that what you can. A kind of aesthetic schizophrenia, I suppose.' He sipped from the glass of Hock he had just poured for himself. 'I have travelled everywhere but in America,' he went on. 'Even, very early in my life, in the Orient. But not in America. And now I am certain I shall not.'

The coffee arrived with a plate of *torte*, and Colman said, 'Travel can be hard work,' because he had little else to say.

'I have always found great pleasure in it,' Von Bleutzen said. 'But I have a frankly splendid home not too far from Garmisch, my ancestral estate, actually, a castle in a setting to which I can never be indifferent or blasé. In fact, I seldom venture from its environs these days; there's more than enough to engage me and to make upon me the demands one needs made on one. It gives me responsibility and various pleasures. And now that I have not even my duty to the university to draw me from it any longer I shall remain there permanently.'

'It must be quite grand,' Adele said.

'It's a matter of taste,' Von Bleutzen replied. 'I admit that I am dismayed by the world in which I now find myself and from which I can close myself off, late in life, as perhaps others cannot. I suppose that is what I wish to do.' He was the slightest bit apologetic because he would need to shut out others who may have been as worthy as himself. 'Perhaps you see that as a form of self-extinction.'

'Not if it suits you,' Colman said, willing to play only a functional role of amiable guest.

'In fact, it may well be,' the count said. 'But often that is what obedience to compelling demands from within amounts to. Of course, I think of it as something else: going behind one's own walls until the barbarians pass on or are killed. As in the days of King Otto.'

'If one has one's own walls,' Adele said.

Von Bleutzen smiled. 'There is that, of course. One must have a place to which one can retreat.' He shrugged. 'But it is a state of mind we are discussing also. And one must perhaps be old to attain it; and to have certain—shall we say, monastic capabilities and interests.' He spoke softly, almost wearily, not boasting, merely explaining. 'The young cannot be expected to understand that,' he said. 'They like adventure.'

Adele said, 'Not all do.'

'Do you?' Von Bleutzen asked.

'Not much,' she answered.

'Merely the pleasures of travel—uneventful holidays in the sun,' Von Bleutzen concluded. 'I assume that you are not Rhinelanders,' he added somewhat facetiously.

'Just on holiday, as you say,' Colman told him. 'I'm with Coca-Cola—the Berlin office.'

'I see.' A noticeable change of atmosphere was suddenly perceivable, the count's expression grown doubtful, his dark eyes deepening as if reflecting the moon gone behind a cloud. 'Then there is something I must tell you,' he said. 'Something I quite obviously owe you. . . .'

Colman looked at him amiably. Von Bleutzen's attention wandered in Adele's direction, her eyes waiting for important, if not life-and-death, information. 'Is there any reason you can think of,' Von Bleutzen said, as if they had been friends for years, 'why the police would be interested in you? Because it happens they are.'

Colman shook his head innocently. 'I have no idea,' he said. 'In me? I can't imagine.'

'In both of you,' Von Bleutzen said. 'Or someone rather like you. An American man and a German woman are wanted for questioning by the Federal immigration authorities and the Berlin *Kriminalpolizei*.'

'That's rather weird,' Colman said.

'This was told to me in confidence by the local chief of police. The name is different, of course, but your presence nevertheless has been noted. There are political police officials and others in the neighbourhood who wouldn't ordinarily be because of all this business. . . .'

'Can't imagine,' Colman said again. 'You weren't told what it was all about, were you? Murder or whatever?'

'No. But I am still His Excellency to people like the chief and my advice has a certain amount of value. I told him, on my own initiative and personal instinct, not to be hasty, because a premature action could prove to be very embarrassing. Authoritatively stated generalities of that kind can be very effective. I assured him that I would know who you were before the evening was through. That was all I said. That I would know who you were.'

'We're exactly what you see. And thank you for the favour.'

'The descriptions were quite like you,' Von Bleutzen said. 'I believe they were sending to Bonn for photographs. No one had any in a place like this. Of course, all this business with the radicals adds to the atmosphere of mistrust and suspicion. There is nothing more dynamic and volatile than young people who wish no part of the past. Perhaps understandably. . . .' He looked at Adele, whose outer calm was almost lyrical. 'Do you agree, *gnadige Frau*?'

'I don't think I understand the question,' she answered.

'Do you find the past detestable?'

'I don't answer questions like that very well,' she said and took a sip of her coffee.

'I know it's rather obscure in some ways. But isn't that what all the unrest among the young is based upon?'

'I can't answer for others,' Adele said. 'My own feelings run differently from that. I don't like ideology—of any kind.'

'Forgive me,' Colman said, 'but it's getting a little bit late' —he was looking at his wristwatch—'twenty past nine, believe it or not. . . .'

'Yes, and you must go,' the count said graciously. 'And so, in fact, must I.' He eyed them curiously but not indiscreetly or as to cause any embarrassment. 'But before we go our separate ways,' he continued, 'I should like to call to your attention that the photographs they have sent for shall be here in the very early morning.' He paused before saying, 'What if they should prove to be pictures of you? . . .'

There was a marked silence as the three of them sat there alone in the dining room, only the steward remaining in the doorway and out of hearing. 'What if it turns out that you are Colman and not McNeil?' the count said finally as if to stir them to a response.

'What difference can it make to you?' Colman asked.

'The difference is you came to my assistance,' Von Bleutzen answered. 'My skin is not necessarily so valuable, but I happen to deeply admire unselfish courage—anyone who takes risks to come to the aid of a stranger.'

159

Colman said nothing and Adele sat perfectly still. She felt moisture on her upper lip and hoped it wasn't noticed.

'I am saying things directly,' Von Bleutzen said, 'because my instinct tells me it is not necessary to be gradual. Truthfully, the woman being sought, whoever she is, is wanted by the immigration authorities because she is an unregistered person from the East. My point is, I couldn't care a fig for that or for the fact that the man, whoever he is, is concealing her. . . .'

'All right,' Colman said. 'Many thanks.'

'But I know, too, because it takes so little intelligence, that surely more lies behind it than that alone. One doesn't run like a thief from something which normally can so easily be resolved to everyone's satisfaction. I am not prying and neither am I motivated by idle curiosity.'

Colman and Adele remained silent.

'I want to help you,' Von Bleutzen said, as if revealing a long-held secret desire. 'If, of course, you wish to be helped.'

'You're assuming we are the people who are wanted,' Colman put in.

'If you were those people,' Von Bleutzen said, 'I could tell you I have lived too long to be impressed by the particulars of a situation in which people are at odds with authority. One either tries to destroy it or run away from it.' He looked at them knowingly. 'The destroyers are self-evident,' he said. 'They are prisoners, generally speaking, of loathsome personalities. They don't look or act like either of you and are terribly boring. They would never be likely to interest me or arouse my sympathy. Do you follow what I am saying?'

'You've been more than candid,' Colman granted.

'I can't conceive of any reason why I should ever regret it. I can tell by looking at you both that you have the stuff of which old-fashioned men and women are made. Which is perhaps a damned strange compliment in your view. And perhaps it is.'

'Taken kindly,' Colman said.

'What matters is that I am ready to give you any assistance I can, if you should require it,' Von Bleutzen went on. 'You don't need to answer either way. Only keep in mind the option which I present to you . . . my unconditional invitation to Schleisstein, now or any time in the immediate future.'

He had taken to studying the configuration of his wine glass as a means of extending privacy to Adele and Colman for an unspoken consultation. When it occurred to him to leave them, all that was possible for the moment having been done, he said, 'If you have no other plans, you might perhaps find it enjoyable . . . coming and going as you wished, staying as briefly or as indefinitely as you like . . . there are twenty-five bedrooms . . . all empty but for my own. . . .'

They looked at him as he rose to leave, Colman rising also. 'It is very near to Fussen,' he said. 'You would have no difficulty finding it. . . .'

He might well have interpreted their silence to mean acceptance, but he didn't reveal this, as if otherwise to make it a touch corrupt—as if it would have been unseemly to suggest he was for private reasons trading on their weakness.

'Why should he?' Adele wondered, after Von Bleutzen had bowed to them and left the dimly lit room, walking away slightly hunched and resigned. She answered her own question. 'But why not? He may be nothing more than lonely,' she said. 'And kind . . . to those he takes a fancy to—if he decides he likes you, that you're what he calls old-fashioned. . . .' She looked at Colman. 'He was a Nazi, I would swear it.'

'You can't be that sure.'

'I'm willing not to be,' she said cryptically.

She appealed to Colman, leaned closer to him. 'Is there anything wrong about accepting such an invitation?' she asked.

Colman looked at her vaguely, still uncertain, one eye on the corruption of safety and ease, of something-for-nothing. Finally he said, 'I don't think, sweetheart, that it's the move for us to make.'

There wasn't a trace of disappointment on her face.

CHAPTER FIVE

THERE WAS, HOWEVER, another move to make and very quickly. Von Bleutzen had provided them with the first true awareness of pursuit. People had issued bulletins; they *were* being sought and, of course, they made an unhesitating departure from the town that very night. They got rid of their suitcases, storing what they didn't need at the train station in Wiesbaden, put on knapsacks, lightweight cord trousers, hobnailed half boots, and began to walk. This helped them to find anonymity, camouflage among the throngs of campers, young and almost-young alike. Colman's beard was soon full grown and very effective; one would have had to examine carefully the new visage to discern the man one had known before.

The tactic offered more varied choices, if a slower pace. They could travel without reservations because there always seemed to be that *Privatzimmer*, that one lady who was willing to rent a room in her own home miraculously never at a premium. Farmhouses, guesthouses, small hotels here and there. Adele and Colman encountered little difficulty. Sunshine, flowers, and tourists were everywhere. Long hair, short hair, no hair; the middle-aged, the elderly, and most of all the young—students and non-students well mixed; dominant, beyond trifling with and poised to take over. 'The revolution is here, *Puppe*, and nothing can stop it,' a young girl said to Adele as they shared an outdoor shower stall at a farm outside of Wiesbaden. 'The establishment is dead. So is *Kuche, Kinder, und Kirche*. But of course that shit has been dead for a long time. But now marriage is dead too. No one needs such conventions because we realize what their purpose was: to enslave, to exploit, to promote wars and racism.' But there was more, the heart of everything perhaps. 'We sleep with *whom* we like *when* we like. We can be free.'

'Free?' Adele repeated, the Puritan values of the DDR never having totally washed away.

'People need change,' continued the unsolicited discourse. 'How long we were forced into an unnatural behaviour pattern. Forever faithful or you are a whore. What shit they heaped on us for all these centuries.'

Adele returned to the attic room in the farmhouse with feelings of disdain and even antagonism. Why would unrestricted, unencumbered partner changing hold such glories for anyone? She couldn't conceive of it as a calculated approach to living; it reeked of failure and boredom and, not improbably, even disease. The sense of personality, of shared understanding, even differences of opinion, had to come before anything else, regardless of how quickly. That was why her loneliness was now as great as it was and made powder out of the speeches about revolutionary sexuality and the new-found freedom to casually copulate with casual, ever-changing partners whenever feasible. It was powder easily blown away by fear of the eventual loss of the one person you gave your body to. She was feeling it right that moment; it touched the very bowels, certified what this one non-interchangeable person meant to her. He was not yet back from Wiesbaden. It didn't matter that she had known in advance that he wouldn't be. She was a hostage to the uncertainties of loving. Maybe it was a bad thing, an affliction one should have hated. But this was the first time they had been separated since the moment he first made love to her and opened all of the locked doors.

What was the essence of love as the liberated *Mädchen* would never experience it? Adele didn't know. She knew only what it felt like. The weaknesses, the fears, and the bodily functions that mocked the spirit were all unimportant. Only the existence of that other person counted; only the captivity which she now cherished, madly and illogically or not, mattered in the least. What bondage this love was, this embarrassing dislocation of oneself so much more disabling and restrictive than even imprisonment. And yet one gave oneself to it with breathless desire and lunatic zeal.

She found herself standing stock-still in the centre of the room and staring into space. She was, she realized, anxious and desperately lonely. The world was a monochromic landscape of longing and solitude. Lovers had grounds to hate and resent each other that no other people had. They robbed each other of immunity to the dormant poison of happiness-through-loving. Nothing else made happiness; merely contentments and minor satisfactions easily surrendered or lost. Three hours apart and here she was withering with loneliness. What but happiness could produce such pain?

As she now stood in front of a mirror nailed to a plywood wall she was experiencing a seizure of panic. 'I can't love anyone this way,' she said to herself in an astonished whisper. 'I shouldn't. . . .' She looked at herself as if at a friend who was in trouble and in need of counselling that she was unable to give. 'It's mad. . . .' And then she smiled faintly and sympathetically. How she did wish he would hurry back.

It was dusk when Colman got off the bus at the crossroads about three hundred yards from the farmhouse. He allowed himself to break into a very fast walk, not much slower than a run.

Looking through the attic window she could see him coming, the voices of other people who were camped across the road playing remotely in the soft early evening air. In a few moments she heard his footfalls on the attic steps. As he entered the room under the sloping eaves, they came together and clutched each other for dear life. 'Oh, my God,' she whispered gratefully. 'I have never felt so alone.'

'I couldn't stop thinking about you,' he said. 'But I'm empty-handed, sweetheart. This fellow Lorenzo—didn't show up.'

'You mean the one who has the credentials?'

'The middleman, the contact. I waited three hours. Finally I tried tracking him down. I exhausted all the possibilities.' He shook his head and felt foolish. 'Something went very wrong. You never can tell with people like that. But it's dead for now. We're back to the starting line.'

'Maybe in a few days. . . .'

'Maybe. But we can't count on it. There's a clearing centre, a little *Kneipe* where he likes to eat right near the Kurhaus. I'll check it a few days from now for a message. But he might not show up for a long time. We've got to be prepared for that. . . .'

'Oh, darling. Does it matter that much right this minute?'

'It could. Not this minute, no. But eventually. . . .'

'But not this very minute.'

'That's right. Not this very minute.'

'Then let's not think about it.'

'I don't want to think about it.' He put his mouth on hers and in a moment touched her tongue with his own, their lips soft and moist, the disappointment thrust aside like a weak opponent.

164

'Oh, Brian. . . .'

'Are you hungry? Do you want dinner?'

'Later,' she said desperately.

In an incredible rush they began to undress. All their articles of clothing came off as if life itself depended on the speed with which they disrobed, being flung aside without aim until they were both naked. He carried her quickly to the bed and deposited her on her back. Her eyes were closed, her mouth contorted with expectation, everything all the more intoxicating for the terrific and unpretending pace at which it took place.

She lay there as revealed and accessible as an open plain, his sudden and effortless penetration consuming all there was to consume of an eagerly yielding citadel. The accommodation was deep and perfect and emollient. This was better than anything until now, Adele murmuring a breathy, prolonged 'Aaah . . . ' the sensation finally pushing her to the brink of a swoon. Colman held her there, her womanhood eagerly entrusted. And when it was done, even after the realities of physical depletion had set in, they knew something special had happened to them, something significant. 'If you go away every day, will it be like this each time you come back?' she murmured when they finally caught their breaths.

'Not after a time, I would hope,' he said.

She laughed. And then she said, almost gravely, 'Should anyone need anyone else this way, darling. So painfully much?'

'Is there a choice after it begins?'

'Is it right? Is it fair?'

'What's the difference?'

'Is it even intelligent?'

'Probably not.'

There was a pause. Then she said, 'One thinks it's make-believe. Because isn't that necessary to all love affairs? I had always thought so. I never could quite believe in any of it. I thought that people conjured it up for themselves. Do you know what I mean?'

'Some do.'

'Yes. But do you know how you know what it's all about,

darling? When only the other person matters; every part of the other person. . . .'

'I knew that, darling . . . the minute I was able to say good-bye to everything else.'

'Even if you were impotent, I would need to be with you,' she said.

'I hope you won't ever prove it to me,' he said.

'But do you understand?'

She waited and he quietly replied, 'Yes. I understand.'

He had never entered into a loose alliance or a casual sexual liaison in his life. That was what had made him what he had been—steady, even demoniac, unswerving—until now. Maybe that was what he had wanted to tell her, as if in some way to document it. But now he could see it had never been necessary.

CHAPTER SIX

IT WAS a *Personenzug* and made numerous stops along the way. They took a first-class compartment with the hope no one else would enter. Their privacy lasted half an hour. They were holding hands, sitting closely side by side, not knowing exactly what was going to happen next. Adele's skin was cold. 'I'm sorry to put you through this,' he said. 'I know it's hard. . . .'

'Being together is all that matters. Even like this.'

'Is it?'

'Maybe it's even better for that, because we know what we have to lose, the way most people never do.'

He looked at her. He didn't share the sentiment but could feel its synthetic allure simply because she did. He saw her as a goddess, pursued and threatened and seductive; and also as a woman whose bodily functions were like those of any other woman. She was this and more. He wanted to crush her in his arms until she gasped for breath. 'I love your voice,' he said. 'Did I ever tell you?'

'My Berlin accent? 'She closed her eyes and gave him a gently amused smile.

'It gets to me.'

'Does it?'

'It turns me into jelly.'

'Will you believe me if I say the same thing to you?'

'I'll believe anything you say.'

She smiled the same little smile. 'You don't believe, then, that all women are liars, darling?' she said.

'I don't believe that all women are anything,' he said, his voice almost an insinuating drawl now just loud enough to be heard above the clacking wheels. He had reached across his chest to hold her arm. He now tightened the hold. Her flesh was firm. 'It's you I know about. . . .' He also held her hand.

'What is it right beneath the skin that comes through the fear?' she said, almost as if in a trance. 'Like some unexpected benefit. . . .'

'If it feels good to you, who cares?'

At Darmstadt three people entered the compartment, leaving only one empty space. After a few minutes Colman and Adele went forward to the *Speisewagen*, which was nearly empty, and sat at a table nibbling at ham sandwiches and drinking beer.

'Sometimes it's hard to remember how you look,' he said. 'I can't recall the details of your face, can't get a picture of you in my mind. It was that way when I was in Wiesbaden, and even for the time it takes to brush my teeth or whatever. I can remember every face in the world except yours. And I know why. Because my memory couldn't do justice to the reality of it. I'm looking at you now. My memory could never compete with that.'

'I wish we never had to get off this train,' she said.

It was about two in the afternoon when they arrived in Stuttgart and went to the hotel directly opposite the railway station and in sight of the vineyard on a slope just above the centre of the town. It was modern and convenient. They drew the blinds.

'Do you want to make love to me?' she said, confident of the answer.

'Yes. But not until I get rid of this beard. I'm going to need to anyway.'

167

They were both very tired and sleep came without delay and extended itself into bewildering darkness. Colman was not easily disoriented; but for just a few seconds upon awakening he was not sure of where he had gone to sleep, everything impenetrably black, the smooth surfaces of his face a new and unexpected sensation. He remained on his back as he found his wristwatch on the table next to the bed. The diaphanous face was vivid, the time was eight o'clock. They had slept about four hours.

He lay there without moving, not wanting to move, enjoying the concessions of her flesh as she pressed against him. 'It's time,' he said.

'Tonight?'

'Yes. We shouldn't wait.'

They easily caught a nine o'clock train for Blauengen, which put them within striking distance of the Swiss border. Colman had come this way before, had travelled this very route, when there had been ice and snow and the singing of sleigh bells. Now it was warm, the night mellow and almost languid.

Adele viewed it through the train window as they came into the valley station. Four other passengers who had come with them from Stuttgart got out at Blauengen. Colman and Adele were left to themselves for the ascent to Brughaffen, the upper station, along the edges of the *Schwarzwald*, dense, massive, now black in the night. Colman had not seen it from this angle before, but he knew where they were in relationship to his previous, long-ago visit. He was clearly oriented, and as the train curved along the edge of a crag he realized they were in sight of the ravine where the body lay, now undoubtedly revealed by the suns of spring and summer, if as yet undiscovered by passers-by and therefore unseen.

She was sitting opposite him, looking at him without even the smallest glimmer in her life about what had happened, of the fact that Colman was more the instrument of her destiny than even she could have dreamed.

They looked at each other like people who each had begun to know what the other might be thinking and feeling under given conditions. His eyes were unflinching and hers were confident of his virtues, denying whatever minor failings he might have had. He wanted to say, 'Adele, it was I who killed Martin,' as though this would give everything size and shape and meaning, purify or consume like the flame which surely such a revelation had to be. But he knew he wouldn't. He kept looking at her and she said, 'Tell me that nothing lasts. Tell me nothing lasts so that I believe it and won't expect anything else. . . .'

'We're just beginning. . . .'

'No. no. I don't want you to be encouraging. I told you I hated hopes that made things worse. Tell me nothing lasts, darling. Tell me that and mean it.'

Colman was able to say calmly, 'Are you that scared?'

'Yes. We shall be caught. I want to understand it before it happens. It's not any good being cheerful and confident. That always makes it worse.'

'You're making a deal with God again, aren't you?' he said with a smile of love and appreciation. 'That's your technique, isn't it?'

'I don't know. It may be.' She was almost dismissive, casting everything aside to take care of the emergency at hand. 'Tell me, please. . . .' She didn't raise her voice or show desperation but was clearly pleading, as one does for something sedative. 'Nothing lasts, does it? And one can't expect anything else.'

He looked at her squarely, unsentimentally and did what was asked of him. 'Nothing lasts,' he said. 'It all comes to an end. The better it is, the worse it feels, the more sudden. . . . Is that what you want to hear?'

'Yes.'

He shook his head as they shared this thing like people testing themselves. 'It's true,' he said.

Her face was beautiful with the desire to go towards what she obviously feared because that was far better than avoiding it until the last moment. 'Nothing lasts,' he said again. 'And we can't expect it to.' He wished they could stay together without end, melt into eternity bound up in each other's arms, entwined without shame or hesitation; or even simply touching fingertips.

CHAPTER SEVEN

CUSTOMS MEN came aboard to examine the passengers continuing on to Switzerland. Colman and Adele debarked and within a few minutes they had begun to walk from the little station towards the road which was not more than two hundred yards in a straight line from the Swiss border. All of their belongings had been consolidated into the Valpak Colman had bought in Wiesbaden.

They crossed the road, which was cut on a terrace between the high rise of mountain on one side and on the other the steep descent of pine-covered slopes, the ravine with which Colman was not unfamiliar. A sign board gave advice to the sightseer. Visible even in the dark were the words ACHTUNG! BEAUTIFUL VIEW TO THE LEFT.

They climbed into the cathedral of forestry, pine needles, ferns, and moss everywhere underfoot, the coolness of night-time in the mountains like breath along their bodies and on their faces, the sharp smells filling the air like incense. They didn't speak but climbed steadily. They climbed as if to a coxswain's stroke and they breathed heavily. Adele's anxiety eased into the process of physical stress, the stimulus of fighting to escape, all her energies directed to that alone. Colman hadn't quite failed to stop remembering when there had been snow and bone-chilling cold in these very trees, on this very spot. He pressed on, the woman to whom he had consigned himself now there at his side only because he had, without malice or knowledge of her existence at the time, killed her husband. There was nothing he would stop at on her behalf, no price he wouldn't pay for possession of her, nothing he would not confide to her, nothing he would not instantaneously entrust or give into her keeping. Except the fact that not one hundred yards from where they now walked he had seen her husband die, had heard his dying words.

They continued moving towards the incline ahead of them. There was unalterable purpose in what they were doing, significant as only undeterrable passion can be. They climbed like pilgrims side by side until they reached the meadow above the timberline.

'Right beyond the top of that hill,' Colman said, gesturing, 'we should be able to walk into Switzerland.'

They never did.

They went halfway to the crest of the last incline, the valley now visible over the tops of the trees in back of them, a light here and there to mark several of the villages below. The pine scent was like a spur; the thought of reaching the summit, the prize of freedom, set their bloods coursing through their veins like an intoxicant. Cold fires burned her cheeks. Colman took her arm to guide her through the meadow grass for those last steps to the top, as if the top were Jerusalem. And then someone shouted: '*Innehalten.*'

Two German border policemen, one above them, one, accompanied by a German shepherd on a chain, below them, had Adele and Colman well trapped.

Colman showed them his McNeil passport, which they inspected by flashlight. Adele was sure her knees had locked and that she would never be able to move from the spot.

As the passport was being examined, the four of them stood there with the dog like figures in a surrealist landscape, the faint light from a crescent moon and the uncontained splash of stars rather than distorting perhaps showing life as it was, as it now looked to Adele. She thought she might suffocate to death standing there, that she would break down and begin to shake and tremble right before everyone's eyes if this ritual went on a moment longer. Colman might have been waiting for the doorman to return the stub of a theatre ticket, judging from his manner. Adele could hardly bear it.

'Everything is in order,' the examining cop finally said, returning the fake passport. 'Why were you up here? There is no crossing at this point.'

'I know. But would it matter as long as everything is in order?' Colman said amiably. 'We just wanted to climb a little bit. We both enjoy the exercise.'

'You would not be carrying contraband of some kind, would you?' the one with the dog suggested.

'We shall be happy to open the bag and empty our pockets for you. . . .'

'That would not be sufficient and we are not inspectors. You must pass through *Zollkontrolle* if you wish to cross over. You cannot do it here.'

Colman gestured in conciliation. 'Just as you say, *Offizieren*.'

The cops watched them move back downhill after casual salutes and an exchange of *Danke schön*'s and *Bitte schön*'s.

'Thank God, they didn't ask to see my papers,' Adele said as the downward slope propelled them back through the trees towards the road. 'Thank God for the male chauvinism of the average German military man.'

'They are border patrol,' Colman said. 'They simply keep people from crossing illegally and arrest those they suspect of something. And I have an idea these areas are crawling with them now—more than ever before.'

'Why is that?'

'Drugs—that's why. They're coming in everywhere, like water through holes in a dyke.'

'Drugs. Yes.' It was disheartening. 'Heroin. . . .'

'Let's stop here a minute, sweetheart.'

'All right.'

'We could still get across,' he said, looking at her in the dark, her features obscured by the night, distant and merely reminiscent, and she was not quite the person he knew most of the time. 'Are you frightened?'

'I'm shaking. . . .'

He placed his hands on her upper arms. 'Listen. There are times when you are stronger than anyone I have ever known. . . .'

'I?'

'Yes. And because you are stronger than anyone I have ever known, I'm going to ask you to try again with me, try to get to the other side.'

She was nonplussed and her eyes widened in the dark. 'You mean now?' she said with astonishment.

'I mean tonight. Say, in ten minutes.'

She didn't speak and he said, 'We can do it, I think. There may never be a better opportunity. . . .'

'But Brian . . . that's mad. . . .' She was sorry she had put it just that way and she said, 'It's reckless.'

'They are probably patrolling a hundred yards or more to

the west of where we ran into them. They won't be hurrying back, they won't be expecting anything—certainly not from two nice, obviously law-abiding people like you and me.'

'But what if you're wrong, if we are caught? We would not be given the same *Gemütlichkeit* a second time.'

'Whenever we try there will be that risk.'

'Yes, but why tonight?' Her voice was impassioned and perhaps even resentful. Like all lovers, like all adored men, he was two people; and so was she. 'Tonight's chance is used up.' And then: 'Oh, darling, I'm sorry. I'm being stupid. I'm forgetting the realities and acting like a nagging wife you'd be better off without. It's because I love you, and that can make someone do and say many things she shouldn't. Especially when she's a coward deep down. . . .'

'Forget I said anything.'

'I'll do what you want me to do. I'll try to do whatever you say, Brian.'

Colman waited about five seconds before saying, 'Not tonight. We'll wait.' He didn't share her obvious relief. 'We had better get to the inn at Brughaffen before it's too late to get a room,' he said.

They walked in silence towards the road, the Valpak having begun to be irritating and burdensome to Colman.

'What shall we do next?' she asked. 'When do you wish to try again?'

'We'll keep moving for a few days. After that, I don't know.'

There was something in his voice that silenced her. With great luck they were able to secure the last room at the mountainside inn about five hundred yards from the bus stop. There was a single bed and also a niche built into the wall, wide enough for one. Adele said, 'What is the matter, Brian?' She was sitting on the bed in the niche, stripped to her panties and bra. She saw the tight set at the corners of his mouth, the sudden dissatisfaction in his expression, and she knew that the stress was at last building up, like a river rising around them. 'Why did you change your mind about attempting it again?' she said.

He looked at her. 'Why? Because I was scared too,' he confessed.

173

'Were you?'

'Do you think I could just shrug my shoulders and go to the movies if anything happened?'

'I'm sorry.'

'For what?'

'Nothing. Everything. I had no right to stop you.'

'Except that each of us is one-half of the same thing,' he said, moving to the centre of the little room. 'It's not me, it's not you. It's both of us. Sounds like bad song lyrics, doesn't it?'

She smiled softly. 'In a world full of people who don't believe in it, I like the way it sounds,' she said.

'It all comes back to the same thing,' he said without a change of tone. 'Mankin. . . .'

Adele frowned slightly and watched him carefully now.

'The man they were going to trade,' Comman went on, the idea tantalizing. 'If only they had got him out somehow, we'd be free and clear now. . . .'

Adele didn't move but continued to look at him. In an effort to break the mood that had overtaken him, she said, 'I may not be available tomorrow, darling.'

Desire was nearly constant even as it was being assuaged. They were indeed the two halves of the same thing.

In the morning they went for a walk along the shoulder of the beautifully engineered road that wound through the vast wooded hillsides. Like any other tourists, a manifestly healthy young couple, they hiked in silence as if they were enjoying the sights and scents of the great forest and were carefree. They themselves might have been momentarily deceived. But only momentarily. And when they returned to the inn they redis-covered the reality of their circumstances. Two men, one in a policeman's uniform, white-capped, bull-necked, the other in civilian clothes, were standing in the vestibule with the *Lederhosened* landlord engaged in intense conversation that had to be about one thing only. Neither Adele nor Colman had gone past the threshold. 'Let's get out of here,' Colman said.

'But all our clothes. . . .'

'They can be replaced, we can't be.'

They resumed their journeying in unexpectedly short order and with suddenly measurable weariness. As they sat on one of the yellow post-office buses out of Brughaffen, Adele said, 'Maybe it didn't concern us.'

'Maybe a dog won't bark at a cat. You can't be sure. It's best not to be.'

'But *why*?'

'If I knew the answer to that, darling— Possibly the border guards mentioned it. Casually. Or even had second thoughts. They might have wanted to question us about something else, just because we've been noticed near the border. The drugs— Who knows? What's the difference? We just can't let ourselves be stationary targets.'

Ludwigshafen, Oberlingen, Friedrichshafen were towns along the edges of Lake Constance, and Adele and Colman passed through every one of them, the Romanesque and baroque churches looming at every turn, it seemed. Clots of vacation people jammed everything—buses, restaurants, hotels, beer gardens, the *Autobahnen*—the ruddy-faced campers, the various foreigners, groups of boy scouts, groups of girl scouts, groups of nuns like blasé penguins, provocative girls and aggressive playboys. In five days they had reached Munich by train, without greater impetus than the need to buy new clothes, and they found themselves in the middle of the *Föhn*. A warm wind blew from an invisible source perhaps thousands of miles away across hot desert lands. It had arrived somewhat early according to the natives.

Perhaps it was this alone that finally governed them. The winds persisted like the endless attentions of a heartless molester. The city seemed at one and the same time lethargic and short-tempered. The air was crystalline but heavy. Banners, wherever they appeared, were outstretched. Birds bobbed in buoyant configurations above the trees, then came to the ground in the Odeonplatz and sat like lead. Colman's eye followed the flight of a pigeon indifferently as he and Adele occupied a table on the terrace of a café in the *Hofgarten* not far from their hotel. 'When will we try again?' she asked listlessly.

'Soon,' he answered, his energies at a very low ebb, sucked dry by the wind, compromised by two failures out of thus far two attempts.

'If only we could stay in one place for longer than a day or two,' she mused. 'If only we didn't need to think about anything or worry about tomorrow. If we could be weak and not strong—just for a little while. . . .'

'I know the moving around is hard,' he granted.

'There is a way we might be able to,' she said directly, her voice dry and even rough-edged and uncharacteristically calculating. She looked at him and smiled wearily. 'But I don't suppose we would want to do that, would we?'

Colman knew what she was driving at but he didn't answer immediately. Then he said, 'I don't know why we should. . . . But I can't give you a reason why we shouldn't. And I know there must be one. . . .'

After a moment or two of silence Adele said, 'Should we think about it?' She was tentative, diffident. But the wishfulness was there.

'You would like it, wouldn't you?' he said sympathetically.

She was afraid to face it. 'I don't know. I don't know if "like" is the word,' she said.

Colman stared across the square towards the globular tops of the *Frauenkirche* several streets away. 'There should have been a way to get Mankin out of East Berlin,' he said, feeling useless.

Adele said simply, 'But there wasn't.'

They sat there with empty coffee cups and didn't say anything to each other for quite some time. But each knew what the other was thinking about.

CHAPTER EIGHT

'THEY DIDN'T TURN OUT to be each other's jailers, the way we hoped,' Brannigan said. 'Remember?'

'Let me tell you something, Red,' Stevenson said, hands in back pockets, walking around to the front of his desk. 'I know all about love, if that's the word. I mean the kind of love those two afflicted people are going through right now. Not the kind you and your Cathy have, nothing like that. I mean the kind that Stendhal wrote about—diffuse, insane, feverish, deranged, and ridiculous. It's a state of emotional and glandular tumescence, and sooner or later it goes sour.' Maybe he remembered his own old afflictions, his eyes on some distant point for just an instant. 'But until it does, there is one thing about it that stands out. It thrives on pain. The harder things are the sweeter; the more suffering there is, the more rewards. The agony is delicious. Suffering for each other is sheer ecstasy. . . .' He snorted. 'That's what I overlooked in my wishfulness.'

When Brannigan had concluded the business that had brought them together, Stevenson sat there with the sensation of moving through an underwater world. He had just lost an appeal to the higher-ups for an agent exchange. He knew what Emmering's price was, but the offer to release an imprisoned East German of some importance (there were a number who fit the description) might well have been too great to be denied. Llewellyn had said, 'No dice, Michael. More and more this business of swapping spies is looked on with favour less and less.'

Llewellyn's locution was interesting but its substance no less depressing for that.

Whatever Stevenson did, all his best shots went unrewarded. Concerted efforts and accord were a thing of the past, perhaps had never existed in the first place. One fought from within these days, struggled with allies and friends, and discovered too late that very different objectives lived side by side, sapping each other into effeminacy in all the big establishments in the West. There had to be people who recognized and deplored what was happening, what had been happening for decades, virtually unnoticed or misjudged. That was why he, who was one such person, hoped he would never become dispirited, that his resolve would never be broken. He wanted his own private 'hot-line', because without it, or some good substitute for it, *détente* was just another word for supine acceptance of a ravisher. Yes, it was not too much to put it exactly that way. But even this thing he had in mind had its limitations. How good—in other words, how effective—would prior knowledge of the evil intent of one nation be to another nation which was inclined not to respond to that evil anyhow? He didn't know.

But such a doubt would in no way deter him. Too many others were already deterred, passing on the fashionable fiats about 'nonmonolithic Communism' and telling themselves all the momentarily comforting little fibs and then the gross and heartless lies that would ultimately bring death. He would never be one of them. He would instead stick with the helm of a ship that might have been destined to sail on and on and never to come into port, possessed, obsessed, and somewhat dismayed by his own solitary figure. But he would not tell himself anything he knew to be untrue and act on it as if it were not. It wasn't a matter of stubbornness, or even mere principle. Because behind it all, behind his devotion to the conclusions about Communist intentions, was deep gloom. Perhaps even fear. The vision of this unchecked, gathering force haunted him. It was not the wind, not the sea, not the spill and flow of deadly lava. And yet it was looked upon as if just that much an element of nature, by people everywhere, in high places and low. And that was what was so harrowing. That was what kept Stevenson where he was. That was what burned in his brain and remained in his consciousness despite anything he might have wished to do about it. That was why he waited now and tried to think of alternatives. And there weren't any. The knowledge of Mankin's arrest would do little to increase Comrade X's confidence in future association. This was a thought Stevenson, as he now sat alone in his office, was entertaining for the first time. It hit him forcefully. He lit a cigar slowly, his visions blurred and distant. The fact that it would all be going on after he was dead didn't seem to matter.

CHAPTER NINE

ROLLING PLAINS gradually became absorbed by foothills, upland meadows, and dark forests. The castle Schleisstein, more baroque than rococo, finally dominated an enormous mound in the centre of an undulating mountain range high above a group of little neighbouring villages. Its isolation was total. The altitude, the woodland stillness, the free flow of air were more a part of heaven than earth, a rugged massif of limestone peaks to the south cutting across the skies of Austria. 'One could never be taken by surprise here,' Von Bleutzen said when Colman and Adele first arrived. 'Or, for that matter, even discovered. There are so many rooms, so many attics, so many passageways. . . .'

Alone but for the seven or eight servants, the count owned all he surveyed for a good distance in every direction. This was his domain, and he seemed, if somewhat airy and even a touch mad, only too eager to share its unending comforts with his two visitors. Unconditionally.

Two massive cobblestoned courtyards lay within the crenellated walls, stables, flower beds, parterres, flagstone paths, and grey-stone staircases characterizing its palisaded enclosure, the enceinte. The entry hall of the main house was large, its grey-stone floor rubbed smooth by generations of feet and scrubbing brushes. The countless rooms served, as much as for anything else, to exhibit paintings on panelled walls, casement windows giving on to various views of the castle enceinte and of the vast forests and mountains and the sky above the castle walls. The main house was four storeys high and overlooked the inner circumvallation where an old stable building now housed two Mercedes and a Ford Consul.

In spite of the count's expressed surprise, there was the feeling that Adele and Colman had been expected. They were given a self-contained apartment which had once been the bedroom of Von Bleutzen's parents. It had, surprisingly, pink canvas walls, french doors leading to a small terrace full of pink and white geraniums, a rosy brick fireplace, cupids on the ceiling, and small gilt footstools. '*A la française*,' Von Bleutzen commented. 'We Bavarians and the French have been *en rapport* for more than two hundred years. You would not expect as much perhaps. But my great-grandfather went to Moscow with Napoleon. . . . The *pot de chambre*, by the way, is ornamental, so don't be concerned about that.'

The number of paintings seemed without end. The count identified some of them in passing along the hallways and connecting passageways: priceless, if authentic, works by

179

German painters like Dürer and Cranach and other people neither Colman nor Adele had ever heard of; others by several Dutch and Italian artists; portraits of the count's ancestors like sentinels watching from every panelled wall—armoured soldiers, ceremonially garbed, titled people, envoys of kings. 'Do you see this Judith and Holofernes?' he said at one point. 'It is said to have been painted by Franz Zwinch. The name may mean absolutely nothing to you, of course. In any case, no one is really certain, but I have always liked it very much.' He clearly relished these many prizes. 'We are much luckier, by the way, than our blighted English cousins,' he went on. 'We are subjected to low death rates and absolutely no estate taxes. Otherwise we should not be able to survive any better than they do.'

They continued the brief tour in an atmosphere of rapidly growing trust and candour and by late afternoon of the first day at Schleisstein, Von Bleutzen had been let in on everything —to the extent only that Adele herself understood it, of course. The roots, however, remained deep in the frozen ground, rotted and unseen. But withholding the explanation of their flight, under the circumstances and given the personality of the count, seemed superfluous to Colman and a needless caution. The candour served to dispel a fog more unnerving than anything it may have concealed. 'So you were a part of *that* deadly game,' Von Bleutzen was moved to say rather sadly as they sat in a beautiful living room whose chief features were a brilliantly polished pinewood floor and a Bechstein grand piano. 'And now you are a part of only yourself.'

'The deadly game is a death struggle,' Colman said defensively. 'It's bigger than the people who fall in love and can't accept its conditions.' He put his hand on Adele's hand and went on. 'It doesn't recognize them. It's history and no one turns it back.'

'I know. But it is already lost. You deceive yourself if you think otherwise. What you have done doesn't appal me. It is historically superfluous. That is why I am here now and shall remain here, too old even to be expected, thank God, to attempt to control any but my own personal history. One cannot, in any case. But that is why you have altered nothing,

I wager, by your personal decision.' He paused briefly and then continued: 'To sacrifice this woman to the tactics of one of history's hopelessly minor moments—the exchange of *spies*—would be so crass, so imbecilic, one can't find words for it. . . .'

An imposing-looking, dark-eyed mastiff reclined at the count's feet, staring thoughtfully into space and seeming to be in accord with the sentiments of his master.

'But you were unable to let that happen, in any event, weren't you?' Von Bleutzen continued. 'Because of what I assume was, first, personal revulsion and, finally, that glimmer of feeling you soon had for this beautiful lady.'

'You can't always make things go together,' Colman said obscurely.

Just as obscurely Von Bleutzen shrugged. 'The old order is already doomed, if not actually yet dead. I don't think even Communism itself is surviving or that the issue of combating it is very compelling to begin with. It is only the passing of an old order which once encompassed many different styles that is foregone—to be replaced with I shudder to think what. . . . And if I am right, to talk of Communism against free enterprise is to indulge in childish babble.'

'You say an old order,' Adele put in questioningly. 'You have lived through rather sharp variations of that, haven't you? What does it actually mean when you say it now?'

Von Bleutzen breathed deeply, his hands, veined and tanned, dangling over the edges of the easy-chair arms like relaxed, obedient old servants. 'What I mean is that a workable vocabulary common to all no longer exists.'

'But did it ever?' she asked earnestly. 'Would there have been wars if it had? Would there have been Hitler?'

'In fact, yes,' Von Bleutzen said. 'One doesn't extol repugnant people but does wish to understand them. What is lost, in other words, is not a Utopian time free of Hitlers but rather the ability to instantly recognize them. Simplicity, you could say. The world no longer knows who Hitler is. Everyone has a different description of him. The old order, on the other hand, made such confusion impossible; even we Germans knew who he was.'

'He was we Germans,' Adele said.

'If you wish—a rare and highly sophisticated view in Germany. Where did you get it? Do they teach collective guilt in the German Democratic Republic?'

'Not precisely. Only that it all did happen. Nothing is left out. But they don't tell you how you must feel about it.' She shrugged, the quick-witted, cynical person usually hidden within now visible. 'They would rather you feel nothing but are too clever to say so. Once you've been given the statistics they let it drop.'

'Then how do you arrive at your conclusion?'

'You come to the West where everyone consciously tries to deny it—all except a strong minority,' she explained with a certain insouciance. 'As a result, the subject is always alive. There's nothing like that on the other side. Socialism absorbs everyone's thought and energy.'

'And do you think the subject should remain alive eternally?' Von Bleutzen asked, as if he were trying to fully gauge the strengths and weaknesses in her character.

'I only know what I myself feel,' she answered.

'What is that?'

'That we are not remorseful enough.'

Von Bleutzen nodded. 'I agree. But is it possible to be remorseful enough, if one's conscience is as strong as your own seems to be? If you have such deep feelings can you ever stop feeling for the victims, for the dead, for those who were murdered? Can you ever be satisfied by admissions of guilt, by commemoration? Can you ever feel that enough penance has been done? Perhaps you cannot.'

'Perhaps I am not supposed to.'

Von Bleutzen nodded again. 'It may be that very thing that attracts this man to you,' he said, 'if I may take the liberty of saying so. You are a rare girl. You were barely born when the war ended.'

Adele lowered her eyes, refusing the characterization. 'The old order you speak of,' she said, 'is the very thing that has forced us into hiding and will separate us for ever if it can.'

Von Bleutzen said quietly but almost votively: 'While you are here at Schleisstein it cannot even find you.'

Adele and Von Bleutzen seemed to be cojoined in contempt

for the systems that had failed them both, however in different ways.

Colman finally said, 'An American intelligence organization facing a deadly enemy has to fight its best fight. It doesn't matter what that sounds like, it will stand up to any examination you want to give it.' He spoke quietly, soberly, relieving the air of various abstractions. 'It has no reason to be kind to anyone—or unkind, for that matter. It's not up to mischief or children's games—I know that for a fact. The man in charge is serious and very smart and completely dedicated. What is important to him is very important to a great many people. It just doesn't happen to be important to me. Not any longer.'

Colman looked into Adele's eyes and found a faint frown. 'Isn't it? How I wish that were so,' she said, candour before the count an evidently easy matter, perhaps because the old man was obviously disengaged and his house like a last bastion; perhaps because heaven and death were so nearby in the most delightful colours imaginable.

'It is,' Colman said. 'You know it is.'

'It is fascinating to realize that, consciously or not, the two of you are opposed in your thinking,' the count observed. 'We all are, in fact. I see history as a hostage to the barbarians proven by the emergence of the new hordes. One of you sees it in terms of a fight against Marxist totalitarianism, the other as the exploitation of the individual by any systematic organism.'

'The last thing that I am in the world,' Adele said smiling softly, 'is an anarchist.'

'Well, here at Schleisstein it doesn't matter,' Von Bleutzen said peacefully. 'Only death can find it and come over its walls. . . .'

'Sooner or later we must leave,' Adele said.

'Leave? If you wish, yes. But if you want to stay, you may . . . for as long as you like . . . a year, two years. . . .' He looked from one to the other. 'Until I die . . . there is no reason why not.'

The exhilarating atmosphere was undeniable; it was not like the flatlands where people congregated in dense fumes of suspicion; and a kind of thin-aired madness pleasantly afflicted all of them, a freedom from normal cautions and social restraints. One could almost feel it immediately, insidious, delicious, and disastrous to the will. The slow fall of summer dusk came on the place like a reassuring blanket, the sounds of woodcocks and other things in trees carrying softly on the early evening breezes. Distant barking brought the mastiff to attention, his great head upright, his collar clicking like the adornments of a medieval sovereign.

'I should hope it would tempt you. I should feel I had done something of value,' Von Bleutzen said. 'You are people of quality. Why should you be swept up in any of what is down there now?' Elite, burdened with greater-than-average understanding, he looked at Colman through the gathering gloom of the unlit room. 'You have said good-bye to all that, haven't you? Regardless of your objective opinions.'

'Good-bye to the business I was in, yes. It got too personal. But more is down there than my small part in the deadly game, as you call it—much more.'

'What do you see?'

'You find out as you go along, I suppose. Up till now I've only been one thing. I'm not an expert at anything else—not that I was very expert at that. But I think you can only hide so long and no longer.'

Von Bleutzen shrugged and at that instant a lady wearing a dirndl entered and switched on several lamps controlled by a wall switch. 'Entschuldigen Sie, Excellenz.'

'Danke schön, Helga.'

Ulrich, a sturdy, grey-headed Bavarian wearing a green cloth long-sleeved shirt, horn buttons, black leather knee trousers, and high stockings, entered a moment later bearing a tray of glasses and several bottles. 'Dürfte ich ihrer, Excellenz, einen cocktail servieren?' he said.

'Nein, danke. Ich werde meinen eigenen zubereiten,' the count said, rising, and then added to his guests, 'There is, as you can see, a rather informal atmosphere at Schleisstein. They are married and have been with me for thirty-five years.'

In a few minutes the count had prepared drinks for them and himself and sat down to the piano. He played Debussy with unexpected and stunning fluidity while Adele and Colman sat in their chairs listening. 'This is *Le Tombeau de Couperin*,' he said. 'Only the prelude. And I try in my clumsy way to imitate the way Gieseking played it. Though I don't for a moment suggest that I am anything but the most rank talented amateur.'

He was gifted, the music filling the air sensuously, no less voluptuous than Debussy can be for all its delicacy. Music works on the senses of some, stirring ashes, igniting flames. Adele and Colman shared the sounds as if their bodies were touched intimately by them, their minds alive with memories of mere feeling, led through lanes of undying love, haunted by unbearable devotion as they looked into each other's eyes, peering into each other's very souls. The music had no mercy, its seduction altogether appropriate, the world effectively shut out for the moment.

Von Bleutzen then played a piece of Ravel and another by Poulenc. It all sounded French. 'I like Wagner too, of course,' he admitted as they went to the dining hall. 'But we're all a little bit mad where France is concerned, as I've told you.' He walked between the two of them, the paradigm of gracious hosts as he continued: 'You know Prince Ludwig? When he built Linderhof he intended to call it Meicost Ettal. I could let you puzzle that out, but I shan't. It is simply an anagram of *L'état c'est moi*. It shows a deranged Francophilia I hope never to share; and which he fortunately didn't ultimately choose to express. Instead, do you know what he did? He dressed up as Lohengrin and sailed in his swan boat in a little grotto on the grounds. Not every day, but often.' He shook his head. 'I shall not do that either. But if there is anything else that would interest you, let me know.'

They then sat down to dinner. They dined on veal cooked in cream sauce that proved to be delectable, the altitude a spur to one's appetite, accompanied by a tingling *rosé*, the meal served by Ulrich, Helga, and a young, deferentially silent steward. A massive hunting scene in sylvan colours and shapes dominated the wall above a serving sideboard behind the count's chair at the head of the large oak dining table, an old, deeply parochial painting of heroic men with their horses and hounds.

A second wine was decanted, and finally, little cakes and coffee were served as the conversation, centring mostly on the count's various enlightenments pertaining to both family and Bavarian history, went unfalteringly forward. The two were actually well intertwined, an outstanding family annal that of the count's father's allegiance to Crown Prince Ruprecht, whom he had tried to persuade to Draconian measures against Hitler immediately after the Beer Hall Putsch. From the first his father loathed Hitler and Ludendorff both and was a far-sighted man for his time and background. The count related as much with manifest satisfaction. He himself had gone into exile in 1933, extending the family revulsion for Hitler and Hitlerism by leaving the land. In the wake of this revelation Von Bleutzen became infinitely more attractive to Adele, his sybaritic nature now tempered not only by talent and intelligence but deep feeling and an admirable sense of human values. He went so far as to imply participation in various clandestine anti-Nazi activities but left the details vague. The remainder of his life included a certain brilliant and beautiful Nicola Renzi-Stiefer, who long ago became his Countess Nikki and who was now dead some fifteen years. As he talked his eyes drifted fondly after the ghostly shimmering remains of a passion he had never rid himself of. And then, consciously to break his mood, he went on to something else—his son and daughter, both married and living in New York, a story about Cuvillies, the dwarf architect who built the State Theatre, and another about Lola Montez, who exposed her breasts for examination at a state ball to allay Prince Ludwig's scepticism concerning their authenticity, finally winding down and obviously ready to retire. He avoided looking at his guests as he said, 'No one will interfere with you here and whatever you wish will be fulfilled in so far as it is possible.'

'We are overwhelmed,' Adele said. 'Isn't that so, Brian?' she added immediately because it was his opinions and decisions which had to come first.

'Altogether so,' Colman said quietly.

'There are horses, if you ride, and places to explore, and most of the modern conveniences. . . .'

'Please, we need no persuasion,' Adele said, smiling.

The count seemed to mock himself. 'I do sound as if I am trying to sell the place to you at that.'

They all laughed amiably and very shortly parted. The French bedroom was killingly seductive, its assaults on one's equilibrium nearly irresistible. 'It's hard to keep one's head, isn't it?' Adele said.

Colman smiled faintly, looked around, said nothing, and Adele said, 'The count is one of the world's most over-privileged people. But I think he is a good-hearted person, don't you?'

'He's not bad. He has insides anyhow. He wasn't afraid of that crew that was after him in the street that day,' Colman said. 'He's the fairy godmother in disguise.' They stood close together and he held her hands in his. 'I could see you beginning to feel it down there, as he calls it. That's why we're here.'

She didn't keep the resentment out of her voice though she smiled when she said, 'But darling, was it that alone? You make me feel like a manipulator. I mean, didn't you want to come also?'

'Yes, I was beginning to feel it too. That's just the point. I like the easy way, sweetheart, just like anyone else. And that can be a trap. Staying here forever isn't even remotely for us.'

'My God, Brian, who said that it was? Not I.'

'Neither is living from day to day, looking over our shoulders every five minutes.' He looked into her eyes. 'We can't go back to that. And we're not going to. I promise you that.'

'You don't need to promise me anything. Don't you see that?'

'I'm promising both of us. . . .'

'But you don't need to. I'm afraid of promises.'

By then the sights, the tastes, and the aromas of the long day had synthesized with the night, the soft lighting, the altitude, and the intake of wine. The two of them were primed beyond reversal; and she urged him on with both word and deed to that for which he required no urging. Nothing else existed, no other awareness, no further anticipations—only this wicked rapture in an opulent, canopied French bed superbly serving its finest purpose.

CHAPTER TEN

THE COUNT sat in his study the next morning, as he most always did, attending to his memoirs. They were important to him for reasons beyond even his own grasp. He worked diligently at the business of setting down the things he remembered, and he hoped that he would have the courage to leave out none of it.

On the walls were several small paintings and some photographs. One of the paintings showed a man encoiled in darkeyed wisdom and ancient scepticism, a prayer shawl on his shoulders—a rabbi by Marc Chagall. Von Bleutzen had purchased it ten years before because, as he had said to the dealer in Paris, 'No Bavarian castle should be without one.' And he greatly admired it.

He shortly joined his two handsome guests in the rockery overlooking an expanse of foothills and rolling meadows travelling down to where villages clustered here and there in undisturbed anonymity. The air was as empty as the inside of a giant soap bubble and the piney scent seeped into one's lungs as suggestive as perfume. 'Do you have a green thumb?' he asked Adele.

'No. But I love plants and flowers,' she answered.

Her eyes shone and her skin was glowing and Von Bleutzen looked at her with evident favour. 'I can teach you certain fundamental things about Alpine plants if you would care to learn,' he said.

The three of them walked down the stone steps of the easily sloping terrace along one of the grassy paths between the rock bed, herbs and shrubs, and various coloured blossoms everywhere. 'It isn't impossible to raise this type of thing,' Von Bleutzen said. 'But neither is it without challenge. Most of them, you see, are not indigenous to the area.'

'It's a wonderful garden,' Adele said, more enthusiastic than she might have been at some other time in some other lesssheltered place. Now everything was like Shangri-La in the old film she had seen on the Hardenbergstrasse a few months before, sitting alone in the dark, draped in scrims of preposterous, painfully wistful dreams. 'They're lovely.'

'Some are,' the count said. 'They must be tough in order to assert themselves up here. And yet they are basically fragile plants and their hold is always tenuous—not all, but some of the better ones. That is the paradox.' He smiled faintly. 'And it is also the chief satisfaction one gets in working a garden like this. When one of them grows and comes to bloom—one meant to thrive, let us say, only in the state of California, such as this white mariposa—something of value has occurred. What exactly, I cannot say, but . . . something has been gained.'

Adele took Colman's hand as the two of them followed the count, his boots, tweed jacket, and gnarled walking stick, to a lower level. Colman had never seen Adele looking as beautiful, as free, as relaxed. She was radiant with a kind of perfection that could only be heartbreakingly fleeting. He had nourished her well the night before, but only facetiously could that be suggested to account for her vibrancy. She needed security and for the moment was enjoying it; her sense of well-being was as distinct as the aromas playing innocently everywhere in this aerie. She squeezed Colman's hand, as if to maintain the secrecy that lovers share in the presence of a third party.

They came to a small plot of ground on a noticeably sharp angle, and Von Bleutzen said, 'I wanted to try something new right here, something whose habitat is South Africa—a daisy called Felicia. It produces a glorious blue flower with a bright golden centre. It is supposed to be sown in the frame, but so are many others I've done out-of-doors. And it happens that this is just the time to begin.' He looked at Adele. 'You could, if you wished, try your hand at this next-to-impossible task.'

'I?' She smiled. 'I haven't the faintest notion about plants. I am an X-ray technician.'

'Are you really? How surprising.'

'Why should it be?'

'Because you look more suited to—flowers. Don't you agree, Mr Colman?'

'Sure. But never trust the looks of anything, Count.'

'Ah, that's for spies and counterspies,' the count said with a good-humoured laugh. And then: 'Of course, the Felicia is only a passing thought, one you needn't feel polite about refusing. A little foolish, perhaps. . . .'

'I shouldn't like to quit in the middle of anything,' Adele said in a genial way.

'You would not be so circumscribed in your comings and goings if you stayed here as perhaps you may imagine,' Von Bleutzen said without suasion, his tone objective and reasoning. 'Actually you could move about rather freely, since your only real palpable risk exists in either attempting to get out of the country or in having bad luck with your *Ausweis* at a hotel in some other unforeseen situation. You could do so many things—go to theatre in Munich or cinema in Garmisch. . . .'

'In a week's time,' Adele said, 'you will be glad to see the last of us.'

The count smiled as if he were her grandfather. 'Do you think so? You mustn't be so self-effacing. But you must, of course, do as you think best.'

At lunch the subject came up again along a circuitous line. 'I am inclined to agree that the English will give you asylum you could not get in Austria or Switzerland—neutral or not. At least, that is my opinion. They would return you on the request of almost any West German authority if you entered either country illegally. Illegal entrants are a particular problem for Switzerland, at the moment.' He paused to eat, then said, 'Perhaps France would be a good place for you.'

'I would count more quickly on the English Parliament than on the French Assembly if any problems about asylum were to come up,' Colman said.

'You think it would come to a national debate?' the count said, his eyebrows arching, his expression amazed.

'I am ninety-nine per cent certain we would be granted asylum—that is, Adele would be,' Colman said, 'even though the pressure might be terrific from British Intelligence, for example, for extradition. They could drum up some phony reason or other.'

'The community of interests between spy organizations,' Von Bleutzen concluded.

'They don't get on that beautifully at all times, actually. But my former boss isn't easily kept at arm's length. He'll try hard and won't let it go because someone gives him a polite but firm no. He'll push.'

The count nodded, put down his knife, his fork suspended in mid-air, and he saw that Adele appeared to be pensive and withdrawn, like a person whose handicap was being discussed in front of her by two physicians. Colman saw the same thing and said, 'Adele knows that about him. . . .'

'Yes,' the count said. 'I would think something of a fanatic was needed for a job like that.'

Colman said, 'He's not a fanatic; a fanatic has private visions and he can't be reasoned with. Not him. He goes on historical record. Some people don't share his conclusions or opinions. But they know what he's talking about.'

'I see the distinction. Perhaps I meant to say tenacious.'

'He's tenacious all right.'

'Then you might lose in the end,' the count said.

'Not the way things are today, I don't think,' Colman said with a wry and somewhat rueful grin. 'The America-haters will love us for this. They're everywhere and they're strong enough to help. It's help I'll take advantage of.' He added: 'That's the way it is. You can't have everything.'

'I see the irony, of course. But what strikes me as most curious is that only this young woman will satisfy the requirements of the situation. Even given the interest of the East German colonel . . . surely there must be another way of securing the release of this man if he so much obsesses your former boss. . . .'

No one said anything and the count sighed audibly, then finished eating, drank some beer, and looked at a pattern of sunlight falling through a casement window and across the stone floor like yellow gossamer. It held his attention momentarily before he said, 'Have you ever stopped to consider what history really amounts to—politics and power? Only sexuality and art.' He gave a shrug. 'Art records history to begin with and then finally is all that is *left* of history—painting, architecture, music, and literature actually *becoming* history. Of course. And sexuality obsessively promotes the historical continuity—not necessarily in practice, but as an objective, a wish, a desired state of attainment. The prodigy of Louis the Fourteenth until he was nearly *ninety* is well known. Everything else —food, shelter, bodily needs—were merely supportive.'

'Hitler promoted history without either one,' Colman said, speaking perhaps because he didn't want to give the topic a chance to reside exclusively in the personalities of Von Bleutzen and Adele; an almost intangible Puritan envy seemed to push him to it. 'So did Stalin.'

'Yes, yes,' Von Bleutzen was quick to reply. 'But only art is finally left—in theory, mind you, in theory only—to those for whom sexuality is not attainable. For whatever the reason. Without either art or sexuality there is an unholy void. And perhaps that explains Hitler and Stalin. Kill others or kill oneself.'

'What of love?' Adele asked. 'When you feel just that, and physical desires comes secondly. . . .'

'Yes, it does exist. But it is hard to define. A king may think he has given up his throne in its name when actually he has done so because of an overwhelming sexual obsession.'

'But how easily they can go together,' Adele said quietly.

'Then let us say they are inseparable,' the count granted. 'It is nevertheless this admittedly animal urge and the power to take physical gratification that we most easily recognize—in ourselves and in others.' Again he shrugged. 'It disappears and the force of its absence can be as dynamic as its presence. Men have second thoughts about their mistakes and turn to other things—to art, if they are so fortunate. Sexuality has deceived them. But, of course, they would let it do so again if they could. . . .'

That was all there was of it, and in the afternoon Von Bleutzen went off to oversee the efforts of several workmen on scaffolding along the north parapets. Adele and Colman visited the horses and then went walking in the nearby woods. Adele knew nothing of riding a horse. Colman offered to give her instruction but she declined. 'We shall not be here long enough to accomplish anything,' she reasoned. 'So why begin?'

'In a few days I'm going to go to Wiesbaden again,' Colman told her as they came to a clearing and sat down on the large stump of a felled fir tree. 'I don't think you should be with me. But I don't know whether you should remain here.'

'Let me come with you.'

'No. It's too tough. It might take days. I'm not sure I'll be able to locate Lorenzo immediately—or, for that matter, whether I can locate him at all. They all may be in jail, for all we know. The whole thing could be gruelling—moving around, killing time, lousy hotels—no, I don't want you on that kind of thing. I want you well placed, out of reach . . safe.' He shook his head. 'I suppose that means Schleisstein. I can't think of anything better, much as I would like to.'

'Why should it have bothered you in the first place? You don't think Richter can't be trusted, do you?' she said with a little smile.

'It's just my conventional upbringing coming back to haunt me,' Colman said. 'But I've no doubt he's attracted to you, if you want to know.'

'Oh, Brian, no. Very remotely at best. And after all, he *is* rather advanced in years.'

'According to him, Louis the Fourteenth was ninety. Remember?'

They began to walk back in silence towards the castle. 'Brian. . . .' Adele took Colman's arm and leaned close to him. 'What if you can't work things out with this man Lorenzo? If we can't get hold of new papers?'

'Let's talk about that when it happens,' he said.

When that very thing did actually take place, Colman and Adele found themselves immobilized. They spent the next seven weeks at the castle, each day one of beauty and peace, without strife, without conflict or friction, without the consequences of life in a tough, antagonistic, everyday world. But the whole thing was all wrong and Colman knew it.

CHAPTER ELEVEN

THEY WERE STILL THERE when the Felicia began to bloom. Colman had succeeded in locating Lorenzo immediately only to discover that a certain key figure in the proceedings was out of the country and was probably not going to return for a very long time, if ever. It was a somewhat fishy story but Colman had no alternative to accepting it. He suspected that the entire operation had died with old man Faubrein.

'We can get across the frontier at Metz and into France,' he told Adele on the night of his return, in a tone meant to encourage and to make the prospect attractive. 'Then we'll either stay there or find a way across the channel, depending on events.'

'Okay, Brian,' she said in a way that was intended to be brave but came out grim.

'We can do it, I'm sure.'

The next morning Von Bleutzen said, 'Why be governed by a preconceived idea? Maybe it needs re-examining.'

'You're wonderfully kind,' Adele said, the three of them taking breakfast at a small, round, glass-top table on the terrace just outside the main house, the early sun at exactly the right angle.

'Don't speak of kindness, it embarrasses me,' Von Bleutzen said. 'It is the last thing that motivates me, as far as you are concerned. So it mustn't get in your way. Think clearly, be sensible, and do, finally, what you think is right for you. . . .' He looked from one to the other. 'One of the problems we all face is those almost hopelessly Pavlovian minds nature has left us with. So what I am suggesting to you now is that you not automatically respond to concepts you may have had six months ago and which just may by now have become useless without your notice. I don't mean to presume upon you, please believe that; I don't wish to appear too much the advocate. I say only that perhaps the risk of arrest in attempting to illegally cross a frontier is indeed one you must take because it is the way to your salvation; and . . . perhaps it is not. In my opinion, that is an issue which may not already be irrevocably decided. That is all I am saying.'

'You see, Richter,' Adele said, 'Brian and I are convinced that it is.'

'You must reach England,' he said sympathetically but with regret for their shortsightedness, 'because you think of that as freedom.'

'Because it is somewhere to be and something to do—for Brian and me.'

Von Bleutzen nodded with sad wisdom. 'I suggest merely that you think about it. Even for a day—an hour. But think about it.'

They thought about it for longer than either of the suggested periods of time. And perhaps they never should have. It wasn't long before Adele felt the resolve slipping out of her like air from a slow puncture. And Colman then began to go from day to day observing her quiescence, not moved to disturb it. The advantages of Schleisstein were very apparent but to his mind inappropriate, if not worse than that. The days passed them by harmlessly, growing one by one into the beginnings of a past as innocuous as the softly painted scenery of a stage setting.

As they sat in the little *Hofbräuhaus* in Garmisch one afternoon, Colman said, 'I feel as if we're in a web. It's made of spun sugar, but it's a web anyway.' He spoke quietly, amiably, a faint good-natured smile on his lips, as if he were discussing a bad golf shot.

Adele said with challenging sincerity, 'I'll do whatever suits you.'

'What is it that suits you?' he asked.

But she had already caught the scent. 'Darling, you're in charge,' she said. 'The one thing you can't be is indecisive.'

'I suppose not many people would complain about a set-up like this, would they, sweetheart?'

She looked at him as if she had always known what was just beneath the surface, a somewhat disappointed smile on her face. 'Brian, darling, do you hate the way we are living?' she said.

'Night after night I sleep with you. Day after day we are together. We do whatever we want to do, when and how we want to do it, and no one interferes with us. How could I hate that?'

'It's possible,' she said.

'I don't think I like that,' he said flatly.

She put her hand on the sleeve of his jacket. 'If you want me to go with you, anywhere at all, I will go right now—this very minute. We can try to sneak through, leave our clothes behind —I don't care. We can send Richter a letter of apology. . . .'

'I didn't say anything like that, sweetheart.'

'If you want to go alone—if you don't want me with you, I'll accept that also, I promise, darling, without any to-do or fuss.'

'If I were somebody who hit women, I might hit you for that,' he said.

'Maybe I said it because I'm sure you wouldn't want to.'

'I don't care why you said it, don't say it again.'

He pressed her hand and neither of them said anything further, and very shortly they returned to Schleisstein by bus, then walked up the narrow lane to the castle. They were silent, taking fairly long strides where the terrain steepened, their bodies angled forward. It was late in the day and they joined their host for the ritual *apéritif*. It was that occasion that the count announced, 'The Felicia has arrived. Come, let us all go to it.'

The blossom was in a most incipient stage of development but unmistakably healthy, blue, and gold. Adele could not help but take delight in it. 'All your doing,' Von Bleutzen summarized. The sense of achievement was justified; but the flower marked the passage of a time without respect to reality. Just two days later reality found its way into Schleisstein like a lengthening shadow just before dusk.

CHAPTER TWELVE

ADELE HAD DECIDED to cut some azaleas and bring them to Von Bleutzen's study. They were in full bloom and particularly beautiful that morning. Without real purpose Colman had preceded her to find the count sitting behind his desk, evidently pleased and surprised by the visit. He had been for his morning ride through a light rain and the place smelled of his damp tweed jacket and the saddle soap with which his boots were kept gleaming and well conditioned. Not two minutes elapsed before Adele joined them with a bunch of red azaleas, and the count rose from his chair, Bavarian heartiness tempering the Latin blood that surely lurked somewhere in his veins. 'In that light, with those flowers, you could be a Renoir come to life,' he said.

'Less than that, I should think,' she said with a mechanical smile, going to a vase lost in the vast surface of his heavily constructed Georgian desk.

'Do you know, I have been considering bringing in more rocks,' Von Bleutzen said, 'and creating a new situation right beneath the azaleas and the catchfly. We could think up something new for the fall. . . .'

'We shall be gone very soon, in any case,' Adele announced, somewhat matter-of-factly, too casually. 'Tomorrow or the next day, in fact . . . Brian and I have decided that it's time. . . .'

Von Bleutzen took it with the deep breath of a man who has been expecting disquieting news but is still not well prepared for it, his dark eyes saddened by a soft smile. 'Of course, I am sorry to hear that,' he said.

Adele continued to fuss with the flowers while Colman watched her steadily, puzzled of course. 'You've been a good friend, Richter,' she said, 'and a brilliant host. But nothing lasts forever.'

'But I shall miss you both,' he said. 'You have been'—he paused, gazed dreamily through the window to where a boy was pitching dung from one of the horse stalls on to a generous expanse of burlap cloth covering the cobblestones nearby— 'my last moments of grace and beauty. Because you are brave and you are in love. I am very glad that I could play a part in . . . your odyssey.'

Colman said, 'We can never adequately express our gratitude. . . .' He didn't know what else to say.

'I am tempted to ask that you never contact me on any account. That way, I shall never have any indication of what becomes of you. I think I should prefer that.'

Colman made a gesture of assent.

'I suggest you try crossing into France. It might be worth the extra journey.'

'Yes.'

'Of course, if I were burdened with English breeding I should simply say, so good of you to visit, tallyho, and carry on. But we Bavarians are crude, straightforward louts, no matter how far we travel.'

Adele poured water from a little pitcher she had brought with her and said, 'It would do no good to say more.' She turned to face him and was not smiling, her lips noticeably whitened, the sun behind her now. 'Some things do not transplant. . . .'

Colman studied her face, a noticeably tense, cautious look about her. She gave a thin smile and added, 'Like some of the Alpines that come from other places.'

'But why so suddenly?' the count asked.

'Why not?' Adele said coldly.

'There is something else,' the count said, quickly dejected, his dark eyes probing or perhaps pleading. 'It is more than just your decision to go elsewhere that is behind everything.'

'There is nothing,' she insisted in return, holding herself stiffly.

'You are disturbed—deeply disturbed. . . .'

'People have their moods. . . .'

'Yes, but you are not in a mood, my dear, you are in a state. You are simply stiff with emotion. I beg of you—what is it?'

'Nothing. Nothing in the world. Your flowers are beautiful, your paintings are beautiful, your castle is glorious, and we are grateful for your hospitality. At a certain point, it was almost life-and-death to us; but now we must leave. . . .'

The count's eyes flashed and then dimmed sadly. 'You have discovered something, haven't you?' he said in a tone of capitulation.

Adele said nothing and Colman knew that the count had struck on the truth, and from Adele's still, cold face he judged it to be less than easy or mild. 'It could be only one thing at which you are outraged,' the count persisted quietly, 'at which you are as shocked as you appear to be. Your lips are white, your voice is tight . . . it is obvious.'

'What is it?' Colman said directly to Adele.

'It is not for me to be anything,' Adele said in a voice not quite steady. 'I have been your guest, you have been kind—more than kind. I am not the conscience of Germany.'

The count shook his head, caught out and old-looking. 'But the fact is, you are, in a manner of speaking. . . .'

'I am sorry,' Adele said. 'I haven't felt well today. Let us just say that and not anything more.'

'You have uncovered,' the count said nevertheless, 'my Nazi past, haven't you?'

Colman looked at Von Bleutzen as one does at an old piece of evidence, unable to conceive at first of the connection. Humanist, if somewhat conservative; philosophical, artistic, generous; could such a person have been a Nazi? The answer always had been, of course he could.

'Ulrich,' she said slowly, looking out the window. 'I asked him for shears . . . small shears. . . .'

'Ulrich,' Von Bleutzen mused, something ludicrous in it.

'I complained, in a joking way, that so well-stocked a house was missing such insignificant items like a set of shears for stems such as these.' She smiled ruefully. 'One word led to another and he then proceeded to tell me, in all candour, how difficult it was to get hold of things in nineteen forty-four, when everything was going so badly, but that *you* . . . were able to work miracles. . . .'

The count looked away, recalling, his face like grey parchment suddenly and about to crumple at a touch. 'Ah, yes,' he murmured, as if he could do nothing about it now. 'So that is it. . . .'

Adele said nothing and Von Bleutzen went on. 'Obviously I was not in exile, but here all the time . . . not a noble anti-Nazi ready to have sacrified all, but simply a disgusting relic of the Third Reich. . . .'

Adele felt choked, unexpectedly confused, shook her head and shrugged her shoulders convulsively. 'Perhaps I always knew,' she said. She didn't look at him and added: 'You gave us peace and shelter. . . .'

'But you wish you had not accepted it,' the count said.

'I think I only wish that I had not found out,' she answered, then walked to the window, watching the boy gathering the dung without actually seeing him. 'Tomorrow we shall be gone. . . . What does it matter?'

'But it does matter. Oh, how I too wish that you had not found out. If only I had thought to drill things into Ulrich's head. Yes, I am enough of a hypocrite to say as much.'

'Colman said, 'Maybe you shouldn't say anything at all and we'll be gone—maybe even tonight.'

'No, no, I do implore you not to depart in haste as if from the smell of death. I harmed no other living being, betrayed no one, I swear. I was merely weak and . . . ignoble, selfish and hypocritical, but not more—not a fanatic, not a criminal, but merely one of those who—went—along.' He was now breathing heavily, his skin ashen, and he was openly shaken and naked. No amount of Debussy seductively played, no amount of knowledge, good spirits, or wit, of cultivated behaviour could overcome what they had found out about him. 'It is important to me that you know I did not for a moment feel anything but loathing for Hitler and the Nazis . . . though perhaps that will seem even worse to you.'

Adele murmured, 'I don't know. . . .'

'I went along—yes; but it did cost me dearly to do so. It was hard to defy them, to resist. I could hardly bear their presence, their vulgarity, and the stench they carried wherever they went.'

'Their stench, you say,' Adele said scornfully. 'How easy for you. *They* had nothing so convenient to fall back on, no high and noble background from which to look down with a shrug. You *hated* them? Yes, then how much the worse at that. . . .'

There was dead silence and then Adele said, 'I am sorry.'

'No, you are right about all of it,' the count conceded wearily, crushed. 'I will not insult you further with attempted justifications.'

The three of them stood there in contemplation of long-vanished devastation whose ruins would not stop smoking. The count, like many others, had out of cowardice and sybaritic, or even Epicurean, lusts sold himself for use by political pederasts than whom he now appeared to be much worse. He had given himself to brutal and degenerate men who knew not of and cared nothing for Debussy or Watteau, given fealty to an act he had no accord with but which failed to revolt him sufficiently to make him forsake his treasures and his pleasures. He had played ball. One really couldn't hate him, under the circumstances, but one was inevitably no longer charmed. Not with Richter, not with oneself.

'I knew in my heart you were one of them,' Adele said. 'But I was willing to let you fool me, willing to believe your well-told lies, because then I could have all of this with Brian and an easy conscience too.' She felt on the verge of tears but held them back.

'You shall not leave here until tomorrow, I hope,' Von Bleutzen said. 'At least let us go together to Munich this evening, as we planned.'

'Munich?' She had forgotten.

'*Oktoberfest*,' he reminded her. 'If you can stand to be with me for just that much.'

'Of course, we can stand to be with you,' Adele granted him sombrely. 'What good does it do more than to see you for what you were?'

'I am not sure I wouldn't prefer your hatred to your understanding.'

'You're not on trial,' Colman said dully, feeling cheerless and dissatisfied with himself. 'And we're not judges and prosecutors.'

'I was quickly cleared through an American investigation of my status, please realize that.'

'All right, that's fine.'

'I tell you mainly so that you do not need to feel too regretful or pained at having lived here with me and having been . . . my friend.'

'That is very thoughtful of you,' Adele said. 'But I would prefer to feel regret and pain about having lived here with you, Richter.' Adele looked at him without rancour, most of her emotion now subsided, her looks grown calm. 'I hate comfort of any kind suddenly, I hate safety. . . .'

The count obviously understood, his sensitivity undeniable. 'I suppose I am Faust,' he said with a nod of agreement. 'It is better not to have one's every wish fulfilled sometimes.'

CHAPTER THIRTEEN

THEY RETURNED to their own quarters and remained there for some time amidst the chenille, the brocaded walls, and the cupids. 'You can't love me twenty-four hours a day,' she said. 'I was a fool to even dream that you could.'

'Oh, but I do.'

'I know, love; but you can't love unending idleness in a grown-up Disneyland—not you. You only agreed to it for this long for my sake, because of my fears. But I know you haven't been pleased, that it went against you. . . .'

They were seated head-to-head and facing each other, she on an ottoman and he at the edge of the fancy chaise-longue, and he caught the aroma of the toothpaste she had just used. 'This was an interlude, at the most,' she said.

He took her hand and said, 'I wasn't that eager myself. Maybe I allowed you to be an excuse for my own indecision.'

'Have you been indecisive, Brian?'

'You saw it yourself a few days ago. You even told me I was.'

'I said it was the one thing you couldn't be. I was being dishonest. I was trying to slip out of the responsibility. I didn't want to leave Schleisstein—not ever. But I didn't have the—insides—to look you in the eye and say it.'

'Let's stop accusing ourselves. Now is now.'

'Yes. I'm sorry for Richter. I would never have believed I would be. But I am.'

'That's the way things like that work out. Somebody is good to you. He's kind and generous and saves your life. And then you find out he's a practising cannibal.'

Adele gave a faint shudder. 'He's not exactly that. And it's hard to sit in judgement when it's the way you describe it. It's so much easier when it's Hitler or the entire petty bourgeois of the nineteen thirties.'

'Yes, it always is.'

'I don't feel that we are running away from him—not in that obvious way. But we do have to leave, don't we? It always had to be that, hadn't it?'

'We have to face ourselves,' he said. 'That's what we'll be trying to do, nothing else.'

She detected something in his voice she couldn't identify, but it gave weight to the simple and overfamiliar words. 'Shall we leave tomorrow?' she asked.

'That's time enough,' he answered, about to let her in on what had gone wrong, on what it would take to fix everything up. 'Tomorrow will be all right. . . .' There was discomfort in passion, even pain, as he had discovered. There were agonies in duty and not less, sometimes, in shirking it. 'But we can talk about it now,' he said, looking at her with the love he had for her, love that had, in a sense, come full circle. 'In fact, we should.'

She looked into his eyes, loving him desperately, steadily, and could feel a tiny nerve shuddering behind one of her eyelids. 'It's either succeed or perish this time, isn't it?' she said, hollow and far away.

'Not altogether. It's different than that. It's all about something else.'

She waited while he took a moment longer. 'We're not going to try to get out of the country,' he said. 'Not illegally.' He shook his head. 'It's not the way, sweetheart.'

She waited and he said, 'I've thought about it quite often during these past few weeks when there was nothing better to do and now I know how to get Mankin out of jail. . . .'

'Yes?' she said warily, inadequately.

'As I say, I have thought about it a lot, and I worked out a full-scale operation I am sure is better than any other for carying out his—call it rescue.'

Again, 'Yes?'

'Obviously, if that could be accomplished, you know what it would mean to us.'

She faltered. 'I think so. . . .'

'We would be free and clear, obviously.'

She was somewhat perplexed. 'Well, of course,' she said with a flutter of her hands. 'But . . . what are you telling me?'

'That I can get him out,' Colman told her. 'That it's what I want to do. So we can be free and clear and out of debt.'

'You? But why? Can't you tell them your plan? Can't someone else do it?'

'It doesn't work that way,' he said.

'Listen to me, Brian,' she said, a slight shake in her voice. 'If we try to cross into France, the worst that can happen is that I would be caught. And that is not much next to what would happen if *you*, darling, are caught on the other side. Don't you see? How can you get such an idea? I am weak in the stomach just thinking about it. It is madness.'

'You don't understand.'

'Don't I?'

'It has to be this way,' he said evenly. 'There is nothing in the world for me that's more certain than that.'

'I see. . . .'

'Not in that tone of voice.'

'I can't control that.'

'Let me make something clear to you: there's no politics in this, not even esprit de corps. I have to close the ledger in a way that lets me say to them, I owe you nothing now. Let someone else do it and good luck to them. I'm through because I earned the right to be.'

'Earned the right by going to prison for ten years or even being killed? I don't understand that.'

'Then maybe you can understand this,' he said, strangely at the edge of impatience with her. Why couldn't she give him exactly what he wanted now, exactly what he needed? Why had he to go through all of this, find himself her adversary? 'A man who was doing the job his government expected him to do—whether you agree with the objective or not—is sitting in an enemy prison because of me alone; because *I* decided that he would—because the choice lay between *his* remaining there and *you* being there. I had the power to make that choice, and I made him pay for my personal feelings, for my conscience, for my desire, for my loving—none of it having the slightest importance to anyone but to me, to us. And I doomed that man to imprisonment when he had every reason to expect nothing of the kind from me, so that we—you and I—could be with each other. Do you see? I did it while I was pledged to do the opposite. So that we will be building our lives on betrayal. Because it comes to one thing: a man who is paying for it whenever we're in each other's arms—whenever we kiss or touch or talk. Right this very minute. . . .'

'I am still weak in the stomach thinking about it. I can't help it.'

'Look, there is no easy way, you know that. Richter took an easy way and neither of us can stand to be near him now because we found out about it.'

'Oh, Brian, how can you compare such terribly different situations?'

'It would be different if I hadn't been a *part* of it—you must see that—you—with that quick mind. I *was* part of it. That's why I don't have the right to you if Mankin pays for it. Oh, I can *take* the right.' He took her arms in his hands. 'But it touches *you* if I do that. I don't want that and neither do you. There are no politics in that.' He was trying to make her understanding greater than her apprehensions; that was why he had invoked Von Bleutzen's compromises, his passive acceptance of safety and privilege while others suffered. 'You do see that, don't you?'

'You make it sound so ethical—like Socrates or something. But Brian. . . .' She shook her head.

'I would do it to him again if there were no other way, and my conscience would be something I'd live with. But there *is* this way and I can't ignore it.'

'It is all so terrible—for him, for you, for everyone in such things,' she said with loathing.

'I was part of it. Not a passing good Samaritan or a boy scout; not a crack-brained adventurer looking for excitement; but part of the whole system that's supposed to back up its own whenever that is possible. And you do see that I always will be part of it no matter how far we travel or how much time goes by unless I do this thing.'

'I am trying. . . .'

'Most people can't tell you why they do certain things. They can't put it into words worth the idea. It all comes out like recitations from a third-grade reader.'

'I understand everything you are telling me, Brian,' she said. 'And I am trying to share your outlook. But that isn't easy. All that makes sense to me is what happens to us—nothing much else.'

'Does the man mean nothing to you?'

'Yes. But he's an agent. He knew the risks.'

'So was I. And I knew them too.'

'I'm selfish, I know.'

'This is how we break all connection with it, darling. After that, they can all forget about me.'

Her intake of breath was audible and dispirited. 'You will never break connection with it, Brian. I think it is more than you are saying it is. I think it is more than you even know.'

He said nothing, was talked-out for the moment and feeling down. And she at the same time felt shut out because he seemed cold and distant suddenly, as he had never been before, as if she had intruded in some way or called attention to an embarrassing blemish or a lifelong inadequacy. It struck her in the pit of the stomach but she smiled faintly and said, 'We were bound to misunderstand each other a little bit, at least, on this topic. . . .' He had said he didn't care any longer, that even though his old views were objectively unchanged none of it mattered, that he had become a bystander, a detached, dispassionate observer in the gallery who would sympathize but would under no circumstances take part. But how much he had kept from himself, how much had remained merely dormant, held down but not crushed, was apparent now. 'Darling,' she said gently, not sadly, 'I have things to attend to —just little feminine odds and ends; perhaps you would like to walk about somewhere by yourself for a while. . . .'

He nodded. 'Okay, darling.'

The act of love needed guidance and faith and couldn't thrive in airless rooms.

CHAPTER FOURTEEN

AS THEY RODE, chauffeur-driven, in the custom-built Mercedes towards the outskirts of Munich, the count, sitting sideways on the plush jump seat he had insisted on occupying, wanted to talk, to bare his breast. 'What a thin line between pain which is intolerable and the pain one enjoys,' he said.

'There is nothing enjoyable about pain,' Adele said.

Lights crossed their faces from time to time as they drew into Starnberg.

'The pain that ennobles, then,' Von Bleutzen said. 'I am trying to cross that line, frankly, but I don't think I am destined to.'

No one said anything more for several minutes and the count finally broke the silence with a summary of the origins of the *Oktoberfest*, explaining it was first held to mark the engagement in 1810 of Ludwig to Princess Theresa. 'Long before he dreamed of building Neuschwanstein, long before they took to calling him mad. I think it is most opportunely available, considering everything. Perhaps it will lighten your departure.' He added with a completely ingenuous sense of discrimination, 'You will need to rub elbows with a great many *nouveaus* and *arrivistes*; but that shan't disturb you, I am sure.'

When they arrived at the enormous tent-covered expanse of the Theresienwiese the count dropped them off, said he was driving on but would meet them at the Bayrischer Hof at midnight if they had had enough by then. He obviously wished to be by himself finally—or at least free of their presence.

The night was on fire with lights and bursting with the unrestrained noise of rambling thousands of people. Everywhere were the billowing beer tents, jammed from wall to wall, the smell of beer itself following every nose till special awareness ceased; a giant wheel dominating the area and swinging through the sky in a circular trail of coloured lights. The shrieks of young female voices seemed to be the leitmotiv within the waves of the noise of human voices, and music from one section of the field competed with music from another at various crossover points like a crashing of weapons.

Adele and Colman sifted through the throngs and said nothing to each other. They moved like floating islands in a sea of perceivable physical appetite and even gluttony, of uninhibited lusting with little regard to prerogatives, stolen privileges covered with confetti and certified by the blowing of party horns and the racket of various noisemakers. The heat of such excitement could hardly be held down. It flushed the faces of the revellers and put everything at a boil. She took his hand. His grip was firm in return. Like reaffirmation.

'I love you, Brian,' she said. 'I know it sounds empty. But you are the only one in the world to whom I have ever said it.'

They were making their way through thick knots of people near the entrance to one of the tents. Their hands slipped apart. 'I love you too, you know that,' he said as they came to rest alongside the canvas wall; a hand reached towards Adele, and Colman calmly batted it down. The person was nowhere to be seen. 'Get me some beer,' she said. 'I shall wait right here.'

'But will you be able to dodge the groping hands of all these gay holidaymakers?'

'I think so.'

He left her and went to the enormous kegs just inside the tent where drinks were being dispensed. Beery breath came at him from a starched white shirt front; big, scarcely covered breasts nestled side by side like smooth-coated, well-behaved dogs right under his nose; a cacophony of conversations and shouted requests went on like the roar of the surf. It took some doing but in a few minutes he returned with the beer to where he had left her. She was nowhere to be seen.

He walked along with the two Löwenbräu mugs, searching without success. The noise of the merry-go-round nearby persisted, strangers going from place to place in a dogged state of euphoria. Some wore traditional Bavarian costumes, others evening clothes like the markings of their urban habitat. They strolled arm-in-arm or while encircling each other's waists, and none of them seemed to have the slightest trouble or care in their lives. As Colman covered more and more ground, his face still, his pace merely steady, the impression of other people's enjoyment grew. In a few minutes he knew that she had deliberately vanished.

She had said goodbye with a certain wistful insouciance to which he was now having a delayed reaction. Only now did the strange little smile, the soft look of goodbye strike his consciousness and become significant.

He came to the location of a women's lavatory and he waited within sight of the entrance, watching the comings and goings for about five minutes, knowing to begin with it was a futile action. She had run away.

He began to move very fast through the seas of people, covering open spaces at a near run, his eyes darting everywhere. What had she discovered about herself? About the two of them? He didn't know. As he raced desperately from one place to another he felt diminished in a way he never had before. Before he had felt only regret, only acceptance in the face of death—his mother's, his father's; a man he had killed But now he had fallen through a trapdoor and he felt small and alarmed. It was altogether different. Hadn't she known it would be?

'Brian, darling,' she thought to herself as she walked along as if strolling behind a coffin, 'I shall be dead without you. Even if I am alive, I shall be dead. . . .'

She was moving towards the Hall of Fame overlooking the festivities, the statue of Bavaria in its forecourt like a giantess in need of a giant who could take away her sword. She was eighty feet in the air. Adele glanced unseeingly at her. She didn't know yet exactly where she was going, only that she had to absolve Brian of his part in her destiny. He would have to realize quickly why she had done it, and she deeply hoped he would find that he was relieved.

She continued to walk along. She didn't know that a set of eyes, disbelieving and eagerly widened, were upon her. She didn't know until the eyes were confronting her, a hand on her elbow. 'Well, we meet again, Mrs Fischer. And in such festive surroundings.' He tipped his hat slightly.

She recognized him immediately. Grey-skinned, inhuman, unredeemable, it was the man who had arrested her. 'This is so interesting, I can't believe it altogether,' Bork said in his marked Berlinese German. 'And yet like poetry, in a way. That it should be you and me and *Oktoberfest*. After all these many months.'

She reflexively began to pull away, jerking her elbow from his grasp. But he quickly recaptured it, enclosing his hand firmly on her upper arm. 'Just a moment. I am arresting you, Frau Fischer,' he announced. 'Just as I did once before. Only this time I may receive a promotion for it.'

'I am so glad,' She sneered at him; none of it mattered.

The Cold War and spies: It was *Scheissdreck*, all of it, unladylike and rough as the description may have been. What had it to do with love? No more than it had in the beginning. And yet now, after all this time, it was occurring to Brian that indeed it did have something to do with love, that without its consideration love somehow was tainted. So the first step had to have been cold and cutting, had to be endured until there was no longer the capacity to register pain.

'You might wonder why you have had such incredible luck,' Bork felt compelled to say.

'I wonder about nothing.'

'The fact is, Munich is my usual station, as a guardian of the nation's security. I am in Munich most of the time, unfortunately for you. Though I still have a suitcase in Berlin, as I am sure you have also. . . . You know how the song goes, of course.'

She said nothing, walked along as if he weren't there, the people, the lights, the noise like a wall around her. 'Whatever drew you to *Oktoberfest*,' he went on, 'led you right to me—or at least greatly increased the chances of our running into each other. Just look around at the types one sees here and you'll get some idea of why we infiltrate. There are dozens of us everywhere. A lot of people from Schwabing need to be watched, you can bet. Spies and subversives posing as *Gammler*. But I see you're bored, so I won't go on. . . .'

'Thank you.'

'But you can't be alone, Mrs Fischer. Surely the brave and true American is somewhere around. Or have you two split up by now? Maybe you have another arrangement now with someone else, *Ja*?' He shrugged, did his nonchalant act, and added: 'Not that I mean to stick my nose in. . . .'

Still no response, none of the rise he so corruptly hoped for. 'But it's hard not to, considering the circumstances. I mean, you would have every reason to split up, if you take it one way. Then again, maybe not. I mean, maybe it didn't matter to you that he murdered your husband. Maybe you aren't split at all. Maybe you are still together. At least, up till now. After tonight, I doubt you will be together any longer.'

Her eyes swam because she immediately believed what she

was told, found no inner reason to reject it or to be outraged by the snake of a man who had told it to her. 'But, of course, you must have been aware of that after all this time,' Bork said with heavy mock surprise, searching her face like a monstrously solicitous friend. 'I can't believe you weren't.'

Had she always known? Just as she had always known about the count. 'You are lying,' she managed to say.

'Then you *didn't* know. How incredible.' He made a clicking sound of solicitude with his tongue and palate. 'I am so sorry, But yes, that is what happened. He killed your husband. . . .' He lowered his voice just enough to balance all the surrounding noise, the clamour and discord, a nearby pneumatic organ pumping out a French love song for the merry-go-round riders. 'I didn't see it, but I assure you it happened. I can't believe you didn't know. I mean . . . a woman being that close . . . not ever suspecting. Or was your relationship platonic, as they say?'

He continued to watch her for a moment or two longer with a curious lack of satisfaction. 'It must be a shock,' he then said with an extra bit of probing to bring the pain to life. 'I gather that he never said anything about it and was—well—being intimate with you and all the time knowing that he killed your husband. Or was he perhaps not intimate with you?'

She made a sudden move and he blocked her. 'Don't be a fool, Frau Fischer. . . .'

'Then be silent, do you hear?' she demanded in a strangled voice, piercing and desperate, her eyes enraged and contemptuous. 'If you don't wish to attract attention, don't say another word to me, just take me wherever you must.'

She had a way of defeating him, first in Berlin that morning and now here, a way of separating herself from him as if he were trash. He smiled unconvincingly, his urge to malice bottomless. He contented himself with her obvious unhappiness and hopeless plight. 'Let's go,' he said.

Somewhere in the core of her she was weeping; somewhere behind the gaze of now steady eyes a wound had begun to throb. She had loved him unsparingly. He had come to her, harbouring the secret while penetrating her body and her spirit. But with what motive?

'My car is in the park,' Bork said as they approached the countless rows of vehicles after several minutes of silence, the crowds thinning out at this point.

In a moment or two they had entered the car park, Bork guiding her in the direction he wished. 'Right here,' he said, and they turned into one of the clearance aisles. 'Do you remember that morning so long ago, Mrs Fischer, when we first met? I guess you do, You looked at me as if I were some kind of inferior. . . .' He simply couldn't let it alone. But she didn't care. 'It doesn't pay to act that high and mighty, because you never know when somebody will have power over you.'

A small black-and-white mongrel with one blue eye and one brown one whimpered, then barked 'happily' as he saw his master's approach to the car in which he was locked up. He bounded gleefully around in the back seat and then stood up, leaned on the window to look through. He had an appealingly stupid face. 'My dog, Schnapsi,' Bork told Adele.

He said no more.

Colman had discovered Schnapsi's presence five minutes before and was waiting for the master's return also, just two slots away; and he greeted Bork with a smashing right hand to the somewhat underdeveloped jaw. It was a quick, paralysing punch, the sound of the blow a terrible thud. He didn't hate Bork; but he found punching him easy enough.

Adele gave a startled cry as it happened. Colman caught Bork before he could fall to the ground and gently lowered him. Bork was out cold.

'Brian, I didn't want you to do this,' she said in a choked voice, back from the dead against her will.

'I can't live without you,' he said. 'I couldn't even try. Don't you see? Hurry. Let's get out of here, Please. . . .'

She swayed a little and now resisted the tug of his hand. 'What is it?' he asked.

'Nothing,' she answered quickly, because she couldn't have said anything else.

Part Four

CHAPTER ONE

'YOU'VE GOT TO BE WILLING to guarantee that you will lay off Mrs Fischer and that she will be treated decently,' Colman said. 'Do that and you'll get Mankin back from the East Germans. But you've got to take a chance—be trusting and kind. It will make you feel good in the long run.'

'Thanks for the analysis, Brian,' Stevenson said. 'Even though I didn't ask for it.'

'I think I can do it. I *want* to do it, what's more, because I owe it to Mankin. But not without the terms.'

'There's still a little man inside who tells you what to do, eh, Brian? But only up to a point. She gave you the air but you're still on the hook. You're different, Brian, no two ways about it, you're different.'

'You don't want to be analysed, so don't analyse me,' Colman said.

But Stevenson went right ahead. 'I'm only saying I know the terrific shock she must have had when she found out. But here you are. And where is she?'

'Where I left her and that's where she will stay.'

'She threw you out, gave you your papers, and I'm not saying she was wrong. But she didn't stick when she knew the truth. It looks to me as if all the obligations have been discharged. . . .'

'You're talking about something you know nothing about,' Colman said icily. 'She didn't throw me out, she doesn't make scenes, she's not second-rate.' There was just a decibel of emotion in his voice. 'She didn't do anything at all. Not anything. She didn't do or say a thing. Maybe you'd have stayed around to explain.' He shook his head. 'I just left her with a few instructions and the money to carry them out.'

'And she didn't stop you. It's the same thing. What more do you owe her? Look; what I'm getting at is simple. The intelligent and relatively painless thing to do would be to give Mrs Fischer back to them. I mean now that you're through with each other. I am not talking about coercion or force, Brian, but consultation. Maybe the idea would appeal to her.'

'What could be more appealing than Colonel Emmering and life in the DDR?'

Stevenson looked at Colman, the two of them on opposite sides of the room of the second-class hotel up in Wedding. One of Colman's people ran the place and it was what was called a safe house. That particular morning, a mild early-autumn day, had been about to melt without distinction into so many which had preceded it during a long, disappointing summer. Stevenson's mind was tired and impatient and he felt as if he were being held in a tight grip—not painful, but oppressive and very boring to suffer. The phone on his desk had rung towards noon and the tight grip seemed to grow slack with the sound of Colman's voice, a ghost cast upon the shore from the watery grave of a long-ago war. He had had no handshake for Colman, merely a look of truce. Colman didn't seem changed after all these months; he looked at you with that same unshockable, tough West Point expression on his face. Stevenson had trusted it once before and was only partially ready to trust it again. Colman stood with his back to the window, watching Stevenson moving around now, in a place that had been of Colman's choosing, looking things over like a fire inspector. 'You may be a genius, Brian,' he said. 'It has scope, imagination, and daring. And it could get you killed.'

'I don't think so.'

'It all hinges on a chance remark made by a man who might have said anything to save his skin at that moment.'

'Mankin is not in Emmering's normal area of concern. Yet he was able to promise to give Mankin back to us. How else if not through pressure?'

'Okay. Strong probability is a point of law, as a matter of fact,' Stevenson said. 'But I haven't the authority to send you into the DDR anyway.'

'Who the hell is asking you? Just take the heat off Mrs

Fischer. I'll do the rest if you will tell everybody to co-operate with me. Whatever happens after that, you didn't know a damned thing about. All right?'

'I would make a last appeal to your sanity, but you haven't any. You have guts. And you even have brains. But not sanity. You want to do the kind of thing that went out with Ben Lyon and Bebe Daniels. For a woman you can't even call your own.'

Colman looked at him and said, 'You actually would *prefer* to do it the dirty way, wouldn't you?'

'I call it the foolproof, bloodless way,' Stevenson answered. 'But you don't want that. So I could tell you to write to your Congressman and there wouldn't be a thing you could do to make me promise you anything.'

'Your keen mind is failing you.'

'No, it's not. You'll go in now anyway. No matter what. You'd be lost if you didn't. Because that's the kind you are. You can't walk away or sit it out. It would wake you up in the middle of the night after a while. No woman, no deal, no Mankin, just limbo and a very inconvenient conscience. I don't really need to promise you anything. All I have to say, out of sheer goodness, is get him out and she's home safe. She can come out into the sunshine. But first get him out.'

Colman was standing in the centre of the room, his hands jammed into his trouser pockets, his eyes on Stevenson. Stevenson was ultimately the best judge of character in the world, and it was astonishing that he had as many problems as he had. He read people as easily as one reads headlines; and he was ruthless, whether it pained him to be or not. 'You would be surprised if you turned out to be wrong,' Colman said feebly.

'Yes, indeed,' Stevenson said amiably. 'But I'm not.'

'You could use someone else if you wanted to.'

'I wouldn't. That would mean I was initiating it. That's out. Besides, it would be like tight shoes for another agent; second-hand. You've thought about it and felt it. You might even carry it off.' He stopped, then resumed. 'You'll do it, Brian, you'll have to. . . .'

'Have you ever heard voices or seen things that weren't there, M.J.?' Colman asked mildly.

'Often, quite often. And so have you. That's why you got this idea. That's why you've got to carry it out. I might not have thought so until now. But now I see the two profiles, Brian. You feel responsible for Mankin. You don't like that. You don't like owing anything to anyone in the world. It's your disease. I should have realized that sooner or later Mankin would have caught up to you. The clue to it was that you had never even laid *eyes* on Mrs Fischer when her widowhood began to eat at you. . . .'

Colman saw the surgical nature of Stevenson's thinking. He didn't feel resistant or resentful. His willingness had increased, if anything, as Stevenson's cranky analysis ensued. He knew all the reasons why, all the dangling ends that needed tying off.

'I wouldn't want to hand her back—I never did,' Stevenson said. 'But I'd be crazy to close out that option with any unwarranted promises. So get him out and it's in the bag.' Stevenson had been straining to hear and see everything for so long that he had begun to perceive things like a cat or a dog, even before they happened. And sometimes he would make something come true by attaching to it a belatedly discovered likelihood. And as he had described Colman's motivations, Colman recognized them as he never had before. 'And yet it's too much of a gem, Brian, and that's what scares me,' the indomitable and seasoned little man mused. 'Too shot full of ironies and jokes.'

'It's better than tying bed sheets together,' Colman said.

'It's so good . . . it shouldn't really work.'

Colman smiled, narrow-eyed and sly. 'Hope that it does, M. J. Because if I abort trying to spring Mankin, he's going to take on importance he never had up till then, and that would be the end of it. It will make him non-negotiable. You wouldn't be able to trade Adele even if you had your hands on her when it came to that point. That just this very minute popped into my head,' he said with obvious satisfaction. 'You haven't any terms to give. . . .'

'Academic, Brian. Theoretical,' Stevenson said, even as he suddenly saw the same possibility.

'One particular man is sitting in an East German prison as a suspected spy,' Colman expounded further. 'Nobody knows what he's worth because they have nothing concrete to go on. But then this breakout is staged—or attempted. It fails. The man is still in custody. The other guy—me, that is—is either dead or in the jug also.' He stopped, took the proper pause, and continued: 'Now, can you imagine anyone over there having enough strength or nerve to barter agent A for anyone less important than the head of our cryptography section? Or maybe Richard Helms? You bet you can't, M.J., not without a gun to his head. It's win or lose with me, M.J.' A thin, faded smile lingered as he talked.

Colman was either right or wrong, so what was the point of hitting it back and forth? 'If you're right, Brian, we really didn't need to have this conversation,' Stevenson said, 'except to find out that we didn't need to have it.'

'Just reinstate me. There wasn't really any more to say than that.'

Stevenson nodded. What the hell? This was better by far than things had been up till now. 'Just one thing, Brian,' he said. 'We never had this talk.'

'What talk?' Colman asked.

Stevenson walked out without another word and went back to Rose Bowl, where he washed some of his parched thoughts down with two fingers of Scotch from the bottle that had been in his desk drawer for three years.

Colman made his various arrangements at the house in Zehlendorf where the research and analysis and the crypto-graphic departments took up three entire storeys of a pilastered rectangle bordered by lawn and numerous trees. He talked to the people he considered necessary to his plans, ordered the things he needed, and then returned to his room. He had dinner, went to bed early, lay in the dark, and thought about Adele. He couldn't help it, of course. The control one has over one's mind is tenuous; there is no thought, once entertained, that cannot recur, no former lover who can be prevented from re-entry, no yearning kept out permanently.

He fell asleep shortly and then awakened to a sleepless hour or two. He turned on his lights, read an American paperback edition of *My Silent War* by Kim Philby, and finally fell asleep again. He awakened twice more before he finally sank into a consecutive four hours that was broken by the phone ringing on the table next to the bed. It was eight o'clock. A voice said, 'Brian, get over here right away.'

In twenty-five minutes Colman had reached Rose Bowl. Stevenson was at his desk and Brannigan was standing next to it when Colman entered the office.

'Brian, we're going to cancel your mission,' Stevenson said. 'Mrs Fischer turned herself in to us early this morning and has requested that we return her to East Berlin immediately. And you might have known she would.'

CHAPTER TWO

'YOU'RE NOT CANCELLING ANYTHING,' Colman said coldly, meeting Brannigan's calm, critical stare. Adele's action meant nothing to him. It wasn't love, it was a gesture of indifference, of exhaustion and disinterest. It would wipe him out and he couldn't let it. 'If you try,' he said, his voice level but seething, 'I'll see that it goes into every ear I can find starting with your various friends upstairs. What you're doing doesn't exactly thrive on publicity. And there are plenty of people who would be happy to scalp you on general principles. So you're not cancelling anything.'

'It's her own choice, Brian,' Stevenson said like the world's most reasonable man. 'No one is being cruel or inhuman.'

'That's fine,' Colman said. 'All she has to do is walk up to any checkpoint and announce herself.'

'What we should have done,' Brannigan suggested, 'was made the exchange fast, not said anything to you until it was over.'

'You might not have succeeded before I was on my way into the Zone,' Colman pointed out.

'So we'd have lost you,' Brannigan said philosophically.

'I like your honesty, Red.'

Brannigan was quietly very angry with Colman. 'I'm a realist. You're a dead loss, Brian. And now you may put us in the toilet for good.'

218

'Here's a chance to extend your lifeline, Brian,' Stevenson said. 'And you won't take it. Okay, let me give you my opinion. Mrs Fischer wants to go back because that disassociates her from you, from ever having known you or been anything to you. It does something towards wiping out the time she spent with you. Call it an attempt at self-induced loss of memory. She's looking for yesterday, bad as it may have been. Be a good friend and don't get in her way.'

'Thanks, M.J.'

'She had that hollow, half-dead, end-of-the-line look in her eyes. Just like the day I first talked to her in Moabit,' Stevenson said and then turned towards Brannigan. 'You could see that, couldn't you, Red?'

'I saw it,' Brannigan said with a baleful look at Colman. 'She doesn't want any favours from you.'

'She wants to forget your very name, I'd say,' Stevenson went on, a doctor diagnosing a bad illness as gently as he could but as forthrightly as necessary. 'And going back to the DDR seems to be her way of doing it. If we don't convey her, she will convey herself.'

'In other words,' Brannigan said in an even, vengeful voice, 'she wants to go back whether you live or die. Get it?'

'Yeah, I got it. And, as they say in court—motion denied. So you may as well release her right now. Unless you want to find out how knives feel as they're going in.'

Joe Fox was waiting for him in front of Europa Centre, and they walked into the courtyard with the ice-skating rink, legions of faces everywhere, people of all kinds moving in every direction, at all sorts of tempos. There was traffic in and out of the various shops, the sound of voices like a continuing hum easily submerged. They strolled side by side around the perimeter of the rink along the colonnade, past the fronts of the arcaded shops, skate blades slicing into the icy surfaces. Fox's aloofness was immediately apparent, his manner that of the faceless contact who is being seen for the first time. He listened with undivided attention, his eyes only once or twice on Colman's face. He didn't have to look, only to hear the words that were being spoken. He gave Colman an assuring professional nod of understanding when the explanation was completed.

'Not too complicated,' Colman finished off. 'But I promise you it will be interesting.'

'Gee, that's swell,' Fox said tonelessly. 'I was afraid maybe it wasn't going to be a lot of fun. I might not have wanted to do it then.'

'What's eating you, Joe?'

They stopped walking, found themselves standing at the guardrail bordering the ice. Fox stared into Colman's eyes. 'Remember how you felt about Stebbins?' he said. 'No mercy, not an inch. His conscience didn't mean a goddamned thing to you, and you were dead right.'

'You think I'm the same thing, is that it?'

'Not at first. But then I started to see what it was, Brian. I'm not the deep type, but I saw that you could rap one guy's conscience because what was bothering him wasn't bothering you. And then all of a sudden it was you who were making the choices because you had a private cause of your own. And now you're back, nice and neat, and just as if nothing ever happened. But tomorrow you might find that something else is eating into your guts and maybe I'll be the one to go. See what I mean, Brian?' This was a coldly caustic Joe Fox that Colman hadn't known before.

'You don't trust me,' Colman said.

'We could have had Mankin out of East Berlin long ago,' Fox explained. 'Why is he still there, if not for you?'

'That's right. I didn't think of it that way at the time, but I do now.'

'You think saying it makes you look different to me?'

'Joe . . . do you want to wash out? Anybody else can handle the job. No hard feelings, just let me know.'

'No, I'll stick with it. The odds are very good. Nothing can happen to me, no matter what.' He added, 'Okay. You asked what's eating me. Now you've got it.'

'I'm paying it off, wouldn't you say?' Colman said mildly.

'Yes, you've seen the light or something, Brian. But in a real squeeze——' He shook his head. 'I would never count on you. You might want to do the right thing. But if a dame came along—even a real lady—I might have to go down the tube. And even for a real lady, I wouldn't want that to happen.'

Colman smiled with genuine regret, his mouth a sad line. 'Think it could never happen to you, Joe?' he asked.

'I'm not that big an ass. Maybe it could. But I don't think so. And if it did, I'd be the same as you, and some other agent could look at me and say the same thing. Except they usually don't get second chances, do they? You're a star attraction, in a way.'

'I'll get Mankin out, and I won't leave any dangling ends. So don't feel too sour about me.'

'What I can't understand is this business about Mrs Fischer,' Fox said, as if criticizing the conduct of a professional operation. 'I've poked around and I know a deal could still be made for her for whatever the goddamned reason. And I can figure out that somehow you're the one who's blocking it.'

Colman was facing the skaters, vaguely admiring the configurations of a man and a woman gliding in blissful unison on the ice. 'I had you all wrong, Joe,' he said. 'I wasn't sure you would work out as an agent. I detected a soft centre—I thought I did anyhow. But if it's there, you've got it well under control. And that's a professional opinion.'

Fox nodded, said, 'Thanks,' and then walked away.

It would have been unseemly to act defensively. Fox had every reason to feel as he did. It was when Colman was back in that world of men doing a tough job together, men who were counting on each other, that he most felt uneasy and punished, all with unquestionable justice. Maybe even Mankin would feel the same way Fox did if he were to know about everything, the act of courage, the effort to make things right at any cost notwithstanding. It was a matter of trust. There was no arguing with it. Except that you never knew until the particular weakness came to light. What he had not done under the touch of Captain Chong's cigarette ends he had done at the touch of a hand. And now the hand was gone. All he had left was Mankin. And that was what he wanted. But it made him feel like a man with a deformity in the grey mood to which such a person must constantly awaken every morning. It wouldn't go away, and you never got used to it.

All his other preparations were completed that afternoon, the various confirmations made, and the next morning Colman went to the airport and waited in the international section for the announcement of his flight.

Holiday traffic had obviously lessened in volume, the crescendo of midsummer noticeably modified. He just sat there. What would happen afterwards he didn't know or care —he didn't want to toy with future possibilities. He had no guidelines left. He could see only as far as the next few days and he thought about what was required of him when he went against the bad guys. He wondered how quickly the bad guys would respond to him. Would the thing work? He wondered about a lot of things. He made a conscious effort to stay with his immediate purpose. It was not easy. He glanced at his watch. A few minutes to go.

He looked up and saw Adele coming towards him across the spacious waiting area, a figure among many but as isolated as the prima ballerina followed magically by that heavenly cone of light coming from nowhere.

CHAPTER THREE

IT WAS LIKE seeing a woman you had made love to when you were very young, intimacy thinned out by time and events —three full days, in this instance, as vast as years of separation. It took a moment to overcome this, but just that long. She was the same, a bit thinner, that was all; her beauty somewhat sharpened, her eyes quicker at the moment. They both now knew something that only one of them had known before. 'I was afraid you'd be gone,' she said. 'I gave myself over to them, but they released me.'

'And you came here? For me?'

'I would go anywhere for you.'

'Even back to the other side?'

'If I couldn't be with you.'

'How did you know I was here?'

'Your friend—the blond one.'

'Joe Fox?' Colman said with mild surprise.

'He said you might be here if only I could get here in time.

222

He said it wouldn't do any harm—if I wanted to see you for any reason, he said. Yes, I can think of a few. . . .'

'Can you?' he said quietly, the sight of her having changed the entire world for him. 'I'm glad. I'm so glad, I don't know what to say or do. . . . I thought something completely the opposite.'

'It was an accident, wasn't it?' she pleaded as if she were intentionally giving away an answer within the context of a question, like a lawyer leading a witness. 'I know it was, so how can I condemn both of us for that? Not that I was ever doing that. But it *was* an accident, wasn't it? Tell me that you fought, you struggled, and the gun went off. It was a gun, wasn't it?'

'What if it wasn't that way? What if I had done it because I thought I had the right?' he said in a grim, urgent whisper.

'Then you'd have regretted it. That's the way you are, darling.'

'If I said I regretted it, I'd be lying. Can you take that?'

Her fondest hopes fell apart, her face went slack. 'What right would I have not to?' she said. 'I said to myself again and again, if only it hadn't happened, if only it hadn't happened. But I couldn't turn away from you, whether you had killed or not,' she said, revealing a horrifying secret, her voice deepened by the gravity of what she was saying, her eyes finally opened to what she really was. 'And that was when I found out about myself. I was sorry for Martin's death, yes, and sorry you had been the one to cause it. But the truth was I was glad, so glad in my heart that it had not been you who died. I suppose I knew that instantly. And maybe that was what appalled me— so that I couldn't say anything to you. I suppose I had shocked myself. Yes, poor Martin. But the truth was it mattered less than being without you did. That was where the real pain was. Not that you had killed Martin. You were gone and that was what hurt. How could I come to terms with that? How could I admit such a thing? How could I face even you with that? I knew you had walked away without a word of defence or explanation because you were so certain that I would be right-fully shocked and repelled. But I wasn't—not in the way you thought. And that's me as I am, darling. Like everyone else— living one lie or another. . . .'

'But you were ready to go back to the Zone,' he pointed out. 'You're not too consistent, are you?'

'What else was there to do?' she said with a shrug. 'It was the only way I had a chance of finding you. And it worked. Even if only for these few priceless seconds together.' She smiled and the mere act seemed to bring incipient tears.

'You came that close to going back. And you wouldn't have seen me. If they had been a little less old and weary, they'd have taken your offer and I couldn't have done a thing to stop it. All I had were hollow threats, believe me.'

'Then at least you wouldn't need to do this mad thing.'

'It's not mad.'

She looked at him. 'I think I would stop at nothing to hold you back,' she said.

'You've lost weight,' he said. She flexed her lips tightly in a quick, synthetic smile, obviously not interested in such trivia. And looking into her eyes, he said, 'There has never been a less risky mission, really. I'm going in well prepared. . . .'

'Yes, I know. . . .'

'There's no other way.'

'People have said that so often,' she said. 'It's as true as one wants to make it.'

'His freedom and ours are inseparable, sweetheart. I owe him something. If I want you, there's a price to pay—a small one at that.'

'Oh, Brian, you damned fool,' she said with impatience he had never seen before. 'You bloody, damned fool. . . .'

'If that makes you feel better, okay. Maybe I am. . . .'

The Zurich flight announcement brought him to his feet, and he took her with him. 'Go to the Sperbisher Hof in Wedding and tell them that McNeil sent you,' he told her. 'Wait there. It's not fancy, but it's clean and safe.'

He kissed her and walked away with the attaché case that so many oddly motivated people carried these days. She stood still, speechless, left behind, an ambivalent look of goodbye caught fleetingly in her eyes. It was as if everything had come about suddenly and as a complete surprise. She kept watching his departing figure until it had vanished somewhere on the tarmac outside the building.

He sat on the plane and found himself recalling their moments of passion. But the recollection shortly began to be a burden and he had to cast it aside as quickly as he could and proceed to the bleak experience ahead of him. For the first time he knew that he actually wished that there *had* been some other way. There wasn't; and nothing could be changed now.

'Coffee, bitte?' the stewardess said.

He looked away from the window and said, 'Nein, danke.' And then sat there waiting for the touchdown at the Kloten airport.

CHAPTER FOUR

THE SHOP OF SACHS HARQUIST, narrow and neat, was not far from the river in a row of glittering windows and polished brass name plaques. Busy Swiss passed back and forth on the sidewalks, and cars and bicycles wended here and there like fish in a stream. Watches, rings, pendants, and bracelets coldly discriminated from their cushions and cases under glass. Harquist, about forty, slick-haired and long-faced, was one of those people who always seems on the verge of a sneer or faintly conscious of a bad smell. It made him autocratic and disdainful on first glance. Colman sat on the opposite side of a display counter from the jeweller, examining two or three wristwatches just like any other prospective buyer. They were twenty-one-jewel, ultraprecision, and the feel of each of them was tempting, their faces almost seductive as the pencil-line second hands broke their endless journeys with barely perceptible, perfectly spaced little beats. 'Webber was ready to sell you out when we caught him,' Colman was saying matter-of-factly. 'He tried to bribe me to let him get away. When that didn't work, he offered to come over to us.'

'That was poor psychology,' Harquist said, unrushed and possibly unconvinced. 'It should have been the other way round.'

'That was when he told me you were his HVA contact. We

were alone. No one else heard it. Later on when he tried to get away, someone shot him.'

'And here you are.'

'That's right.'

'Quite a lot left out in between, isn't there?'

'I'm just offering certain things for sale. They can be judged for themselves. Here. On neutral ground. I don't need to go over there and they don't need to come into the Federal Republic. That was the way Webber handled everything—I know because he told me—and that is the way I want to handle everything also.'

'Yes, but why? Just profiteering or is it something else?'

'What's the difference?'

'I do my little bit for them, as a matter of fact, because I wish them luck,' Harquist said somewhat superciliously.

'Are you telling me you work for them out of conviction?' Colman said, examining a watch in the palm of his hand.

'Well, certainly not for the kind of money it pays.'

'Very interesting.'

'I came from Leipzig while one still could, because I couldn't stand the life. It was too much for me. My conscience bothers me less now.' He smiled. 'I'm not a Socialist type, but I think they may have the right idea.'

'They'll pay plenty for what I've got.'

'Careful with that watch.'

Another customer came into the shop and Colman sat by himself for fifteen minutes while Harquist sold a small diamond ring to a man who looked like a car mechanic in his dress-up suit. Then he was back with Colman. 'Where can I reach you?'

Colman gave him the name of the hotel along the Bahnhofstrasse and then left the shop.

He sat that evening in the crowded hotel dining room, the chandeliers hanging like giant crystal fruits, a wall of mirrored panels enlarging everything. The dinner cart pushed by one of the waitresses came to his table and he had veal and egg rolls. A glass of white wine accompanied the meal. Two stock-exchange types shared the table with him, one of them reading the *Neue Zürcher Zeitung* even after his food had arrived, the newspaper folded into quarters and propped against the mirrored wall to his left. Colman took passing note of the man's absorption with the commerce of a society Colman had been engaged in trying to protect for so long, capitalist-imperialist henchman that he was. In the mirror Colman could see Joe Fox seated about ten tables away, enjoying his dinner in the company of three total strangers. It was Colman's first glimpse of him since Berlin. They met in Fox's room shortly thereafter.

'Did it go all right?' Fox said.

'They'll contact me, but I don't know how. Maybe tonight. Maybe tomorrow. But I may not have a chance to tip you off, so you're going to have to be watching pretty carefully. You're going to have to haunt that lobby.'

'When?'

'From the minute I leave you and go back to my room until at least one a.m.'

'If they come after that, what?'

'I'll be able to call you from my room at such a late hour before I let them in—that is, assuming someone comes directly to my door.'

'Good enough.'

'But stay in the lobby until one.'

'Okay.'

'Oh, and thanks, by the way.'

Fox wasn't being altogether open about anything yet. 'They had her out in Zehlendorf and I saw her when they told her she could go,' he said as if it was a trivial matter. 'I just asked her if she would be interested in talking to you for any reason . . . I figured you for the morning flight.' He shrugged. 'It's none of my business.'

Colman wanted nothing more of it; Fox had casually, and for murky reasons, played God. 'I'll talk to you later,' he said.

'Where can she be reached right now, by the way?'

Colman stopped in his tracks. 'Who?'

'Mrs Fischer.'

Colman frowned. 'Why?'

'Just on the off chance that something happens to you. . . . Who is going to tell her?'

Colman didn't answer immediately. He didn't like the suggestion. 'Thanks, Joe. She's at the Sperbisher Hof,' he said.

'In Wedding.'

'Yeah.' Killing time was the next step in the proceedings.

Harquist telephoned Colman the next afternoon from the hotel lobby and said, 'Mr McNeil, I am downstairs and I have the shockproof dynamic we discussed—with the alarm and the silver trim. Could you perhaps join me for a few minutes and I can show it to you?'

Joe Fox watched them from a chair against the glass-panelled hotel front next to the revolving door, the street visible behind him. Colman examined the watch and listened while Harquist said, 'We will sit here for a moment or two and then walk out together, and I shall leave you at the appointed time and place.'

Their destination then took them past the façades of the great banking houses, the elaborate displays of capitalist goods and various enticements common to affluence in the windows of the dazzling shops, an ocean of temptation surrounding them. 'Do you think all of this luxury is really of value to the human soul?' Harquist said. 'All of this opulence?'

'You seem to be at home with it,' Colman said, faintly impolite.

'Ah, yes. I fear so. I can't resist living in an atmosphere like this. But I question it. Other people are starving all over the world. Yet I can't resist.'

'Don't even try. I won't say a word to anyone.'

'Shall I tell you something? They have the right idea on the other side. Oh, they do it badly. But luxury corrodes the soul. The same way passion for a beautiful, heartless, and cruel prostitute does. Do you understand what I mean?'

'You may be right.'

'Socialism is an absolute necessity. It must come. It *should* come. But I know I shall despise it when it does. That is quite a dilemma, isn't it?'

'I guess it is. But, frankly, I would rather talk about where we are going and who will be there.'

'You will see.'

'I won't deal with anyone but *the* man—that didn't slip your mind, did it?'

Harquist looked at him with sidelong hauteur. 'That was

perfectly understood. Do you think I am someone who would trick you?' he asked.

'I think you are someone who is a very odd bird,' Colman said.

Harquist didn't reply and they continued in silence until they reached the train station, walked through the building, and proceeded to the garden of the National Museum across the street. The trees and flowers and little paths made very pleasant surroundings and the light was still quite bright in an off-blue sky.

Colman and Harquist stopped at a tree next to a bench. 'Just wait right here,' Harquist said. 'Not very long, so be patient. Oh, yes. You forgot to return the wristwatch. . . .'

His hand was out and Colman, having absently deposited it in his pocket, returned it with disinterest. Harquist smiled and walked away as if he had somehow exposed a case of capitalist corruption. Colman took a deep breath and sat down.

Only seconds later he saw the approach of Western Operations Chief Main Department II, Colonel Gerhard Trauner. Fat, hardly unobtrusive, but coldly confident, and coming directly towards Colman, handling his bulk with strange grace.

CHAPTER FIVE

THEY SAT SIDE BY SIDE, Trauner wearing a dark-brown summer suit made of a very un-Socialistic-looking shantung, his manner that of an impresario granting time to someone who wanted to better himself. 'Before you say anything else,' he instructed, 'I want to know who you are and why you have contacted us.'

'How would you know if I'm telling the truth?' Colman said.

'I may not. But I'll know something about the turn of your mind even if you are lying. What do you claim to be, in other words? A mercenary or someone who has discovered the virtues of Socialism?'

Colman saw that this adulterated-looking man spoke in

earnest. 'From the looks of that suit you're wearing I'd say things are picking up in the Socialist camp.'

'This is a DDR-manufactured garment, as it happens. But, please, don't be facetious.'

'You didn't ask a very sensible question.'

'Shall I rephrase it? All right. What proof do you have that you're not here to plant false information or in some way to discredit us?'

'None. And you must have guessed as much from what the jeweller told you. So why did you come?'

'Because I was frankly curious to see who it was that killed Martin Fischer—or Webber, as you may call him—and perhaps find out why.'

Colman grew stony and his face went blank.

'You did kill him, didn't you?' Trauner said.

'I've already said I would answer only sensible questions,' Colman said flatly.

'You didn't say that. And I suppose you won't answer, even though it would be easy to lie. Because *you* know and *I* know that too much evidence points to it. The mere fact that you've gone to this trouble underlines the distinct possibility. You killed him on order and we both know who gave the order and now is trying clumsily to involve me in some stupidly elaborate intrigue for reasons best known to himself.' Trauner never raised his voice and his eyes remained still.

'Go on. I'm spellbound.'

'Are you really? Then let me ask you why you should think that I, personally, am the only one you could talk to about anything as trivial as a list of old names, most of which we already know about and whose locations aren't even reliable any longer and the remainder of only minor significance at best?'

'Because, my dear Colonel, it is not about that at all,' Colman said. 'What I really have is of value only to you. It answers every question of importance you could conceivably ask. It is nothing you would want me to turn over to anyone else. I had to tell Mr Harquist something he could handle, you'll agree, I'm sure. . . .' Colman shrugged. 'I thought you'd come anyway. I thought the mere mention of Webber's name would get you here. You have nothing to lose, no risk, it's neutral territory. Of course, I didn't anticipate that you would come at me with all that wild business about murder plots and the rest of it.'

Trauner was caught but was a careful predator and revealed nothing save moderate interest indicated by his suddenly avid silence. Colman waited for a reaction, got none, and said, 'But I know who you're referring to, as a matter of fact.'

Trauner waited, skilled and experienced. Colman picked up a pebble, jiggled it around in a loosely closed fist, and then tossed it into the grass. 'There happens to exist,' he began, 'information and documented evidence about a certain Colonel Ernst Emmering . . . that could ruin him. . . .'

Trauner continued to listen, and Colman looked at him and said, 'What would such material be worth to you, Colonel?'

'What makes you think that such a thing would interest me?' Trauner said, a little too indifferently.

'Whenever you have internal security side by side with an espionage organization you have people who cannot get along too well—under the best of circumstances, whose toes have been stepped on, who might even hate each other's guts.' A pause and then: 'It's the natural law of departmental conflict.'

'Is it?'

'I see I haven't shocked you too much.'

'Go on.'

Colman nodded. 'Two: I assume that you would consider it a duty to expose the sort of thing I'm referring to. . . .'

'What exactly *is* it you're referring to?'

'Things.'

'Photographs? Documents? What?'

'Maybe both. Enough to destroy Emmering if one were interested. . . .'

Trauner shrugged his massive shoulders as if they amounted to nothing. 'One is always interested. In duty.'

'How interested?'

'Quite.'

'How?'

'Don't be silly. You don't put it on a scale to see how much it weighs.'

231

'Sure you do.'

'Ah, yes. . . .'

'It would cost money.'

'I assumed.'

'Not an inconsiderable amount, Colonel.'

Trauner shrugged again, waited, was obstinately shrewd and reserved.

'Do you want the figure?' Colman asked.

'Why not?' Trauner replied, not yet more than audience to a somewhat interesting anecdote.

'Ten thousand dollars—cash. Half in advance. Also two American passports.'

Trauner shook his head with a puckered smile. 'You don't come cheap, do you?'

'Do you think it should—a chance to destroy an enemy who might destroy you otherwise? Perhaps your *only* chance. . . .'

'You assume a great deal,' Trauner said, shifting his weight a bit and removing from his pocket a nasal inhalator which he proceeded to use quickly and noisily and then put away. 'Pollens. They are rather dense suddenly.'

'What have I assumed, Colonel?'

'Colonel Emmering and I are professional men. It took some time for all of us in the German Democratic Republic to learn because we were not trained managers. Only the Nazis knew how to make things work, you see, and we were Socialists, very young and learning from our elders, who also had limited experience in running government departments. But we have finally reached a level of efficiency not far behind anyone's. And Colonel Emmering and I *are* professionals, and our primary concern is in loyalty and service to the state. We understand each other. We're collectivists and personal animosities don't get very far.' He spoke, never forgetful of Emmering's pressures and intimidations and blackmail.

Perhaps it showed despite his best efforts, and Colman said, 'Now why, Colonel, does that sound like bullshit to me? . . . Could it be because I know better, because I have it from no less an authority on the subject than Webber—Martin Fischer, that is?' He added, 'You even started out by accusing me of being under Emmering's orders.'

232

'I mentioned no names.'

'Coyness doesn't become you, Colonel. Will you pay for what I'm selling—at my price and at my terms?'

'In theory.'

'Meaning?'

'Meaning I would certainly need to know more about it: I would have to have some indication of its worth.'

'Okay. Do you know that Emmering is a pervert, a thief, and a blackmailer, and that he has used his office for reasons of self-interest and various types of profit over and over again.'

Trauner, though still cool, rose to it. 'You can document that?'

'Are you aware of it?'

He snuffed a breath of air and said, 'I have never wished to believe such stories, of course. . . .'

'Then you don't believe it's true?'

'I didn't say that.'

'Here's your chance to strike a double blow—one for the German Democratic Republic and one for yourself.'

'Where is your evidence?'

'I'll present it to you at a prearranged time and place of your choosing—*if* you're willing to admit your interest in it.'

'I would have to know where it came from and how you secured it.'

'I promise to give you all of that with the evidence itself. There will be no doubts left in your mind about anything.'

Trauner gave it under five seconds of consideration and said, 'Done.'

'Where?'

'The Hotel Royal. Room two-oh-seven. When can you come?'

'Nine o'clock this evening, if that suits you.'

'That will do.'

'I will only have part of it with me, understand that,' Colman said, the show of caution like the necessary touch of garlic in a salad. 'If you want the whole thing with the conclusive evidence, you'll need to pay me half the money in advance.'

'I shall decide on that when I see what you have to offer.'

'There's one thing, Colonel. And this is absolutely crucial to the arrangement. Because if your answer is no, we can say good-bye right now.'

Colman looked into that abundant face now touched with incomprehension, the eyes waiting calmly enough.

'If what I have to offer,' Colman went on, 'is all I claim for it, in your judgement, and is strong enough to put Emmering where you want him . . .'

'Yes?'

'Will it make any difference to you if it all isn't absolutely . . . genuine?'

'You mean a forgery? False evidence?'

Colman raked his lower lip with his teeth and shook his head up and down deliberately to make sure there was no misunderstanding. 'That is exactly what I mean,' he said.

Trauner, his languid manner screening vast energy and drive, rose in a slow upward motion and with un-Germanic sangfroid, said, 'How dare you?' And stared with icy contempt at Colman.

'I take that to be a negative reply, Colonel,' Colman said like a professional who knew when he was licked.

'What do you take me for?' Trauner said.

'A man without sentiment, Colonel,' Colman said. 'That is, I did. . . .'

They stared at each other in silence for a moment or two and then Colman, defeated and acceptant, walked away from Trauner and stopped to stand next to a railing meant to block the unhampered passage of children through a small flower bed. He looked at the blossoms and thought of Adele. He tried not to think of her. Thoughts of her sapped him, diverted him almost as sexual relations did and were meant to do. But he had to think of something more appropriate now. He didn't know what his next move would be, but he had to have Trauner's full accord. It was the mortar without which there could be no building.

He felt Trauner's presence and he turned to face him so he could be sure he was not going to fall prey to some desperate and conclusive decision on the part of a man he may have been unwise to tamper with. Trauner's expression was unchanged. 'Bring what you have,' he said. 'I'll be waiting.'

Colman was insistent. 'Even if it's a frame-up?'

Trauner's hesitation was nominal. 'If it's good enough,' he granted, 'that won't matter.'

The fat East German intelligence officer marched away, the act done without strain or trepidation. After all, the only falsification existed in the mere presentation. The assertions were all undoubtedly well founded.

Colman couldn't visualize the same degree of ruthlessness on his own side: the Stevensons and the Llewellyns would never frame each other. Their ruthlessness took different forms, different directions. They would double-cross one another into perdition, ruin each other's lives to protect a position, to implement a scheme, but they would never consider forgeries and outright lies as weapons. And yet Trauner did not seem corrupt; only willing, perhaps for reasons of what he considered to be high principle, to use the devices and the means he had been brought up with. Colman was using devices and means, on the other hand, that he had *not* been brought up with, things that he had learned and was now willing to do. Not to the enemy as much as to himself. It looked as if it might be easy work but not one ounce of satisfaction derived from it. It was something to be got over and done with, never to be recalled or spoken of after that. Right now there was no place in his thinking for moralizing. He needed no justifications. He was a man as much without sentiment as he knew Colonel Trauner to be.

Joe Fox had sat in a rented VW on the quay angling along the north-east border of the park and somewhat beyond the museum itself. The straight line between his position and the place where Colman now stood was unbroken save for a few trees here and there. A few minutes later Colman waited across the street from the railroad station facing the front of the museum until Fox drove by and nodded to him. Then Colman walked through the station, with its clacking footfalls and expectant air, the luggage carts, the porters, the travellers, and back to the hotel. He gazed thoughtfully into space as he walked along, the word *Lindt* harmlessly attracting his attention, and he was uncomfortable suddenly with his relationship to Trauner. But comfort had nothing to do with it, had it?

Fox and Colman took their dinners together in the hotel dining room because caution was no longer necessary; whether or not Colman was the solitary figure he had pretended now didn't matter. 'When Fischer said they were at each other's throats, he knew what he was saying,' Colman declared, staring recollectively.

'What if he had never brought it up?' Fox wondered. 'If he hadn't gotten on to that subject you never would have known. None of this would be happening now.' He dipped into the fondue he had before him and ate it with relish. He used his napkin at the corners of his mouth and continued: 'He could have skipped it very easily and given you some other line. And, of course, he might not have run at all. What if he had used his head and hadn't made *that* suicidal move?'

Colman said nothing.

'That's what everything comes back to Brian—the fact that Fischer decided to take a chance and make a break for it. Everything that happened to you after that—the very reason we're sitting here right now. Did you ever stop to think about that? About what a weak thread things hang by?'

'Why stop there? Why not go back to what made Don Stebbins tick?'

'Because that had no direct bearing on it. Only when Fischer decided to run the complications set in. At least, that's the way I see it.'

Colman sat there and remembered that he had fired to save the names that Trauner now considered both trivial and obsolete.

'But what if it had been some other agent, not you, who went up there to meet Fischer?' Fox continued to speculate. 'And the same thing happened, let's assume. The aftermath might have been entirely different, Brian. In fact, it would have to be, if the laws of probability are taken into account.'

'How does anyone ever know? And anyhow, Joe, right now I don't care.'

Fox leaned in closer to the table, facing Colman. 'All right, Brian, let me put this one to you,' he said. 'What was it that really set you off? What's that mysterious thing that goes on inside that says, "I don't want this but I've got to have that"?'

'I don't think it's worth the trouble, Joe,' Colman said, sensing something he didn't want to go into. Maybe there was brandy or benedictine in the fondue.

'I got to see your friend Gerda after you left—by accident, at first, and then we went out together a few times.'

'What for?'

'Why not? I'll tell you frankly, she was really in a state about you. I found her drinking *Molle und Klaren* in one of the Hilton bars when I first ran into her. And that's not for girls who are light drinkers.'

'Why are you telling me all this?'

'Because was it that only Mrs Fischer's chemistry matched yours? Or could it have been any woman whose husband you'd have—done it to? I mean, why not Gerda? I've never seen anyone better-looking. She's smart and loyal. Why wasn't it her?'

'You're starting to sound fuzzy, Joe.'

Fox wasn't telling Colman everything, but it was easy enough to guess at. Fox hadn't attained what he was after, possibly didn't even know what precisely it was. Maybe he was remembering the mists of unrequited passion in Gerda's gaze. 'Okay,' he said. 'But one thing she told me, you might like to hear. She said that nothing ever happened between you, not even a kiss.'

Colman made a little gesture of faint appreciation.

'Did you ever hear of Young Werther?' Fox asked.

'Yes, I've heard,' Colman replied.

'And Frederick Barbarossa?'

'Yeah.'

'Well, when she talked about you she said it was as if Frederick Barbarossa had turned into Young Werther. That was the first I had heard of either of them.'

'Look, Joe. There's only one thing on my mind, so I'd appreciate it if you'd cut out all that shit right now,' Colman said. The last thing he wanted to get into was the labyrinthine world of Joe Fox's ideas on human behaviour and the "hots" he just possibly might have had for Gerda Hantzmann.

'Try not to be edgy, Brian.'

'I'll try, Joe.'

CHAPTER SIX

TRAUNER WAS STANDING and waiting in the middle of his hotel room when Colman arrived. He had his hand on a beautiful handwrought Czechoslovakian automatic in his jacket pocket as he said, 'Come in,' in answer to the knock at the door.

Colman looked at him guilelessly. Trauner behaved as though he were about to observe a vacuum-cleaner demonstration as Colman placed his attaché case on a table and said nothing. 'I assume that case contains the material,' Trauner said.

Colman nodded, said, 'This is it,' and unsnapped the lid. He then removed a small spool recorder, about six by eight, in a black plastic case and looked at Trauner. 'I'm going to switch this on and you can judge it for yourself.'

'I assumed as much.'

Colman pressed down the starter key and immediately Trauner's voice was heard saying:

'Bring what you have. I'll be waiting . . .' followed by Colman's voice saying:

'Even if it's a frame-up?' followed by Trauner's voice saying:

'If it's good enough, that won't matter. . . .'

Colman clicked off the machine and explained:

'I began at the end of the tape because—of everything on it, those three brief speeches are the most damaging to you, and cannot, in any circumstances, be explained away.' He pushed the rewind key, saying, 'We can listen from the beginning so you can fully appreciate just how potent the whole conversation is. . . .'

Trauner's equanimity was quickly out of the window as, with wild-eyed shock, he lunged like an enraged whale to pick up the compact machine, rip the tape spool from it, and dash the machine to the floor. In unsparing frenzy he then unreeled the tape and tore it and twisted it and flung pieces of it here and there. But he suddenly stopped what he was doing, as if shocked by himself more than anything else, the realization that he was achieving nothing corroborated by the way Colman was standing quietly off to one side, watching and waiting for

238

an end to the performance. Colman looked into the still-angered but sapient eyes and confirmed the unspoken thought. 'Yes, there's a copy,' he said.

He removed from his pocket a cube-size transmitter to which Trauner needed no introduction. 'You were talking into this,' Colman told him. 'A few hundred yards away, in a parked car, the tape was made and then put on a duplicating device.' He added: 'There is no *Schadenfreude* in this, Colonel. But if it gets into Emmering's hands, you are finished, from all I know of him. And I know quite a bit.'

It couldn't be denied. Trauner's willingness to collude in Emmering's downfall through the use of forged evidence, his manifest wish to destroy Emmering literally spoke for themselves. The threat was enormous, Colman's hold on him painful and easily wielded. The realization could be seen in Trauner's demeanour as he panted for breath more from emotion than exertion. 'My claims of efficiency and professionalism were obviously hollow boasts,' he said, guided by the principle of the necessity of self-reproach for errors.

'Not necessarily,' Colman said with inexpensive generosity. 'How could you even remotely have anticipated this? And you still can't know what it's all about.'

'I shall find out quickly enough, I imagine.'

'I want safe conduct in and out of the DDR under your personal protection and guarantee—something you can grant me with the snap of your fingers.'

Trauner actually didn't place the highest premium on personal safety, having lived underground in Frankfurt as a then-lean youth because he believed in Communism, as had his musician-father before him. But the idea of his revealed guilt in the proposed frame-up of a fellow Socialist, a *Genosse*, made him a bit sick. He said nothing and Colman went on:

'I could be one of your operators, an informant, or anything you want to make of me, and not a soul will question it. All I'll need is a few hours. Not more—just a few hours.'

'You can't seriously believe I would entertain such a preposterous idea.'

'But I do.' Colman gave him a tight, mirthless smile. 'Don't make me get tough. You know what the alternative is.'

'I could explain,' Trauner said with unreal nonchalance.

'Like to try?'

Trauner manufactured a look of contempt. 'I was, in reality, trying to suck you in, as I would any other suspected imperialist spy,' he suggested convincingly.

Colman wasn't convinced. 'If you had listened to the tape from the beginning, Colonel, you wouldn't joke like that,' he said. 'In no way could your reactions be considered anything but spontaneous and unrehearsed, not arranged in advance or anticipating what took place between us. Especially your strong suggestion that I killed Fischer on order and that the same person who gave the order was now trying to involve you in an elaborate intrigue, etcetera, etcetera.' Then: 'Be sensible, Colonel, be sensible.'

'I won't do it,' Trauner said defiantly.

'Then I suggest you will be better off not going home tonight, or any other night. If you like I can arrange a meeting between you and the right people in the West. Have you ever considered coming over? It might be the answer to your problem——'

'But I can't do it,' Trauner exclaimed in suddenly visible despair, almost moved to tears. 'I am not a traitor! I would shoot myself first. . . .'

Colman knew this man would never extend mercy to anyone under similar circumstances or feel any sympathy. To have felt sorry for him would have been absurd. 'That would be quite a gift for Emmering,' Colman said with patronizing detachment. 'Why give it to him?'

'Trauner's eyes narrowed. 'Just what is it you're after?' he said.

'You're better off not knowing. But nothing very big.'

'You expect me to take that as an answer?'

'Look, Colonel, if you want to stand here and talk, fine. Why don't we send down for some drinks and you can tell me all about your devotion to duty. We can talk all night. But it'll come to the same thing in the end.'

'Let you roam at will, eh?' Trauner snapped back. 'Go freely from place to place and blow up the city if you wish, eh?'

'No aggressive plans, Colonel. No violence or theft, believe it or not.'

'Then *what*?'

'Would *you* tell *me*, Colonel? As one professional to another?'

'I might need to or lose.'

'If the positions were reversed you wouldn't want to clutter up my decision with another weight on my conscience. You'd want to keep it simple and not too tough for me. And that's what I'm doing for you.'

'How kind.'

'The objective is very small. No one will give a damn in the long run.'

'And yet all of this . . . for a very small objective. Must you insult me too?'

'Do you want to end up where they all do when they get into these scrapes?'

'Maybe it is right and proper that I should,' Trauner said as if it were a private thought spoken aloud.

'What does that mean? Is Emmering a better man than you thought? Were you a bad boy to want to do him in?'

'I've behaved without dignity, that's all that's important. I've trafficked with an agent of Western imperialism, of German revanchism. . . .'

'I'm none of that, Colonel. But even if I am, it's beside the point. If you think you've been bad and want to be punished, I won't hesitate to punish you, because that is the way it works. We are nothing to each other—ciphers. Either I get in and out of East Berlin with your blessings or you will be in deep disgrace by tomorrow morning and even worse off than that not long afterwards.'

'I deserve disgrace,' Trauner said quietly. 'I deserve whatever the state deems as proper.'

'Say the word and I'll see to it,' Colman said as if promising to do a favour.

Trauner had begun a hard wrestling match with himself, one that might go on for years. His eyes searched coldly for guidance that simply wasn't to be had, and he walked across the room to stare out towards the lake, the luxury of whose purchased view was for a Socialist in a class with venial sin.

241

He stood like that with his back turned, not speaking, and Colman knew that the colonel was not quite ready to let his Socialist soul be cleansed at any cost, not utterly. Colman would shortly be walking around in East Berlin more safely than one of its own citizens.

CHAPTER SEVEN

HE LANDED AT TEGEL on a Swissair twin-engine jet. It was ten in the morning, muggy and grey for this time of year, and noticeable dampness lay on his skin like importuning hands. Strong temptations assailed him. Not more than minutes away Adele could have been touched, had, loved. Should he telephone her? Just that much. He went through customs in seconds, his luggage consisting of the single attaché case containing discarded socks, undershorts, a shirt, and a set of rather uninteresting-looking bank statements. As he walked out to the taxi rank he could feel pangs of longing like recurrent fever. They all but cut off one's breathing. He got into a cab and directed the driver to Charlie. It was the only place to cross without attracting too much attention. The other checkpoints were for West Germans, West Berliners, or for interzonal business.

The driver cut through the Tiergarten after he had reached the Ernst-Reuter-Platz. And from the Potzdamer Platz he followed the weavings of the Wall. The letters KZ were sprawled in angrily applied red paint countless times along the way; crosses, black wreaths, and occasional flower bouquets fled by in silent accusation at the places where desperate men and women fell and died. And finally at Friedrichstrasse Colman got out of the cab and walked towards the *Schupo* and the American MP who were on post just outside the inspection hut. He showed them his diplomatic ID and they waved him through along the pedestrian path towards the NVA guards, who watched his approach with bland faces and the expectable withering silence. The unseasonably stifling air didn't improve anyone's disposition very much.

The *Vopos* checked the same ID, all in order, just outside their yellow inspection shed. Concertina wire stretched in endless reaches off to either side of the street, a lookout tower about thirty yards away occupied by a *Vopo* manning a mounted machine gun. Colman was passing through the Death Strip, the stone and steel barriers everywhere, the pitfalls and wire fencing almost ludicrously preventive and forbidding. Three or four cars were lined up to enter, one having come from the other direction hoping to leave. The diplomatic ID pierced the wall more quickly than any other. In just a few minutes Colman was sitting in one of East Berlin's checkerboard-striped taxicabs driving first north, then in an easterly direction through a city teeming with jackbooted, high-collared *Volksarmee* troopers. They wore Russian helmets, as if to qualify as a different breed of German for that alone. You could hardly miss the open spaces and the islands of neatly piled rubble.

Colman got out of the cab in front of the Berolina tour office and went inside. There were posters behind the counter exalting Poland, Rumania, the Soviet Union, but not Hungary or Czechoslovakia, as far as Colman could see. ENJOY YOUR HOLIDAY IN RIGA, one said; SEE THE BLACK SEA, another tantalized. A surprising number of people were interested enough in just such suggestions and blandishments to keep the clerks busy. One of the latter, wearing an SED emblem on his lapel, responded to Colman and on request gave him a sealed envelope addressed to B. Zeissner, and when Colman returned to the street he had in his possession a Ministry of State Security A card. Which meant that he was, in most everyday matters of freedom of movement and access to certain key places, almost invulnerable. No SSD goon or *Vopo* could detain or even persist in eyeing him suspiciously; he didn't have to look over his shoulder or wonder when the axe might fall; it could only from very high above.

The Alexanderplatz was where the regime seemed to have put its best face: the tremendous TV tower, a complex of new shops and department stores, and whatever glitter could be effected with a couple of new-looking hotels which Colman could see on the street running east from the big circle he was now crossing, with little vehicular traffic to impede his progress.

Red banners and ribbons adorned everything—building cornices, store windows, brick walls—and the catalogue of Socialist slogans were attached like ownership tags. THE REPUBLIC NEEDS EVERY WOMAN, EVERY WOMAN NEEDS THE REPUBLIC. AMIS GET OUT OF VIETNAM. WE ALL SUPPORT REVOLUTIONARY STRUGGLE WHEREVER IT MAY TAKE PLACE. It was as relentless as it was banal, as dismal as the heavy air and the low-hanging grey skies—especially in the face of those jackboots and high Prussian collars so much a part of the atmosphere.

Colman would not have made a move without Trauner's official seal, the protective invisible shield—the small, concealed plastic plate bearing ironic resemblance to a Bank Americard. It bore Trauner's name and his ministry rank, was specially treated and unforgeable. It got Colman into the very core of Rummelsburg Prison.

Guards and officials deferred to it without question, and Colman found himself escorted from the main building across the catwalk overlooking the exercise yard and into the processing and maintenance building. He waited in a small room with a table and several chairs until Mankin was brought to him from the cell in the very long barrack which could be seen from the window. Colman watched him coming across the yard in tow of one of the guards. He didn't look bad at all, no visible slack in his gait or break in his posture. He was about forty, flint-eyed, rock-jawed, hard, but unmistakably scholarly, his vast educational background discernible in the quiet surface toughness that marked him. He was as smart and adaptable as anyone to be found anywhere, and that was why Stevenson had picked him for this particular assignment. Only the treachery of a Stebbins could have accounted for where he was at this very moment.

When he entered the room and saw Colman he showed only faint surprise and a flicker of suspicion. Colman knew he was someone who could be counted on, that he was built for speed and wouldn't take long in catching up to things. 'Hello, Jim,' Colman said simply, sympathetically.

244

'Hello, pal,' Mankin chose to say in a noncommittal tone.

'I'm sure you're a little surprised to see me here,' Colman said. 'But it'll all be clear to you in just a moment or two.'

'Will it?'

'I think so. Why don't you sit down? We can talk.'

'About what?'

'Various things. How are you being treated, by the way?' Colman was sure that Mankin already knew that nothing was out on the table and was prepared to take all of his cues from whatever Colman did and said.

'All right,' Mankin answered, eyeing Colman warily. 'Damned good, as a matter of fact.'

'No one bothers or harasses you in any way, do they?' Colman said cajolingly.

'That's a fair description of it.'

'The food is good?'

'Adequate.'

'Why don't you sit down, Jim?'

'What do you want?'

'Okay, Jim. We'll stop evading the issue now and come right to the heart of the situation. But why don't you sit down?'

Mankin sat down next to the table and kept looking at Colman as Colman said, 'The last you knew I was one of *us*. And now you see me from out of the blue and you don't know why or how. You're sitting in jail, cut off, out of communication month after month and then all of a sudden you get a surprise visit from one of your old sidekicks who simply walks into the middle of a DDR prison as if he's Comrade Ulbricht. And you don't know what to make of it, do you, Jim?'

'Maybe I do,' Mankin said insinuatingly, a thin layer of contempt on his words.

'Jim,' Colman said, sitting down on the opposite side of the table, 'you never know where life will lead you. . . .'

'That's damned profound, pal.'

Colman smiled a little and said, 'Try to understand what's happening. Power is shifting constantly. People change their minds, their outlooks.'

'You said something about the heart of the situation, I believe,' Mankin said with open hostility.

'I thought it might be easier if it were I who talked to you about certain things,' Colman said. 'That is, I suggested it. . . .'

'You're the friendly go-between, is that i?'

'Call it that.'

'They figured someone from home builds confidence, the familiar face, the old associations.' He nodded with a nasty grin. 'Everything for the misguided imperialist's comfort, Stalinism now in disrepute. . . .'

'Look, Jim,' Colman said grimly, 'do you want to get out of here?' He looked into Mankin's eyes with not one but several messages. 'I am in a position to know that no one is terribly interested in keeping you here indefinitely, but without some sort of propelling device, they're almost forced to.'

'Here comes the kicker, if I'm any judge.'

'A very simple one, Jim.' Colman opened his attaché case, removed an envelope, withdrew from it a folded sheet of paper, and extended it to Mankin. 'If you will just sign this statement —a very innocuous one, at that, as you will see for yourself. . . .'

Mankin coldly and with strong, gnarled fingers held the document open and his eyes followed it unemotionally as Colman explained, 'It merely acknowledges the fact that you were sent into the German Democratic Republic by the CIA for purposes of securing information, though not necessarily to commit an act of espionage.' Colman paused and splayed his hands in a gesture to deride the importance of such a thing. 'Not much of a concession to make, you must admit.'

Mankin admitted, 'It isn't a very tough statement as these things go,' and finished reading the contents of the page.

'It's not much to ask, Jim. I'm glad you agree with that at least.'

'Oh, sure.'

'Then what do you say?' Colman asked.

Mankin folded it, handed it back to Colman, and looked at him with a self-satisfied light in his eyes. 'In the tongue of Donne and Dryden and Shakespeare and Swift,' Mankin said, 'I say, fuck you.'

CHAPTER EIGHT

COLMAN ENTERED the huge, coldly Socialistic, recently constructed building of the Neue Königstrasse. Two *Vopos* parted
in the entry at the sight of the magic ID and then Colman
was clacking across the marble-floored vestibule, police per-
sonnel like the occupants of a hive passing back and forth.

An elevator run by a hefty young woman with a sombrely
pubescent face took him to the floor he requested, and at the
end of the corridor a man sitting at a desk and wearing an SED
lapel pin (they were everywhere) checked his ID quickly. A
uniformed man bearing a sidearm stood nearby. Once this far,
Colman knew he could go anywhere until he came to the last
bastion of this particular section of the internal security community. There his unquestioned passage would end and
something new would need to come into play.

It was like any other government official's office, any other
place of police administration. Two solid-looking Germans
with hard-looking foreheads and tight mouths sat at face-to-
face desks poring over reports or records of some kind, the fates
of others in their hands, like detectives in any station house, a
long-faced middle-aged woman at a typewriter behind a railing and just outside the door to an inner room.

Both men looked up questioningly and Colman flashed the
ID. 'I'm here to see the colonel,' he said.

One of them frowned as if straining to place Colman's accent,
and the other said, 'Why don't you try telephoning ahead of
time?'

Colman gestured understandingly. 'Sometimes it's difficult
to do that.'

'You people think you're above protocol,' the first one said,
the second one still frowning. 'We're not as special and free-
wheeling over here. We go in for procedure. That might come
as a shock to you, I know. But don't bother to sit down.'

'Maybe we shouldn't be quite so demanding, Franz,' said
the second one, blond, thoughtful, and still thinking hard.
'After all, he is one of the *Super-Genossen*. We have to mind
our manners.'

'If I may inject you with a small amount of liberal reform,'

Colman said good-humouredly, 'we say *Kollegen* in our department these days.'

'What do you want?' the first one said.

'I've already said.'

'If it's some kind of cross-indexing, there's no need to see anyone but us.'

'Do you usually keep the colonel wrapped in a cocoon like this? Or only when one of us *Super-Genossen* walks in?'

'Where are you from?' the cerebral one said. 'You have an interesting accent.'

'And interesting clothes,' the other observed.

Colman smiled tolerantly, a part of the game but a little uncertain as to how he should play it at that instant: tough? smooth? put out? It would not be a good idea to open up anything to these two, to in any way endanger Emmering by setting noisy underlings in motion. 'I think you'd better tell him that someone from Colonel Trauner's office is waiting to see him.'

The woman had staunchly continued to type all this time, but when the inner door opened she stopped and looked up. Emmering's gaze went directly to Colman, unhesitatingly and unemotionally surveying him from top to bottom. Emmering was built, Colman could see, like a middleweight wrestler. His skin was toneless, his hair pasted flat and black and straight back, his eyes like lumps of coal in a snowman's head, and Colman was eager to get into a room alone with him. 'I'm Zeissner, Kollege Colonel,' Colman said, relaxed, hands at his sides, a friendly expression on his face.

'Zeissner?'

'From Comrade Trauner's department. . . .'

'You are here to see me?'

'Briefly, if I may.'

'I was on my way to lunch. But step in.'

It was an office like any other, like Trauner's own must have been in respect to Ulbricht's photograph on the wall, a smaller one of Erich Honecker below and to the left; not large, two chairs facing the desk, one behind it, a sweeping view of the Alexanderplatz far down the street and to the west out of the single window.

'Can we be heard?'

Emmering assessed the question briefly and answered with a touch of annoyance: 'No; what is said in here is heard in here. Not elsewhere.'

'Good,' Colman said, as if they were on the same side. 'There's a man sitting in one of your cells in your Berlin Rummelsburg Prison whose name is Mankin.'

Emmering reacted to the name, became stock-still as he stood in back of his desk.

'You will be interested to know that he is ready to swear that you are a West German agent in the direct pay of FIA and that he, as a member of American Intelligence, was about to contact you when he was arrested by Trauner. And that you then prised him loose from Trauner and took over his incarceration yourself until you could figure out just what to do with him. Yes, he is ready to swear to just that. . . .' Colman looked out of the window momentarily and waited for the message to sink in.

Emmering, stocky, stolid, unruffled, glared with those turbid eyes at Colman. 'Who are you?' he asked with no show of fear.

'I am one of Trauner's people,' Colman said and displayed the million-dollar ID. 'So you're getting a good break.'

'You must be crazy. I don't know what you're talking about. But I know that you've made a fatal mistake—you and Colonel Trauner both.' He quickly and easily took a gun from his desk —a snorkel-nosed automatic of some kind—and said, 'I am going to arrest you this very minute and then I shall talk to Trauner personally and effectively without delay. Don't move, I could shoot you dead right here or in front of a hundred people and never have my judgement questioned. That power goes with my responsibility. Trauner has overstepped himself.'

'Trauner doesn't know a thing about it, as you'll be able to ascertain for yourself if you can bring your nerves under control and allow me to give you some facts. If Mankin accuses you of being a double-agent, you are through, Colonel. You and Trauner are far from friends. You have enough on him in your files to make him do tricks and he would give his right arm to be able to find a neutralizer.'

'It's a foul-mouthed lie,' Emmering said in that same

equanimous drone. 'No one would believe Mankin, they would know it was some sort of attempt to subvert. And anyhow, why *would* he, to begin with?'

'To get out of the DDR, Colonel, that's why.'

'What?'

'And to keep him from saying such things about you to Colonel Trauner or anyone else, you're going to see to it that he *does* get out, safely and in perfect health. As you've pointed out, you have so much power you could kill me in front of a hundred people without even apologizing. In comparison, releasing someone like Mankin is easier than lighting a cigar. Oh, you will do it, Colonel. If you don't you'll lose a lot more than your edge on Trauner.'

'I'm not in the least frightened of this rubbish you are talking. . . .' Emmering was defiant but making no aggressive moves. 'It's a preposterous lie.'

'Is it?' Colman said, sensing the tenacity that must have still been operating in respect to Adele; this was someone who didn't leave things alone very easily. Colman tried consciously to feel no personal satisfaction as he took a thick letter-size folder from its tuck in his belt. He tossed it on the desk and said, 'Then how will you explain the large amount of money you have in the Swiss-Romande Bank of Geneva? Twenty-five thousand dollars deposited in various sums over the past three years.'

Emmering handled the material as if untouched by the loathsome and base experiences to which duty forced him, superior and sceptical.

'You will notice the account is numbered, Colonel, rather than under a name, which is customary to many of the accounts in Swiss banks since so many of the depositors have reason to keep what they are doing a secret. Also you will notice a mailing address: E.E. in care of the post office on the Franzosiche-strasse. That's in case of some urgent reason to contact the depositor. Those, I believe, are your initials, aren't they?'

'But this is a forgery! I have no account in Switzerland!'

'Lower your voice, Colonel, and put away the gun before it goes off by accident.'

'You won't get away with this, whoever you are.'

'The account is as legitimate as twenty-five thousand dollars can make it. It exists. The dates go back over three years and can be corroborated, if need be. It can all be verified without much trouble. What *can't* be verified is the identity of E.E. The bank doesn't know who its depositors are unless the depositors want them to. Part of the service is anonymity. And the account of E.E. is real. But *no* one could tell you who E.E. actually is. It might, therefore, easily be you. The accusation would be tough to disprove, especially if the American sitting in your jail right now turns out to be the paymaster whose facts and figures exactly coincide with those in your hands. And they do. He's ready for it. So you can see how it would be no matter how you protested and no matter how many people might even want to take your word—Colonel Trauner excepted, of course. It simply is a losing proposition, it always is. A well-documented false accusation?' Colman shook his head knowingly. 'Practically impossible to recover from. Few people ever do. The garbage dumps of history are piled high with their bodies. Some of it always sticks. And in *your* position? No, Colonel. It's more than you could handle. And if Colonel Trauner came into possession of it—well, he would use it as a yoke or a noose. . . .' Colman shrugged. 'It's not worth it, Colonel.'

'What if I just kill you and Mankin both?'

'You're not sure of yourself or you wouldn't ask.'

'Maybe you've no convincing answer.'

'Corruption and malfeasance, followed by a double murder to cover them up. Grow up. You don't think for a minute that it starts and ends with Mankin and me, do you? That there's only the two of us? Grow up, Colonel.'

Emmering, an expert on the use of force, stood there silent, smouldering and frustrated.

Colman said, 'You were going to walk him out anyhow a few months ago—at a price. Now the terms are slightly altered, that's all.'

Unexcitedly, Emmering slowly replaced the gun in his desk drawer. Colman watched him without speaking. Emmering said, 'How do you happen to enjoy Colonel Trauner's confidence to the extent that you seem to?'

'He thinks I've defected. And it would gain you anything to tell him I haven't. I'm sure you can see that for yourself.'

'It's very clever. If it works successfully, you will be rewarded, no doubt. Money. Promotion. But such a big risk for so small a return. What can it ultimately mean to you?'

'Why do you do *your* job, Colonel?'

'I'm on the winning side. You can't turn the tide of history. Hasn't anyone told you?'

Colman wasn't interested. 'You should be able to release Mankin in minutes, Colonel. He's not under sentence and there are no specific charges against him—just a tip from one of our turncoats, right?'

'What value does this one man have to you, you people in Section Two? I begin to wonder. I begin to believe that perhaps more is there than Colonel Trauner's counterespionage experts realize.'

'I wouldn't know,' Colman said. 'But I advise you not to get into that with Trauner unless you're anxious to become a martyr on an anthill. And nothing would suit Trauner better.'

Emmering shook his head with an almost somnolent air. 'Trauner wouldn't survive me, I assure you,' he said.

'So you would take him along with you. You look too practical to do a thing like that. No, it's what we call a Mexican standoff, Colonel. At least until Mankin and I are out of here. After that you're on your own. But first there is that. Otherwise copies of the charges against you, fully documented, will be sent to the chairman of the *Staatsrat* and his deputies, to each member of the Politburo, to the editors of *Neues Deutschland*, and to Colonel Trauner. To avoid that, what I am asking of you is a cheap price to pay.'

Emmering didn't argue. 'But how stupid of him to have been so easily convinced. I would have thought you held something over his head.'

'Don't underestimate him.'

'You must have presented a very convincing case.'

'I'm considering coming over, as a matter of fact.'

'Is that meant to confuse me?' Emmering said. 'I am wondering actually why he is so taken in by you. How long have you known each other?' He began slowly to pace the room.

'Where did you meet? . . . What did you say to him to so utterly convince him of your worth to him?'

'You're beginning to think too much, Colonel.'

'Am I? Habit, you understand. Slow, methodical, reasoning. That's what a man in my position has to be.'

'It won't matter in this case. No matter what you come up with, you still have to face'—Colman gestured towards the banking statements lying poisonously on the desk—'that.'

'It's something else, Zeissner, isn't it? Something you are holding over Trauner, something so strong that you are able to enjoy his protection.' Emmering was suddenly smiling a thin, unexpected smile that turned his eyes into those of a saddened clown. 'He thinks I don't know he travelled to Zurich a few days ago. . . .' He stopped pacing, looked directly at Colman, and said, 'Did he meet with you while he was there?'

Tenacious was the word. 'You're cold, Colonel,' was all Colman could say.

'That's too bad,' Emmering said, and it was impossible to know what he meant or if he meant anything. Then, as if he didn't mind very much at all, he said. 'I am going to need to do this later in the day . . . when less people are about and the various ministries are not—in full swing, shall we say.'

'That's up to you.'

'It will be better that way—for me. For you too, possibly. I am sure Trauner is not in on this with you, and perhaps it would be best if nothing changes in that regard.'

They were suddenly co-conspirators and Colman listened carefully. 'You had better not be seen with Mankin. Don't leave with him, let him cross at Friedrichstrasse by himself. I'll arrange the credentials personally. . . .' Emmering conducted everything with efficiency and professional devotion, even plots against himself.

'How will I know?' Colman asked.

'You will see him. He will come into the Café Moscow for a drink. Wait there at eight o'clock. Watch him leave.'

'You might pick him up again five minutes later.'

'What would be the point?'

'Why all the circles?'

'Allow me to be the judge of why all the circles. I think you

have everything else the way you want it. You are getting him
out. How is up to me. If you don't mind too much.'

It was now a matter of Socialist pragmatism, and Colman
was willing to defer to it under the circumstances. If Emmering
felt any rage, he didn't show it. 'Actually,' he said, 'there is no
practical reason why you should not return to West Berlin
immediately. It will all go the same way.'

'Thanks. But I'm not in that big a rush, Colonel. I don't
want to be told about anything later on.'

CHAPTER NINE

IT TURNED OUT to be a long, empty wait. Its full dimension
couldn't have been foreseen. Colman did some sightseeing,
noticed a few Americans here and there accompanied by
guides assigned by the Information and Organization Bureau.
Sitting at a sidewalk table on Karl-Marx-Allee, he spotted
someone whom he took to be shadowing him—a young, thin,
bureaucratic-looking man with blond hair swirled to a
pompadour in front, a washed-out complexion, wearing glasses,
reading *BZ am Mittag*, but not escaping Colman's notice. Colman had ordered a citrus-flavoured soft drink and was reading
a copy of *Neues Deutschland*, which bulged with the unbelievable
language and the stories of the Communist never-never land:
crude editorials about Washington-supported Nazi resurgences,
detailed reports on new approaches to crop rotation. But most
of it was white-hot stuff. Diatribes against the United States
were not in short supply.

The young man followed Colman to the HO department
store on the Alexanderplatz, a fairly sizeable walk. Colman
stopped and confronted him where the man stood pretending
to study a window displaying toilet soap, Chlorodent toothpaste, and a home hair-permanent set. The air of joyful discovery and optimism in all of this had a distinctly false ring. It
gave the feeling of another time and place vanished very long
ago in a haze of German impressionism. 'Get off my tail,
Kollege,' Colman said, flashing his ID. 'I'm on assignment.'

The other said nothing, assented with a slight nod, and walked away. Colman browsed through the dismal and limited goods in the store and then went by tram to the Friedrichshain Park, where he sat and watched East Berliners taking pleasure in the huge public swimming pool. He occupied a bench in the bowl-shaped stadium looking down on the swimmers and splashers. His Western look, the suit and shoes, gave him away. A thickset thirty-five-year-old man sat down next to him, open collar, baggy pants, feeling the seventy-eight-degree heat. 'You wouldn't have any cigarettes, would you, chum?' the man said in English. 'Camels or Chesterfields?'

'I don't smoke,' Colman said.

'I mean to sell.'

'No.'

'Or anything else we can't get over here? I used to live in Cleveland, would you believe it? My father was a Socialist and we came back here in forty-eight.'

'Really?'

'You are on a visit, of course.'

'Yes.'

'It's not so bad, to tell the truth. Prices are sky high on a lot of things, but they will never have to open soup kitchens for the unemployed. I mean, everybody has a job if they're not old or sick.'

'That's something.'

'Well, it's security, you see? I like that for the kids, I have three. But then, on the other hand, I would like to be able to get a bottle of good Scotch for less than twenty bucks. That's right. Twenty bucks on an average. Can you believe that? You can get it for about ten or twelve marks across the Wall. . . .'

Colman listened for a while and then got up, said good-bye, and walked away from the noticeably disappointed former resident of Cleveland. He went by S-Bahn to the centre of the town and at a self-service cafeteria at the Bahnhof Friedrichstrasse had a helping of bockwurst, which was good enough in an emergency. A discarded paper called *Wohin in Berlin*, picked up and scanned idly, sent Colman by cab to Marienkirche, a large church, austere and unadorned. Here he sat in a back pew and listened to organ music for about two hours. By then it was six o'clock. He had been aware of the music only vaguely, as one is of sleep, dreaming with open eyes but not quite off guard. Music for perfect love in a garden with a virginal young girl whose beautiful face is later indistinct and leaves the dreamer haunted. It was a weird sensation—organ music to carry you away while you wait in a near-empty theatre for the movie to begin. You could almost forget exactly what it was that you were *actually* waiting for. Almost. The last minutes, as they began, were the hardest.

In the bar in the Moscow, at a quarter to eight, he ordered a steak which turned out to be the smallest of its kind that he had ever seen. It was good enough, and he washed it down with some East German beer. Two couples were dancing to an uninspired recording of 'These Foolish Things' the way people did in the thirties but with the somnambulant look of the reconciled. He watched momentarily and then saw Mankin walk in, as scheduled, his suit rumpled, his thinning grey hair matted, a neutral, austere look on his face, a man fluent in five languages including Russian, experienced, tough, valuable. He gave Colman an unrecognizing glance and went to the bar. The whole thing was almost done; Colman felt elated; it all had greater meaning than ever before. Until now there had been dreams, desires, and guilts; sins to wash away; a dark, uncompromising force from within that called for that transcendent act which had to take place whether fully understood or not. The sight of Mankin, released from that black, anonymous recess of police arrest in a people's democracy put everything else into the shade. Mankin was real, was human, was a friend, and his ordeal was at an end. You couldn't help feeling something new, something greater than the abstract significance of summary reports, of tactical moves, of planning boards and flags to mark the moves. Colman was glad he had got Mankin out for more than just the benefits, whatever they may have been, to himself.

Emmering came to his table as if they were meeting for a convivial drink or two and a little inconsequential conversation. Colman hadn't expected him. He looked at Colman with the same unrevealing expression that both his adversaries and whatever friends he may have had contended with at all times. He had undoubtedly taken advantage of it in the past and perhaps, on occasion, had tried to break out of it when the man inside wanted sympathy and understanding, wanted to be taken for something else. 'You will see him leave in just a few minutes,' he said to Colman. 'A tram will take him to Friedrichstrasse in a matter of minutes and he will be safely across. But what guarantees do I have in return?'

'The fact is, you're in no position to ask for any. But you will receive a photostat of the bank statements and a record of withdrawal of funds and cancellation of the account by the real depositor. That should show the whole thing up for what it was and no one could ever use it against you. And we wouldn't want to.'

'You couldn't, as a matter of fact. I would fight it if anything greater than this were at stake.'

'That's probably true.'

'The one thing I have learned is that the best interests of the greatest number of people come first in the kind of society we are building. The turmoil and mistrust such a vicious attack would cause could damage more than just me personally. Your man *is* a small price to pay—he always was, valuable though he may be to you.'

Another way of saying do nothing unorthodox, show no independent idealism, take no risks in the hierarchical arena. He was a well-trained *apparatchik*.

Colman merely said, 'Yes, I can see what you mean.'

'Not altogether, I don't think. There's more.'

Colman saw Mankin finish his quick drink and walk out of the place. If nothing went wrong, Mankin would shortly pass through the checkpoint like someone ending an uneventful visit. 'There's no doubt you could say a lot about all of it,' Colman said absently, ready to follow Mankin. 'Anyhow, Trauner will never know. You're too strong for him.'

'I'm referring to something else, as a matter of fact, something which, in my slow, methodical way, I realize is behind this situation. . . .'

The two of them now looked at each other and Colman, for the first time, was acutely conscious of who Emmering really was, and he looked different suddenly. Colman remembered vividly Adele's various accounts and descriptions of her early life.

'If I am right, you saw Trauner in Zurich,' Emmering said, an unexpected sense of unwelcome intimacy overcoming Colman. 'I associate a man named Martin Fischer with similar meetings in Zurich—not with Trauner but with Trauner's department. Did you know him? I have a feeling you did. Zurich and Trauner and you all come together for me, and I am willing to go on that supposition.'

'What difference does it make?'

'I have been thinking about this all day. Mankin *was* to be exchanged, as you said earlier. But something went wrong.' He looked at Colman as if he were studying him. 'I didn't know at the time just what it was. But I found out soon enough. The exchange prisoner . . . escaped . . . and you people had to lose the chance. And now . . . here you are, and it's all about Mankin again—just as it was before, but with an entirely different set of tactics.'

Colman said, 'That's the way it is.'

'The point is, it was Martin Fischer's wife, an illegal immigrant in the West, who was to be exchanged.'

'More than possible.'

Emmering leaned in closer, because this was something one had to emphasize, give some importance to. 'It was you, wasn't it, who interfered with that process? You took her into hiding, but you wanted to get Mankin out of prison anyhow, some other way. This way. . . .'

Colman couldn't bring himself to deny it.

Emmering said, 'You embarrassed yourself and your superiors and now you are making up for it. If I am wrong you just have to tell me as much. But I must know if that's the case. Only that, not more.'

'What if it is?'

'Are you ashamed to admit it?'

'I know all about you. If you're not ashamed, nobody should be.'

'They say we Germans are too analytical,' Emmering said with what passed for a thin smile. 'That we question and pick

258

things over too much. But you Americans are exactly the opposite. And that's how you get fooled over and over again. It's why you make mistakes more often than anyone else.'

'I hadn't noticed that.'

'You've answered my question. You said you know all about me. We both know the source.'

'What more is there to say?' Colman said.

'Don't take us for crude fools or knaves, Mr Colman,' Emmering said, using the name for the first time. 'I have known Adele for a very long time, and I will only tell you this —that her background was such that she could not ever make a good Socialist. She didn't have the ability to feel with the people, to submerge her own bourgeois tastes and desires to the greater good; no sense of social duty. No matter what she told you, that is why she and Fischer, who was even worse, fled to the West.'

Colman looked at him, unable, of course, to know whether he sincerely believed what he was saying or not. In any event, even the truth of it would have had different meanings for each of them, taken on different tones.

'If you had known her mother you would understand it,' Emmering went on. 'A Socialist view, Mr Colman, is the closest thing to objective truth in this world. We make mistakes. But we have the only possibility for the solution of most of the meaningful questions. It protects us against petty and personal distortions; and it provides an understanding that both Adele and her mother were incapable of.'

'Why go into this now?' Colman asked, though he knew it was the need for a day in court that was motivating Emmering.

'Because you have undoubtedly been told a great deal. I want you to know that we are not what she says we are, that the injustices she may have recounted are based on the weaknesses within herself.'

'She's been pretty fair, I'd say.'

'I suspect you may be ready to accept anything she says.'

'Would I be wiser to accept everything you say?'

'I think you miss the point.'

'As a matter of fact, she doesn't say that much about it, Colonel. Why fret?'

'I personally don't care. It's the regime that counts for me. Whether you believe that or not is of no importance to me once you have heard me say it. You may not understand that I am talking as a Socialist, but I am. That is what matters.'

'All right, I believe it.'

'Perhaps you do, perhaps you don't. But I want you to know one thing more. And it is simply that if Adele had been unwilling or incapable of taking up her life as she should have done in the DDR, I had *no intention* . . . of doing anything other than seeing to it that she was allowed to emigrate from the DDR to wherever she wished to go.' He paused and said, 'I hope you will tell her that. And think about it yourself, for that matter.' He rose from the table and said, 'Don't always believe everything you hear. Even when people are not deliberately misrepresenting the truth, they may be labouring under a misapprehension. . . .' And he walked away. That was what he wanted to get across, and Colman half believed him. It was perhaps the only way he could defeat her rebukes, the only way to salvage himself. He might have done exactly as he said he would had the situation actually come to pass.

Colman suffered no regrets about it and wasn't decided on whether he owed Emmering a good character reference to Adele or not. He left a moment later, looked around him on the strangely almost deserted wide avenue, and then walked towards the Schillingstrasse U-Bahn to pick up one of the taxicabs stationed at that point. The night was starless and the street lighting was as poor as so dead an atmosphere could be expected to warrant. One could walk in perfect safety anywhere, if one had anywhere to walk to. Colman could think only of Adele, who would be waiting, who even now, within reach, seemed like a dream.

At the checkpoint two *Vopos* trained machine pistols on him from two different directions while an inspecting guard said, 'I am sorry, you are under arrest,' scarcely having considered his diplomatic ID.

CHAPTER TEN

MISTAKEN IDENTITY, he thought to himself; it had to be. But it came with a minor jolt anyhow. 'Under arrest? That's insane. What for?' he demanded without raising his voice.

And then he saw inside the shed and standing right next to a poster proclaiming THE FIRST GERMAN PEACE AND FREEDOM STATE the clerical-looking, frail, blond young man who had been tailing him hours before. His unimpassioned, businesslike eyes were fixed on Colman unflinchingly. He had apparently identified Colman for this detention on sight, was in the inspection shed at the checkpoint for solely that purpose. Why? Colman couldn't imagine the answer. The striped barrier was all too far away. The big sign on top of the Graphic Trades Building flashed beckoningly, but Colman didn't make a move. 'You will be told soon enough,' the arresting guard said.

For the first time he felt hemmed in. The delay was on the wrong end of things, tougher to withstand at the last minute than at an earlier moment. It made no sense immediately. Who was behind it? Where had he missed a step or left something out? Adele was waiting.

'Come with me, please,' said the young man with the blond pompadour.

'Where to, and why?' Colman snapped irritably.

'You have nothing to worry about. Come along, please.'

Two other tight-suited, hatless men joined the gathering to give emphasis to just what kind of a situation it was. Colman didn't quite believe what was going on yet. He was being stopped in his tracks, freedom, peace, and love just inches away. What in hell had happened to break up the smooth pattern, to destroy the step-by-step inevitability of the thing?

He could do nothing but get into the back seat of a waiting car behind the inspection shed and then sit alongside a pre-dictably unsympathetic goon, bulky and packing something in his jacket pocket where his hand remained without moving for the next twenty-five minutes. The young man in charge sat in a bucket seat next to the driver, turned halfway to be able to face the rear without necessarily looking at Colman directly—in fact, avoiding doing so. The line of the modified pompadour hadn't moved even a single strand since Colman had first seen him earlier in the day.

No one spoke and Colman knew he had a hard time ahead of him, that getting out of East Germany was not going to be the carousel ride it might have been, that he improbably had come to believe firmly it would be. The sickeningly familiar landmarks and streets now came back mockingly as the car travelled through the nearly traffic-free city towards the east: the Linden Corso, the Unter den Linden, Marx-Engels-Platz —he hadn't expected to see them again—dimly lit, oppressive, a kaleidoscope of boredom and hopelessness. It soon became obvious that they were leaving the city, always a sign of special urgency, and Colman waited somewhat fatalistically for the final destination. A farmhouse in the midst of vast, ghostly acreage, the crops indiscernible in the darkness, a wooded area perhaps three hundred yards away in back of the barn. The main house was brick and stucco and had a gabled slate roof. A gravel road led to the front door. The car continued on past it and around to the back of the building, which faced the barn some hundred feet away.

Everyone, including the driver, got out of the car like polite escorts and waited for Colman, who was the last to alight. No one prodded, pushed, or threatened. The door that opened led directly into the kitchen, a good-sized room whose refrigerator looked about thirty-five years old and whose large black iron stove was a wood-burning relic. At a six-place table in the centre of the room sat Colonel Gerhard Trauner, looking right at Colman, waiting with almost judicial calm, large and immovable. An aide of some kind stood at the swing door probably leading to the front of the house. An overhead lamp hung from the ceiling and gave the place moderate light, most of which fell sharply in the table area.

Colman looked at Trauner with a brazen absence of concern, and Trauner said, 'I want to assure you at the beginning that you are only somewhat delayed. I am sorry for the inconvenience, of course.'

'Be sure you know what you're doing,' Colman warned him.

Trauner nodded to the blond, who went through the swing door to another room, the two others remaining outside where the car was parked. Only the man posted at the swing door stayed in the kitchen with Colman and Trauner. 'I shall come directly to the point if you will just sit down,' Trauner said, and when Colman had done so, continued: 'Some months ago it was suggested to me by Colonel Emmering that a certain American agent who was in the custody of the state on suspicion of crimes against the German Democratic Republic be released in a prisoner exchange. It was, at the time, his contention that this man, James Mankin, was of no value to us but that the exchange prisoner was, because she could shed light on a number of urgent matters, not the least of which was how she and her husband had been able to breach the protective barrier separating the Democratic Republic from the neo-Nazis, revanchists, and cartelists of Bonn. . . .' A kind of buoyancy emerged as he talked, a sound of conviction in the cool, orderly way of speaking. Colman sighed deeply and deliberately. 'Try not to be bored by this, it's more than mere words, as you will see.'

'How about the words I might have to speak?' Colman asked, pointedly looking towards the nearby attendant.

'You can say whatever you like in front of Walther,' Trauner told him. 'But you'll see that all of that is immaterial very shortly.'

Colman sat there and waited.

'There *was*, quite true, nothing specific against James Mankin, and Emmering's argument might have had some substance. But since this same James Mankin has only just two hours ago been released on Colonel Emmering's direct action with no apparent reason, with no visible return from the other side, new questions arise. Questions which you, it happens, can be the one to answer.'

'We had better talk in private, Colonel,' Colman reminded him.

'No, we hadn't. It's not necessary. Not any longer. I can't stand by and let this great a corruption go unchecked, you see, regardless of what it may cost me personally.'

'Oh, another martyr, eh?'

Trauner made a disdainful face. 'Don't be so—wisecracking. The fact is, it's all different now. You might say the point of balance has been passed; and my sense of duty is weighing more heavily than other considerations.' He had known that some day that would happen, had warned Emmering of it, in fact. He shifted in his chair, calling attention to his bulk, and leaned forward on the table, his face thrust towards Colman. 'You visited Mankin in Rummelsburg,' he pointed out. 'Then you contacted Emmering. Emmering, just hours later, personally supervised the release of James Mankin and the invalidation of any further investigation pertaining to him. That all has a very strong pattern to it, of one action following logically from another. If so, the only thing missing is why. Not why, in fact. We know why. You told Emmering he must do it. That is why. What I am now asking you is—*exactly* why? What is it you are holding over Emmering?'

'Not a thing.'

'That is one question. The other is, Why, after all, is this man Mankin so important to the CIA? That they would go to these extremes to get him from us, that they have tried twice to do so suddenly places everything in an urgent category. I ask myself what we have given away through Emmering's corruption. Emmering himself might or might not know as much. But *I* must know. And I must know what it was that forced Emmering—if indeed he was forced—to co-operate with you in the action. You can see how heavily it weighs, how irresistible the responsibility suddenly has become. All the rest is nullified. But you are free to continue on your way as soon as you answer the two questions I have put to you: What did you threaten Emmering with? And why is Mankin so important? Why had they to get him back, at almost any cost, it seems?'

'I don't have any idea. All I did was to say hello to Colonel Emmering, as I was asked to do.'

Trauner slammed his hand down on the table and was suddenly almost as maddened as he had been in Zurich. 'Now listen to me, McNeil,' he raged in a hard, strangled voice. 'I have, after all these years, which you know nothing about, decided to put my arm in fire, if need be, in order to uphold my oath to the people. I have made small compromises, but none that wouldn't let my conscience rest. I always intended to do what had to be done to serve the people and the Party, to prevent, at all costs, significant damage to the Socialist cause. If it were my final act, I would carry out that duty as I see it. So to think you can banter with me or find great patience for your evasions and refusals is utterly ill-conceived on your part. I won't tolerate it for an instant. Be aware of it.'

'None of this is worth your suicide, Colonel,' Colman said calmly. 'You're taking too much for granted. I don't know anything about any of it. I'm just one of the drones.'

'Don't lie.'

'If I'm not back soon, Colonel, things are going to happen—things you won't like, and you know what they are.'

'McNeil, you are playing with fire. I have tried to explain that none of that counts any longer so that you would be able to make new and realistic judgements. But either you can't or won't accept it. You're making a mistake you shall regret, I promise you.'

Dedication to a principle had taken hold and could be seen in Trauner's eyes and heard in his voice. Colman said, 'How will you explain it, Colonel? Are you willing to face that?'

'I shall tell you once more and not again. There are mitigating circumstances: Emmering's corruption, exemplified by your adventuristic tactics—first with me in order to get to him, and then with Emmering himself. The justification for even my own questionable actions in association with you I think lies in what is clearly Emmering's criminal behaviour. Can you understand that?'

'It's wishful thinking, Colonel.'

'I think a people's court would grasp the implications, particularly in the light of the evidence you will supply.'

'*I* will supply?'

'At this moment, I mean. . . .'

'You're sure you didn't mean in trial in a courtroom? Or was that just a slip of tongue?'

'This is growing needlessly out of hand. Give me the information on which I can proceed against Emmering, and you will be in the West within half an hour. You won't be needed beyond that point. What is Mankin's importance to the CIA? And why did Emmering see fit to so hastily release him? That's all you're required to tell me. Why hesitate?

Mankin is safely across, and you have my personal guarantee of safe conduct from the DDR the very minute you answer.'

Colman sighed and shook his head, unable to answer the one, unwilling, for some reason, to answer the other.

'Well?' Trauner demanded.

'Colonel, I don't have any idea why Mankin is important. Would you expect me to? Do you think I would want to? What do you think we are over there? A discussion group?'

Colman's impatience and consternation came through convincingly, and the argument may have made sense to Trauner, who said, 'For the moment then, set that aside. But you can't expect me to believe the same innocence applies to your other reply. You surely must know what it is you said when you spoke to Colonel Ernst Emmering this afternoon at one fifteen in his office. You can't seriously hope to convince me that you remained alone with him for twelve full minutes merely saying hello.' His voice tightened and rose indignantly. 'You're *not* going to sit there and be that asinine with me, are you?'

The man at the door, tall, square-jawed, his expression disapproving and impatient, hadn't moved. His hands overlapped each other like fig leaves. Colman glanced towards him, then looked at Trauner. 'Colonel,' he said with a faint, sympathetic smile, 'they will get you. It won't work out the way you're hoping. Let me go before you can't turn back.'

'You can go. It is in your hands.'

'I mean without the melodrama. Otherwise the Zurich tape will be the people's property tomorrow. And you will be done, Colonel. The best you can hope for is a job as the manager of a warehouse in Stettin or an island in the Baltic Sea. At worst, five or ten years in prison. . . .'

Very deliberately, staring fixedly at Colman, Trauner said, 'It does not matter. Do you understand? That tape is no longer a card for you to play.'

'Then you're ready to take whatever comes,' Colman said reasonably, respectfully. 'Fine, Everybody to his chosen fate.'

Trauner then exhibited the preternatural patience of that man who is finally just about to erupt, to go up in smoke with rage. 'Don't, McNeil,' he advised like an old friend. 'I am willing to overlook your blackmail. But that is all.'

266

'Colonel, I can't help you. . . .'

'What did you say to Emmering?' The voice rose again, the face became enlarged, the breath was audible and angry. 'Tell me.'

'I told him you wanted Mankin released.'

'That is a lie!'

'He seemed to believe it, but it took some talking. I told him you had damaging information about him. He didn't argue.'

'You *won't* tell me, in other words—you refuse.'

'I *am* telling you.'

'It is almost as if you are protecting him.'

'Not a chance. Why would I protect *him*?'

'That's all that makes sense to me. Why else would you resist such a simple, inconsequential request? Just to answer this one question—we can forget the other permanently—and be able to go back freely where you came from. Why, if Emmering isn't someone you wish to protect, should you refuse? You *can't* make up anything I won't see through. So you are saying nothing. Why—if not to protect . . . a double-agent, perhaps? Don't you see that it finally comes to that?'

'Wrong,' Colman said, finally forced to go further than he had wished to. 'I had him in a frame-up. I threatened him the same way I threatened you. Only this was out-and-out forgery —completely false material, counterfeit from start to finish. Not one shred of it was based on truth, or even a half-truth, understand; he was completely innocent. But what a hell of a terrible time he would have had proving it. So he gave me Mankin because it was the only thing he could do. And that is the truth.'

'What *chutzpah*. . . .'

Colman had heard the word and knew what it meant; many people in Berlin used it. He didn't reply. Trauner said, 'Now it's starting to ring true. Yes. . . . And what did this counterfeit item consist of?'

'Just one of those carefully built-up pieces of forgery no one can tell from the genuine article.'

'Come, come. . . .'

'You've got the answer, Colonel. I can't give you more than that.'

'You mean you don't wish to.'

'I made a bargain with Emmering. He kept it. I'm keeping it too, just the way I'll keep the one I made with you. Basically, he's innocent—you've got to accept that. That is, as far as my connection with him is concerned. He may otherwise be the worst son-of-a-bitch in the world.'

'You're not making sense. You're either lying again or you're insane.'

'I gave you everything of importance.'

'But not the means of coercion—to my mind, the most important part of everything.'

'That's just it. You might be tempted to use it against him. That's double jeopardy—not nice. . . .'

'What difference would it make to you?'

'It *does* make a difference.'

'Aren't you suddenly very fastidious? You are surely not taking a moral position——'

'You can do what you like with Emmering. But not with my help. Not in these conditions. Now come on, Colonel, and give it a second thought. If you do you'll see you're on the wrong scent.'

'You are going to tell me what I want to know, my imperialist friend, or you will be with us indefinitely and until you decide what's best for you.'

'Emmering might not like that.'

'Emmering won't even know.'

'And when the tape comes to light?'

'*You* will come to light also. Along with the true story. And your voice on the tape with mine. I am quite ready for that.'

The implications were like a vapour in the ensuing silence. Colman said nothing, nibbled the inside of his lip fleetingly, sat there straight-backed and as if they were talking over the terms of the sale of a house. Trauner sat still, his breathing a bit more noticeable than anyone else's, and he calmly studied Colman. They seemed to have entered into a period of normal deliberation. The particulars had been gone over; the move was now Colman's. He looked at the man at the door, who looked back at him sullenly. The silence continued. Only a distant barking dog demanded any attention. Nothing else. This place was lonely and purposefully removed, its twin utilities being tranquillity and dirty business when necessary. Not more than forty-five seconds elapsed.

'All right, Colonel,' Colman gave in. 'I'll give you the details. Then I expect you to drive me right back to Checkpoint Charlie.'

'I said you would be free to leave. Now talk, and leave out nothing.'

'The physical evidence, as far as I know, is in Emmering's possession. But there's more to it than that. It's a numbered bank account traceable to Emmering. Or at least that's the way it's supposed to look. . . .'

CHAPTER ELEVEN

TRAUNER SAT QUIETLY listening, enrapt and grown deadlier somehow, more massive. In just a few minutes Colman had described the entire thing just as he had to Emmering—the figures, the dates, the post office mailing address; he even described his visit to Mankin in the prison and what Mankin's part was to have been, all of it. 'It was all there in the letter I showed to Mankin,' Colman said. 'There I was, under your protection—an American defector interrogating an American prisoner, trying to get him to sign a simple confession. Anybody listening or watching us would never have guessed it was anything else. Mankin sat there reading his instructions. . . .'

'I have to say . . . congratulations,' Trauner said with an admiring glint in his eyes.

'But now Mankin's gone, Colonel,' Colman summed up. 'So you don't have that all-important corroboration.'

Trauner smiled with a sense of accomplishment. 'There is something as good, perhaps better. The mere fact that Emmering, with *no good reason* on behalf of the state, the Party, or the people—released an imperialist agent. Why? You can see how well it holds up even without Mankin's actual presence —perhaps, as I say, even better for his absence. . . .'

'Then you are going to try to use it?'

Trauner looked at Colman with sneering but somehow clinical eyes. 'What a strangely childish side there is to people like you,' he said.

Colman found the comment unexpected and he didn't answer.

'The sudden, incomprehensible display of purity and Western ethics,' Trauner went on analytically, ironically. 'Romantic ritual takes hold in the midst of utter ruthlessness. And for so odd a reason.'

'I do a job just as you do. You must have some dos and don'ts of your own.'

'Our actions are collectivist, and we are never faced with imperialist dilemmas. We have an historical understanding, so our dos and don'ts aren't the inconsistent and bourgeois nonsense yours are.'

'Congratulations,' Colman said with a nod, anxious to get out of there quickly.

'You are suddenly in the curiously anomalous role of protecting the position of an enemy,' Trauner said, drumming a series of rippling sequences with the four fingers on his right hand. It slowly punctuated everything for a moment or two longer as he spoke, summed up the peculiarities of the capitalist personality. 'One whose existence is not even a matter of expediency. I find that symptomatic of great shortcomings in the way people like you approach everything. I also find it encouraging. We are right; in the end you will lose.'

'Look, Colonel, I gave you what you asked for, didn't I? As a reward, spare me any further delay.'

'But you did so with reluctance. Protecting Emmering seems such a strange cause to fight.'

'I wasn't protecting Emmering. He can fall off a cliff, I don't care. But destroying him was not my objective—only using him. I said, "Do exactly as I tell you and such and such will be the result. Otherwise it's your head." He did as he was told. He earned the right to a kept promise. That was all. There is no reason for us to cause his death or downfall, do you see? *You* can cause it, that's just fine with me. It's just that I did not want to lend *myself* to it.' He shrugged. 'But I did. And now good-bye, all right?'

'But you haven't really,' Trauner insisted, somewhat languorous for just a moment. 'And once you are on the other side, I can see just how quickly a disclaimer would be made. That's all it would take and the case would fall to pieces. You know that. That is why you were suddenly so co-operative But don't you think I could see the same loophole? Of course, I could.'

There was something in the air Colman didn't like, something almost toxic. 'I think you would feel moved to abide by your imperialist concept of honour and fair play,' Trauner went on. 'You can lie, cheat, murder, exploit, and commit blackmail, but at a given moment, out of some peculiar bourgeois concept of decency and ethics, won't break a promise. . . .'

'I already did.'

'No, you haven't. You would to me; I'm an adversary. But not to Emmering, because he made a bargain with you. You're a breed apart.'

'What's your point, Colonel?'

'That we must detain you further. I am sorry, but it's impossible to do anything else. . . .'

'Then you've simply lied to me,' Colman said with no show of emotion.

'No. I have been forced to discard one position for another.'

'Same thing. I know you won't care either way.'

'We have a doctrine. You live by romance and self-deception. Don't expect that of us.'

'I don't expect anything of you,' Colman said reasonably, standing up like a man ready for his fate or about to routinely step out for a bite of lunch.

Trauner watched him with an odd lack of curiosity as he took hold of the kitchen chair, without any sudden or unusual movements, and with it smashed the overhead porcelain-covered lamp.

There was a shattering of glass and immediate darkness. And outcries—shocked, angry, garbled. The chair went heavily through the air towards the man called Walther, struck him, and caused him to swear in great rage, Trauner heaving to his feet, Colman springing towards Trauner.

Colman smashed him an open-handed chop across the nape

of the thick-layered neck, just hard enough, and took from him the automatic he was in the process of drawing.

The others were then flinging open the doors from opposite directions and Walther had his gun out to fire. Trauner sank to the floor and Walther fired twice, the bullets thudding somewhere behind Colman, who had ducked down alongside the stove, quickly spraying back three shots of his own, two towards the swing door, one at the back door leading out of the house. The reports shook the air in the confinement of the room.

As quickly as he had burst in, the blond man withdrew to the living room, the two sentries retreating to the black of night, Walther falling to the floor, hit by at least one of the bullets Colman had fired.

Trauner lay like an incapacitated elephant, his breathing stertorous and helpless. Less than fifteen seconds in all had elapsed. There was cold-blooded, suffocating silence. Except for Trauner's intakes and expulsions of air as he lay there in a semi-conscious state, counted out in a fight, of course, but not seriously damaged at all.

Colman crouched right next to him, as to a cover of sand-bags or a fallen horse, his only intention that of escape—to somehow get back to West Berlin. Adele was there, no longer under threat. He had to get back but he knew he might not. He wasn't as well prepared for that now as he might have been at another time long ago, and it made him a little more dangerous to both himself and his adversaries.

Very swiftly he removed his belt and tied Trauner's wrists together behind that hummocklike rump. The man, like a fallen monument, lay there on a vast cushion that was himself, his head turned to one side, his great, heaving breaths ebbing and flowing audibly.

Now in the lurid darkness Colman waited mere seconds, under barbed wire, to where Walther had fallen, keeping himself below the |line of 'possible fire through the kitchen windows.

The man who had evidently enjoyed Trauner's confidence was lying on his back, an arm flung out, one leg bent at the knee and hooked under the other. Colman had seen him go down fast, as if jerked from underneath. It could be dimly ascertained that he had been struck twice, once in the face through the left cheekbone, once probably just below the sternum, blackish blood soaking both his shirt front and his suit jacket. He was dead. The others were hiding, lying in wait, waiting to attack or to ambush, everyone poised to kill.

It was gruesome and unreal and desperate—a set of conditions one couldn't withdraw from even had one wished to do so. Trauner had had to take things this far, but Colman couldn't have anticipated it, didn't know the extent of Trauner's devotions, how stifled he had been, how he thirsted for expiation. Colman couldn't help having a reaction but then thought to himself, The hell with it. The moment wouldn't go away by itself with handshakes and smiles all around.

Colman took Walther's gun in his free hand and now had two of them. Walther's seemed to be a .45 automatic. He felt both weapons for a few seconds and then lay there thinking out a next move. He needn't have. The move came from the other side, the outside door smashing open with the entrance into the room of a searchlight beam which instantly found Colman for the benefit of double bursts of fire from the guns of the sentries.

Colman moved with the crash of the door, turning on his belly with reflexes sharpened by the will to survive, miraculously escaping the raking hail of bullets.

He answered from where he still lay on the floor, firing both guns simultaneously three or four times into the stupidly open doorway, the .45 in his right hand and rocking on each shot, Trauner's fancy weapon unhampered by any recoil. Colman hit both men and they cried out as they were driven back by the bullets into the barnyard, one of them staggering a few feet before hitting the ground to die.

Two more shots rang out in the near darkness to which one's eyes were now accustomed. They came from the gun of the frail blond young man who was crouched and firing into the room through a two- or three-inch opening to which he had pushed the swing door giving on to the front of the house.

Colman was on one knee and his response was instantaneous, immeasurably quick, no pause having taken place in the shooting from the very second the back door had swung open.

He fired both guns in reply to the shots from the living room directly at the swing door panel. A single cartridge had been left in the .45 and two slugs in Trauner's automatic. The young man pushed the swing door open again just enough to fall into the kitchen with three bullets in his body. He moaned pitiably and then was silent.

Colman had gone to both knees now and remained that way, the stinging presence of cordite in the air, and he knew he was hit, superficially at least, somewhere on the right side above the hip. He dropped the empty guns and was feeling for the wound. His hand came away dripping, warm, vaguely sticky blood on his fingers.

There seemed to be no pain and he was able to get up without difficulty and to go to where the blond lay like a boy not to be outdone by his companions, dead or in a coma, almost as if he had had by oath to join them in death. His pompadour was smashed, of course. Colman picked up his gun and knew from its weight that the magazine contained cartridges. He began to feel a twinge of pain which told him that obviously he had to move with maximum speed.

'Trauner, you're going to get me past the *Vopos* at the checkpoint,' he said as he untied the other man's hands. 'If you don't, I'll shoot you dead.'

'You're wounded, aren't you?'

'I'm lucky at that. Come on, get up and let's go.'

He comforted the open flesh with the palm of his left hand and held the gun in his right as he and Trauner proceeded towards the car. The pain was now incessant but not unbearable, and he didn't feel mortally wounded. The other two men, the sentries who silently had brought him to this place, were sprawled on the ground, one of them not quite dead but nearing his end. 'Don't look and you'll be much better off,' he advised a now hesitant Trauner repelled at the sight. Colman's legs were growing shaky and he was glad to be able to sit down in the back seat of the car while Trauner drove. The key had been in the ignition, obviating the need to search bleeding bodies for it.

'You killed three, possibly four men,' Trauner said in cold, trancelike tones.

'Not because I wanted to. . . .'

'We were only going to detain you. . . .'

'Don't be a hypocrite. . . .'

He did what he sincerely believed he had to do. But he consciously hoped he could keep it from Adele, that it would never be revealed to her. She must never know how efficiently and quickly he had killed again—even those deadly, unhesitant men who would otherwise have killed him as one stamps an official document. They would have killed him automatically. And he had killed them, left them lying in the blackness, ruptured, torn apart, and as oblivious as the unborn. He was sorry, not for those men, but because death was so easy and he wanted never again to be its direct cause. He wasn't sentimental and he didn't believe in so many of the soft-minded pronouncements of unrealistic people. But he was nevertheless not sure he could have shot Trauner now, even in self-defence. Mainly because there would have been no sense in it. He needed Trauner, would be doomed without him.

He was feeling sapped and he wanted no more, not ever. There was an end, as he knew long ago, to how many decisions one could take, how realistic one could be, how willing and able to do what undoubtedly had to be done. And yet how comfortable would refusal make one? There were those whose very existences were based on refusal, perhaps because they knew others wouldn't refuse on their behalf, or perhaps because they believed that refusal beginning with themselves would spread to others, drift like pollen, impregnating flowers of refusal everywhere—until no desperate and indecent killer weeds were left in the world. Colman didn't know, of course, as he sat there in the back seat with growing hopes, the gun in his hand, his blood coursing, his strength grown shaky, a dream hovering like mist above the reality of the pain of his wound. All he wanted was to get back to his woman. He had given everything and he wanted only that in return. Half an hour would be long enough to resist the misty dream.

'What will you do when we get there? Don't you see that merely on a mechanical level it can't be accomplished?' Trauner was saying.

'Yes, it can. You'll identify yourself to the guard. Then

you'll drive across with me. I get out and you drive right back to your own side. One wrong move out of you and we're both dead, believe me.'

All he had to do was hold on to the last glimpse he had of her three days ago. He would be laid up, perhaps for weeks, after he got back. But then their lives would begin again. Love would shut out everything. All he needed to do was remain conscious, to keep from being drawn into that all-enveloping mist where the pain would lessen and disappear, the mist like healing vapours. The alternative would find him coming back to life in the bed of a DDR hospital, the doctor, the nurse, and Trauner looking down at him, caught and ready to cook. So he held on to the pain, let it throb dullishly, concentrated on its cruelty. He refused to escape. He told himself that Adele's well-being, her happiness depended on his feeling this pain to its fullest. Blood seeped through his fingers, but he was holding his own.

'I told you in Zurich,' he heard Trauner saying, 'that perhaps I deserved disgrace and punishment. I did then and still do. I would let you shoot me now and that would be an end of it. I am not that afraid to die. But I owe something to the state, to the people: my own confession of failure and the removal of Emmering, who sits in power and betrays his trust. You wouldn't be able to do this otherwise, rest assured. But I could not leave behind four brave and loyal dead comrades, and Emmering still presiding and untouched. I could not do that, much as I would like to take vengeance against you. . . .'

Colman heard the drone to which Trauner's high-pitched tenor voice had been reduced and understood perfectly, and without malice muttered, 'That's very commendable. . . .'

'When one has faith, one has everything. And we have a faith—not a blind, primitive set of superstitions, but a living, growing system for making a better life for the greatest number of people, not merely for the Rockefellers and Standard Oil.'

Maybe the reaffirmations were pouring out because Trauner was badly shaken by the shattering events, the unreality of the last hour. He needed to bandage a wound of his own, perhaps. Colman knew that losing four men that way must have been hard to bear no matter what your politics were. Was it only

276

that morning, he marvelled, that he had come into East Berlin? Protected, in perfect health, reasonably certain that everything would go all right.

'In effect you owe your life, at this particular moment, to Marxism-Leninism—a supreme irony, you must admit. Otherwise you would need to shoot me and be left to bleed to death. . . .'

Colman could see the dimly lit city going past, the car having reached its environs ten minutes earlier. Soon they would come to the corner of Unter den Linden and Friedrichstrasse, a few minutes later to face the challenge of Checkpoint Charlie. Colman had to keep awake until they were through. He kept exhorting himself to that preponderant truth. Get to the other side and then pass out, not before. Breathe slowly, keep still; don't use anything up too quickly.

'You think you've had an enormous victory. But it's hollow for one reason: it represents nothing. People aren't behind it, only Chase Manhattan Bank, only Wall Street. Not people. And nothing can sustain without benefit to the many. Everything else is rotten at the base and soon crumbles.'

'Why don't you hold free elections?' Colman mumbled.

'Ask the Negroes what they think of your free elections. . . .'

Trauner then drew a welcome curtain of silence between them, as if this had been the final impeachment, and he turned into Friedrichstrasse and understandably grew expectant and tense.

Colman knew Trauner had not abandoned the natural inclination to a last-minute reversal of the situation. The concept of turning the tables dies hard, especially when you're at gunpoint and someone who can help you is within the perimeter of your very breath. 'Don't try anything,' Colman told Trauner quietly. He would, he knew, not hesitate to shoot after all.

Trauner didn't answer and simply continued to drive along the rather wide thoroughfare towards the checkpoint, still some distance away. The silence extended towards the Wall at Checkpoint Charlie. And then the moment was at hand.

The MP's and the *Schutzpolizei* on the West Berlin side saw the car halted momentarily by the green-grey uniformed guard of the NVA. Then without special interest they watched the striped bar swing up in the air, the car, led by its dimmers, come across the intervening piece of territory, finally reaching the American inspection shed.

The driver of the car, obese and obviously ill at ease, wasn't aware of it, but the MP's could easily see immediately that the passenger in the back seat was dead.

CHAPTER TWELVE

JOE FOX was the one to tell her. He came to the door of the Wedding hotel room, dim and plain, but safe just as he had said it would be. Before Fox spoke, before he said hello, she knew why he had come. She began to shake inside and she thought she would faint, but only for an instant. She forced the whole thing into a distant setting, making it something with which she could sympathize but was not wholly a part of. She took a deep, deep breath and hoped she would be able to keep this up for just a little while longer. Fox was honest-eyed, respectful, and solemn. Brian had already become a myth to him, she could see. 'He was the best man I ever knew,' he told her.

'Was he?' she said, her eyes brimming with tears, her stomach tight and cold.

'I don't know what else to say. I know that nothing helps.'

She couldn't survive the belief. It was without mercy and it was there to stay, time finally frozen, as she had so often childishly wished it, death and condolence passing between two total strangers. He was dead; there was to be no variation on that. 'I want to see him,' she said, not demanding it, merely expressing a lost hope.

Fox nodded, ready to give help. 'You can. I can take you there. . . .'

It was a clear, sunny day into early autumn, and the air was bracing and inviting and heartbreaking. A *Leierkasten* was being operated by a man with a small capuchin monkey on a lead, a group of children gathered around. The music lilted and she hated it. Fox took her by taxi to the police morgue in Schöneberg.

Jeremy Colman was there—tall, somewhat like Brian but missing that element that was Brian, naturally; yet like Brian, Brian's traces in him; without awareness of her, without that cognizance.

They both looked at Brian, untouched, handsome but pale, and Adele's eyes closed as if to hide from the agony and perhaps to imagine another time, protect herself from the full impact of the image, keep from weeping aloud in front of Jeremy Colman and the morgue attendant. That wasn't for this tundral place with its echoes, its death everywhere. That was for later on, for the nights and days ahead.

'I'll want to move him tonight,' Brian's brother told the attendant, his face long and his lips thin and white.

'We can have him ready whenever you wish,' came the answer in English.

'I'll arrange to have a hearse here at seven o'clock. . . .'

She didn't hear all the details that passed between them and she walked out to the vestibule of that dreadful building, its footfalls cracking with disrespect for the dead. Brian had looked as if he were sleeping, as if he had no thoughts or memory of her. How could he have deceived her so? He said that there had never been a less risky mission. How could he have? Oh, Brian, I loved you so and love you still. All I want is to stop or to die too.

Jeremy Colman caught up to her at the doors to the street. He was as tall as Brian, a few years older, less vibrant, on the surface more cautious, sympathetic, troubled. 'I'm going to take him back with me to New York tonight,' he said. 'And I'm not even sure that's what he would want. He could be buried in Arlington National Cemetery. But again, I'm not sure. . . .'

'Does it matter?' she said.

He didn't answer, just looked at her, sharing a regret, his eyes reflective, slightly distant. 'He wrote me one letter in which he mentioned you,' he said. 'From Wiesbaden.'

'Yes. . . .' She recalled the very moment he had written it.

'Could we sit down somewhere and talk for a few minutes?'

She wanted to be alone in a closed room or at the top of a hill so she could discover all of her pain without witnesses, have what could only be a private experience. Once you had uncovered it, taken it out of concealment, so to speak, it became a part of you and you could do with it whatever you needed to. But Jeremy Colman was one of those people who cared in his quiet way; he wanted one last link with Brian, and she couldn't deny it, perhaps shouldn't have. 'I hadn't seen him in some time,' he explained with sorrow just beneath his dignity.

'Yes, if you like. . . .'

They went to a place near the Town Hall and in view of the vast encampment of the canvas-topped produce stalls, a few thousand people milling here and there, the buying and the selling now in lively, noisy progress. Friday was a market day. Dimly it occurred to her that she had been anticipating the week-end as one does the fulfilment of a lifelong desire.

He looked across the small round table, making no show of studying her, or trying to find anything. He wasn't a man to make demands. She was aware of this, as little as she was able to concentrate on him at all. 'He didn't say much about you,' he was assuring her quietly. 'Only that . . . you were together.'

'He could have said whatever he wished,' she said simply, almost carelessly, as if to sum up everything.

'Yes. . . .' He lit a cigarette and glanced uselessly around him. 'I didn't know what he was doing specifically, though I suspected.' He shrugged, his face said. 'I can see now that my suspicions were right. It's the U.S. Mission, of course, that informs next-of-kin, as if he had been an ordinary government employee. . . . I suppose that's a matter of security.'

She made a cynical mouth. 'Or because they want to keep the truth from themselves. . . .'

'I wouldn't like to believe they were that self-deceiving. . . .'

'What do you want of me?' she asked straightforwardly.

'Nothing. Anything. Is there something I can do for *you*?'

'No. You are very kind. . . . I don't know what I can tell you—at least, at the moment.'

'That's all right.'

They had nothing to talk about and seemed to realize as

much. Strangers couldn't easily survive silences; they couldn't hold hands or kiss or feel confidence. But then the coffee arrived, and as he stirred his cup absently, Jeremy Colman recalled: 'We were close friends in many respects, and yet I never knew what made him what he was. . . .'

'Who ever does know that about anyone?' she challenged in a voice so low it was barely audible.

'We were an Army family, as you may know,' he said. 'But he didn't need to be in it if he hadn't wanted to. He didn't have to be in any of *this* business. . . .' He was undoubtedly critical in tone, but out of love and admiration and perhaps even some dormant old envy. 'I suppose I'm trying to find out what sense, if any, there was in his death. And I'm sure that's impossible.'

'Perhaps there was for him but wouldn't be for you.'

He looked at her. 'Is there any for you?'

'I know that he did what he wanted to do. Nothing else makes much difference now.'

'Did he tell you that?'

'Yes. I can tell you this. He had to go into East Berlin to get a man out of prison—a man to whom he felt obligated.' She remembered that part of it for the first time. 'I don't even know whether he succeeded or not. . . .'

'You know all about it, don't you?' he said, as if this somehow confirmed her, gave her standing.

'I am from East Germany. A defector. I was to be sent back in exchange for one of Brian's colleagues who was in prison over there, do you see? To save me from that, Brian tried to get him out through very dangerous means, at the risk of his life. That is why he is dead,' She spoke from the need to put things out where they could be seen so they would not fester. Jeremy Colman's eyes never moved from her face. 'I tell you this so that it can either make some sense to you or give you someone you can blame and even hate if it will help you. . . .'

'Hate you?'

'It wouldn't matter. We won't ever see each other again anyhow.'

'Why would I hate anyone he loved that much? I would sooner hate the situation, but even that is a waste of time, isn't it?'

'Yes. It does absolutely no good.'

'Then he had a reason all right. The best I can think of.'

'You're a kind person. I am sorry for your loss.'

'I am deeply sorry for yours.'

He took her back to her hotel, where she insisted on being left to herself despite his solicitude, his offers of assistance, his invitation to contact him in New York any time she wished. He was an architect, married, the father of two teen-agers. She let herself weep for hours.

Three days later Mrs Stransky, whom she had finally contacted, prevailed on her to move into the apartment with her until she could find something that suited her better, decide what her life was to be about. To Adele's initial hesitations, Mrs Stransky said, 'You would be doing me a favour. It would be a joy to have you keep me company—I mean, whenever you feel like it and could bear to be with me. Please, don't think of it in any other way. . . .'

This flat of Mrs Stransky's, only ten years old though it was, was heavily draped in the past. Adele felt as if she were at a memorial, felt the spell that guards the sites of vanished greatness or courageous follies or sheer horror.

'I must leave,' Mrs Stransky confided as they sat drinking coffee that first night together in the kitchen. 'As I get closer to death, I realize that. . . .'

'To Israel?'

'Yes. . . . And you?'

'Where could I go?' Adele said without self-pity. 'I am a Berliner, with neither pride in it nor shame. I can't help it.'

Mrs Stransky smiled. 'Come with me. . . . I'm only joking, of course.'

'I thought you couldn't live anywhere but Berlin.'

'The blood calls, perhaps. . . .' The words came from the lips of a survivor who lived in a universe of ghosts and lingering anguish despite her miraculously benign face with its twinkle of intelligence and the small non-accusatory voice.

Adele was sure ghosts and anguish were never completely laid to rest. Several days had gone by when she realized that she needed to pay a visit to a doctor, that she had a condition which required investigation. She remembered now the very source of it, its beginnings during the last weeks they had spent at Schleisstein. She had not mentioned it to Brian at the time. Mrs Stransky lent her a sympathetic ear and gave her the address of a doctor in the neighbourhood.

CHAPTER THIRTEEN

STEVENSON'S FLAT in Charlottenburg-Nord overlooked an entire housing estate laid out amidst trees and various grassy configurations. It was a bit too perfect, too symmetrical, perhaps, but he wasn't very critical about it. The single contention he felt with the neighbourhood lay in the memorial wall at the church in the Toeplerstrasse.

Sixty-five feet long, it commemorated what Stevenson found to be a curious grouping of historical violences: Golgotha, Auschwitz, Plötzensee, and Hiroshima.

Hiroshima, with what he felt was clear justice, deserved a far different association than this solely on the basis of the perversely ignored fact that Hiroshima was part of a military and political bastion in desperate alliance with those very people condemned for Auschwitz and Plötzensee. Only a kind of lunatic illogic could ignore as much and arrive at such a confusion of sentiments; only a conscious or unconscious effort to blur the truth and discredit the United States could support it. Which was neither new nor extraordinary, of course. It had been a staple in the diet of a certain kind of international politics since almost the very day the Second World War ended. One might have regretted Hiroshima, yes, but no more deeply than Rotterdam or London or the Katyn massacre or Babi Yar; or the slaughter at Nanking; and without lending it to the deeply unscrupulous and sinister connotations it now enjoyed among the weird and the warped, and the merely bathetic and addictable, the sheep of all nations. An Arcadian and peace-loving people dangling their fishing poles in idyllic waters were suddenly set upon, having given no provocation, by unspeakable and sadistic beasts motivated only by the compulsion to torture and destroy. The agonies of Christ: of six thousand

Jews a day; of men pierced and left to dangle from meat hooks; all that and the American war effort too. Unless one had lost all fire and disgust of fraudulence, one's blood had to boil. Stevenson's did. Shameful deceits and lies garnished with lip service to enlightenment and humanism polluted the atmosphere as surely as automobile exhausts and factory emissions. The open societies of the West had served the Communists well, undoubtedly beyond even the Communists' wildest dreams and most graceless boasts. The ingredients were ignorance and vanity, the absence of a sense of consequence that one needed only to look to the United States to discover.

But he took note of it with a greatly lessened response that morning as Kagen chauffeured him from one underground garage towards the other across West Berlin. The clues it offered to history and the behaviour patterns of people were really academic finally and only the day-to-day acts counted for anything. It was at that moment that he just happened to see Adele Fischer from the back seat of the cruising Mercedes as she was walking along not too far from the Grünewald. He had intended for the past few days to call on her personally. 'Drive alongside of that woman, Kagen,' he said.

In a moment Adele had accepted with evident reserve, with extreme emotionlessness, Stevenson's invitation to join him. He got out of the car to extend it and held the door open for her entry. 'I wanted to see that you were all right, Mrs Fischer,' he told her as they drove towards the huge state forest. 'Your status is settled, of course, and you'll be able to do whatever suits you. Something you've always deserved. If there's anything you need. . . .'

'Nothing,' she said, looking at him. 'You think people are chess pieces, don't you?'

'That's a bit overdrawn, don't you think so?'

'I find it natural to say.'

'All right. But it's not true, Mrs Fischer. The contrary happens to be the case,' Stevenson said. 'Life is not chess at all. Did you ever read *War and Peace*, Mrs Fischer? I bring it up now because in it Tolstoy tells us how very different life and chess actually are—for those of us who might have thought otherwise. He says it through the character of Pierre on the eve of the Battle of Borodino. He points out that in chess two pawns are undeviatingly stronger than one, and the result is never in doubt. But in life a battalion may prove stronger than a regiment in one instance and weaker than a mere company in another.'

'Why do you tell me this? Do you think it will mean the slightest thing to me?'

Stevenson confronted the beauty, the agony, the restrained, and therefore all the more potent, contempt. He kept from quavering or backing away from all of it but understood and respected it. Quietly he said, 'My point is that I never think of any human being as a chess piece—that whatever I do, I do only with the hope that it will turn out well and only after all the less hazardous possibilities have been squeezed dry. Every move cuts like a knife. And when a man dies, I don't shake my head philosophically and light a cigar. . . .' He had said something of the sort to Senator Davis. 'But I try to remember the seriousness of the decision that caused it, the circumstances for which he died. . . .'

'No one believes in dying any more, Mr Stevenson—if they ever did. There is never anything worth that sacrifice, not to the one who dies . . . not politics, not systems.'

'You're talking with personal grief now,' he said gently.

'What does that make me? A stupid woman and a coward? If so, I don't care a damn.'

'No, no. The truth is we never really know anything with complete certainty. Yet we still pursue our ends even when we're not sure what they are. That sounds absurd, and even inane—*quatsch*—I know. But it's the hinge, if I may put it this way, on which everything swings—that all action turns out to be inexplicable because we are human beings, and human beings are capable only of short-range thinking, even at its most far-seeing. Yet no alternative exists, does it? And for me, personally, a certain outlook demands my . . . accord, call it. Oh, not my full, idiotically unquestioning accord. But more of it, by far, than I can give to the discredited certainties of Marxism, or the abdications of Oriental religion, or the taking of drugs; or the acquiescence in nihilism masquerading as enlightenment. I prefer my own kind of torment to any of those. . . .' He waved his hand. 'Okay, I didn't mean to make a speech.' He shifted in his seat next to her to give emphasis to what he wanted to say next. 'There was an important reason for Brian's mission—not just for what it meant to you and to him personally, but to the extent that human actions and ideas can be called important, and granting the possible ultimate folly in all things. With all that, an important mission. Brian thought so also, though he didn't know to what an enormous degree. I am sorry Brian is dead—deeply sorry. But he wanted to accomplish this mission. I give you my word on that. And he did. Maybe you can find some meaning and comfort in it.'

'May I get out here, please?' she said.

Stevenson had gone as far as he could have and he knew it was no use. He was glad he had tried. Or perhaps he should not have. Why had it to be so laboriously explained? Why wasn't it self-evident?

He sat there after she had alighted, left with the perennial residue of bitterness and regret attached to so great a part of human behaviour, whatever one's motives. It was a banal conclusion, but shared understandings were rare and all commitments were dangerous.

Adele walked along, briefly recalling the atmosphere of Schleisstein, its isolation. Had these indeed been responsible for the failure to renew the simple, revolutionary prescription? Made her forgetful? Only six days had elapsed at the time. She didn't dream it would matter. And now she sat down on a bench in the Grünewald and waited to feel the growth of life. That morning the doctor to which Mrs Stransky had sent her confirmed once again the continuing cycle of grief and joy and desire.

She was gravid and redeemed. She even felt a touch of triumph, a sign of approval from a heaven whose God was deeply deficient but better than none perhaps.